SHERRILYN KENYON

AND

DIANNA LOVE

WHISPERED LIES

D0348642

POCKET BOOKS

New York   London   Toronto   Sydney

Pocket Books
A Division of Simon & Schuster, Inc.
1230 Avenue of the Americas
New York, NY 10020

This book is a work of fiction. Names, characters, places, and incidents either are products of the author's imagination or are used fictitiously. Any resemblance to actual events or locales or persons, living or dead, is entirely coincidental.

First Pocket Books paperback edition April 2010

POCKET and colophon are registered trademarks of Simon & Schuster, Inc.

For information about special discounts for bulk purchases, please contact Simon & Schuster Special Sales at 1-866-506-1949 or business@simonandschuster.com.

The Simon & Schuster Speakers Bureau can bring authors to your live event. For more information or to book an event contact the Simon & Schuster Speakers Bureau at 1-866-248-3049 or visit our website at www.simonspeakers.com.

Cover design by Lisa Litwack

Manufactured in the United States of America

10 9 8 7 6 5 4 3 2 1

ISBN 978-1-4391-6994-0
ISBN 978-1-4165-9754-4 (ebook)

We're dedicating this to all the thousands of wonderful fans who come out to meet us on the road that makes all that traveling worth it—you're the best!!

ACKNOWLEDGMENTS

From Sherrilyn Kenyon

Thank you to Dianna for being such a good sport and always making me smile. I never thought I could cowrite anything, but given that we often share a common brain (LOL) you made it not only easy but a joy. Thank you so much for all the support.

Thank you to Kim, Jacs, Tina, Brenda, and Retta for reading all my manuscripts and making great comments. And let's not forget Tina, Carl, Eddie, Aimee, Brynna, Kim, Judy, Soteria, and all the others who make my message bbs a living community where all are welcomed. Thank you, fans, for coming back day after day. You guys rock!

To my husband for being my shelter in the storm. You are my rock and I'm grateful every day that I said yes when you asked me out to see a movie I couldn't stand. For my kids who are always my comfort and my greatest source of pride. May God bless and keep you all.

From Dianna Love

It was great to write a second BAD Agency story with Sherrilyn. She's one of the most creatively generous people I know. Thanks, Sherri, for all that you do and for being a wonderful friend.

I also want to thank my husband, Karl, who supports everything I do and supports all my writing buddies as well (his cooking is becoming as legendary as the wit he shares with us).

A special thanks to all the fans who gave our collaboration a chance and wrote such wonderful notes about *Phantom in the Night*. Your enthusiasm and excitement for this series means so much. Su Walker and Leiha Mann—thanks for the laughs and endless support, the next martinis are on me. A big hug to my dear friends Walt and Cindy Lumpkin, and Dave and Gail Akins, for always being there for me and the many dinners. [Note for anyone traveling to my area in Peachtree City, you'll find one of my favorite restaurants mentioned in this story. It's owned by Pascal who helped us with details on France.] Thanks also to all my super family—James (brother) and Teri Love (sister-in-law, who also reads for me), plus my nieces Ashley and Tiffany, who understand without complaint when I miss family events and am typing during holidays.

From both of us

We appreciate Lauren McKenna's support and faith in our ability to cowrite this book. In addition to being a terrific editor, she's a wonderful cheerleader, always ready with a positive word.

Thanks also to Merrilee Heifetz for all the hard work on our behalf and her amazing skills as an agent.

A big thanks goes to author Mary Buckham who is always willing to read the first [bumpy] draft and critiques with a surgical ability that is deeply appreciated, and thanks to her husband, Jim, whose knowledge of rare information and Italian elements still surprises us. The talented Cassondra Murray is always willing to read and share her feedback when needed, plus explain weapons from a female perspective. Her husband, Steve Doyle, provides us with expert advice on Special Force operations and weapons, plus feedback on our romantic adventure from the male perspective. Keith Morgan shared his extensive knowledge of electronic forensics in a way that even Dianna could understand it <grin>.

Pascal Le Corre was an enthusiastic resource for us on France. He grew up there and returns every year. After seeing that country through his eyes, we want to go. A voracious reader of many genres and dear friend, Manuella Robinson dropped everything to read the final pages on short notice that really helped with our deadline. Kim Newman is an ESL teacher originally from South America who is a friend and a valuable resource and graciously reviewed pages to assure we had things like the regional Spanish correct.

Hope Williams once again gave us an early read and some of the best cookies you've ever eaten. She's always a big help. Wes Sarginson, who recently retired from forty-six years as an NBC newsman, is a limitless fountain of information. He's a good friend who helped with details about congressional media events. Thanks to Annie Oortman, who provides great live story reviews for readers. We hope we haven't missed anyone. If any detail is incorrect, it is our fault. Great resources and terrific first reads play a huge part of creating an exciting romantic thriller.

To the RBL Women—thanks for all the support, laughs, and martinis. You are too much fun! Congratulations to Kathryn Collupy, who won the "name in our book" raffle.

We love our readers!! You are the reason we work so hard to create a story you'll lose yourself in for hours. A huge thanks to all of you who have sent us notes of encouragement, excited about this collaborative effort, and who read our books, allowing us to do what we love— write stories. You are the best!

ONE

If he had to die today, he'd have preferred a warm climate and a bullet between the eyes over this.

Carlos Delgado had no one to blame but himself. He *had* agreed to take the lead on this screwed-up mission.

The routine HAHO—high altitude, high opening—jump from a C-130 came with a standard set of risks. First, his team had to hit a tiny spot in the French Alps near St. Gervais. Second, a midnight op upped the ante. Last, parachuting into a snowstorm kicked in the high-octane factor.

And those weren't even the best reasons for labeling this op suicidal.

He stretched his legs and lifted a hand to scratch his face, but stopped. The Gentex face mask itched like a son of a bitch, but breaking the seal between skin and mask would immediately lower the raised nitrogen level in his blood. That meant he'd have to abort the jump and scrub the mission since this op was planned with a minimum number of operatives.

With the mood his three teammates had been in when they went wheels up, someone would immediately accommodate his wish for a quick death.

But they'd show some restraint since none of them wanted to waste a day off for his funeral.

Carlos checked his watch. Just after lunch on Sunday in the States. Headquarters should have new intel by now. He was ready to get moving as much as he hated making the jump.

He'd made the leap more times than he wanted to remember, but the stakes were high this time. The only thing worse than flying in an airplane was exiting one during flight . . . and at this altitude. An adrenaline junkie's dream. Not his.

He slapped a sideways look at Korbin Maximus, sitting next to him on another uncomfortable canvas seat. Their resident adrenaline junkie and insertion specialist for BAD—Bureau of American Defense—wore an identical oxygen mask. His night-vision goggles were shoved up on his forehead.

Slouched, eyes closed above a perpetual five-o'clock shadow, and arms casually crossed, Korbin appeared at rest, but Carlos knew their point man was not asleep.

"What's the matter, Korbin? Job puttin' you to sleep?" Reagan "Rae" Graham's British lilt came through the commo headset they all wore. Perched across from Carlos and Korbin, Rae was the only female on this op and no petite miss at five-eight. She could more than handle herself in hand-to-hand combat, cool as an ice cube under pressure. Few men would suspect the trim woman packaged with all those lush curves to be so lethal, but she was one tough babe from the short, sandy brown hair to a mile of legs . . . to the G36C rifle strapped across her chesty flight suit.

"Just reserving my strength for later." Korbin lifted a dark lash long enough to send a whispered wink at Rae.

"For the op or some sweet *thang?*" Rae chided in a poor imitation of his Texas drawl that sometimes carried shades of Korbin's Mexican heritage.

"I'm always up for a sweet thing, especially one loaded for bear." Korbin's eyes crinkled in challenge.

"Yeah, right. In your dreams." Rae flipped a droll don't-waste-your-time glance at him.

Carlos rolled his eyes at the pair. The banter and verbal poking had gone on for the past six months. Why hadn't they found a room yet? Should be a perfect match since both of them considered dinner reservations a long-term commitment.

BAD did have a "No fraternizing with team members" rule, which wouldn't normally faze most agency operatives, who considered breaking rules part of their job description.

But the first commitment of every agent in BAD was to protect teammates, which would be damn hard to do if one of the agents caught in cross fire was a loved one.

Carlos had no problem steering clear of relationships with females on a mission. Emotions complicated an op and jeopardized lives.

He'd learned that lesson the hard way and never made the mistake again. Never would.

"Besides, Korbin, you haven't made it to the *R's* yet," Rae piped up. "Who is it this week? Jasmine, Kelly, or Lisa?"

Korbin scowled, eyelids still at half-mast.

Rae's gaze twinkled with undisguised gloating over the direct hit.

"Is that what you're doing?" Gotthard Heinrich, the fourth operative, broke in. As the beefiest member of the team, he packed an easy 275-plus of solid muscle into that granite body and a temper not to be tested. "Gayle two weeks ago . . ." Above the clear oxygen mask, Gotthard's diamond-blue eyes narrowed in sharp concentration. "Haley last week . . . Isabelle . . . two days ago. Damn! You *are* working your way through da alphabet. You son-a-bitch." He spoke perfect English, French, German, Russian, and Italian whenever he wanted, a faint German accent slipping into his English only when in a secure situation.

"Thanks, Rae," Korbin growled, anything but appreciative.

"Hey. You're the one with the itch and a predilection for patterns."

"Must be nice to be single," Gotthard grumbled.

"Depends." Korbin shifted his slouch. "I don't have someone to go home to *every* night."

"Makes two of us." Gotthard dropped his head back, eyes shut.

Banter eased tension on a mission, but Carlos grimaced over Gotthard's slip. The few agents aware of the big guy's turbulent marriage also knew Gotthard did not discuss it openly.

BAD was a covert organization the U.S. government would never acknowledge that protected national security and saved lives, to put it in pretty terms, but the bottom line was they did whatever it took to get the job done. That way of life generally torpedoed serious commitments, in spite of a few couples that had managed to make cohabitating look possible. Most of the time even the best relationships fell victim as unavoidable casualties.

The one married teammate on this mission was slowly realizing that and getting an earful from his wife about being home for Thanksgiving in four weeks.

Wouldn't be so hard if Gotthard could tell his wife the real reason he'd missed the last two holidays. That he didn't really design interiors for aircrafts, but that sufficed as a cover.

Gotthard sat up, tense lines daggering the bridge of his nose.

"Incoming?" Carlos asked before he could stop himself, but he needed better intel, now. Gotthard had the only link to headquarters and had probably just gotten a vibration from his wrist unit.

The big guy gave a curt nod as he shoved the pale gray sleeve of his flight suit back, exposing his wrist video. The satellite-linked video device looked like an oversize square watch similar to the V-Rambo unit worn by Israeli soldiers and alerted the wearer of an incoming message by vibrating.

But this electronic baby had been customized and developed just for BAD operations, all financed by a silent investor Joe knew. With a name like Joe Q. Public, no sense of humor when it came to his name, and a background most agents only speculated about in hushed conversations, no one questioned the director's supplier for BAD toys.

Gotthard was their communication specialist, who could all but talk to NASA with a piece of aluminum foil and tin can if they needed to reach an astronaut. When the wide-bodied agent finished reading the text on his arm piece, he lifted his gaze to Carlos, then his deep baritone came through the commo set.

"Heads up, everyone." Perfect English this time.

Korbin straightened next to Carlos, alert and ready. Rae cut her eyes at Gotthard, who continued once he had everyone's attention.

"New information is coming through in chunks. The transmissions are breaking up as we move between two satellites." Gotthard's gaze shot down to his wrist video. "Package . . . is confirmed missing from origin . . . stolen goods."

Carlos nodded when Gotthard glanced up to see that he understood. The *package* was Mandy Massey, the missing seventeen-year-old daughter of an American diplomat currently in Uruguay working on a military-site agreement the United States needed in that region. The diplomat thought his daughter was still traveling across South America with friends, but she was also known as a hellion who had disappeared from time to time from her private school in Europe.

BAD intercepted a kidnapping tip from an anonymous source known only as Mirage. The message indicating Mandy as a target of kidnappers had been sent with specific electronic markers, obviously meant for international intelligence agencies scanning for suspicious communication. BAD instituted a covert search across South America, which ended at the last place Mandy had been seen. Another electronic tip followed hours later, warning if the young girl went missing to look for her at a château in the St. Gervais area of the French Alps.

The BAD mission room had sounded more like a bar brawl in the making twelve hours ago when Joe first informed them of this jump. Carlos couldn't fault his companions for arguing against sending a team to jump into a blizzard when the missing renegade daughter had disappeared twice before then shown up later as if nothing were wrong. But the minute Joe shared that the second intercepted missive from Mirage stated Mandy would be given to something called a *fratelli*, the room had quieted, all agents ready to go.

Added to that, Mirage had been correct too many times to ignore the validity of the message. The very reason every intelligence agency in the world searched for this unknown person. No informant ever just shared intelligence freely.

They all had an agenda.

BAD needed to find out what Mirage stood to gain from sharing this information. What game was going on?

The team knew all too well that the reference to a *fratelli* in the tip could well mean the *Fratelli de il Sovrano*, which translated into Sovereign Brotherhood, number one on BAD's most-wanted list of dangerous organizations.

During the past year every agent had seen what this maniacal group could do to human beings. Men, women, and children had been used as guinea pigs for the Fratelli's biological terrorist attacks. The virus unleashed had turned the victims' bodies into hideous forms as they drew their last breaths pleading for death.

Making tonight's HAHO jump was no longer under debate with the chance of saving this young woman from the Fratelli, plus the obvious bonus of finding a link to this organization of monsters.

But no one had located Mandy in South America so the second, and possibly only, shot they had at rescuing her was tonight.

Carlos ran over every step in his mind, again, looking for anything he might have missed. He'd spent the past five days coordinating this op from BAD's headquarters in Nashville, dispatching agents to investigate possible châteaus in St. Gervais based on occupancy and activity. The ground teams had quickly narrowed the choices to six and kept each site under surveillance, watching for unusual movement.

He received word twelve hours ago of four snow-mobiles and a Range Rover arriving at one château now protected with armed guards. Bingo.

Thirty minutes later, Carlos and his team were wheels up. The mission felt rushed and unplanned, but that's what dropped it squarely in the hands of BAD. They could—and would—move on a hunch when other agencies had to go through proper channels.

"There's more coming through," Gotthard said, his eyes locked on the small monitor. "Another notice received . . . this one identifying courier . . ."

Courier was code for the identity of the kidnappers suspected of delivering Mandy to the Fratelli.

"Have they found the messenger?" Carlos asked, indicating the identity or location of the mysterious informant Mirage.

"Not yet," Gotthard replied without looking up as he scratched on his notepad.

If misinformation from this Mirage character sent his team into an ambush or put Mandy at risk, Carlos would be looking for blood when he returned.

If they returned.

Gotthard hit a button on his wrist unit, ending the connection. "Here's the courier." He lifted the paper he'd written the kidnapper's name on for everyone to see.

Anguis.

Rae's lips moved silently mouthing *ahn-gee* as she absorbed the information.

Carlos blinked. He stared at the letters, trying to make them mean something else, but there was no mistaking *Anguis*. Not the largest organized-crime family in South America, but one of the most dangerous to cross. *Merde!* If the tip was correct and the men guarding the château worked for Durand Anguis, they might recognize Carlos. And if they did . . .

"Pilot just radioed a ten-minute warning," Gotthard announced.

Everyone went into motion, forcing Carlos from

his shock. Could the Anguis really be involved with the Fratelli? This smelled like a setup, but who would know to set *him* up? He switched his 0_2 tube from the console to the bottle attached to his jumpsuit and accepted the busted hand he'd been dealt, then focused on his role as team leader. "Sound off."

After making the same oxygen-supply switch, Korbin nodded. "Check."

Rae and Gotthard both confirmed.

"Synchronize altimeters." Carlos gave his reading and finished with "Six minutes."

The next check would be two minutes, then showtime with no second takes.

Carlos adjusted his goggles and strapped on his helmet. "Korbin is on point, me, then Rae. Gotthard sweeps cleanup."

Irritation fumed in Rae's gaze.

Carlos didn't care what she thought of him putting her in the crib position, the safest slot in an assault.

One woman had died in his arms years ago.

He wouldn't be responsible for another.

Highly skilled and lethal as any man on this team, Rae was more than capable of protecting herself. A damned good agent. But Carlos had seen too many women die in inhuman ways, one grotesque example only three months ago. A female informant had missed a meeting then disappeared, until Carlos discovered her inside a building in a remote mountain range in Brazil where rebels hid a stash of weapons. And caged women.

But the rebels were killed in a skirmish with the government over a week before Carlos and a team located the building.

Carlos could still smell the baked stench of rotting bodies. He found the weapons and the informant along with seven more women in chain-link cages waiting to be sold. The metal building had turned into an inferno when the temperatures roared over a hundred degrees every day. One nineteen-year-old female's fingers clung to the chain-link where she reached for help.

Nightmares were the vanguard of his conscience and every decision he made.

Carlos shook off the morbid vision and focused on the living. "Two minutes." Time to head for the rear.

Korbin moved forward, careful not to tangle his feet in the loose hoses. Everyone filed in line behind Korbin toward the rear of the cavernous fuselage, the silence now filled only with the roar of the jet engines. The aircraft's transponder pinged a signal to local air traffic control that this was a commercial flight delivering cargo.

The ping just didn't elaborate on the lethal capability of the aircraft's cargo.

Carlos forced a long, easy breath through his lungs. Anything to slow the blood slamming through his veins from the shock. Anguis soldiers could be waiting at the château. One had seen, and recognized, him in the past sixteen years. That man hadn't lived to tell anyone.

Because of that incident three years ago, surgical alteration had been necessary. Durand's massive soldier nicknamed El Toro, the bull, had recognized Carlos during an undercover operation in Argentina before Carlos saw him.

The six-foot-seven Anguis soldier had once taught him how to hit a baseball as a teen, but when he encountered Carlos in the undercover operation, all El Toro saw was the half-million bounty Durand offered to deliver him alive. The Anguis soldier planned a perfect ambush with an additional man. Jumped on his way to meet Gotthard, Carlos refused to go down without spilling blood, most of which was his. But he'd managed to send a double-click radio signal to Gotthard for backup. Two minutes later Gotthard arrived, neutralizing the men, and found Carlos beaten close to death, his face hamburger.

Agents were at their most vulnerable while undercover, which influenced Joe's orders for the plastic surgeon to create a new look to protect his man in the future.

The face that stared back at Carlos from a mirror was at times similar and other times startling. Different enough no one would easily recognize him and put his team at risk, his only true concern. BAD operatives were some of the most highly skilled, and dangerous, in the world. He'd stake his life on them, and had many times.

He couldn't ask for a better team tonight.

But Durand Anguis operated like no other criminal entity, using the most unexpected tactics.

The rear load ramp groaned open. Icy air blasted in as a precursor of what to expect. When Korbin moved forward, so did the team. A bottomless black void loomed beyond the gaping hole to suck them from the aircraft. Carlos shifted closer to the roaring wind. The half-pie moon shone down on a low-hanging blanket of clouds dumping fresh snow across the French Alps.

Folding each finger into his gloved hand as he silently counted down, Korbin closed his fist at five—the signal to go.

Carlos followed suit, a buffeting thirty-degrees-below-zero wind jarring him. Legs tucked in a sitting position, he yanked the rip cord, deploying his ram-air parachute. When the square canopy caught, the sudden change of airspeed wrenched his body backward and up. Jaw clenched to keep his teeth from banging together, he lifted his hands and grasped the risers, instinctively maneuvering the parachute.

His heart drummed faster than a machine gun with the trigger pinned. Adrenaline exploded through him, then he drew a deep breath and settled in for the ride. To be honest, he did enjoy this one part of jumping, loved the sudden quiet and sense of floating in ethereal peace. Seconds evaporated faster than the moisture on his goggles as the team glided twenty kilometers toward the landing spot. He lived his life in minutes, one op to the next, watching over his shoulder for the past sixteen years, waiting to be killed.

If things went to shit tonight, the wait could be over.

He squinted. Two tiny lights appeared in the greenish view of his night-vision goggles as Gotthard's wide shape and Rae's long form came into focus. Where was Korbin?

A flicker of light dropped diagonally across his path at last. The adrenaline junkie settled into the front spot. All lights were extinguished, radio silence in force.

Alex Sanderson, the fifth operative, known as Sandman for putting the enemy to sleep, was an ex–Air Force combat controller, otherwise known as an assault weatherman, highly trained. Sandman would be in place by now setting the infrared strobe as a beacon for the landing spot. He'd been on the ground two klicks from the target for the past week camping in a spider hide, invisible to everyone while performing reconnaissance vital to the mission.

If Sandman was not where they expected him, he was dead.

At thirty-one thousand feet Korbin banked left and Carlos followed. Still no strobe, but trust ran deep in this team. Each agent would continue toward the objective with the absolute knowledge the others performed their part of the mission without fault.

Carlos squinted as they broke through the wall of white and closed in on the undetectable patch of earth.

A pulsing strobe came into view. *Thank you, Sandman.*

In the last thousand-foot drop to the mountainside, a ferocious wind gusted up from the canyon below. Carlos hit and rolled through two feet of snow. He released the chute that was dragging him and planted his feet. When he swiveled around, searching for the team, Gotthard was already standing and consulting his wrist video. Korbin was plowing his way toward Rae, who lay sprawled backward on the snow.

Carlos started toward her. A sick thought that her body might have hit a boulder in the snow flashed into his mind. But by the time Korbin reached her, Rae sat up and knocked away his offered hand. Prickly woman when it came to help in any form.

She and Korbin reached Carlos as Sandman strode up

to the team, weapon hanging across his chest. Sandman raised a gloved hand Rae slapped for their usual high-five "hello." Inside the dark mahogany skin beneath his dove-gray snow camouflage suit was a man Carlos always wanted on his side.

Sandman had two personalities. One could turn a female into his angel for the night in a blink, and the other could make a terrorist piss himself.

Once all the chutes were stowed out of sight, Korbin waited for the thumbs-up "all-set" sign from everyone, then struck out, leading the hike. A hundred meters from the three-level home, Carlos signaled to gather. The team closed quarters behind a mound of naked boulders.

Gotthard produced a compact thermal infrared camera and raised it to his face. He began passing information through hand signs: *Two guards outside, walking—one on the east side, one on the west. Four bodies inside, two on the second level. Two on the third floor, one was horizontal and motionless*—probably the female hostage.

Carlos signaled each operative to move into position. He'd rescue the young woman and protect his team first. Saving his own ass came last . . . if luck shined on him one more time.

He steeled himself and moved forward, ready to find out if the men guarding this château really belonged to Durand Anguis.

TWO

Had her e-mails gone through in time?

To the right people?

Gabrielle Saxe stood and paced from the workstation to the window in her rental house. A dreary Sunday. Heavy mist from a slow rain hovered over Lake Peachtree, blurring the dock lights. Peachtree City, a planned community in Georgia south of Atlanta, had been the best place she'd found to hide since living on the edge for the past ten years. She missed her family home in France, but the occasional fog here in the South made her long for her flat in London even more.

She missed her freedom, too, but safety came with a cost.

And not just hers. She'd do anything to keep her family in France safe, too. That was one reason she'd gone into hiding ten years ago. Right after her divorce from a rising Italian screen star who had charmed her into getting married with only one intention—to use her. The honeymoon lasted two months, then things started to sour between them. She met the true Roberto Delacourte. First came the verbal abuse on how lacking she was in the bedroom even after she'd tried to meet his expectations. She'd had no experience and hid her revulsion at some of his ideas. When she'd awakened tied to the bed and suffered the equivalent of rape, she started hiding from him.

Six months into the turbulent relationship he back-handed her across the face and punched her stomach.

Gabrielle had braced herself for more violence when she demanded a divorce and threatened to put him in jail.

He'd calmly laid out the terms for divorce in intricate detail, having clearly planned many things in advance. As he'd spoken, she realized how in her naïveté she'd been played for money and social connections he used to further his career. He explained how he would inform the media that *he* was asking for a divorce and that she would pay him an exorbitant settlement from the trust fund her mother had left her. All details of the divorce would remain sealed unless he chose to share something, and she could never say a negative word against him.

She screamed that he was insane, which earned her another blow to her ribs. Then he warned her what he'd do to her and her family if she did not meet his terms. He reeled off a list that included releasing lurid stories about her supposed perverted sexual appetite to the paparazzi with doctored photos of her in compromising positions and alluded to having underworld contacts who liked small children, such as the two girls her father and his new wife had birthed. She wouldn't allow anything to happen to those children. And with her father in a close campaign race for a high position in the French government, the scandal alone would cripple his career.

She'd been young and truly feared Roberto, afraid of how far he would go to get what he wanted.

Gabrielle would have fought Roberto if only her life and reputation had been at stake, but not her family's. And Roberto had garnered a list of prominent people who would vouch for him in a public venue. Her fault. She'd introduced him to the cream of London and Paris, all of whom believed he was a wonderful husband since she'd been raised to keep her personal life private. He was a rising star who wanted enough money and platinum contacts to shove him onto the big screen.

And he'd known she'd sacrifice all for those she loved.

She hadn't been planning her moves the way he had, hadn't been careful to protect herself against a monster. Gabrielle had brought him into her family's world, so she had to get him out. She swallowed her pride and agreed to his ultimatum, thinking money would get rid of him for good.

If she'd only known just how ruthless he could be, she'd have realized he would never be satisfied with a simple divorce settlement of $5 million.

Turning back from the window, she stared at her laptop, willing it to give her an answer. She fingered the oval locket dangling against her neck from a thin gold chain and checked the online site again.

Why wouldn't someone—such as the CIA—post the message on the bulletin board as she'd asked? So much for appreciating the risks she'd taken to feed a message into the right channels, key words included for a suspicious eye. Anyone in the intelligence community knew better than to let a pipeline to information dry up. She'd secretly helped other agencies in the past, but she wouldn't stick her neck out for the Americans again if they weren't going to do their part.

Mon Dieu! What was their problem?

Cuckoo . . .

Gabrielle jumped at the broken silence. She had to turn off that clock when she went to bed. She never slept in the afternoon, but her body begged for the reprieve right now. Rest hadn't been possible for the past fifty hours since receiving a postale card that almost stopped her heart in midbeat.

She rubbed her stomach where a mass of squirming nerves was doing a bang-up job of making her nauseous.

Maybe tea would settle her stomach.

Two days of sleep would do more good.

She scanned e-mails. Nothing, just mundane chatter that ranged from IT questions generated by articles she wrote anonymously for online publications to the rare personal e-mail.

Her gaze snagged on an e-mail from Fauteur de Trouble that read, "Call me soon—I'm being exiled and you're the only one who will understand . . ." Gabrielle smiled. Babette had chosen an apt electronic name. She was definitely a troublemaker, but in a lovable way. Gabrielle doubted drama queen Babette, one of Gabrielle's two half sisters from her father's second marriage, was truly being exiled.

More likely, the rebellious fourteen-year-old faced being sent to a relative's home for the holidays to give her father some peace. The headstrong teen was turning his hair gray, which Gabrielle found amusing.

Go Babette. Unfortunately for their father, he'd spawned another female who refused to be crammed into a mold and stamped out like a perfect child. That designation belonged to eleven-year-old Cora, Gabrielle's youngest half sister.

She hated that term—*half sister*. What was the other half? Both her sisters meant the world to her, regardless of the percentage of blood they shared. If it was safe to do so, Gabrielle would enjoy seeing her sisters more often.

She'd pretended to be a recluse, which her father interpreted as her never having got over her mother's death. She'd understood his confusion and grief, but was still hurt by how after the funeral he'd sent her to live in a school with strangers, rather than deal with a heartbroken child.

Her first thought upon waking each morning in school was that her mother's killer walked free. Her second was a vow to assure that someday the Anguis paid for their crimes.

Gabrielle fingered the stiff postale card from Linette propped against her monitor base. She smiled at the memories that drifted through her mind of the young girl she'd met at the private school . . . Linette Tassone, her only family for several years. Who then vanished.

Where was her dearest friend now, and how had Linette known about this girl Mandy being kidnapped?

The photo of a palomino horse running free decorated the card front. Linette had loved horses, always dreamed of owning a ranch. But more than that reminder had been an absolute confirmation the card came from Linette—the tiny handwritten words at the closing, *bee happee*, with the double *e* that had taken Gabrielle's breath.

She and Linette had agreed to only use *bee happee* in dire circumstances to assure the message came from one of them.

Gabrielle had laughed back then, calling the signature a secret handshake, but Linette loved the secrets they shared.

Good thing.

Anyone other than the two of them would likely dismiss the neatly written message as an odd language, not a code.

Gabrielle had started the whole code business, adding a cryptic word in each personal note to Linette, who quickly guessed the words, genius that she was. What else were two lost souls ignored by wealthy fathers supposed to do while huddled in their dorm room on holidays when most of the other students went home to their families?

The old fifteenth-century castle that housed their school in Carcassonne, France, had been torn from the pages of a fairy tale, with precious tapestries, exquisite Louis XV bedroom furniture in the dorms, and gourmet delicacies prepared by chefs. She and Linette had giggled their way through the first quarter, accepting the rigid security as necessary for their protection.

Life seemed pretty ideal until Linette disappeared

along with all of her personal belongings just before her seventeenth birthday.

No one answered Gabrielle's questions until her persistence landed her in the dean of women's office, where she was warned of disciplinary action if she mentioned Linette Tassone to the staff again. From then on the fairy-tale castle's stone walls had felt cold and suffocating as a prison. No wonder she'd been so easily duped by a charmer. She'd been alone so long she'd been easy prey.

For eleven years she'd searched, wondering what had really happened to Linette, unwilling to believe the story Senor Tassone had told about his daughter.

But how could she argue with no evidence to the contrary?

She'd finally buried the memories, accepting that she'd never again have anyone she could trust like Linette. Until this card arrived. Gabrielle might not be able to help Linette, yet, but she wouldn't let her dear friend down in the meantime.

She flipped the card over, decoding the first line again.

Gabrielle — You can't help me, but I need you to save others from ending up where I am.

She didn't need to read the rest, knew the text by heart now, including an odd reference to the kidnapped girl being sent to the *fratelli*—an Italian term for "brotherhood." The card had arrived at a postal delivery center in Peachtree City after being forwarded from her father's ancestral home near Paris. Gabrielle quietly thanked him for forwarding the occasional mail he received for her, or Mandy might have had no chance at all.

South American kidnappers were after the young American woman, but Linette had said Mandy was in "grave danger" and "no one will know" about the kidnapping, which made no sense. Regardless, Gabrielle had faith in Linette, so she'd fed an electronic message into the right channels, those scanned by trained intelligence observers.

She'd made it beyond easy for the intelligence agencies.

So why hadn't they posted online to confirm they were acting on the information or that Mandy had been found? If Gabrielle didn't hear something soon, she'd . . . what?

Call the CIA? They would dismiss it as a crank call if she called anonymously. Sending a second e-mail would be too risky. Might as well just send the intelligence world her address since another electronic link *might* lead them right to her, if the first one hadn't given her away.

Okay, so she was a bit anal about this, but she'd protected her anonymity too many years to get caught now.

She scoffed quietly at herself. A rare few in the world could track her electronic trail; so far, none of which were employed by intelligence agencies had. Stop worrying.

No one had found her during a decade of hiding.

But she wouldn't take an unnecessary risk. She'd already put herself and others on a bit of shaky ground, so the damn spooks needed to do their part.

She'd done all she could.

Few people, even those in the intelligence community, could have found out as quickly that the men in South America after the diplomat's daughter belonged to Durand

Anguis or that Mandy would be taken to a château in St. Gervais, France.

But then no one in the intelligence community would have spent the past decade committed solely to finding a way to bring down everyone connected to Durand Anguis.

Gabrielle rubbed her gritty eyes. Her skin rippled with an eerie sense of something not right. She ran her hand over chill bumps pebbling her arms and glanced around.

No sensor had been tripped or an alarm would have sounded.

She reached for her laptop, tapping two keys to bring up the digital video cameras monitoring the outside of the house. Crime was so low in Peachtree City she thought of it as Pleasantville. Her protection devices weren't for the run-of-the-mill burglar.

A thief's first priority wouldn't be to slit her throat.

Images popped up from all six cameras. Nothing but the drizzly wet exterior surrounding the house. If someone had approached from the driveway or come up through the woods, the intruder would have tripped one of the many sensors she'd hidden. That would trigger outside floodlights. Then an inside alarm would sound with two quick dings like a phone ringing continuously until she cleared the alarm. The property was a virtual Charlotte's web of underground wiring.

She hit the keys once more to bring up the bulletin board on her monitor and searched for a message from REBOUND that referenced Mandy as "the babe," the name she'd told them to reply with. And there it was finally. . . .

Her heart thumped hard. The message read, "Babe in danger of being lost. Needs your help. Now."

Oh, mon Dieu!

—⁓—

Once the two guards outside the château were neutralized, Carlos signaled Sandman to patrol the perimeter, then Carlos and the team inserted.

Inside the dimly lit garage, a Range Rover and four snowmobiles were parked, ready to drive straight out. Carlos slipped off his goggles and drew a breath of musty air. Snow shovels and other household tools hung from one wall above an empty washtub with too many rusty holes to be useful. Faded blue cabinets and a workbench filled another stretch of whitewashed wall.

Gotthard produced a valve-stem puller and squatted down to begin disabling tires. He'd remain behind to cover the exit point and have the snowmobiles ready on word from Carlos.

Korbin slipped up the wooden stairs and into the house with Carlos and Rae on his heels. The toasty smell of logs burning somewhere inside swept through the warm air. At around four thousand square feet, the building fell short of spectacular by wealthy standards, but the owner wasn't slumming either.

When Carlos reached the first landing, he motioned with hand signals for Korbin and Rae to deal with the guards on the main floor, secure the building.

Taking down a guard should cheer up Rae.

As Korbin and Rae started to move, shouts in the house froze all three of them. One guard was yelling to the other in Spanish, "She's bleeding . . . get me bandages—"

Carlos took the lead, waving to Korbin and Rae to follow him, until they reached a hallway where they were faced with the option of going up a wide staircase to the third floor or to the kitchen on the right.

Drawers were being opened and slammed shut in the kitchen, followed by cursing between two men.

Carlos sent Korbin and Rae to the right, then he raced softly up the stairs. At the next landing, he caught a deep voice muttering snarled curses down the hall to his left. Carlos followed the sound to a room where the sharp smell of fresh blood hit him as he quickly took in the scene.

A massive guard in a black turtleneck and matching cargo pants intent on his task was hunched next to a heavy mahogany bed. Chunks of broken glass from a shattered water goblet lay on the nightstand and the floor as if the drinking glass had been struck against the edge. A shock of blond hair spilled over the side of the bed alongside the man's leg.

Carlos slipped his knife from its sheath and entered silently. He moved two whispered steps and reached for a fist of thick, black hair. As he whipped the man's head back, exposing his throat to the razor-sharp blade, Carlos got a clear shot of a young woman lying still as death— Mandy—her wrists bleeding profusely. *Merde.*

The guard arched up, but Carlos finished the kill before the man's next breath and shoved him out of his way, then checked for a pulse on Mandy. Weak, but she wasn't dead. Yet. He yanked up the flannel bed linen covering her limp body and started hacking several long strips. The teenager's camo T-shirt barely moved with each faint breath. Her gray bottoms looked like a child's pj's.

The white sheet had more color than her bloodless face.

Damn those bastards for whatever caused her to do this.

"All clear," Korbin announced, entering the room with Rae.

Carlos nodded, too busy trying to keep Mandy alive to answer. At least radio silence was no longer an issue now with the resistance neutralized.

"Find a snowmobile suit," Carlos ordered.

"I saw one downstairs." Rae snapped out the statement on her way out the door.

Korbin lifted Mandy's wrist, allowing Carlos to bandage her faster and finish by the time Rae raced back in with a snowsuit that would swallow the teen. Exactly what Carlos wanted. He crossed her arms over her chest to keep the injuries above her heart, then used more sheet sections to wrap her arms to her body so they wouldn't flop around.

They used the suit like a cocoon, sliding Mandy inside and leaving nothing exposed. Carlos lifted her into his arms and followed Korbin out the door. Rae covered everyone's back down the hallway to the stairs.

"All clear here, we're heading out," Carlos said into his commo transmitter for Gotthard's benefit. "Package is damaged. Fire up the rides."

At the bottom of the stairs, Carlos cursed. "Check for—"

"—marks on the bodies," Rae finished. "The three I searched all had the tattoo on the left chest area."

Carlos never slowed on his way to the garage, thrumming with the urge to see the bodies himself if not for one problem.

He couldn't question another team member's assessment.

And he sure as hell couldn't explain why he had to see the tattoos for himself.

The informant had been dead-on. How? He'd kill for some time alone with Mirage, who'd been so accurate about the kidnappers, the teenager, and this location, about everything right down to the Anguis. Anyone who knew that much about the Anguis family probably had an ax to grind with them.

And anyone who knew that much about the Anguis was a threat to Carlos's existence and the secret he shielded. Durand killed anyone in his path, especially a snitch, so how could the informant have known Anguis business well enough to rat him out and still live?

Carlos growled deep in his throat. If only the tips had come through early enough for his team to reach this child before she slit her wrists. He prayed she'd live.

In the garage, Gotthard had the overhead door open and the snowmobiles outside and running. "Sandman sent the signal for the helo to meet us at the extraction point in one hour," he told Carlos, who nodded, hoping Mandy would survive that long.

The chopper would have a medic on board, but she might need more blood than they normally carried. He handed Mandy to Gotthard. "Strap her to my back."

Carlos pulled his goggles back into place and settled

on the lead snowmobile with his feet on the running boards.

Gotthard wrapped Mandy's snowsuited body around him, fastening the long, empty sleeves in front of his chest with a wire tie. Carlos felt a belt looped around his chest, drawn just tight enough to snug her close to him.

Gotthard secured her legs and slapped Carlos's arm. "Go."

Carlos thumbed the accelerator sharply, grimacing over how lifeless her body lay against his back when the machine roared into action. He glanced behind him once more to see the other snowmobiles following, loaded with his team.

All alive and accounted for. Mission accomplished.

Except for the chance to inspect the bare chests of the guards. To see if they *only* had a snake-and-dagger tattoo over their heart marking them as Anguis soldiers or if a scar intersected the tattoo as well, indicating they were blood-related to Durand Anguis.

Just like the scar across the same tattoo on his chest.

———

Inside the château's garage, the washtub moved up on one side then slid off the trapdoor to the basement. Pushing the trapdoor harder, the man lifted his head up and took in the silent room now empty except for the Range Rover. That had flat tires.

He sighed and withdrew a cell phone.

Report first. Find transportation next.

His boss was not going to be happy.

THREE

Gabrielle's neck hurt. Her arms hurt. Everything hurt.

A dream shouldn't hurt, should it?

She fought through layers of drowsiness, struggling to open her eyes. Sleep pulled at her, but some annoying sound kept poking at her to wake up.

. . . *cuckoo, cuckoo, cuckoo.*

The clock. How many times had that bird chirped?

Her brain flickered to life. She lifted her head from the desk. She swallowed against the icky taste in her mouth and rubbed her sore eyes, blinking to focus. Fish swam across the monitor screen on her laptop. Life should be so happy and free.

The smile she started to indulge vanished.

Computer. Bulletin boards. Mandy!

She reached for the mouse, moved it, and tapped, bringing up the message board. She read quickly. Thank God.

They—whoever had received her first warning on Mandy—had asked for more help last night, specifics on the château and the Anguis. She couldn't add anything new on the château, but after convincing herself Mandy's life was worth the gamble, she'd shared a little more of what she knew on Durand that must have helped. The message posted to the bulletin board at just after ten this morning now read, "Babe in safe hands."

Would have been nice if she'd received that at six this morning when she'd finally crashed at the computer. She could have slept in a bed.

Gabrielle squinted to focus on her cuckoo clock. *Almost four o'clock?* Light leaked into the room through cracks in the blinds. So, that would be four in the afternoon? Monday. No wonder every muscle ached. She'd only slept a handful of hours in the past three days and that had been bent over the desk.

A bath, some food, and she'd go back to bed for a while.

Food first or she might not make it through the bath. She scrounged around the kitchen, considered having food delivered, then changed her mind when she found Thai leftovers and a glazed doughnut for dessert.

The bath was almost as refreshing as brushing her teeth. She spent every day in T-shirts and sweatpants, what she called frumpy comfort. But to sleep she slid on a silk camisole and lace panties, her little self-indulgence. Never having to think about her appearance was just one perk of living in seclusion. A sad chuckle escaped at the sarcastic logic.

Gabrielle whipped back the covers on her bed, snuggled down beneath them, and drifted right off to deep sleep.

An annoying noise infiltrated her swirling dreams.

She tried to ignore the sound. Her body pleaded for her to ignore it, but the stupid sound wouldn't leave her alone.

She'd have to disconnect her clock.

Ding, ding. Silence.

Ding, ding. Silence.

Gabrielle's eyes flew open. Not the clock.

The security alarm.

———

Carlos grabbed his bag out of the overhead bin and filed into line exiting the airplane and headed for customs at Atlanta's Hartsfield-Jackson International Airport.

He checked his cell phone for the local time—4:00 p.m.—then keyed a text message to headquarters, informing the director he'd arrived and would head to Nashville as soon as he made a stop at home.

Calling the expansive four-bedroom cabin in the north Georgia mountains home was a stretch since he didn't own or rent it, but that was all he had. Telling lies about his past, such as that he'd grown up in Bolivia instead of Venezuela, hadn't protected his identity. He'd even kept an apartment in Nashville at one time, until the Anguis soldier recognized him three years ago. After that, he stored his few belongings in the cabin, which served as a safe house. The only possession he truly cared about—the

photo of him and his little brother when they were kids—
was in the cabin's safe. A rival of the Anguis's had shot his
brother to retaliate for a slight by Durand the day before
the kid would have graduated, with honors, from college.

The cabin served as one of BAD's many secure residences where any agent could spend downtime or take a
prisoner temporarily.

All Carlos needed for a home.

All he'd ever risk having.

He scrubbed a hand over his cheek, scratching at the
whiskers, too tired to bother shaving when he'd showered
eleven hours ago. And if he didn't get a haircut soon he'd
have to start pulling his hair back into a ponytail. The
yawn caught him off guard.

He'd stolen a catnap on the flight back from Charles
de Gaulle Airport in France, but it hadn't been worth a
damn. His mind had refused to let him forget the lifeless feel of Mandy's body when he'd carried her onto the
helo . . . or the gruesome image that blossomed when he'd
cut her out of the snowmobile suit. The sharp scent of
blood had clashed with biting-cold air. He'd sucked in a
breath at her washed-out skin and blue lips, the makeshift
bandage soaked with what had appeared to be every drop
of blood from her body.

A sick ball of failure had crashed through his gut.

But miraculously she'd still had a pulse. The medics
started an immediate infusion and kept her alive until they
reached a secure facility outside Paris where he'd left her.

Mandy's prognosis sucked, but she hadn't died in his
arms.

She had a chance.

Gotthard would send word on Mandy as soon as he landed in Nashville. Korbin and Rae should be hitting D.C. and New York about now, everyone returning on separate flights for security.

Carlos stepped up to the customs desk and gave all the standard answers to wary-eyed officials. Did they practice looking suspicious in mirrors?

Welcome to the United States. Don't even think about chewing gum the wrong way.

He maneuvered around pockets of weary passengers flowing toward the exit like a lazy stream and had reached the upstairs main terminal when his cell phone started buzzing.

When he flipped it open, one message popped up.

Call office immediately. Translation: Urgent.

Carlos keyed the speed dial.

"You through customs?" Joe said without any salutation.

"Yep." Carlos pushed through the glass exit doors of the terminal. Smokers flooded the humid Atlanta air with nicotine as they sucked on either their first or last cigarette.

"We found the source."

Mirage.

Last Carlos had heard before flying home was that BAD had traced the IP address to a computer in Russia, where Joe had extensive contacts. That could mean anything or anyone. A UK team from BAD had also been closing in on a London location right before his airplane lifted off. Which one found Mirage?

Carlos snapped to attention. He checked his watch, calculating the possibility of catching an international flight at this time of day.

"Great. Fly to Gatwick?" Carlos strode quickly to the other side of the airport thoroughfare where traffic flowed between the parking garage and the terminal. He could be headed anywhere in the world since the post had been bounced to a hacked computer system in Romania, then Russia. But the minute BAD had pinned down the Russian IP and gained authorization to trace the path from there, a team of agents on the ground and in BAD's headquarters had waited on Mirage to make a mistake.

"No," Joe told him. "That's why I sent an urgent message. The bulk of our immediate resources were shipped to the UK as a starting point since language data programs we ran the posts through indicated our source could be from there, but that might have only been to throw us a curve." Joe was saying the informant was either not in the UK or not from the UK.

"Where?" Carlos shook off any last exhaustion with that word, ready to track the bastard down.

"Georgia. Peachtree City."

"Are you serious?" Carlos spun around and rushed up the ramp to the parking deck.

"Yes. That's why I called you. I've only got one local asset and he's on the way to the location." Joe paused and sounded as though he sighed. "I sent instructor Lee."

Carlos jammed his parking ticket into the payment kiosk and stuck his credit card in next, willing it to process quicker. "*Instructor? When did that happen?*" *Instructor* was code for "field agent" since this was not a secure line. Lee couldn't be ready for prime time yet.

"Today. No choice. Nobody else close enough besides you."

"Where is he?" Carlos snatched the paid ticket the minute the machine spit it out and picked up his pace, eyes searching for his steel-blue 750i BMW.

"Ten minutes away from the meet spot."

"Send him a message to wait, no matter what—"

"I gave him guidelines. You'll get a text with the meet location next. He has the rest."

"I'll be in touch." Carlos shut the phone and found his car. Just in time to toss his bag into the trunk, climb behind the wheel, and release a scalding curse.

Welcome home. Deposit any hope of the day ending on a good note and charge toward a situation with as much planning as a train wreck.

The only redeeming factor?

Carlos got first shot at interrogating the snitch on Durand Anguis. To find out what angle Mirage was working. Informants always wanted something, always had an ulterior motive.

And he hadn't met one yet that wasn't a criminal.

He could list four countries off the top of his head that would jump at the chance to get this one. They could have him as soon as Carlos got what he wanted.

—⁂—

Gabrielle jumped up, tossed on a gray long-sleeved T-shirt and sweatpants, then shoved her feet into sneakers with Velcro clasps. The perfect shoes for quick exits. She glanced at the clock on her nightstand, which informed her she'd slept a half hour.

How long had the security alarm been sounding?

She hit the wall button to shut off the repeating double ring, then ran to the closet and snatched up a backpack that held clothes, money, passport, and a few more necessities. Always.

On the way to the living room, she took her hair out of the clamp at the back of her head, then twisted her hair up and stuck a cap over it. Swallowing was difficult. Fear climbed the constricted muscles of her throat and threatened to strangle her by the time she reached her desk. She lunged for her laptop, working the keys in between slinging a scarf around her neck and shrugging on her knee-length khaki trench coat. Two clicks of the mouse and her monitor split into six screens, showing the areas scanned by digital video cameras positioned around the house.

Five frames revealed nothing unusual.

Number six covered the yard leading up to the front door . . . where a giant man in an ill-fitting brown suit walked up the first step to her porch.

Slow, heavy steps thumped on the wooden boards.

Gabrielle snapped her laptop shut and shoved it into a case with a shoulder strap that held all the accessories. Where to go? She'd always planned on having enough notice to reach her four-wheel-drive Jeep and take a path through the woods, one advantage of living in a community with eighty miles of golf-cart paths. Her gaze slashed to the picture window at the rear of the house, filled with a serene image of Lake Peachtree and a boat dock with a runabout tied up. With a full gas tank.

She'd make a perfect target alone on the lake.

Knock. Knock. Knock.

He couldn't be a salesman. The sign next to the mailbox at the head of the driveway stated clearly NO TRESPASSING, VIOLATORS WILL BE ARRESTED.

Knock. Knock. Knock.

Gabrielle grabbed her car keys on the off chance she could reach her Jeep. Which would already have happened—if she hadn't been so exhausted, the alarm could have roused her faster.

From the other side of the door, a deep voice said, "Law enforcement. Open up."

That froze her. FBI? If they'd tracked her electronically, he could very well be CIA since she'd routed everything through several bounced locations to an IP in London.

"The house is surrounded."

Her heart jumped a foot.

Bloody hell. Options ran through her mind at blinding speed since she only had two.

Running, option one, was pointless.

Gabrielle accepted option two, turned around, and went to the foyer, hoping to bluff her way out. She plastered a smile on her face and opened the door.

"Can I help you? I was on my way out—" She paused to stare up six and a half feet off the floor at a face that would launch a million nightmares. Pocked skin, hulking posture, and a thick neck. Salt-and-pepper hair.

"You don't look like Harry Beaker," he said.

"I'm not. Harry isn't here, but I'll be happy to take a message for him." More smiling. Could she be so lucky he was only looking for Harry? She clutched the door with one hand and the door frame with the other to hide her trembling.

"And you are?"

"Gabrielle Parker. I'm just a renter. I'll make sure Harry gets your message, but I need to go or I'll be late." She'd call Harry the minute she got free if this guy really was looking for him. Harry was pushing ninety, an ex-marine and feisty. She doubted even the CIA could intimidate him.

"I'm not looking for Harry. I'm looking for you," he said.

Her skin prickled at the threat in his voice. "Who are you?" That hadn't come out like the demand she'd hoped for, but had been the best she could do with a dry throat and staring at someone who might be from Durand Anguis.

He reached inside his jacket.

Her heart thumped a panicked beat.

"Special Agent Curt Morton with the DEA," he said, flipping his badge out for a couple seconds before closing the case and shoving it back inside his jacket. He offered her a smile she wished he hadn't. Those big teeth and crooked nose were almost as scary as his flat gray eyes. "Sorry if I gave you a start, but I wanted to be sure before I said too much."

"Sure of what?" she asked, breathless as someone who had just finished a five-mile race. Or close to hyperventilating.

"That you're the one who's been sending electronic messages to intelligence agencies about Durand Anguis."

Busted. And exposed. Durand would find her for sure now.

—⁂—

Carlos motioned for Lee to follow him when he closed the door on a dark blue Suburban and stepped away. The vehicle was parked just off a private driveway in Peachtree City and hidden from the road by a copse of trees. With an unconscious driver.

His feet and hands were bound with flex cuffs, which would hold him until Carlos had time for a full interrogation. The driver had a DEA badge on him, but the credentials were phony.

Carlos couldn't pull the thug's real name to mind, but he'd seen that face and cauliflower ear before. The driver had been part of an electronics bust last year. Hired muscle who offered bargains.

Discount muscle was like eating cheap sushi.

A risk to your health.

Sticks snapped. Carlos cut his eyes at Lee, who grimaced at the noise. Rookies were a risk, too, but Joe wouldn't send someone wet behind his ears. And Lee had ancient eyes in a young man's face. Hard eyes, but he must have come off the streets and lacked experience in wooded terrain.

Waving a hand, Carlos dismissed the misstep and moved ahead, sorting through his options.

Someone had clearly beaten them to the informant. Who? And was the driver's partner here to grab the informant . . . or meet with him? At least two had to be involved. The guy in the car was likely a lookout, a poor one, so the partner could be at the house by now.

Carlos moved quickly through the woods, parallel to the driveway. Light faded faster with each step, tossing shadows through the sparse woods.

Who had beaten him here?

He paused at a curve in the driveway where an open area—the front yard—appeared in the next twenty feet.

He turned to Lee. The young guy's sharp hazel eyes burned with determination. Not quite eye level with Carlos or as heavy-built, Lee stood just over six feet tall, trim, muscular body dressed for the task in camo pants and long-sleeved, dark green shirt.

In spite of all that, this kid was too clean-cut for Carlos's taste. What were Joe and his codirector, Tee, thinking these days?

Joe had given Lee strict marching orders about following anything Carlos said, without question. To that, Carlos had added one simple order—if things went bad, he wanted Lee to back off and contact Joe.

Do not, under any circumstances, play hero.

Voices percolated from the open area just beyond them, too soft for Carlos to make out what the two people said.

He signaled with his hand for Lee to stop and back him up, but stay out of sight. Lee palmed his weapon and nodded. Carlos pulled his own 9 mm from the small of his back, and silently edged forward toward the pair talking.

—⚬—

"I d-don't know what you're talking about." Gabrielle tried to chuckle, but the sound skidded close to hysterical.

Special Agent Morton wasn't smiling. "You're the one who sends information on Durand signed 'Mirage.' We'd like to talk to you."

"I really don't—"

"Miss Parker. Right now you're considered an ally of the United States, but if you refuse to help, your status might change to being considered an accomplice to the Anguis crimes. We've obviously tracked you as the Mirage to this point electronically." He stopped speaking, wisely allowing time for that little warning to settle in.

Accomplice? She swallowed, panic quivering just under the surface of her practiced calm. At least he was with U.S. authorities, not Durand, but leaving here with him would not end well. "*C'est des conneries!*"

"What'd you say?" His thick eyebrows bunched in confusion.

She clutched the shoulder strap of her bag in a tight fist. "This is bullshit. I have done nothing wrong." After years of shielding her identity from the Anguis, she'd lose her anonymity the minute the DEA processed her. Roberto's attempts on her life would pale compared to what she believed Durand would do. "Can we just talk here?"

He shook his head.

"Do I need an attorney present?" Not that she had one, but she could buy time hunting one.

"No. We want to keep this as quiet as you do and protect your anonymity."

Who could argue with that?

She looked past him. "Where's your car?"

"At the entrance to your driveway. Saw the warning. Figured I might risk a flat tire by coming down the drive."

"Is the house really surrounded by agents or police?"

"No, but I do have backup." The gruesome smile appeared again. Why did he even try?

She reached around and pulled the door closed. "I don't know what you are talking about, but I'll cooperate. I'll follow in my car."

Special Agent Morton shook his head again. "We ride in mine. I'll have you driven home." He moved an arm to point toward the driveway as if the way to the car wasn't obvious. When he did, his jacket shifted open, exposing a shoulder holster with a gun.

If she made too big of a fuss, he could just arrest her.

She fumbled with the key, finally locking the dead bolt after two tries. As they said here in the States, just go with the flow for now.

He waited as she walked down the steps ahead of him. Each pace away from the house hurt. This had been the best place she'd lived. She couldn't come back here. Harry's rental house was one of the original homesteads in this planned community, with a paved drive a quarter mile long and hidden by trees on both sides. She trudged through a fresh layer of leaves covering the front yard she'd raked just yesterday.

Striding alongside her, the DEA agent flipped his phone open, punched a key, and waited.

"Why do you think I'm some Mirage person?" she

asked. Where had she screwed up, and who else might have caught her mistake? When he didn't respond, she looked over her shoulder. He'd slowed, but extended those long legs twice, then stopped next to her so she stayed put.

He punched buttons on his phone again, and since he used it like a two-way radio, she could hear the ringing at the other end. No answer.

The flash of suspicion he turned on her now twisted his ugly features to truly evil.

Chill bumps spiked along her skin.

Carlos waited silently as the two men walked side by side toward the driveway. The tall one could have played Lurch on *The Addams Family*. The smaller guy was maybe a couple inches over five feet tall. He wore a khaki trench coat and carried a laptop shoulder case plus a backpack.

And little guy's voice had been high when he said, "Why do you think I'm this Mirage person?"

Damn. Could he be the informant everyone in the intelligence world was searching for?

Carlos slowed his breathing, completely silent so he could hear the conversation. Lee had become perfectly still.

The mismatched pair paused ten feet from where Carlos stood without moving a muscle. Lurch had punched his cell phone and waited. When no one answered, something registered behind that flat forehead that flipped his pissed-off switch.

Two things hit Carlos at the moment Lurch snarled, "Who did you alert that I was here?" at the little guy.

Lurch was Baby Face Jones, a master electronics felon who contracted out for special side jobs, such as kidnapping and torture, when the coffers ran low.

And the little guy—the possible informant—was a woman.

Her face turned a pasty white. She mumbled, "No one."

She sure wasn't what Carlos had imagined.

Baby Face grabbed her by the arm. "Come on." He lifted his phone with the other hand to key it with his thumb.

Now for the train-wreck part of this operation since Carlos couldn't risk that Baby Face would bring in more men.

"Stop right there." Carlos stepped from the brush, his weapon pointed at the pair.

Baby Face's head whipped to Carlos. He released the woman and his phone in one movement and drew a weapon, finger on trigger. Firing.

Carlos shot first, catching Baby Face in the shoulder, the only option he had to knock the incoming bullet wide and not kill Baby Face or hit the woman. But the bullet passed close enough for Carlos to feel heat brush his ear.

The woman screamed, eyes startled in horror at Baby Face, who hit the ground, howling.

Lee jumped into view.

Carlos spun to Lee. "I hit his shoulder. Stop the bleeding and—"

"She's running!"

Carlos whipped back around to see her legs chewing

up ground toward the far end of the one-level brick house. "Son of a bitch." He ran after her.

She was quicker than he'd have guessed. She raced around the corner, disappearing.

When he made it to the backyard, she'd already reached a long dock and flew down the wooden walkway, skidding to a stop before the bench at the end. She tossed her computer bag and backpack into a small runabout and jumped in. He could see her now, but in another fifteen minutes the twilight would fade into night.

Without slowing a step, Carlos shoved his weapon inside the waistband at the small of his back, freeing his hands since she hadn't appeared to be armed. He reached the spot where the boat had been tied just as the outboard she was yanking on caught with a low growl. She shoved off and stood, heading for the steering wheel while the boat floated in neutral.

When his foot hit the last section of dock closest to her, he used that step as a springboard, going airborne. He cleared the six feet of space to the boat, catching a handful of her on the fly, knocking her overboard with him.

She screeched, "No!" as they hit the cold water on the other side of the boat.

Carlos surfaced with a hand still clutching her jacket.

She twisted around, coughing, then fought and kicked loose, catching him in the ribs with her shoe. He grunted, lunged, and snagged her again as she sank. He yanked her around until he had her back to his front, but she was sinking both of them.

"Stop it," he ordered.

She kept flailing her arms and gasping for air. "Help!"

He locked one arm around her middle to free his other arm. The boat was closer than the shore by now, but neither would be an option until she stopped fighting him. "Calm down or we'll drown."

She was gulping for air and squeezing out terror-filled shrieks that died in a mouthful of water. "I . . . can't . . . swim."

Oh, hell. "I can . . . if you don't fight me." He was kicking his legs so hard to keep them afloat his muscles burned.

She stopped moving, all except the deep, wheezing breaths.

Carlos glanced around, hoping Lee could deal with Baby Face and watch both their backs at the same time. The informant shook so hard against him, he expected hysterics any moment. He didn't know what her story was . . . yet, but he had to keep her alive long enough to find out.

"Take it easy," he said, this time in a calmer voice. "I'll get you to the boat."

"Who . . ." She breathed hard a couple times. "Are . . . you?"

"Do what I say and you won't get hurt."

She stiffened at that, then seemed to realize she'd slowed their progress and relaxed some.

He pulled her along as he swam until they reached the boat. She leaped to grab the side as if this runabout were the only life raft in a raging sea.

He'd heard this was a shallow lake. How deep could it be here? Six feet?

But if she thought the water was a deep lagoon, he wasn't telling her any different.

Carlos put his hands around her waist and moved his lips close to her ear before lifting her. "When I get you in this boat, do not make any sudden moves. Don't try to run away or put the boat in gear or I'll throw you back overboard. Do you understand?"

She nodded. Her knuckles were turning bone white from her death grip on the boat rail.

Threatening to put her back in the water wouldn't help calm her down, but it might prevent her from doing something really stupid like trying to use the oar on him.

He kept his voice calm. "When I give you a push, roll into the boat."

Another silent nod.

He lifted her and she lunged into the boat, legs kicking to the point he had to duck or lose his head. As soon as more of her was in than out, he hoisted himself up and over the side.

She huddled in a ball at the back. Cap gone, her hair hung in wet clumps.

"Come up here where I can see you." He motioned toward the passenger seat with his hand.

No movement.

"Now."

She raised belligerent eyes wild with fear.

Carlos shoved a handful of soaked hair off his face. She was still freaked-out. He'd have to go get her. He never let anyone sit behind him, definitely not a felon.

He moved to reach for her, but she held up a hand to

stop him, the action almost regal and elegant in spite of the soaked trench coat and sneakers. She pushed up and teetered her way to sit in the plastic passenger seat, her wide eyes never leaving him.

Fair enough. He wasn't taking his eyes off her either. He sat on the top edge of the driver's seat and shifted the outboard motor into forward, cruising back to the dock. Cold air seeped through his wet clothes. He glanced at her huddled form shivering against the chill and thought about the blanket in the trunk of his car. She should be okay until then.

When they reached the wooden planks, he cut the outboard motor, tied up the boat, and jumped out, offering her a hand.

That she refused.

She grabbed her backpack and computer bag, then climbed out, careful not to get too close to him.

"Let's go." He waited for her to move forward.

"What will you do with me?" She had a lush French voice, laced with a sophistication that carried a soft British accent. But those exotic blue eyes and high cheekbones were decidedly French.

"Haven't decided that yet."

"You murdered a—"

"He's *not* dead," he said before she could accuse him of murdering Baby Face. "Takes a lot more to kill him than a bullet in the shoulder." Carlos pointed the way he wanted her to go and she finally started moving.

She trembled with each step.

Carlos had to clamp down on the urge to comfort her.

She'd been leaving with Baby Face Jones, a known electronics felon who made his living by online pirating and financial scams.

Had Baby Face come to kidnap her or was she cutting a deal with him?

She'd appeared to be leaving voluntarily.

Baby Face was a genius when it came to electronics, but Carlos doubted even Baby Face could have found the informant without aid from someone with deep pockets. Someone who could give him access to megacomputers equal to The Monster, BAD's computer supersystem Joe swore was unmatched anywhere else in the intelligence field. Just one of many questions Baby Face was going to answer once Carlos and Lee took him into headquarters.

Was this woman really the infamous Mirage?

Had the entire intelligence world been overlooking something obvious Baby Face had stumbled on?

Hard to accept that possibility, which meant he'd had help.

When Carlos rounded the house, Lee was nowhere to be found. What the hell was he doing?

Carlos directed the woman to keep moving a step ahead of him toward where Baby Face lay on the ground. There was no sign of Lee or anything stuffed on Baby Face's shoulder to stop the blood flow.

She reached Baby Face first and backed up, whispering, "*Mon Dieu.*"

Carlos stepped up ahead of her. Baby Face bled profusely from a sliced throat.

Something had gone very bad.

She inched away, making noises that normally preceded gut puking.

He didn't have time for her to be sick. In fact, Carlos would bet they were lucky to even be alive and that Lee had not fared as well. Whoever grabbed Lee might not have realized Carlos had been around the backside of the house chasing this woman into the lake.

The thought of Lee dead sucked, but if Carlos stopped to think about the waste of a young life, two more would be snuffed out next.

He grabbed the front of his captive's wet jacket, spinning her terror-rimmed eyes to his, then spoke low. "Listen up. We've got to go. Whoever killed him might come back."

Shock blanched her face even whiter before her eyes sharpened to two angry slits. "You mean your buddy didn't do this?"

"No, he's probably dead, too."

That stunned her. "Who would kill both of them?"

"We can talk or try to get out of here alive." When that registered on her face, he asked, "You got keys to that Jeep?"

"I'm not helping you." She whispered the words, underlining *you* at the end with a slur.

"Oh, yes, you are unless you want to end up with *your* throat slit . . . or worse."

That struck a nerve. She shook like a wet dog and took another step back. White showed all around the iris of her eyes, the perfect picture of a terrified woman.

If tears followed, hysterics wouldn't be far behind.

Merde! He had no time for that or to calm her down. Carlos grabbed the lapels of her coat, pulling her so close he could see tears hanging on her silky eyelashes. "You can either hand over the keys or I'll strip-search you right here." He hated to use that threat, but it did the trick.

She didn't cry.

The mean look she gave him would force a rabid dog to back down. She shoved her hand into the pocket of her coat and produced a small ring with two keys. One was for an automotive ignition and the other looked like a house key.

Carlos took the keys, then latched on to her arm and towed her across the yard to where a ten-year-old dingy-white Jeep Wrangler was parked. With a freakin' soft-top, but at least it had the little half doors on each side. If he didn't have her to deal with, his chances on foot would be better, but getting this informant to headquarters in one piece was his sole priority at the moment.

She was BAD's only connection to the Fratelli.

And he had to find out just how much she knew about the Anguis.

He hurried her into the Jeep and watched to make sure she stayed in while he circled to the driver's side. When he slid behind the wheel, he told her, "Scoot down to the floorboard."

"Why?"

"You'll be less of a target. I don't have time to answer questions and keep you alive, so do what I tell you when I tell you."

"Why?"

He cranked the engine. "You got a problem with your hearing?"

"No, I hear just fine." She sat perched on the seat, pure defiance in contrast to the fear pulsing from her in waves.

"Then you must be dense," he muttered, steering out to the driveway and watching everything at once.

"No, I'm not dense."

"Then what exactly are you having a problem understanding?"

"Why don't you just kill me right now?"

He tossed quick glances at her as he eased the Jeep past the body on the lawn and started down the driveway with the headlights off. He had enough twilight to see the path.

"What makes you think I want to kill you?" he asked, his gaze sweeping everywhere for a threat.

"You're Anguis, right?"

FOUR

Carlos clutched the steering wheel. This was exactly why he had to get the first crack at this informant, find out what she knew about the Anguis. How had she recognized him when no one else in the past sixteen years had?

He'd never even met this woman before today. He slowed the Jeep, still needing to get her tucked down beneath the dash. "Why would you say that?"

She scoffed, but the raspy sound came out on a slip of terror. "I've been waiting on Durand to send someone."

Carlos released the breath he'd been holding, expecting to hear how she knew him. She only thought he'd been sent by Durand to kidnap her.

"You think just because I'm Hispanic that I'm part of Durand's group?"

She swung around, squinting at him as she churned on his answer. "You're not?"

"No. Now, will you scoot down before someone blows

your head to pieces?" He gave the Jeep gas and eased forward.

Gabrielle tried to comprehend what he was saying. Not Anguis? Then who was this guy? His last words finally registered—the comment about getting her head blown off.

She scrunched her body down into as small a ball as she could make, but she'd never been small so the ball was more a misshapen blob.

The man driving had all the attributes she'd ever mentally assigned an Anguis soldier, from the olive skin to thick black hair and lashes to a body built for power.

Danger radiated from him in shock waves.

He cut his gaze at her for a brief moment. Keen eyes assessed her with concern that didn't fit the image she'd conjured of an Anguis soldier.

She would have expected mean, beady eyes.

Brisk air buffeted collar-length black hair around his neck, the soft locks a sharp contrast to the hard jawline and tense mouth. Attractive, in a deadly sort of way. What would he do with her?

A shiver ran along her spine.

If Durand hadn't sent this rogue interloper, then whom was this guy working with? Not law enforcement or he wouldn't have shot Agent Morton.

She glanced up when the Jeep took a curve around the broken poplar tree that had snapped in a recent storm. That meant they were close to the street . . . where someone might be waiting for them?

Such as the person who had cut the DEA agent's throat?

"What about a bullet hitting you?" Gabrielle asked her captor. If this guy was shot while driving and wrecked the Jeep, she might end up a human pretzel.

"I'll be fine. No more talking," he ordered, but in a less menacing tone.

He wheeled the Jeep in an abrupt left turn off the driveway before reaching the mailbox. She stretched her neck to see why.

The Jeep idled next to a dark-colored sport utility parked in the woods. He leaned over, stared at something inside the vehicle and cursed, then backed up to the driveway . . . and cursed again. He accelerated hard, lurching the Jeep forward, and spinning a wheel when he swung onto the street.

A loud ping echoed before the windshield cracked and spider-webbed.

She lifted up.

"Stay the hell down!" He downshifted and rammed the accelerator again, fishtailing the Jeep one way, then the next.

Another shot ripped through the soft top and zinged off the dash.

Gabrielle ducked her head and clung to the seat. She pressed a hand on the wall next to the floorboard to wedge herself in as tightly as she could. Air roared through the open windows.

"Where are we going?" she asked. Her fingernails dug into the seat cushion.

He ignored her.

After two more turns, he floored the gas then skidded

to a stop. Stinking rubber filled the cab. He quickly shifted the Jeep into reverse and backed up as fast as they'd been going forward.

Tires on another vehicle close by screeched against the pavement.

Speeding in Peachtree City was not a wise idea since this small community had its own police department that patrolled the highways. Tangling with law enforcement would make her an easy target for Durand, but getting arrested had a certain appeal when people were shooting at her.

Hard to decide the lesser of two deadly options, but she doubted this guy was going to give her a choice.

Another shot pinged off the inside of the windshield. This one drew a snarl of curses in Spanish from her driver. Blood trickled down the side of his cheek.

Help him or not?

She didn't even know who he was or whom he worked for. He'd shot a DEA agent, so what did that say about him?

Bad guy, to put it in simple terms.

Still, he was working real hard to keep her alive and out of someone's hands. Maybe Anguis soldiers.

Gabrielle reached under the seat for a rag she kept there to clean the windshield when needed and handed it up to him. "Here."

He glanced, did a double take, then snatched the rag and wiped blood that had run into his eyes. He tossed the cloth down against the base of the shifter and yanked the wheel hard to the left.

She barely caught herself. What seemed like forever had probably taken all of ten minutes when he finally slowed down and said, "Think we lost them."

"Can I get up?"

"No."

Antagonizing this guy was not a bright idea, but she had to find some sort of mutual ground for any hope of catching him with his guard down so she could escape. Couldn't let him know how terrified she was.

She licked her lips and tried again. "Where are you going?"

"Not where I'd originally planned."

How about a straight answer? Gabrielle unclenched her fisted hands and took a couple breaths. Now was the time for patience, not ripping at him, but she was edgy from exhaustion and vibrating from the quick release of an adrenaline rush.

She kept silent while he made two sharp turns, then parked. He left the engine running and switched the headlights off. "You can get up for a minute."

About time. She arched her back and tried to get traction with her knees.

"Here." He reached over, cupped her under the arms, and lifted her out of the hole. That he did it so easily told her just how strong this guy was, because she was no lightweight.

As soon as she had some balance, he released her and flipped open his phone, text-messaging someone. He scowled.

"What's wrong?" Her pulse jackhammered in her ears.

"No signal."

She took deep breaths, trying to calm herself, and looked around. The first street sign she recognized meant they were located in the south end of the city, just off Peachtree Parkway. "This is one of two areas I always lose calls. Think we're in a pocket between cell towers."

Sirens whined in the distance.

Her stomach growled.

His look of surprise would have been funny in different circumstances. "Hungry?"

"No." She'd had one meal in two days, but the thought of eating right now nauseated her. She propped an elbow on the door frame and supported her aching head on her hand.

"Who are you working with?" He gripped the steering wheel with one hand, tapping a finger and eyes distant as though he worked on a thought.

"I don't know what you're talking about."

"*Don't* jerk me around," he warned.

Getting yelled at snapped the last link to her patience. Damn the consequences. She lifted her head and turned to him. "Well, I don't know anything about you other than you killed a DEA agent, so I'm not in the frame of mind to be jerked around *either*."

"I didn't kill him," he muttered, then paused and hit her with a look of disbelief. "You thought the guy I shot was DEA?"

Her stomach did a roll at the incredulity in his voice. "He had ID. He is ... *was* Special Agent Curt Morton."

"Shit."

She *really* didn't like the sound of that. "I don't understand."

"Curt Morton has been missing for two weeks, which means if Baby Face had his ID then Curt is most likely dead."

She rubbed her head, trying to piece it all together. "Who is Baby Face?"

"The man you were leaving with was Baby Face Jones."

"Who is he . . . what does he do?" She had a sick feeling she wasn't going to like the answer.

"He's a . . . mercenary who does errands."

"Like kidnapping?"

"So you weren't leaving with him voluntarily?"

She shook her head. "No. I thought he was DEA and he threatened me if I didn't go with him. So *is* he a kidnapper?" *Sacre bleu, sacre bleu* . . . she'd been walking into a trap.

"Kidnapping is side work. His real expertise is electronic crimes, plus he tortures intelligence agents for marketable information when he can nail one."

Dots floated in her vision. "Who are you?" she asked in a strained voice. "Are you with the DEA?"

"Carlos. I'm not DEA. Who are you?"

"Gabrielle . . . Parker."

"Right." That snicker of skepticism was in his voice again. "We have to move. I need a tower."

"Was that sport utility in my driveway yours?" she wondered aloud. Everyone seemed to show up at her rental house on foot.

"No." He scanned around them while he put the

Jeep into gear and flipped the headlights on. "Scoot back down."

"Who sent Baby Face?"

"I don't know and don't care until I find out where my partner is."

"Do you and your partner work for—"

"—no one you'd know."

That wasn't encouraging. "What do you want with me?"

He ignored her again. "Get back down."

Going to the police would create all sorts of problems for her, but she was starting to reconsider that if her next best option was dying or being tortured.

That didn't even take into consideration what this Carlos had planned for her. Where did he stand with law enforcement?

"We could knock on a door and ask the residents to call the police," she suggested. Not a bad idea since it would give her a chance to escape this guy.

"No police." Carlos turned a grim face to her. "If we get out of here alive and find a freakin' tower, I can contact my people."

No police. My people. That sure as the devil didn't sound like someone aligned with law enforcement.

She pushed her body back into a wad between the seat and the floorboard, wet, cold, and scared. Mostly scared.

He kept his speed moderate, driving as if he were a model citizen for several miles. She wrenched her wrist around to see the time, clenching her teeth to stop the chattering.

She took advantage of his silence to plot where to find public transportation and which way to head for a new hiding place once she broke free of him. Accessing funds would take time, but she kept money stashed in several remote locations.

Planning for survival beat thinking about how close she'd come to being caught by Baby Face or wondering what Carlos had in mind for her.

Carlos punched numbers in his phone whenever his shifting hand was free. Something must have gone through since he started talking.

"Lee check in?" he asked without even saying hello. Pause. Curse. "Send cleanup to the location. I've got the source, but I'm in a traffic jam. I need—" He pulled the phone from his head, stared at the tiny cell phone, and lifted it as if to slam the device against the steering wheel.

But he didn't, closing the phone with a finger.

Lost call again?

Gabrielle couldn't see streetlights any longer from her position. Just pitch dark. "We're not in a traffic jam. We're in the country."

"Yep."

"I'm getting up if no one is chasing us."

He reached over and used one hand this time to lift her out of the hole. His grip was strong, but he handled her . . . gently. She would have pulled away when she plopped on the seat, but he released her immediately, his large hands returning to the task of driving.

Gentle hands . . . capable of killing.

Carlos hadn't harmed her. Yet. Was he any safer than

Baby Face? She shivered, glad not to have gone with that monster.

That had been too close.

She stretched her back muscles and rubbed her cold arms. Her clothes had reached that damp, icky state.

"Now what?" Gabrielle swiveled her head, squinting to make out landmarks. They were on Highway 54 just south of Highway 16. Wide-open pastures and rolling countryside spotted with stately homes.

"Soon as I get another tower, I'll get us out of here," Carlos told her. He sounded irritated, and tired.

She shouldn't care. Maybe he was tired because he'd kidnapped a couple more women tonight already. But he was standing between her and death so she'd help as much as she could until he proved to be a threat.

Confidence had been easy when she hid from the Anguis behind a computer. The keyboard had been her sword and anonymity her shield. But survival now depended on showing her strength in spite of quaking inside.

Escaping this guy would take more skill than she possessed.

Familiarity bred confidence. No matter how many one-word irritating replies he gave her, she had to keep him talking and hope he finally started communicating.

"Any signal yet?"

He shook his head without looking at her.

"Reception is even spottier south of the city." She regretted sharing that information when his jaw flexed with frustration.

"I can check my phone for a tower," she offered, reaching where she had it hooked on her pants waist.

"Is it waterproof?"

"No, but—" She pressed the power button since it was dark. Nothing happened. "It's dead. Is *yours* waterproof?"

Carlos gave her a look that questioned her IQ level.

She pitched her phone into the back and sighed. Thank goodness her laptop hadn't been drenched. She'd run solo for ten years. No help, no real friends, since she'd moved every two years to make tracking her more difficult. With the exception of rare visits to see her family, she'd spent more time with this guy tonight than with anyone else in years.

If Carlos hadn't come along, she'd have been gone and no one would have known. She fought against the idea of trusting this stranger, but had to admit she didn't have much choice right now. So far, he'd earned *something* from her even if she couldn't call it trust.

That didn't mean she'd stick with him if she saw a chance to run, but no harm in playing along in the meantime. Her stomach growled loud enough to be heard over the buffeting wind.

She rubbed at her pounding head, then reached between the seats for her backpack, which was now on the rear floorboard.

His hand shot out to stop her. "What are you doing?"

"Getting something for my headache," she snapped before she could check her tone. Not a bright idea to yell at a man with a gun. Gabrielle sighed. "Getting shot at tends to give me a headache."

The corners of his eyes narrowed as if in question, then his face turned hard, but he released her then thumbed a button on his phone. He watched every move she made. Once her hand returned with a small travel tube of aspirin, he settled back into his seat, wrists flexing with tight control on the steering wheel.

She lifted the tube to unscrew the cap.

He suddenly stuck his head out the window, looking over his shoulder, then jerked back inside. She paused.

An approaching whomp, whomp, whomp reached her ears.

She stuck her head out her side. Wind swatted hair all around her face. She shoved a handful out of her eyes in time to see the lights of a jet helicopter bearing down on them.

"Get inside!" Carlos stuck the phone into his jeans pocket and downshifted. *"Buckle up!"*

Dropping the aspirin, she wrenched the belt across her chest and stabbed twice before she clipped the buckle. The minute she did, popping sounds hit the rear of the Jeep.

Gunshots.

He grabbed her around the shoulders as the Jeep took a hard left toward a pasture. When he pulled her toward him, his hand cupped her face protectively just before the Jeep crashed against a wooden gate in their path. Busted wood slapped the windshield and debris pelted her arms, but she didn't feel a cut. As soon as they were through the fence, he released her and fought the steering across the rutted field.

The helicopter dropped out of nowhere to hover just

above the ground at fifty feet, blocking their path to dense woods. Wind lashing off the rotors shook the Jeep.

Gunfire ripped loose, boom, boom, boom. Bullets struck the hood.

Carlos spun the Jeep to the right, lifting up on two wheels, then slammed back down. He gunned the accelerator, but the helicopter roared overhead and dropped down again to land between them and the clearest path to the woods.

Moonlight glinted off three men spilling out of both sides of the helicopter, including the pilot. They ducked under the slowing rotors, and every one of them held serious-looking weapons. Machine guns?

Popping sounds erupted. One bullet ripped through Gabrielle's side of the Jeep, but missed her.

She would have screamed if she could breathe. They were going to die.

"Tuck down!" Carlos spun the Jeep in a one-eighty, shooting his handgun as he wheeled around.

She obeyed immediately, wishing she could disappear. With her head turned to the side of her lap, she could see beyond the half door that offered no protection.

One of the shooters went down.

The Jeep took a hard left, then plowed ahead full speed into the woods as if Carlos had found a path.

She popped upright. No path.

The older pine and oak trees with thick trunks were at least spaced wider apart than the width of the Jeep, so far. Her heart bounced with the hope of escaping this bunch. Then, God willing, she'd get away from Carlos. He might have been right about the DEA guy being Baby Face, or he could have been lying to her.

All of them could be lying to her.

She twisted around, looking for anyone chasing them.

"*Fuck!*" Carlos skidded the Jeep to a stop and slapped the steering wheel.

No translation was needed this time to alert her things had just gone severely downhill. She took one glance at the ravine in front of them flooded by the headlights and agreed with his assessment.

He rammed the shifter into reverse and started backing up wildly. Or at least it would have been wild if she'd been driving, but he seemed just as in control backing through the woods at sixty miles an hour as driving forward on a highway at ninety.

He slammed to a stop and wheeled hard to the right, running along the ravine, snapping saplings with sharp cracks.

A loud explosion boomed right before a smoke screen billowed in front of them with no chance to avoid it. The Jeep ran up on a stump that lifted the two passenger-side wheels off the ground.

Her body tilted toward the driver's door.

She clamped her teeth against the scream gushing up from her chest and grappled for anything to anchor herself.

Carlos released the wheel and threw his weight toward her, grabbing and turning her body to his. Glowing dash lights lit his face. "I've got you."

In that one fleeting instant, she thanked whatever

angel had sent him to her. She didn't know who he was or whom he worked for, but this man was trying to protect her with his life.

He held her tightly, still shielding her as their Jeep hurtled out of control.

The Jeep slammed a tree on the left, jarring her teeth, then counterbounced to the right, throwing her body back and forth, but he never let her go. The cab hit another tree and knocked it sideways, spraying broken glass everywhere.

His arms and body had covered her, preventing her from being injured.

When they stopped moving, she was clutching him and trying to breathe.

His chest expanded with a couple deep breaths, then settled into a rhythm of control she envied. He released her and tried to gun the engine forward, then in reverse. They were stuck on top of something and didn't have enough traction to get free. He cut the engine and turned to her; his eyes took her in with one quick sweep.

"You okay?" The concern in his voice might be her imagination, but she needed it right then.

"I think so." She still clutched him.

He reached across her arms to grasp a triangular glass shard stuck in his forearm and grunted. Blood gushed from his arm the minute he yanked the glass plug loose. He tossed it aside and calmly unclipped her seat belt, then unclenched her fingers so he could release his buckle.

She took a couple deep breaths to calm herself, but all things considered, she wasn't doing half bad. She was holding herself together, prepared to face whatever came next.

At least, she was until Carlos brushed her hair back out of her eyes with a tenderness that threatened to unleash the hysteria curling up her chest.

Her face must have given her away.

He leaned forward and kissed her on the forehead. "Don't panic. You okay?"

The kiss comforted her almost as much as seeing an army charge to the rescue. "*Oui*" was all her strained mind could come up with. She had to pull herself together. Now!

"Let's go."

"You keep saying that as if it were no big deal and it only gets worse." She scrunched her nose at the acrid smell left from the smoke screen they had broken through.

"Don't make any sudden moves." He lifted his cell phone, listened, sighed, and stuck it in his pants pocket. She had no idea where his weapon came from, but he had a lethal-looking gun in his hand again when he stepped out of the truck.

She'd never been around weapons and couldn't get used to seeing so many of them.

He kept gazing all around the Jeep while reaching in with one hand to help her out on his side. Hers was crunched. He cut off the headlights.

"Do we still have a chance?" she asked in a whisper.

"Not right now," Carlos answered just as softly.

Two men stepped into a shaft of moonlight flooding a rise fifty feet away. One carried a rifle he pointed at her and Carlos. The other guy held what she would guess was a grenade launcher—based on what she'd seen in movies— at his shoulder. Now that she thought about it, that was probably what launched the smoke bomb.

"Follow my lead until we get a chance to escape," Carlos whispered. "You're just some chick I dated. Got it?"

Just when Gabrielle was ready to admit defeat, the confidence in those words stoked another rush of belief in this man. She nodded, ready to fight as long as he did.

The two men strolled forward until the one with the automatic weapon held on them stopped a few feet away. "Hello, Carlos."

"*Hola*, Turga."

"Toss your weapon and cell phone away."

Carlos complied. "You have a falling-out with Baby Face?"

Gabrielle hid her surprise at how Carlos and this man talked like old friends.

"No' really." Turga would be invisible if not for the whites of his eyes. He was black everywhere, face and hands, clothes, knit cap, boots and weapon. A heavy smell of cigarettes burdened the fresh air not tinged by the smoke bomb. His English came out in a choppy Turkish accent. "Baby Face became unavoidable casualty. Good thing he found *her* first."

"What do you want *her* for?" Carlos made it sound as if Gabrielle's only value had been supplying him with a vehicle.

"Very funny. You after same thing."

"After what?" Carlos snorted. "Baby Face had business with me, not her."

"Really? So you know of his *big* deal?" Turga eyed him warily, but Carlos had planted a seed of curiosity.

Carlos shrugged. "Didn't get a chance to hear the whole deal and didn't really give a shit when I caught him trying to grab my woman."

Turga snorted as if unconvinced.

"Let her go, Turga. She just made the mistake of getting involved with me."

Gabrielle gave Carlos her solid vote right then. She didn't know who Baby Face or Turga were, but Carlos was the only one in present company who hadn't tried to kill her.

"You think I'm stupid?" Turga asked in a tone that rippled across Gabrielle's skin. "Prove she's your woman."

How could he possibly prove that? Not that Gabrielle wasn't prepared to back him up and agree to anything Carlos said, but doubt took root in her exhausted mind.

Carlos sighed. "Fine."

He turned to her. She looked up at his face, determined to do her best to convince Turga they were together.

But she wasn't as prepared as she'd thought when Carlos pulled her into his arms and dipped his head. He covered her mouth with his, kissing her with more passion than any other man she'd ever kissed. He held her safe, protected.

She hadn't been held or hugged in years.

Her defenses fell without a battle.

Her heart raced along with the frenzy of nerves and wild desire that spiraled up out of nowhere. She curved her hands around his neck, clutching. He drew her closer.

The kiss overwhelmed her senses, drowning her in pleasure.

She moaned.

"Okay, *enough*," Turga ordered, then scowled when Carlos continued. "Give me a break."

Carlos slowly lifted his lips from hers, paused, and touched her lips once more briefly, then peeled her off him.

When he moved her to his side, he kept his arm protectively around her shoulders.

She worked to keep her knees from buckling.

Carlos tightened his grasp on her shoulders, which she took as a silent message to hang on and pull herself together.

She reached around his waist and squeezed to let him know she had it together.

One side of his mouth curved up, acknowledging her message. "Let her go," Carlos repeated. "She won't say a word."

Turga stepped close to Carlos and smiled, the white teeth glowing against his dark face. "Don't think so. You cost me good man. Eye for an eye, and all that."

"Don't tell me you actually care about losing someone."

Turga's grin widened. "Very funny. No, but he was better shot than that one." He tilted his head at the other guy holding the grenade launcher.

"Unavoidable casualty." Carlos smiled sarcastically.

Turga flipped his rifle quickly and used the stock like a club to ram Carlos in the stomach.

He broke away from Gabrielle, bent double with a pained grunt, then sucked a breath and straightened.

She reached for him and Turga grabbed her.

Carlos snarled and moved so fast Gabrielle had no idea how he'd jerked her away from Turga and pushed her behind him.

Turga flipped the rifle up in just as quick a motion, which ended with the tip of the barrel an inch from Carlos's nose.

"Should kill you right now, but only a careless man wastes a resource without first bleeding it dry. One wrong move and I wound her. Start walking." Turga motioned toward the helicopter with his rifle.

She let Carlos take her backpack, but Gabrielle wasn't handing her laptop over to anyone as long as she had a choice. Carlos walked them both ahead of Turga and kept a snug grip on her arm. When they reached the edge of the woods, an explosion rocked the ground.

She swung around to see flames bloom from where her Jeep had been and the second guy running toward them.

Guess that *was* a grenade launcher he toted.

Sirens wailed from the highway, growing louder.

Gabrielle stumbled on the rutted ground next to the helicopter, and Carlos caught her at the waist. He lifted her inside the craft, then climbed in, settling next to her on the backseat.

Turga pushed the dead body in at their feet.

She drew back in revulsion.

Carlos leaned close. "Look out the window and breathe through your mouth."

Turga shoved his rifle out of the way and turned a handgun on them that looked like the one Carlos had carried. Turga's partner climbed into the pilot's seat and started the motor.

Two police cruisers and a fire truck raced along the highway, then the lead car skidded into a turn as the helicopter blades hit full spin and caught air.

One cruiser cut through the now open gate, bouncing toward them.

The jet helicopter lifted with a lurch, flying barely over the top of the cruiser, then picking up altitude as they swung in a wide arc and flew over the woods where smoke rose from Gabrielle's poor Jeep.

An arm circled her shoulders.

She turned to ask Carlos where he thought they were going, but her teeth were chattering so hard she was afraid she'd bite her tongue if she spoke. Shock had set in and cold clothes weren't helping. Her whole body vibrated.

Carlos was warm, though. Why wasn't he cold?

Who cared? She soaked up heat and comfort from his imposing body.

Gabrielle couldn't believe she'd been so naïve as to think Durand Anguis was her biggest threat.

Warm breath brushed along the skin of her neck when Carlos leaned his face near her ear and spoke. "Just do what they say. I'll figure a way out of this." He rubbed the hand on her shoulder up and down her arm, then brushed a lock of hair off her face with a finger.

Her brain stumbled at the endearing action. How was she supposed to interpret his moves?

"So who is she, Carlos?" Turga raised his voice over the roar of the motor.

"I told you." Carlos cupped her face and kissed her gently again. Had that been to soothe her or convince their kidnapper? Lifting his gaze to Turga, Carlos pulled her close, possessively. "Just been dating."

Emotions scurried to find a home, but she couldn't sort through the rash of reactions his touch and kiss provoked.

Carlos was trying to divert their attention from her so the least she could do for now was play along with his charade. She slipped an arm around his waist and hugged against his chest, her gaze jumping to catch their kidnapper's assessment.

Turga made no sound or action to indicate his thoughts.

Moving his free hand to the arm she'd wrapped across his chest, Carlos rubbed up and down slowly then kissed her hair.

She was in over her head in this deadly game, but playing along with a man who looked like Carlos was no hardship. She'd sworn off hot men for relationships, which hadn't been difficult since her lifestyle made dating unrealistic. Pretending with Carlos was safe. But marrying a male icon ten years ago who was just last year listed as one of the world's top fifty most desirable men had been emotional suicide.

To-die-for faces and ripped bodies hadn't appealed to her since divorcing that jerk Roberto.

But she did feel an odd pull toward Carlos that she could only attribute to the situation she was in. His very presence screamed strength and confidence.

Now that was attractive and tempting.

She believed he just might get them out of this.

Indecision camped out in Turga's gaze. "You don't keep women for more than one night."

"Got comfortable." Carlos leaned down and kissed her cheek, so tenderly her insides turned mushy. His arms tightened around her and her heart skipped a beat. She'd never felt protected or cared for. Not the way she did at this minute.

Even though Carlos was pretending, he was doing a better job than her miserable ex-husband had on their wedding night.

But Carlos was not with law enforcement.

Like that really mattered right now given their dire situation?

"We shall see." Turga didn't say another word until they landed fifteen minutes later in the parking lot at the rear of a building with a FOR LEASE sign on several doors. The pilot left the rotors spinning slowly and climbed out.

Turga jumped down from his seat, his rifle slung over his shoulder and the handgun pointed at her. This whole scene was too bizarre to comprehend. Guns, grenade launchers, jet helicopters. Deaths.

She couldn't think about that and function.

Gabrielle waited on Carlos to climb down first, then he turned to help her. When he lowered her to the ground in front of him, he pulled her into a quick hug and whispered, "I won't let anyone hurt you."

Rather than risk losing a grip on her emotions, she nodded. She didn't know this man, didn't know why he had come for her or whom he worked with, but he was diverting all danger from her.

"Enough. Walk," Turga ordered.

As they backed away from the helicopter, the pilot peeled black vinyl off the tail section that had covered the aircraft registration numbers. Carlos kept his arm around her waist and guided them both to the closest doorway.

Gabrielle wanted to assure him she was ready to fight with him. She kept her voice low. "I'm okay. I can do this."

"Open the door," Turga ordered.

Carlos squeezed her waist in reply and gave her a look of admiration that warmed her. He released her to extend his hand and turn the knob, then held the door for her to enter. She stepped out of his grasp and walked boldly through the doorway.

The first thing that hit her was an overpowering metallic smell that gagged her.

The second was the image of a bloody body hanging thirty yards away against a wall.

Her knees buckled.

FIVE

Carlos caught Gabrielle—if that really was her name—under her arms before she sank to the floor.

He'd found Lee.

Gabrielle was making those gut-wrenching noises.

She'd been doing so good, holding up far better than he'd have expected from any civilian. He turned her to face him and held her against his chest. "Breathe through your mouth."

Carlos felt the cold barrel of his own 9 mm poke his neck.

"Keep moving," Turga said.

Carlos held her arm as she stepped along with him, slowly, not a drop of color in her face. "Don't look at him," he told her, wishing he could vanish the image of Lee strapped to the wall spread eagle.

Lee's head rolled to one side. He was alive.

Classic Turga location. This would be one of no less

than three spots in the area his men would have scouted out for this night.

His men must have found Lee with Baby Face while Carlos had been out in the lake with Gabrielle and assumed Lee had shot Baby Face and knew what the electronics felon was after.

At least Turga and his men weren't a professional snatch team that would have known to cover his and Gabrielle's heads with pillowcases, then separate them. Turga was the equivalent of a vulture and he hired bottom-feeders.

Carlos had met him a few months ago when Turga tried to hire Carlos for an operation he declined. If he'd accepted the first time, Turga would have been suspicious, so Carlos had expected a second meeting. Just not this way.

When the chopper pilot entered the building, Turga waved his weapon, indicating a spot where he wanted Carlos and Gabrielle, over to the side. Once Turga was satisfied with their position, he spoke quietly to his pilot.

Carlos averted Gabrielle's gaze from Lee's naked body, covered in lean muscle and bloody gashes. His face had already swollen to a hideous shape.

Tattoos scrolling across his shoulder and down one arm explained why Joe had taken him in. BAD didn't recruit from colleges like the CIA and the FBI.

BAD would be more likely to hold a job fair at a prison.

Joe had drawn Carlos in from the street by offering him a chance to legally use his skills at things like breaking and entering. BAD needed an expert on South America, someone who could move around the country undetected.

One thing about Joe, he had timing down to an art. Having refused to choose a gang in San Francisco, Carlos had been living on borrowed time since he poached on all territories back then.

But Lee had clearly taken a different path.

Lee's inked designs belonged to a Chicago gang known as the Firing Squad, which dealt in interstate drug trafficking, car thefts, shakedowns, and money laundering. A tight group no one undercover had been able to break into.

To become a member, a man had to pass only three tests.

One was to be under the age of twenty.

The second was to be vouched for by a member with five or more years in the gang.

The final and defining test determined if he could kill to survive. The gang pledge had to challenge a member of a rival gang to kill or be killed in thirty days. Sort of the street version of international athletic competition, but in this one the gold chain went to the last one breathing.

The losing opponent won a one-way ticket to hell.

Once the challenge was made, Lee would have had to remain inside the city limits and keep a visible profile for a month with no support.

If he lived, he was in.

The chances of survival were so small it was laughable.

But Lee had made it or he wouldn't have the ink, because no tattoo artist was stupid enough to ink a gang design without authorization.

But Lee must have turned the corner somewhere. Joe had seen something decent in the kid to bring him into BAD.

Maybe the same thing that had caused Joe to prevent Carlos from going to prison and give him a chance no one else would.

Dammit, Lee couldn't be over twenty-five.

Why did that seem so young when Carlos was only thirty-three?

Because he'd lived a hard thirty-three years.

Someone moved into view close to Lee. Just as Carlos had suspected, Turga had backup inside the building. Bald, not quite six feet tall, another stocky, dark-skinned Turk.

This guy had tortured Lee.

He would die first.

Carlos glanced around for a place to put Gabrielle so he would have his hands free. The only chairs were next to a table beside where Lee hung. Carlos wasn't letting Gabrielle anywhere near that animal who had tortured the BAD agent.

What had Lee given up?

Carlos would know soon enough.

"Sit over here." He moved Gabrielle to a crate and she followed without a word. If she went deep into shock where she wouldn't respond, getting her out of here unharmed would be tough if he got a break.

He'd deal with that when the time came.

If the time came.

Deep voices murmured behind him. Carlos had to find out what Turga wanted and determine what, if anything, he could negotiate. But he couldn't leave Gabrielle yet.

He cupped her face with both hands, forcing her to

look up at him. Violet-blue eyes stared back with the full force of her terror. But he'd expected a glazed look, so that was promising.

Before he could say another word, a howl of pain from where Lee hung clawed the air.

Carlos clenched his jaw.

Gabrielle jerked. Her face changed from pale to a sick green, but she was holding up damn good for a woman obviously not trained for this. He'd seen men in similar situations completely shut down by now.

"Keep your eyes on me," Carlos instructed her, then waited on her nod before he turned around. The pilot was gone.

"Why was he with you, Carlos?" Turga asked, indicating Lee. "You share your dates?" Mockery dripped from his tongue.

"Just hired some muscle to watch my back while I stopped in to see her. We were on our way to a job. I caught Baby Face at Gabrielle's house looking for me. If you'd have waited five minutes, I'd have been back around the house. This"—Carlos pointed at Lee's battered body—"wouldn't have been necessary."

Turga merely smiled. "*You* paid this kid to back you up? You insult me." He scowled and turned to his torturer. "What you find out, Izmir?"

"This one claims the same thing." Izmir shrugged. "Said he made some quick cash to help. Hired to watch the woman's house. Took some work, but he did give me Carlos's name."

Carlos would not fault Lee for that. In fact, he commended him on keeping the story straight and only using a first name. This way they were corroborating each other's story.

Turga jerked his head in a sign for Izmir to come to him. When Izmir reached Turga, they spoke quietly.

Turga was a poacher, an opportunist who waited for someone like Baby Face to make a deal and do all the work before Turga showed up at the last minute to snatch the prize out from under everyone. His success depended on timing. Right about now, he was trying to figure out if he'd made a mistake by jumping too soon before he found out what Baby Face was after.

Turga would have given Baby Face one chance to tell him, then cut his throat since he was too damn big to carry out easily.

Carlos glanced at Lee, who lifted his head an inch and angled his face toward Carlos, but there was no way to tell if he could actually see anything out of those bloated eyes. Carlos gave him a slight nod he hoped translated into a promise that he'd make that bastard pay.

Lee moved his chin up and down a fraction, just enough to let Carlos know he had seen something.

Carlos glanced at his watch. How could he use the fact that it was eighteen minutes to six?

"Ask him more," Turga ordered.

Izmir walked to a table next to Lee where a couple towels were piled. To clean up his hands when the blood got too sticky?

You will pay, asshole.

Izmir lifted a pole with a loop on the end like the kind

used to catch a snake, except the loop on the end was a wire that ran to a machine plugged into the wall. Carlos flinched, guessing at what Izmir had in mind. The bastard moved the loop toward Lee's genitals.

"Stop!" Carlos ordered.

"You want to talk?" Turga asked with so much humor Carlos shook with the need to rip him to pieces.

"Turn him loose and we'll talk," Carlos offered in as even a voice as he could muster.

"Don't think so."

"You're going to kill all of us, Turga. I'll give you what you want if you leave the kid alone."

"So you'll tell me your deal with Baby Face? I know it was big score, something that electronic ferret lucked into."

So Baby Face had found Mirage for someone else he planned to shop her to and Turga didn't know.

Hard to imagine that the woman behind Carlos was the infamous electronic informant, but to be honest he'd seen stranger things.

He made a production of checking his watch, then sighed. "Okay, here's the deal. Baby Face offered me a cut to help him make a risky trade. He wanted professional backup, not the clowns he normally dragged around. He had to contact someone by six tonight or the deal was off. I was out of the country. Just got back and found out he was offered more money to deliver sooner, and I know who has the money. So he was trying to snake me on the deal. You cut the kid loose," Carlos said, nodding at Lee, "and I'll tell you the deal, names, everything. In trade, no torture, just a bullet between the eyes."

Turga glanced at his watch and back at Carlos, his eyes twitching as if he couldn't decide whether to kill Carlos or make a deal. He finally cursed something in Turkish.

"If you lie, you look worse than him when I get through with you." Angling his head at Lee, Turga's face creased with confusion, the time element now causing him grief. "Not like Baby Face to pick up an asset himself. Don't fuck with me, Carlos. Only reason she not strung up *yet* is I'm still not buying this girlfriend bit. I no risk damaging merchandise in case she *is* what Baby Face selling. If not, she all mine."

Carlos forced himself not to charge Turga. Fury rode up his back, demanding immediate payment for Lee's bloody body. And, yes, for Gabrielle's terror even if she had put herself in this predicament.

"Take him down and I'll tell you what Baby Face was really after and how to cut the deal . . . or risk missing Baby Face's deadline." Carlos delivered that with a venomous finality that assured he was through negotiating.

Turga finally nodded at Izmir, who grumbled, then tossed his stick to the ground. He produced a switchblade and cut Lee's ankles loose, then his wrists.

A hiss of pain and moans escaped when Lee fell to his knees before his arms and head slapped the floor. He didn't move.

Carlos had covered several steps toward Turga while his attention was turned.

When Turga cut his gaze back, he waved the 9 mm. "Stop there." A jingle played, interrupting the tense silence. Turga dug a cell phone out of his front pants pocket and answered with "What you find out?" After a pause, he smiled and said, "*He* put out a bounty? No, no, we're old friends. I contact him soon. Good work. You almost as good as Baby Face." He closed his phone and shoved it back into his front pants pocket.

"I thought we were going to talk." But Carlos knew deep in his gut that call had complicated things.

"Yes, yes. First, you tell me what she knows about this Mirage Durand Anguis has bounty on."

Hell. Wait. Turga thinks Gabrielle only knew something about the Mirage.

Carlos offered his most arrogant smile. "That's what I was trying to tell you. Durand made Baby Face a new offer for more money to deliver her to him. Durand's far more persuasive than Izmir when it comes to making someone talk." He ignored the feminine gasp behind him and continued, "Baby Face figured he'd save what he was going to pay me and make a bonus amount by picking her up. Not a bad plan even for Baby Face. As you said, he doesn't normally do his own dirty work."

"So *she* has information?" Turga's smile gleamed with anticipation.

"You're smarter than that." Carlos doubted the possibility, but hoped a threat would force Turga to hesitate. "Touch her and Durand will take your balls off with a pair of pliers."

Turga shrugged. "So, no reason to keep you alive, eh?"

That was a tricky one. Carlos needed a minute to come up with an answer. "Go ahead and shoot me."

Turga smiled, shoved the gun inside his waistband, and swung the rifle up.

"But it will cost you," Carlos said quickly.

That unglued the bastard's smile. "What you mean?"

Good news? Turga's greed outweighed his intelligence.

"Let's sit down and talk." Carlos started forward, angling toward the table and chairs, gaining another two steps closer to Turga.

"Stop. We discuss nothing until Izmir tie your hands so you no make one of those moves you famous for."

"Me famous?" Carlos laughed, keeping his eyes on Izmir, who grabbed a length of cord he snapped with pleasure and headed for him.

"I hear stories." Turga scowled. "I would keep you alive if not so risky. Bet someone has price on your head, too."

Carlos shrugged as if he couldn't care less about Turga's debate to kill him or shop his head. He put his palms together, lifting his wrists in front of him all compliant and nice.

Turga's gaze danced past Carlos to where Gabrielle sat behind him.

Carlos turned his head to look at her.

Gabrielle frowned up at him, lips parted in total confusion.

He winked at her.

She blinked, then closed her mouth and gave a tiny dip of her head. A nod he took to mean she was still on the same page with him.

He turned back around and used the opportunity to shuffle another step forward. Izmir stepped between him and Turga, lifting the cord to wrap around Carlos's wrists.

It was now or never. He could only hope Lee had a breath of life still in him.

Carlos swung a feigned look of shock toward Lee and yelled, "No, don't!"

Izmir jerked around to Lee, who amazingly lurched to his feet.

Turga swung the weapon at Lee. "In a hurry to die?"

Lee lowered his chin to his chest, submissive.

Turga grunted with satisfaction, so confident with a gun against a naked and beaten man.

Just stay there, Lee. Carlos used the two seconds he'd been given to curl his fingers tight and lunge, ramming a fist into Izmir's throat, snapping his windpipe. Out of the corner of Carlos's eye, he could see Lee move, but Izmir grabbed at Carlos with one hand and clutched his choking throat with the other.

A gunshot—Turga's rifle—exploded, echoing against the concrete walls.

Screams ricocheted behind the echo. Gabrielle's.

Izmir sucked air, staggering back, eyes bulging. Carlos spun and kicked high, knocking Izmir back at Turga.

Another gunshot. The bullet ripped through the middle of Izmir, catching Carlos across his side, a gash at worst.

The air reeked with curses, screams, and fresh blood.

Izmir tottered. Carlos ran headfirst, ramming him all the way into Turga. The gun exploded again, so close Carlos lost his hearing, but the bullet deflected high.

Carlos crashed down on top of Izmir, who landed on Turga with a heavy thud. Rolling over, he pushed to his feet.

Turga struggled to squirm free of the dead body pinning him. His hand still clutched the rifle. Carlos slammed his bootheel down on Turga's wrist, satisfied with the snap of bone and the howl of pain that followed. He kicked the rifle out of reach and found his 9 mm nearby on the concrete floor. Turga cursed, yelled, and beat his undamaged hand against Izmir, who didn't move. Carlos wanted to kill the fucker, but that would be murder. He had to get to Lee to see how bad he was. Izmir's bulk had Turga pinned.

Carlos hurried to Lee's sprawled body. Fresh blood poured from a hole ripped into his chest. His first duty was to get Gabrielle out of here, but she'd live.

The kid wouldn't.

Dropping down on his knees, Carlos gently lifted Lee's ravaged body into his arms. When he did, his fingers slipped into a gaping wound in Lee's back no bandage would plug enough to save him. Warm liquid gushed down Carlos's arm and pooled on the floor.

"You just had to be a hero, huh?" Carlos said in a voice raw with regret.

Lee's lips twisted up on one side, teeth missing from the perfect set he'd had just an hour ago.

Carlos pulled him close to hear the whispered words Lee struggled to form.

"Sorry." Lee drew hard for a gurgling breath that shuddered through him. A scarlet trail of blood trickled from the corner of his mouth. "Failed . . . first time."

"No." Carlos swallowed against the lump in his throat. He'd never get used to watching the young die. "You aced it."

"Carlos!" Gabrielle yelled.

He swung, instinctively lifting the handgun as he did.

Turga had somehow freed himself of Izmir and was running at him with a knife.

Rage blinded Carlos.

He unloaded four shots in succession . . . all into the lower hips and genital area. Not the spot a marksman of his ability would normally aim for, but Turga didn't deserve a bullet between the eyes.

Turga hit the ground, hands grabbing himself. Guttural howls rocked the warehouse for several seconds, then he just cried, rolling from side to side.

When Carlos turned back to Lee, the kid's lips were moving, his eyes bright. Carlos leaned his ear close to Lee's mouth.

"Thanks" wheezed out, then one hard shudder racked the broken body before Lee's soul passed on.

Carlos dropped his chin to his chest, breathing hard. His eyes stung. There was nothing more helpless than feeling the last breath of someone he held, knowing he couldn't do anything to save that person.

Just as he couldn't sixteen years ago.

Pain knifed through him, dredging up a memory from the past with brutal clarity. He'd held another battered body, that of the young girl he'd loved with all his being, as she'd drawn her last breath.

His heart beat erratically, aching in his chest.

Light footsteps approached him. Not Turga, who had finally silenced. Dead at last.

Lee was no longer in pain. Carlos still had a job to do

and another woman to protect. He eased Lee to the floor. With one phone call, BAD would have a cleanup crew here in a half hour. He couldn't wait that long and risk one of Turga's people coming back.

Leaving Lee uncovered just seemed wrong, but Carlos couldn't expend the time to put his clothes on him.

He stood and turned to Gabrielle, the informant everyone wanted. She'd stopped on the other side of Turga. Chestnut brown hair scattered from having gone overboard and drying in a wild wind. Face white as a ghost and hands trembling, she sure as hell didn't look the part of an international operative. The baggy work-out clothes underneath her open trench coat were still damp.

Turga lay dead on the floor between them, the room littered in carnage.

She lifted misery-filled eyes to his, punching him in the gut with her suffering. "Is he, is he dead?"

Carlos wasn't sure which *he* she referred to, but since they were all three dead he just said, "Yes."

The blank stare worried him. They had to go. Chances were they'd have to interact with someone in the public once they were out of here. He needed her lucid.

When she showed no real signs of coherence, he stepped over Turga to reach her. He held her shoulders, careful not to get blood on her. Considering everything, she should be screaming her head off right now or completely catatonic. Her eyes drifted past him to where Lee lay silently.

"I'm sorry," she whispered.

"Me, too. He was a good man." Carlos shoved his mind back into gear. "We have to go before someone else shows up."

She nodded, but when he started to move around her, she pulled out of his grasp.

"What?"

Gabrielle didn't answer. She just took her trench coat off as she stepped over Turga, then draped the coat over Lee's body.

Nothing could have endeared her more to Carlos in that moment. He swallowed down the lump in his throat and waited until she returned to his side.

She stopped short and stared at him. "Is any of that your blood?"

"Not enough to bother with." However, he couldn't walk around in public like this if he didn't want to draw attention. "Go get your bags."

She took a deep breath that seemed to fortify her, then she walked past Izmir to where she'd been sitting.

Carlos grabbed the towel already soiled with Lee's blood from when Izmir had cleaned his hands. He made quick work of wiping the worst of the blood off his arms and searched the floor beyond the table for Lee's clothes. Ignoring the twist of guilt over taking Lee's clothes, he yanked off his turtleneck and pulled on the long-sleeved T-shirt that had been tossed aside. He exchanged his jeans for Lee's, which were close in fit, and spread his bloody shirt over Lee's face, then walked back to gather up Gabrielle and her belongings.

No point in worrying about DNA at this point since

his blood was in the mix and BAD *should* get here first to clean up.

He reached for her computer bag and she came alive.

"No." She snatched the bag to her chest. "Thank you, but I'll take it."

That reminded Carlos of just whom he was transporting. The Mirage. A woman with a bounty on her head, including one from Durand.

Right now she was a woman he didn't believe had ever been this close to guns or killing. His informant needed fresh air soon or once her shock passed, the sick smell of death would overtake her.

"Don't look at anything but the door." He pointed that way to get her moving.

The slash of disbelief she cut at him brought a flare of color back to her cheeks. "What? You think I'll have nightmares? Like I missed seeing any of *that?*"

He sighed. She might have seen gunshots and some bodies hit with bullets, but her eyes had been glazed when she stood within inches of the blood surrounding Turga and the lower half of his mangled body. She hadn't actually *seen* the gore.

"Do you want to see it again?" he challenged, sure of her answer.

"No, of course not."

"Then keep your eyes on the door." He walked her to the exit and opened the door halfway, then dropped her backpack on the floor. "Stand here, breathe in some fresh air, and close the door immediately if you hear a car or see anyone."

She grabbed his forearm right where the glass had cut

it. He managed not to curse, but snapped at her, "What?"

"Don't leave me," she pleaded in a whisper.

"I'm not." He gently pried her fingers off his gash that would now seep blood again. "I'm going to get Turga's phone and make a call."

She exhaled a sigh that partnered with the relief in her eyes. "Okay."

Carlos moved carefully around the bodies to stay out of the blood. Turga had kept his cell phone in his right pants pocket. The one shredded to pieces. Part of the phone had fallen out of his pocket into the plasma puddle.

Well, hell.

He checked Izmir, whose phone had been in his vest pocket before Turga blew that to shreds.

What did it take to get just one break on this freakin' job?

Carlos shoved his weapon inside the front waistband of his jeans and strode back to where Gabrielle faced out the door opening. He could hear her taking deep breaths. When he touched her shoulder, she yelped and bumped her head against the door.

She turned a panicked face to him.

"Sorry."

"What now?" she asked.

Underneath the fragility glistening in her eyes, she made a damned impressive effort to pull herself together.

"We leave." He opened the door. "Let's go."

"What about . . . them?"

"No one's phone works. I'll send someone to get Lee and deal with this as soon as I get a phone."

"Where are we going?" She finally started walking when he put his hand to the small of her back.

"Somewhere safe." Guess he'd earned the dubious look she gave him, but she continued without question until they reached the end of the building.

Hallelujah. A break.

A dual-cab pickup truck was parked beyond the security lights that shone over the lot.

"Stay here." Carlos eased her against the wall in a deep shadow, then hurried over to the truck. He dug around to all the normal places a guy would throw a set of keys if he didn't want to carry them. The key ring was under the driver's seat. Probably Izmir's truck since the interior stank of strong European cigarettes and the goon would have left his keys in easy access in case he'd had to run.

Carlos waved Gabrielle to the truck. She rushed forward and climbed in on the passenger side. He tossed the backpack on the rear seat.

Once he pulled the truck out and motored to the opening of the industrial center, Gabrielle said, "We're in Tyrone."

"Yep. What's the fastest route to the library in Peachtree City?"

"What? You've got an overdue book?"

He couldn't believe the spark of sarcasm in her voice. "No, that's where I left my car. I figured you might know a quicker way since you live down here."

"To the right, then stay on this road. It will merge into Highway 74 southbound."

"Thanks." Carlos gave her points for not trying to steer

him the wrong way. "Dig around in the glove box, under the seat, anywhere you think someone might stick a cell phone."

She started searching. "Who leaves keys and a cell phone in their vehicle?"

Anyone who lived on the wrong side of the law. "All of Turga's men," he answered, speculating as much as lying.

"Really?" She paused, seemed to process that, then kept searching. "Unbelievable."

Carlos did a double take at her soft curse. "What?"

She stared at him with new respect as she pulled a cell phone from the glove box and handed it to him.

"It's not that unusual. These guys carry three or four of everything they need." Carlos flipped open the phone and damn. A signal. He punched in numbers for Joe's direct line.

When the ringing stopped and no one on the other end spoke, he said, "It's me, Carlos."

"Glad to hear it," Joe snapped. "What about Lee?"

Carlos didn't say a word.

Joe muttered, "Shit."

Carlos gave him the address in a coded phrase. "If you don't get there first—"

"Hold on." Joe rattled the address and orders to someone, then turned back to the phone. "We'll get Lee and handle cleanup."

"What about the first bunch?" Carlos asked, indicating Baby Face and his backup's body plus their SUV at the place he'd found Gabrielle.

"Already gone. You on your way in?"

"No. The source is in rough shape and I need some sleep. We'll head in tomorrow."

"Going to our secure location?" Joe asked, indicating the safe house in north Georgia where Carlos had been heading earlier.

"Yep. I'll text a new contact number in about ten minutes." Carlos also had another phone in his car.

"Want backup sent to meet you?"

"No." Carlos didn't want another human being to keep alive for the moment. "I've got this. I'll fill you in later on everything."

"Your call," Joe said, letting Carlos know he understood until they had the chance to speak over a secure line.

Joe would let him know at that point what he planned to do with Gabrielle. Carlos doubted it would make any difference she was a female if Joe and Tee decided to lock her up tonight.

In spite of how Joe had left their conversation, there could very well be an unmarked van with two armed security guards at the cabin waiting to take her into custody by the time Carlos reached north Georgia.

For the first time since signing on with BAD, he faced having to make a decision he hesitated on. Could he really hand this woman over to guards after all she'd been through tonight?

Carlos ended the phone connection and glanced at Gabrielle. He read her body language—arms wrapping her body, eyes staring ahead, rigid posture—as withdrawing.

Why that pinched him, he couldn't say.

"What are you going to do with me?" she asked, turning her head to finally look at him with suspicious eyes.

"We need to talk to you."

"*Who* wants to talk to me?"

He didn't answer at first, debating on how much to say. No point in trying to get anything out of her right now when she was probably holding herself together with sheer will.

"I can't get into all that until tomorrow," he said. "You have to know by now I'm not going to harm you or let anyone else. I'm taking you somewhere safe for the night. That's all I can tell you."

She didn't make a sound of acknowledgment or to argue.

Carlos kept his speed within the limits. The roads intersected, just as she'd said. Once he was on the main highway, he knew where he was going. A thought popped into his mind.

Was anyone waiting to hear from her?

"Gabrielle?"

"Yes?" That answer came out on a weary sigh. She sagged against the passenger door, a rag doll that had been dragged through the muck and run completely out of batteries.

"Who knew you were living in Peachtree City?"

"No one but the man I rented from and I never see him."

The mumbled answer combined with her sad voice tugged at his insides. She was connected somehow to all of this. That put her squarely on the wrong team.

A sigh escaped on a cough . . . or a sob. No, she hadn't cried yet. He hoped like hell she wouldn't now.

The adrenaline power charge he'd been relying on was spent. He rubbed his forehead, aching from jet lag, seventy-two hours of running a mission without sleep, and the last few hours of fighting for their lives.

Not to mention finding out the informant everyone wanted was a woman who could more easily pass as a schoolteacher than someone involved in international espionage.

She leaned against the door, her head touching the window. He fought the urge to draw her next to him and tuck her close out of reflex.

Not exactly protocol for taking a felon into custody.

They both needed sleep tonight, but he didn't know what waited for him at the cabin.

He also couldn't allow her to see where they were going.

The throb behind his eyes pulsated. Taking down an armed felon would be easier than treating her like a prisoner once they reached the safe house, but he still had a job to do and couldn't risk letting his guard down.

Not after finally capturing Mirage.

She slumped back against the seat. He shouldn't have looked over at her.

The tear running down the side of her face started a war between his conscience and his duty.

SIX

Where is he taking me now? Gabrielle sat upright as Carlos pulled into the Peachtree City library parking lot. He obviously knew something about this area.

She swiped away the tear, hating the show of weakness in front of him, but images from tonight kept bombarding her. Such as that poor guy in the warehouse they'd tortured who had died.

And the way Carlos had held the young man, comforting his partner as he drew his last breath. She had a strange feeling few people saw that side of Carlos that conflicted with the hard man who had fought all night to keep them alive.

Where was he taking her and what did *his people* want with her? Was Durand Anguis at the center of this game she'd become a pawn in? Carlos knew of Durand. Was there a chance anything Carlos had said to Turga was true? That he was delivering her to Durand?

She didn't think so. Baby Face had clearly been surprised to see Carlos at her rental house.

One thing was clear. Carlos *had* saved her life. He'd treated her decently even if he had threatened to strip-search her at one point. In hindsight, he'd only been trying to find the Jeep keys so they could get away from the house quickly.

"Hope my car is still here," Carlos muttered.

"Be serious," she answered absently, hooking the strap for her laptop case over her shoulder.

"What do you mean?"

She glanced up at his surly tone. "Peachtree City has to be one of the safest cities in Georgia." She frowned at him. "At least until *you* came to town."

The truck's headlights fanned across a lot three-quarters full of cars when Carlos turned down a parking lane. He studied her for a minute, then winked at her again.

Her heart did a skip.

That was so wrong. He was the enemy.

Gabrielle searched for anything to look at besides Carlos. Her insides did a crazy somersault routine every time he looked at her. Must be a post-traumatic stress syndrome of some sort.

She closed her eyes. That was a mistake.

Images pelted her of Carlos charging Izmir and Turga shooting his man with the clear intent of sacrificing Izmir to kill Carlos. She blinked her eyes open and found a normal scene of teens clustered outside the entrance to the library on the other side of the fountain, oblivious to any danger.

She'd been just as naïvely happy at that age and hoped they never had to face what she had.

They would be much safer once *she* left this city.

Carlos parked the truck in a spot and lifted her backpack from the backseat. "Let's go."

Gabrielle almost smiled, getting used to his standard limited directions. She followed him to where a silvery blue BMW 750i was parked. Didn't it just figure a man so hot he could stun women with a glance would drive that land rocket?

"Stand here. I'll be right back." He strode to the front of the car and ducked out of view. She'd seen enough tonight to know better than to think she was ever out of his sight.

Besides, she was both too exhausted to try anything and needed that backpack to survive. She doubted he worked for Durand, but that didn't mean Carlos was *completely* trustworthy.

He said he was taking her somewhere safe. She could extend that much trust, to believe he hadn't lied to her about tonight.

Fatigue slugged what energy she had out of reach. With the adrenaline rush wearing off she was both hungry and nauseated to go with a headache that refused to quiet down. All she had to do for now was to stay alert and put a lid on the irritation bubbling up. Then watch for a chance to escape.

Carlos returned with keys and a remote car-door opener in his hands. A soft click sounded before the trunk popped open next to her. He reached in and lifted out a blanket, then dumped her backpack inside.

"Put this on." He held the blanket out to her, patiently waiting.

She would have snapped at him for giving her another order if not for the concern in his eyes. But she was tired of being dragged around against her will. What was this man's organization? Now that they weren't dodging bullets, she should start questioning more, like why he was being so considerate. What did he want from her?

Living on the edge for so long had changed her, but not as much as having married a manipulating liar.

Was all this nice-guy routine just Carlos trying to lower her defenses, invoke a false sense of security? Sadly, it was working. She might keep her mind better focused if he didn't wink, smile, and comfort her.

They were adversaries and she had best remember that.

He'd keep chiseling at her defenses unless she backed him off. Put some emotional distance between them. She'd never cared to be a shrew, but that was one quick way to chill a charmer.

Gabrielle held her hands out and used clipped words. "What? Worried I'll catch pneumonia at this point and you won't get as much for me?"

His dark eyes went from warm-brown patient to black pits of irritation.

She drew back at the shift in him. In fact, he looked tired and seriously annoyed. Not a good combination for a dangerous man. And Carlos was deadly.

"No." He sounded disgusted. "I just don't want wet clothes on my leather seats."

His charm turned to icy indifference faster than his wink.

He continued to hold the blanket and now cocked an eyebrow ripe with challenge.

Rather than give an inch or antagonize him, she stepped sideways, lowering the laptop to her feet so she could shove the sleeves of her T-shirt up on each arm. The damp clothes were starting to chafe.

He moved behind her and wrapped the blanket around her shoulders quickly.

The thick material warmed her as fast as a summer day. Her limp muscles would melt into a puddle if she didn't get in the car soon. She admitted defeat without a word.

Carlos kept his hands on her shoulders and leaned close to her ear. "I've had a long day. The last few hours haven't improved it by any means, so let's call a truce for a while."

His deep voice was gentle, soothing the raw edges of her nerves. And there he went comforting her again, his fingers lightly massaging her shoulders. She couldn't rally a snotty comment when the person who had stepped between her and death now offered a truce and sounded as exhausted as she felt.

Plenty of time tomorrow to battle him.

"Deal." She waited for him to release her. Sooner would be better than later or she might be tempted to lean back against his wide chest.

His hands dropped away and she had to ignore the disappointment. She lifted her computer bag and followed him to the passenger side, where she sank into the heavenly seat and dropped her head back.

He circled the car with the smooth stride of a man in control. He slid in behind the wheel, filling the interior to capacity with his presence.

The engine roared to life.

Gabrielle focused on staying awake while he maneuvered through the parking lot, then out onto the highway. At Highway 74 he turned north, likely heading to Interstate 85. Heat purred around her legs and soft music shushed through the cockpit.

No sleeping. Watch the route. Her mind knew what she had to do, but her body was not a willing party. She fought to stay alert, observing their route until he reached Interstate 85 and gunned into the northbound traffic flow. Unless he changed course, Atlanta was twenty miles ahead.

The smooth ride and quiet did her in.

Anxiety drained from her body in one fast sweep. She drifted off. Disjointed images flickered in her overloaded mind. Computer entries whirled around coded messages. Linette's signature—Jane of Art—appeared on a bulletin board, finally after years of Gabrielle hoping to hear from her again. She lunged to answer the post, but when she typed on the keys, a bloody body hanging against a wall appeared on her monitor.

The man's head lifted. She froze when she recognized the battered face.

Carlos.

She beat against the computer, yelling, "No!" Her screams echoed in the dark room.

Someone caught her hands. He called to her in a low, urgent voice. "Gabrielle, you're safe. Wake up."

She blinked her eyes, heart pulsing.

Carlos had her against his chest, telling her softly, "It's all right. You're safe."

She took a shuddering breath, realizing he had pulled the car onto the shoulder of the road and come around to her side. Her heart raced out of control.

He rubbed a hand up and down her back.

Such a foreign feeling . . . to be comforted. She'd forgotten what it felt like to be hugged. A real hug, not just a polite hello kind. But he was the enemy. She had to remember that or she'd never get out of this.

Gabrielle breathed deeply. She reached for a strength that had kept her alive over the past ten years and out of the deadly grip of Durand Anguis.

"I'm okay." She pulled away, foggy from the hard sleep and hungry. "Where are we?" She couldn't help the surly tone and didn't particularly care if she sounded unappreciative. The nightmare was his fault, plus she was both sick to her stomach and needed to eat.

He released her and returned to the driver's seat. Before putting the still-running car into gear, he reached across her for the seat belt. When he paused, his cheek was next to hers, so close it was like an intimate gesture.

Instead of being frightened, as she should have been, in that one moment she felt secure and protected. She was clearly losing her mind.

His eyes widened with some intuitive understanding, then narrowed before he moved back across to the driver's seat, latching her belt in the same motion. For a man so intimidating in size and solid muscle, his every move was smooth and fluid.

He cleared his throat. "Want something to drink?" He put the car into gear and moved smoothly back into traffic.

"Maybe a water." Gabrielle searched for a landmark as the car quickly reached cruising speed. They were on Interstate 75 and had just passed under the north 120 Loop overpass, which meant they were in the Marietta area, northwest of downtown Atlanta. She'd slept at least forty-five minutes, but didn't feel very refreshed. Sort of like on those rare days she grabbed a nap in the afternoon after spending half the night online.

Carlos took the Interstate 575 split and turned off at the Barrett Parkway exit. Fast-food and retail stores choked the one-mile stretch so close to a popular Atlanta mall.

"Hungry?" he asked.

"*Oui.*" She sat up, searching the many options on each side of the road. "But you have to park so I can visit the loo."

He pulled into a McDonald's and parked, then came around and helped her from the car. She hurried ahead to the ladies' room. When she came out, he was camped outside the door with a bag of food. Her mouth watered at the smell. She did love fries. They ate in silence with her watching Carlos, and his gaze tracking everything that moved.

Back on the road, he pushed the car up to cruising speed again. "Now that you've had a nap and food, let's talk."

"About what? Thought you wanted to wait until I met *your* people."

He shrugged. "You could fill in a few blanks tonight."

"Like what?" Less was better than more.

"You're the electronic informant Mirage." He didn't ask, just tossed that out, and added, "Where are you getting your intel?"

"Who are you and who do you work for?" she asked rather than admit anything, but she couched her questions more politely to encourage an exchange of information.

"If you're worried about Durand Anguis, I'm not in his pocket."

A nonanswer. She tapped her fingers on the door handle. "I sort of figured that out in the last few hours. That doesn't tell me who you *are* working with . . . or what you want with me."

"And, I'm not the one who has to answer questions."

She got that, but she still needed to know whose team he played on. "Are you CIA or FBI?"

"No."

"Are you wanted by either of those?"

"No, but I do work for an agency that protects American security."

She sighed and dropped her head back. "That's something, I suppose. But I might be more willing to talk if I knew what agency you were with."

"Let's just say, no one you'd know." His eyes crinkled with mirth, but the rest of his features remained as stoic as ever.

"Do the CIA and FBI know about you?"

"No."

So was he really with some form of law enforcement?

When Interstate 575 ended, Carlos took Highway 5 north.

Warm air curled around her shoulders, distracting her. Between the meal and the heat, her eyelids felt heavy again, but she had to stay vigilant. Any hope of getting away from Carlos depended on knowing where she was and which way to run.

She rubbed her eyes, letting them close for just a second, just long enough to rest them.

"Why were you in Peachtree City?"

His question snapped her awake. She stretched her face and eyes, trying to come alert. Bad sign that she'd fallen asleep so easily again. "What?"

"Peachtree City. Why were you living there?"

"I liked the area," she muttered, then cleared her voice. "It was quiet with pretty parks and great food. They have miles and miles of paved paths so you can travel all over the city in a golf cart or on a bike. Good food, too. I'm going to miss eating at Pascal's Bistro. That was my favorite—"

"That's not what I meant," he interrupted in a wry tone that poked at her patience.

Gabrielle crossed her arms. "It was just a place to live where I felt safe. No special reason that had anything to do with espionage, if that's what you're insinuating. I didn't know anyone except my landlord, who I rarely saw." She sat upright. "Good Lord. Harry might stop by this weekend. What about Baby Face's body?"

"There are no bodies or cars on his property right now that don't belong to him or you. What did you tell Baby Face?"

"Nothing."

"What exactly did he tell you?"

"That the DEA wanted to talk to me about . . ." She forced her mind back over what everyone had said, trying to make sure she only shared what Carlos already knew. "Durand Anguis, but I don't know why."

"So Baby Face tracked you electronically—"

"Lucky hit." She scoffed then frowned. She'd just admitted too much.

"You didn't just let something slip," he assured her.

She refused to reply since he picked up on every little thing she said and any reaction.

"Really," he continued. "We *know* you're the Mirage. Baby Face was an electronic mastermind with resources all over the world. He tracked you *and* so did my people. There's no telling who else was close to locating you." Carlos rode in silence for a bit then added, "You're lucky I found you when I did."

Gabrielle couldn't argue that point. How *had* those two groups found her?

Answering that last post about Mandy needing her help gave someone a break who was watching for a second post, which Gabrielle had provided them with. That's when Baby Face and the group this Carlos was aligned with figured out about the bounce from Peachtree City to Romania to Russia before the message was fed to several UK and American IPs.

She'd bet the emergency message she'd received about Mandy had been sent by either Baby Face or Carlos's group.

Stupid mistake, but she would stick her neck out again to save a child.

Carlos *had* shown up in time to keep her out of Turga's hands, but her appreciation was going to disintegrate if she found out *his* people were behind the post about Mandy last night.

That his group had lured her into a trap and exposed her to people like Durand.

Until she figured out what Carlos wanted and whom he worked for, she couldn't let his protective nature continue to cloud her survival judgment.

"So, where are you getting your information?" he asked again.

She shrugged. "The Internet, where else?"

His scoff of derision rode on a laugh. "I don't think so. Not all of it. You've passed information to the CIA, MI5 or MI6, Interpol, FBI, and a slew of other groups that couldn't have been found randomly on the Internet. Pick a new answer."

She would not tell him about her associates in South America who had fed her information for the past four years. Contacting Ferdinand and his son for help with Mandy's kidnapping had been risky after all the trouble she'd gone through to set up a secure process for the Diaz men to feed information to her.

A one-way electronic street. Taking the initiative to contact them first opened a channel someone could track.

Please, God, tell her she hadn't put Ferdinand and his

son in danger by breaking protocol, but Mandy wouldn't have been found without that information.

Had the young woman even been found? Had anyone, including Carlos and his group, even cared about what happened to Mandy? Was the young girl really safe after all this? As far as Gabrielle could see, everyone was more interested in Mirage's contacts than anything else.

But asking Carlos about Mandy right now would only confirm what he was fishing for.

She would not give up her South American contacts no matter what his people threatened. Please, God, give her the strength to match that conviction if it came down to torture.

Her mind wandered with disjointed thoughts.

Sleep crooned to her like a lover. Her eyelids drooped.

Carlos ground his teeth against the throb in his temple. He didn't particularly care what they discussed right now since Gabrielle would be answering every question at BAD headquarters tomorrow. He needed to keep her talking until they were close to the secure residence BAD had in Hiawassee, then she could drift back off to sleep while he drove to the cabin.

Otherwise, he'd have to make a wide circle of the area until she faded again. Or blindfold her and tie her hands, which he really didn't want to do.

He glanced at her out of the corner of his eye. Exhaustion underlined her striking eyes that were such an odd shade of blue-violet at times.

A skilled observer would be hard-pressed to choose her exact age. She wore no makeup and could be anywhere from early to late twenties. Loose hairs from the brunette mane she'd twisted up onto her head with a clamp now fell in restless wisps along her neck. Her oval face wouldn't turn every head in a room, but she'd force a few discerning male gazes to linger while they considered the possibilities.

This was the informant who had broken through international intelligence communication?

Wedge that firmly enough into his psyche and he'd have an easier time interrogating her tomorrow.

Her bottom, deep-pink lip puckered softly as if in thought. She leaned an elbow against the base of the window and propped her head, struggling to stay awake, probably trying as hard to figure out where she was going as Carlos worked to keep his cabin location secret.

The blanket slipped off her shoulder to pool around her waist. Her baggy gray pants and oversize T-shirt sure as hell didn't camouflage the curvaceous body.

Especially the damp T-shirt that clung to her breasts.

Carlos felt a stir inside his jeans and scowled at the purely male reaction. Not the time for his body to remind him he was way overdue for some R and R.

He bumped the heat a little higher even though the warmth fed his body's need for sleep as well, but he could stay awake another half hour.

Her eyelashes fluttered against the cream-white cheek.

The minute her breathing fell into a constant rhythm, Carlos turned off the main road. The night closed in around the Beemer headlights as he slowly wound his way up a lonely ridge road.

Gabrielle's soft and steady breathing filled the silent car. He reached over and lifted the blanket back around her shoulders. The urge to keep her safe thrummed as strong as it had when bullets were flying earlier.

An urge that was in direct conflict with the job he'd have to do at headquarters.

But for tonight, she'd be safe from everyone.

When he approached the secluded drive to the cabin, he hit a button in the headrest panel that opened an electric gate. He entered slowly, watching to assure the gate closed behind him.

At the house, he let the car idle in the circular drive while he lifted a remote from the console between the seats and pressed a series of three buttons. Had one signal come back in a default of any kind, he'd have continued around the circular drive and left immediately.

All clear.

Once he had the car inside the triple-door garage, Carlos locked the doors and left Gabrielle while he opened the house. He made a physical check of each room, then returned to her side and opened her door slowly to catch her. Unclipping her belt, he lifted her into his arms, grunting at the stab of pain in his forearm and side. The jagged bullet gash and glass cut would need stitches tonight.

He carried her to the master bedroom, where he'd already drawn the covers back on his first pass through. She didn't stir while he removed sneakers and her sweatpants, which had finally dried. When he lifted the edge of her top, he found the tail of a silky undergarment, so he took the T-shirt off, too.

She curled up in a ball of smooth skin, candy-red lace underwear, and a matching silk camisole.

How could someone who looked like a librarian wear sin underwear? He debated over how to secure her for the night.

She could rest unbound while he was awake, but he needed sleep and would crash hard once his head hit the pillow after so many hours on his feet.

The safest thing would be to cuff her hands and arms to each corner of the bed, especially if armed guards showed up tonight to take her into custody.

The vision of her cuffed spread eagle in that red lace rushed through his brain then charged south to his loins.

And that kiss still lingered on his lips, in his thoughts.

He really had to straighten out his thinking about her, starting with not thinking about her mouth . . . or her underwear.

Carlos pulled the covers over all that temptation.

The information she'd shared electronically may have led them to Mandy, but he'd never met an informant who was simply a Good Samaritan with no hidden ulterior motives. They always wanted something and couldn't be trusted since their allegiance shifted with the best deal being offered.

So think enemy.

He glanced back down at her sweet profile and regretted having to stake her to the bed, but he couldn't leave her free or she'd run at the first chance she got.

There was another option. But she wouldn't like it.

Hell, he wouldn't either.

His head hurt too much to make one more decision, so Carlos dug a quarter out of his pocket and flipped it.

SEVEN

Durand knelt on a wool blanket to keep from ruining his black dress pants. He lifted the L96A1 sniper rifle, settling it against his shoulder, then centered the crosshairs on the head of his six-foot target standing two hundred feet away. The wind slipped through trees on each side of him that created a canopy of relief from the afternoon heat weathermen had warned would reach the high nineties in nearby Caracas today.

Like fall in Venezuela was not always hot?

Ankle-deep grass stretched between him and the target so small against the lush tree line and the imposing mountains farther back. So vulnerable. When his breathing slowed to shallow breaths, Durand gently pulled the trigger.

The explosion rolled across the empty field and echoed against the ten-foot-high stucco wall at Durand's back. Sulfur odors stung the air. His target's head burst, pieces of clay flying in all directions.

Cheers went up behind him.

Durand grinned, then swung around, making a theatrical half bow for his audience of four elite Anguis soldiers he'd chosen to train with the new rifles. They wore an assortment of jungle-camo fatigues, black cargo pants, dark T-shirts, and sleeveless camo shirts. With their ages ranging from early twenties to late thirties, there wasn't a spare ounce of fat among them.

"I only buy the best for you," Durand said softly, his smile growing. "And in return, I expect the best. *Entienden?*"

They answered a resounding "*Sí,*" all confirming they understood. More than that, their eyes beamed with respect for him. Durand constantly proved to his men he was a cunning leader with vision. A man who put family above all else and treated his soldiers as his family.

A man who deserved uncompromising loyalty and would accept no less.

"You are the *mejor,* my finest marksmen," he told them, watching each man silently accept his praise. He waved them toward a row of tables displaying rifles, scopes, silencers, ammunition, and more. Everything a marksman needed. "Choose your weapon and begin training."

He frequently spoke English in his compound to lead by example. The better a man understood anyone outside his camp, the more formidable an opponent he became.

Durand left his men joking and laughing as they picked through weapons and accessories like children given free rein in a toy store. He strode toward the rear of his private compound enclosed by the butter-yellow wall built to match his hacienda it protected. Spiked, black wrought iron ran along the top ledge interlaced with cascading bougainvillea that perfumed the warm air. A landscape architect had designed the rock gardens with tropical plants that ran low to the ground along the exterior base of the wall, hiding trip wires.

But the exterior was nothing compared to the landscape artistry inside his fortress.

At the arched oak door that allowed rear access, two guards in pressed khaki shirts and pants held H&K assault rifles at the ready. The older of the two men lowered his weapon to pull open the ornate door carved with scrolled vines, which hid a core of solid steel.

"*Hola*, Ferdinand. How is your son's knee?" Durand paused before passing through the doorway. The grayhaired soldier had come to him many years ago, asking for help. Ferdinand's wife needed medical care that Durand provided for six months, but her cancer had proved too advanced and she died.

"He still uses the . . ." Ferdinand's wrinkled forehead drew tight in heavy concentration. "Sticks."

"Crutches?"

"*Sí.*" Ferdinand sighed and wiped a bead of sweat from his forehead with a cotton bandanna. Fifty-eight years of living had carved deep lines in his forehead and around his mouth that lifted with a smile whenever he spoke of his son.

Durand was only six years younger and eye level with Ferdinand, who stood five feet eleven inches and was still strong for an old hombre. But the similarities stopped there, because time had been hard on Ferdinand's face. Durand was still a virile and attractive man. He kept his body fit and wore his silvery mane tied back with a leather thong. Women admired strength in a man just as his business associates respected power in a peer.

Ferdinand shrugged. "You know how a young hombre is too proud to ask his papa for help, but I go anyhow. I tell him working in the pawnshop when I leave here is better than doing nada at home. He will be much improved in a few days."

Durand frowned over his man having to work all day for him then nights and weekends for his son. "You may have this week to go help him, then come back Monday."

Shaking his head, Ferdinand argued, "No, Don Anguis. I do my job."

Durand patted him on the shoulder. "Go, old friend. I want you to. When your son is better, tell him to come see me. He can make more here than at that pawnshop. *Sí?*"

"*Sí.*" Ferdinand swallowed, then nodded. "*Gracias.*" He backed away then to hold the door open.

Once inside, Durand strolled along the stone-paved walkway that snaked through tiered gardens. Two acres of paradise. Nothing like the filthy hovel he grew up in. Three of his five gardeners trimmed hedges, shaped the bougainvillea, and planted fresh flowers. Celine, his latest *novia*, liked something to always be flowering.

A small price to pay for what she can do with that mouth.

Guards stood at each corner of his nineteen-thousand-square-foot hacienda, a magnificent two-story stucco backdrop to the pool that stretched the length of his

Mediterranean-design home. Double glass doors in the center of the lower level opened. His sister pushed the wheelchair with her son Eduardo outside, wheeling the chair to the far left under a cabana next to a kidney-shaped pond with rare fish Durand had personally selected.

He started each day by sipping coffee at the pond, watching his fish play. He found it peaceful.

Maria insisted her son needed a daily dose of sunshine.

Durand headed their way, but his eyes strayed to the foot-long bloated body of a dead fish partly hidden beneath the leaves of a water lily. His favorite scarlet-and-white one he'd raised from a guppy size.

Stopping next to the pond, he fisted his hand.

"*Qué te pasa, Durand?*" Maria called to him.

"*Nada,*" he answered, then corrected himself. "No problem." He relaxed his fingers and made a mental note to have Julio deal with it. His bootheels clicked against the hand-painted ceramic tiles covering the concrete perimeter of the pool as he reached the pair. His nephew lifted his head and gazed Durand's way before averting his eyes.

That boy was such a waste. Durand regretted that Eduardo wore the tattoo of an Anguis soldier with the scar of a blood relation. His life was full of regrets, such as Alejandro, who had walked away from his family rather than take his rightful place.

He asked his sister, "Did you confirm your plans?" Heat burned through his silk shirt from the sun bearing down on his back. Why didn't his sister put Eduardo out here if he needed sunshine?

"*Sí, nosotros—*," his sister started to answer.

Durand interrupted her by shaking his head. "Please, Maria. In *inglés*."

Her mouth turned down in a frown until she caught herself and quickly recovered to nod, a passive mask in place. She had never been a beauty, but she was not unattractive either at forty-eight. Her head reached his shoulder and she had a full womanly figure a man would like if she allowed someone to date her. He'd given several men permission, but she refused any invitation.

Dios mío. Durand hated the submissive droop in her shoulders. She was his baby sister. He loved her. He did not tolerate insolence from his men, but he would never raise a hand to her.

"Sorry." She kept her hand on her son's shoulder. "Yes, everything is confirmed. We leave on Thursday."

"How are you today, Eduardo?" Durand asked for Maria's benefit. The boy got on his nerves.

"*Bien.*" A paraplegic since an accident in his teens, Eduardo could use his upper body. He *could* raise his head and look his uncle in the eyes, but no.

Durand sighed. He'd had the pool built so the boy could be wheeled into it from the far end, but Eduardo refused to go into the water.

"Do you need me to do something for you?" Maria never failed to draw his attention away from Eduardo, ever the protective mama.

As if she thought her own brother was a threat?

"No." He scratched his chin. "I must speak to Julio."

"I saw him in his office on our way out."

Sweat ran inside the open collar of his silk shirt. Durand excused himself with "Until dinner."

Inside the hacienda, he ran into Julio in the two-story hallway, who said, "Were you looking for me, patron?"

"*Sí*. I have an errand for you." Durand explained about the dead fish, finishing with "Find that pond keeper Tito and kill him."

Julio nodded, but before walking away he shared, "The Italian called to say he was on his way and should arrive in the next fifteen minutes."

Durand dismissed Julio and headed to his office. This meeting would determine if he and Vestavia would remain partners. He'd settled into the leather chair behind his burled-pecan desk and had finished making a call when heavy footsteps approached.

"My associates aren't happy." The stocky Italian entered his office on a sweep of anger. A few inches taller than Durand, Vestavia was not a huge man, but he was thick like a bull.

"I expect better manners in my home," Durand warned. Few people were even allowed to step on his land in central Venezuela. Even fewer were invited inside the compound.

"You want better manners? Give me better results." Vestavia shoved an uncompromising gaze back across the desk. The black-rimmed glasses he wore belonged on an accountant, not that bulked-up body covered with a tailored suit designed for boardrooms in New York. The rough-cut, dirt-brown hair reminded Durand of American cowboys.

"Please." Durand pointed at the inlaid-wood humidor on his desk, silently inviting his guest to choose one of the ten most exquisite cigars made in the world.

Instead of answering, Vestavia withdrew an OpusX cigar, ran the premium blend below his nose with the intimacy of smelling a lover. He used Durand's engraved snipper from the desk, lit the cigar, and took a seat in one of the two liver-colored leather side chairs.

While his guest settled, Durand twirled a stiletto between his fingers. Vestavia should respect his elders. Vestavia could be no more than late thirties. The respect was due.

"We both suffered losses." Durand pulled his lips tight in a grim smile. This man Vestavia had shared little about the mysterious group he represented. But the money and underworld connections he brought to the table were too substantial to dismiss. "You think I am pleased to have lost fine men?"

"You assured me you could do this project," Vestavia countered.

"And you assured me you could locate Mirage."

Vestavia quieted, his lips not moving until he blew out a stream of smoke. "We did find the informant. We—"

"—may have located the informant, but you do not have him. Excuse me for interrupting, but I believe I know more about the outcome than you do." Durand placed the stiletto on the desk and selected a custom-rolled cigar from the humidor for himself.

That drew a brief flicker of concern into Vestavia's gaze that dissipated just as quickly. He puffed, watching

Durand with the eyes of a predatory bird patiently waiting for the perfect moment to attack. "Go on."

"As I understand it, Baby Face found a connection, which I assume was due to some help you must have given him since all my people claimed Mirage could not be found without access to supercomputers." Durand paused until Vestavia gave a slight nod of his head in agreement. "I have men looking for this informant as well. Everyone with a computer and a weapon on both sides of the law is after Mirage. Baby Face was brilliant, but his ego became a liability. He bragged online about, as he put it, 'hitting the mother lode' or some such. This allowed Turga to catch scent of the deal and cost Baby Face his life."

"Who is Turga?"

"An old associate who will unfortunately not see his next birthday. He is what you would call a poacher, who shows up to snatch a prize at the last moment, then auction it to the highest bidder. I understand he *was* very hard to kill, but he is also dead. His helicopter pilot was the last one to see everyone alive. He told my people that Turga caught a man and woman who escaped Baby Face. This pilot is on his way to meet with me. By tomorrow, I will have an artist's sketch of the man and woman from his description."

Vestavia's face never changed, eyes as flat and cold as the first time Durand had met him. But this man's vision for the future—or his organization's vision—was exceptional, a world where the Anguis family would thrive and rule in Venezuela, then all of South America.

If he and Vestavia could reach a point of trust.

"So we have both been disappointed, no?" Durand continued. "As for Mandy, my men did their job. She was delivered to the chalet on time, but a black-ops team ambushed my men. I will find who was behind the attack."

"Going to be hard to do that with all your men dead."

"No really. I never send my men in on a new operation without surveillance."

"What do you mean?"

"I sent Julio, my most trusted soldier, ahead of the team. No one knew he was inside the house. He entered before they arrived and used lipstick cameras that fed to a terminal in the basement where he stayed the entire time."

Vestavia sat forward, tense. "Why did you send a spy?"

"I am a cautious man."

"No." Vestavia moved his head slowly from side to side. "I think you don't trust me, which I find insulting."

Durand smiled. "Trust is the question between us, yes? I have not known you long. What kind of leader would I be if I do not assure of a way to make someone pay for ambushing my men?" He drew on his cigar and exhaled, sending wavy circles into the air. "Using Julio keeps my men sharp. I tell them things about their missions they think I cannot possibly know. They respect that. You see, respect is like trust, it must be earned."

Vestavia was one of those men who exuded power in silence.

Durand would not be intimidated, not even by a man whose money, contacts, and powerful organization could help him bring the Salvatore family to their knees. He would soon have the throat of that squealing Mirage pig in one fist and Dominic Salvatore's cojones in his other fist.

But in the meantime, he did not want to create an enemy of this Vestavia.

"I provided projects to make you high profile for Mirage," Vestavia offered in a conciliatory tone Durand knew better than to believe. "Kidnapping Mandy was moved up just to give you more exposure to Mirage since the informant seems to take a particular interest when a female and the Anguis are involved."

"True, but our deal is not one-sided," Durand cautioned. "My men have made two successful attempts on our oil minister's life appear as if the Salvatore family is behind the attacks. Killing the oil minister would be much simpler than pretending to. I do not want the Venezuelan government on my doorstep. I admit I am happy to put Salvatore's cojones in a vise, but these attacks are very risky. What is the purpose?"

"I don't explain myself to anyone," Vestavia warned.

Durand hid the urge to choke this man. To show anger was a sign of weakness. "I only suggest that if I understand your reasoning, I can better support your cause since I have a finger on the Venezuelan pulse."

Vestavia studied on that a moment before speaking. "My organization is quite pleased with the results so far, but it's imperative the pressure is kept up. The United States is under scrutiny for their attempt to secretly partner with Venezuelan oil production behind the Venezuelan government's back.

"Both candidates for the next U.S. presidency are

opposed to financing a partnership with Venezuela to produce more oil. Both are pushing the platform about America becoming a more green country since that's the new hot button for voters. The media is fueling rumors that one of the two political parties is funding Salvatore to assassinate your oil minister. No one can figure out if the Democrats are behind the attacks to show how the Republicans are trying to partner with an unstable country for oil instead of going green or if the Republicans are behind this and plan to produce evidence the Democrats were behind the attacks simply to lay the groundwork for a major shift to going green."

"How does Salvatore fit in your plans?" Durand leaned back, arms draped along his chair. A pose of confidence.

"It appears the Salvatore Cartel is sitting back until the elections are over to see if a coup does indeed overthrow the government. If so, that's when we'll find out if the new U.S. administration actually forms an agreement with Venezuela for oil. Salvatore can be an impediment in the oil ministry's plans or the two could team up to form an agreement that assured the oil production industry was protected from rebel attacks as long as Salvatore's drug shipments passed through safely."

"Yes, yes, I stay informed through my contacts." Durand tapped his cigar on the edge of a crystal ashtray. Salvatore had been an obstacle in *his* plans for many years. "I have no care what America pays for a gallon of fuel or the presidential election next week. I *am* concerned with the future of the Anguis and believe we can help each other." He let that sink in.

Vestavia had come to Durand. Not the other way around.

When his guest didn't comment, Durand repeated, "We *both* suffered a loss in France. The question is how will we both recover our losses? Someone *will* pay for mine. If we work together, we can recoup and make an example for others who might think to interfere again."

"No one *ever* screws me over and lives to brag." The brutal cold in Vestavia's voice could freeze a hot ember.

"Then work with me to find these men who have killed mine and taken Mandy, because together we will find them."

"You're certain about Julio's allegiance?"

Dios! This man had better be worth the aggravation he caused. Durand smiled. "Julio was the only person who knew about the chalet in advance and I stake my life on my cousin's loyalty. Blood is everything in my family."

"Did he get any good photos of the black-ops team?"

"Julio is processing everything now."

"Send me what you have and I'll put our people on identifying them." Vestavia had said more than once he had limitless resources.

Durand nodded politely, but he would not share photos or anything else of significance until he could strike Vestavia's name off the list of suspects for the ambush.

"Someone got the information to Mirage very quickly that you were behind the kidnapping," Vestavia pointed out. "Sounds like a snitch inside your group."

"I have people on that as well, but you also have a problem," Durand countered in a calm voice. He suppressed a smile at his guest's scowl. "My men did not know where they were taking the girl until they were in route, and since all were killed, is it not logical to assume their innocence?"

Durand paused to draw on his cigar, letting the rich tobacco flavor flow through his mouth. He exhaled and said, "Before you accuse me of failure, you must explain how anyone knew of the chalet meeting spot. The elite team who killed them showed up in less than eleven hours of my men arriving. How did the informant get *that* information so quickly?"

Vestavia didn't answer for a minute, his tiny brown eyes shifting between narrowed slits. "If there is a leak in my organization, I'll find it and deal with that person. But if I learn that someone in your camp betrayed us, my associates will expect his head or yours. And I mean that literally."

Durand smiled conspiratorially. "If someone I know killed my men—one of whom was my younger brother— you may have the head and any other piece . . . once I am finished with him. You cannot have mine, ever. And if it is one of your people, I will expect the same courtesy in return."

"Fair enough. In the meantime, continue as planned. I'll personally interrogate Mirage once that informant is captured."

Durand waved a finger back and forth. "Nada. The Mirage is mine. Delivered alive."

Vestavia grunted, neither agreeing nor disagreeing and reached down into his briefcase. He withdrew a thick manila envelope. "Your next contract."

Durand did not move to take the package. "I no joke about this informant."

"Fine. Alive. No promises on the condition of the body."

Durand took the package and opened it, withdrawing the photos. "Another female. No problem."

"Maybe, but this one won't be quite as easy to grab."

Durand studied the teenager and wondered yet again what Vestavia's purpose was for the teens, but his alliance with this strange Italian depended on better results with less questions.

"What is our time frame?" Durand lifted the photo sheets into view. Pretty, but nothing notable.

"Two days. Mandy was intended for a side project, but this girl," Vestavia said, his gaze going to the photos in Durand's hand, dark eyebrows dropped low over mean eyes, "is needed now. No missteps."

Vestavia lifted his briefcase and turned to leave.

"It would be in your best interest to find the snitch before I hand over this girl," Durand warned quietly.

Vestavia stopped, breathing slowly during the long silence. "Threatening me is not a healthy idea."

"I only offer incentive to move as quickly as you expect my people to. If you do not locate this Mirage first, then you will owe me, yes?"

Vestavia left without another word.

Durand tapped his cigar. This would never be an easy alliance, but the truly strong ones took work and finesse. He pressed a button on the radio function of his cell phone, calling Julio, who answered immediately.

Durand asked, "How are the photos from the château coming?"

"Most are fair, but one is no bad. It is the man who I believe was in charge of the team."

"Bring all the photos now."

"*Sí*. I am on the way."

Eight

Gabrielle curled closer to the warmth, hugging the pillow. The cloth smelled so . . . masculine?

She kept her eyes shut, allowing her mind to sharpen while she mustered the energy to pull away from the deep sleep tempting her to stay.

Now that she could actually process information, she realized the pillow wasn't soft at all. The surface was hard and carved.

Last night . . . they were driving somewhere . . . then nothing once she dropped over the edge into deep sleep.

Carlos had been talking to her. When did they get out of the car? Her face moved up and down when the sculpted surface rose and fell in a gradual motion.

Her senses sharpened all at once. She couldn't be where she thought she was, or better put . . . on top of . . . *him?*

Gabrielle opened her eyes, peeking at the left side of her body, and found she was at least wearing her underwear. She'd been undressed. Not acceptable, by her rules, but she didn't think anything had happened. She lifted her head slowly to figure her chances of sliding out of bed without him noticing.

Zero.

Alert dark brown eyes stared back from a shaved face so seductively male she couldn't break her gaze. She was spread across Carlos's chest, hugging him like a lover, and afraid to move or speak.

When was the last time she'd been in this position?

So long ago she couldn't recall, and never with a man whose body turned her gray matter into complete mush.

He was propped up on pillows, studying her with a quiet gaze so unlike the deadly face she'd witnessed yesterday.

A strong arm banded around her, his hand rubbing along her back, slowly, soothing. She had to get out of this bed, clear her head, and figure out what the devil she'd got into.

But his fingers were gently kneading the tense muscles, turning her body to jelly. Her limp muscles lost all tensile strength. Moving from this spot would take a monumental effort.

Who was this bloody guy?

He winked. All thought of reprimand over this impropriety stuttered in her mind.

She sighed. *Isn't it against some set of rules to be in bed with the prisoner?* His magical fingers dismissed that question. She should be ranting at him, but honesty forced her to admit she enjoyed his touch and wasn't particularly distressed at the moment.

Considering what she'd experienced yesterday, this wasn't that strange.

He stopped rubbing her back, but left his arm looped over her shoulder. The silence continued. The formidable gaze that swept through his eyes now was no softer than the hard chest beneath her. A muscle twitched in his cheek.

Was he laughing at her?

She narrowed her eyes into what she hoped sent back just as formidable a message, though she had a feeling his was better. He'd probably had more practice at looking intimidating.

"You're much calmer than I expected." His chest continued to move slowly up, then down. His breath smelled like mint. She'd noticed the tin of strong mints he kept in the car last night. Must keep them near the bed, too.

"Why am I here?" she finally asked.

"I told you I was taking you somewhere safe."

"Don't be obtuse. I mean *here*, in this bed."

"You needed rest." His eyes softened. Amused. "Trust me. Nothing happened."

Why had that sounded so definite? As in, he wasn't the least bit interested in her sexually.

That should be a relief, right?

It probably would have been if his deep voice didn't engage the wrong part of her brain. The part that considered it a perfectly sound idea to lounge in bed with a sexy stranger who had kidnapped her. All right, yes, she did sort of trust him after he'd constantly protected her yesterday, but that didn't excuse a lapse of sanity.

The point was to get out of this predicament, not feed his ego by remaining compromised.

He drew a deep breath quickly, lifting her up so fast she hugged her right arm to him out of instinct to maintain balance.

Not the message she wanted to send him, so she pushed up with the same hand to get away.

That's when she realized she had a cloth wrapped around her right wrist. When she jerked her right hand up to inspect it, he scowled. Her wrist jangled.

"Wait a minute." He grabbed her wrist with his left hand.

"You"—Gabrielle leaned her elbow on his chest, enjoying the grunt—"*handcuffed* me to you? Let me go." She jerked away, but couldn't get leverage from her position.

He rolled her over swiftly, pinning her with his body.

Any humor or concern had vanished. The black gaze raking her now stunned her into silence. Here was the man who had killed without hesitation yesterday.

"Don't start this morning fighting me or today won't go much better than yesterday," he warned in a voice rough from deep sleep.

Think. Say something to back him off. She couldn't process a thing with him so close. His eyes blazed with a different heat all of a sudden. The look was so charged with arousal her hormones went on alert for an early morning treat.

Now she was the one not thinking like a prisoner.

Carlos studied her with intense interest that left her feeling he could see right into her mind, then his gaze relaxed. He asked in a gentler voice, "How can you be afraid of me after yesterday?"

She worked on breathing steadily, in, out, in, out. When was the last time she'd been this close to a man in bed? Anywhere? One so overtly sexual she didn't think he could prevent it. She swallowed, preparing to ask him, nicely, to let her up.

He must have misread the action and thought she still feared him when he lowered his head, those chiseled lips so close she could taste them. "Truce, remember?"

He kissed her.

The man had kissing down. He could give lessons. She'd sign up for an ongoing program. His mouth played across hers softly, teasing, then paused and sealed her lips with his. She sensed him holding back, then raw, masculine heat poured through the kiss. His tongue slipped into her mouth, moving with slow erotic motions that sent a wave of lust spiraling down to pool between her legs.

His fingers drove into her hair, holding her.

She shivered and clenched with the raging need for more.

Years of hiding and loneliness interfered with the message from her brain warning her to stop now.

With her hands free, she reached for his shoulders to pull him closer.

One hand made it. The other slapped back to the bed, still handcuffed to his wrist. That broke through her erotic haze.

She stopped kissing, priding herself on that one feat since her lips didn't want to leave a mouth like his.

"Let. Me. Up," she demanded through clenched teeth, trying to regain some self-respect. She twisted her body back and forth to make it clear she meant *now*.

He scowled a curse, which she figured out a bit late. Moving her hips with their bodies so close had the opposite effect of what she'd intended.

His legs were on each side of hers, locking her into place. The only barrier between where their hips met was her lace underwear and his shorts.

And one impressive hard-on.

She was in no mood to be impressed right now. Her heart thumped so hard the beat should have been echoing off the walls, but she would not feed his ego by letting on how much he affected her. "Get off me."

A weary sigh rushed out of him on another mint-flavored breath. He eased up on his elbows and knees, but kept her legs locked between his.

"Calm down." His eyelids lowered in a droll frown. "I am *not* interested in taking advantage of you. I had to handcuff you to something last night. You kept sleeping on your stomach so I cuffed your right hand to my left hand but you scratched the hell out of me—twice—when *you* crawled up on my chest."

She lowered her gaze to his shoulder and saw two red marks that disappeared inside the gray tank top he wore, then lifted her eyes to his. *I am not apologizing.*

"So I finally uncuffed you and waited for you to settle down in one spot before I cuffed us again."

When she didn't say a word, he snapped, "*You* picked the spot, not me."

She shouldn't feel embarrassed for climbing all over him, but couldn't convince herself to take it in stride. He sounded put upon to wake up with her wrapped over him when it was just as much his fault as hers. She'd slept alone for so long she was used to having the entire bed at night and normally ended up on top of a big pillow.

Besides, she stung from how he was "*not* interested" in her body. He could have just said he'd kept his hands to himself. She knew she didn't have some buff body.

"Don't kick, hit, bite, or do anything else and I'll uncuff you. Agreed?" He'd issued that offer as an order.

She nodded.

He just shook his head and reached over to the nightstand, returning with a key. He unlocked his wrist first. She noticed a red welt where he hadn't wrapped his wrist protectively.

Her wrist was fine since he'd wound soft jersey material around it, taping the material in place. Or had he done that because her wrist was narrow and he thought she might slip out of the cuff during the night?

That made more sense.

She was his prisoner, not a kinky date.

The minute she was free, Gabrielle scrambled off the bed to stand.

He was still crouched on the bed. His gaze swam across her from head to toe. What was he thinking?

"The bathroom is over there." He nodded to the left. "Get in there. I'll bring your clothes."

She went rigid at the disgust in his voice. As if he couldn't stand the sight of her.

"Move. Now!"

Gabrielle stumbled trying to hurry to the bathroom, but caught her balance. His curse followed her into the room so she slammed the door. Childish, but it still felt good.

Her body was far from perfect, but he didn't have to act so revolted that he ordered her to get out of his sight. She should be cheered by his lack of interest, not insulted.

The bugger was probably angry she realized he'd become excited lying on her. She refused to feel bad about her body. Other men had found her attractive.

One anyhow. A jerk.

Gabrielle shook her head at the direction of her thoughts. She was a prisoner with more problems than wounded vanity. Turning around, she scoped the bathroom, made of stone, teak, and glass. Slate tiles covered the floor and walls of the shower not encased with glass.

The oversize Jacuzzi tub in white marble with pink and gray veins matched the sink counters. Taupe and gray tiles covered the walls not hidden by teak cabinets.

And a wide-screen television monitor.

Someone with money ran this operation. Who, and what did they want? Trepidation shivered over her skin. Her gaze landed on her backpack, sitting next to the base of the cabinets.

What about her laptop?

Well, if he'd tried to access anything on it last night, he'd have had a nasty surprise.

Gabrielle gave the possibility of escaping through the bathroom a brief evaluation, but even if she had her laptop in hand, the windows were narrow, horizontal jobs with fixed glass.

She rubbed her arms, scanning the sink counter. A wrapped toothbrush, new toothpaste, shampoo, brush, and anything else she could hope to find had neatly been stacked.

She leaned her hands on the sink, fighting despair. She could do this. Linette needed her to be strong. Gabrielle had to regroup and plan. Going through everyday actions lent a hand to her confidence, but this was not an average day.

Get showered and dressed first. Find her laptop.

Then be ready to run.

Carlos stepped into a pair of jeans, careful as he drew the zipper closed to prevent putting himself into any more pain. He jerked the tank top over his head and snatched up the cotton shirt he'd left on a chair last night, shoving his arms through the short sleeves. He buttoned the front of his shirt on his march to the laundry room.

What was he thinking last night?

That he was a freakin' ice man?

More like the iron man right now.

Should have locked Gabrielle spread eagle on the bed and slept in another room.

She might not have rested, but he would have.

No, she wouldn't have. Every time she'd started moaning, he knew a nightmare was tearing her up. All he had to do was take her in his arms to calm her down. She was so exhausted she never even woke each time he'd slide her back onto the bed at his side. By midnight, he couldn't listen to her cry out in fear again and desperately needed a few hours' sleep himself so he lifted her over his chest and clipped their wrists.

She slept like a babe the rest of the night.

Better than he had with the lush curves of a warm female draped over him.

Next time he got another brilliant freakin' idea like that one, he'd just slam a door on his hand. Couldn't be any more painful than watching her jump up from the bed in all that red silk and lace this morning, knowing he couldn't touch her. He must have been wiped out last night to think she was just sweet or cute.

That body had been made for hot sex, hours of it.

And he'd been disgusted with his lack of physical control.

She had to think he was a roaring bastard after yelling at her, but goddammit. He'd spent half the night trying not to think about how unbelievably pliable she felt in his arms.

He'd spent the other half of the night not touching her.

She better damn well be smiling the next time he saw her.

Fat chance of that.

Not after snapping at her to get in the bathroom, but every man had his limits.

There she'd stood, wearing sex-on-the-floor red he couldn't touch and wanted to so bad he doubted his family jewels would ever get over the disappointment.

Gabrielle needed to get dressed and keep all that skin

covered up. The minute this op was over, he was taking the leave he'd turned down the last three times.

One long, hot, physically draining week of R and R should trim his baser needs and return the level of discipline he was known for.

Carlos lifted her T-shirt and warm-up pants out of the dryer, where he'd stuck them last night. He'd left the clothes washing while he'd sewn up the gashes in his arm and side. Right before he'd fought for thirty minutes with the freaking e-mail that would not load up and send. He stopped by the office to check, and, no, the e-mail had not gone through.

He hated technology on the best of days. Laying her clothes on the desk, he closed the program, reopened it, and loaded the e-mail, which went through without a hitch. Damn fickle thing.

The coffeemaker he'd set last night gurgled with the last drops of water through the system. He looped her clothes over his arm and walked back to the kitchen. When he stopped at the sink to pour a cup of coffee, Carlos gazed out the windows, facing a serene view from the rear of the house. Fog hovered over trees blanketing the mountain range. The peaceful moment helped him reorient his mind and priorities.

After chugging a couple gulps of coffee, he set the cup on the black granite counter. Exhaustion was as much at fault for his libido breakout as not having a woman in a while, but he was rested and better under control.

So he shouldn't make the mistake of giving in to his conscience again, which tossed out ideas like kissing her to take the sting out of his words. But she was the reason behind the edge in his voice to begin with, so why was he suffering this stab of guilt?

Because he'd barked at her like a tyrant for not moving all that hot body out of his view when the real problem was that he wanted her and couldn't have her.

He scrubbed a hand over his jaw and face. She was not a guest here. Might as well establish their positions from this point on. The worry he'd indulged last night was understandable, the same he'd have felt for any woman who had been through yesterday's ordeal. And things could have been worse for her if Joe had sent an armed team to haul her off in the middle of the night.

Gabrielle had put herself in the middle of this somehow. Not him. He'd saved her ass. That ought to count for a few points toward forgiveness.

Besides, he was the freakin' ice man from here on.

She was a prisoner until Joe determined her status.

Carlos paused. Joe and Tee didn't release *any* prisoner back into society as a free person. That was standard for anyone who learned the identities of BAD agents, and before this was done, Gabrielle would see more agents than him.

He shook off a twinge of remorse over what would happen to her. He had a duty. American security depended on how well he performed.

And Gabrielle had information on the Anguis that could jeopardize the lives of loved ones he'd spent his life on the run to protect.

Carlos headed to the bedroom, ready to see her as he should—a detainee waiting for interrogation.

A screeching alarm blared as he entered the room. Annoying sound, but he'd set the clock alarm on "obnoxious" in case he overslept.

As he reached over to hit the off switch, the door to the bathroom opened and Gabrielle rushed out, holding a towel in front of her, not wrapped. Her hair hung in wet links around her shoulders. She looked refreshed. Innocent.

Like a rain nymph.

"Clothes?" She squeezed out that one terrified word.

Merde!

He slapped the alarm, silencing it, dumped her clothes on the bed, and walked out.

Ice man, my ass.

Carlos scowled his way back into the kitchen, then got busy putting breakfast together. He ate his food while he cooked hers. The secure phone line to headquarters beeped in the office on the other side of the great room. He lifted the extension next to the sink and shoved the receiver under his chin. The clock on the microwave indicated just after 8:00 a.m.

"What's up?" Carlos asked since Joe shouldn't expect him to be mobile for another hour. "I just got the damn e-mail with the files to send a few minutes ago."

"I'm downloading them now," Joe confirmed. "I sent the team to you. They should all arrive in the next half hour. I'll be there close behind."

"Why?" The cabin was secure, but Carlos didn't like the idea that he might be holding up the team.

"New developments came up overnight I want to

share with everyone together once we talk to the informant. Rae, Korbin, and Gotthard got more rest than you so I put them on the road early this morning. Of course, they haven't seen your reports yet."

They would have if Carlos could have held a gun on the computer to make that piece of shit send an e-mail.

Joe added, "What have you gotten out of the informant?"

No rest. No sex. No information.

"Not much, but she was pretty beat up last night," Carlos told him.

"She?"

"Yeah, and she's not what I expected. She comes across as untrained to be in the intelligence field."

"She admit to being Mirage?"

"Not in so many words, but she hasn't denied it either." Carlos flipped a saucepan lid over Gabrielle's plate to keep her breakfast warm.

"Hold on." Muffled voices filled the break, then Joe was back on the phone. "Got to go. I'll have anything new sent to Gotthard along with your files."

As Carlos hung up, soft footsteps padded into the kitchen.

He turned around to find Gabrielle standing on the other side of the island, dressed, thank you, God. Her hair was twisted up in a plastic clasp, the smooth hairstyle accentuating her high cheeks and extraordinary eyes on her pensive face. She moved with an elegance he hadn't noticed yesterday when she'd been running for her life.

"Hungry?" He loaded his empty plate into the dishwasher.

"Not particularly, but I'll eat."

He ignored the contradictory comment and slid her plate over the island counter toward a seat across from him. He uncovered her dish, revealing scrambled eggs, bacon, and toast.

She lifted a fork and pushed food around for the next minute, using the paper towel he'd given her to dab her mouth in the same manner someone would use a linen napkin in a five-star restaurant.

Little was leaving her plate.

"You should eat," he prompted. This might be another long day.

She raised pained eyes to him.

Hurt? Hell. Hurting a prisoner's feelings had never been an issue for him, ever, in all his years with BAD.

She lowered her gaze back to her plate without a word and picked at the food some more.

Carlos folded his fingers tight in frustration from watching her. He'd only yelled at her to go in the bathroom. She'd shown more backbone in the face of death yesterday.

Where was the female who had snapped at him last night?

He didn't know, but he did have to get this interrogation moving along. If only he could raise the anger he'd felt forty-eight hours ago in France.

The urge to browbeat their informant had simmered.

He'd feel like the lowest of animals if he used normal interrogation tactics on this delicate creature. But he had a job to do. Appearances aside, if Gabrielle really was the person who had connections to the Anguis and the Fratelli, she was a threat to American security.

"Where's my laptop?" she asked in a whispered voice.

"Downstairs."

When she pushed back, he stopped her with "It's locked up. I haven't touched your laptop. I know enough about *your* kind to know the program would likely disintegrate if I did."

Her mouth thinned at the "your kind" comment, but she scooted forward again and shoved the plate away, food half-eaten. "What do you want from me?"

"To begin with, your real name. And a word of warning, lying will not help your case." He really doubted her name was Gabrielle Parker. "We know your online code name is Mirage."

She said nothing. No reaction at all.

Carlos sipped his coffee, considering his next question. The monitor on the wall activated. A mechanical voice said, "Guests arriving," indicating someone had sent a gate-access request from a cell phone.

Guest was code for "BAD agent." Carlos pressed a remote to disengage the security and open the gate so they wouldn't have to wait. The entire security would return active again once the gate closed.

A sleek, crème-colored Lexus SC 430 pulled through the now open gate as Carlos pressed a remote to disengage the sensors along the driveway. Rae's ride.

Korbin's 1978 gold Road Runner pulled through next, the custom mufflers rumbling with a throaty growl that warned all challengers he had a HEMI under the hood. Gotthard brought up the tail with his deep-woods-green Navigator sport utility.

"Who are they?" Gabrielle stared at the monitor.

"Guests. Stay where you are. I'll be right back." Carlos sauntered to the front door and opened it to the trio climbing out of their cars.

"Mornin', luv," Rae said, striding up the steps in a warning-flag-yellow, wispy blouse and jeans that fit her long-legged frame as if shrink-wrapped. She carried a Starbucks cup in one hand and had an alert gaze for someone who had slept one night in the past three days.

Just like the rest of the team.

"Rae." Carlos held the door for her. At the top of the steps, she strode right on past him.

Korbin's dull-white ostrich-skin cowboy boots clicked decisively on each step. He paused at the door, his eyes taking in the scratches still evident along Carlos's collarbone and the stitches on his forearm. "I hope for all that you got something out of the informant."

"Not enough." Carlos smiled.

Gotthard followed Korbin inside with nothing more than a grunt and nod at Carlos, but the big guy was never much of a morning person and probably caught hell at home for leaving again so soon. The computer case dangling from his fingers might as well be an appendage since he was rarely without it.

When Carlos walked back into the kitchen, he found three agents looking at him as if they were in the wrong house.

"Who's she?" Rae asked with an eyebrow hiked up in accusation.

Carlos frowned at her. Gabrielle wasn't handcuffed to indicate her status, but did Rae really think he would bring a woman he was dating here?

"This is Gabrielle," Carlos said. "Also known as Mirage."

Gabrielle sat as still as a mouse staring down a roomful of hungry alley cats.

"Really?" Rae chuckled. "This shouldn't take long."

Gabrielle angled her chin up in an unyielding manner in reply that drew a feral smile to Rae's lips. Carlos clenched his teeth to keep from snapping at Rae for frightening Gabrielle, whose face lost color.

But Rae was only doing her job, intimidating the witness.

He had to do his part and run this show. Unfortunately for Gabrielle, that meant as of now she was on her own.

Carlos turned to the trio. "Okay, everyone downstairs." He waited until they vacated the room to speak to Gabrielle.

She jumped up first. "What's down there?" The panic in her voice ate at him.

He'd never hated his work, but using that fear against her was part of his job. He wouldn't like it, but he'd do it.

"Just a room. We're going to ask questions. Nothing sinister." *Not unless you don't give us what we want.* He squashed the sudden urge to reassure her everything would be okay. Lying came with the job description, but he didn't have to terrorize her unnecessarily.

Not yet.

NINE

S omeone was leaking Fratelli information.

Fra Vestavia pressed the button on his private elevator, which ascended subtly to the thirty-second floor. Who had interfered and now had Mirage?

Who could possibly be leaking information from within the Fratelli de il Sovrano? Someone brilliant and ballsy.

A perfect description of Josie.

He pondered that all the way to his suite of offices occupying the top floor that included a secured access to the helo pad on the roof. Plus a 360-degree view of Miami and the Atlantic Ocean from a prime spot along Brickell Avenue.

The elevator doors swooshed at the thirty-second floor, opening into the central foyer for Trojan Prodigy, a business purported in national magazines to represent state-of-the-art electronic counterterrorism software and antispyware.

True, but not the whole story.

Vestavia had started Trojan Prodigy twelve years ago, back when international companies were desperate for technology to protect them from sophisticated hackers. They welcomed his people with open arms and access to their operating systems while he was busy splitting his time between playing the role of DEA special agent Robert Brady and Vestavia, a loyal Fratelli supporter.

He abandoned the DEA identity last year when he disappeared after successfully executing a Fratelli mission and was now considered a wanted felon. As of next month when he had surgery, Agent Brady's face would no longer exist and his fingerprints on file had been altered years back.

Timing was the most critical element in any plan.

He abandoned the DEA just as Trojan Prodigy received significant military contracts that made him the best choice to take a seat at the table of the twelve North American Fras when one died unexpectedly.

Every continent had its own ruling body of twelve Fratelli, who headed up businesses with international influence or had stockholder seats or strategic government positions—everyone had to bring something to the table once he proved value as a leader.

Vestavia stepped from the elevator and sank into carpet that reminded him of walking on clouds. The air smelled pristine and untouched. Samuel, a male assistant of slight build, sat behind a monitor at a contemporary workstation trimmed out in gold. He typed so quickly the sound was lost in the rush of water pouring down a twelve-foot-high slate wall directly behind him. Running the width of the twenty-foot-wide space, the waterfall shushed in peaceful reverence.

When Vestavia neared, Samuel came to attention, brown eyes alert, hair cut short, business-neat, slate-gray suit blending into the background. They shared an interest in archaeology, but Vestavia had no time for casual conversation right now.

"Messages?" he asked the young man.

"Yes, sir. On your desk in order of priority. And Josie Silversteen is waiting in your office. She said she has something for you." Samuel spoke in a hushed voice used in places of worship.

Josie here? Vestavia checked his watch. "I'm expecting her." Not really, but Josie knew he'd want answers on what happened to Baby Face and Mirage. Anyone else would have called in that update rather than face him.

Josie was like no one else.

He hoped his trust had not been misplaced.

"Shall I bring coffee or tea?" Samuel asked.

"No. This will be a short meeting. Hold my calls for a half hour."

Vestavia strolled down the wide hall, passing a virtual gallery of art by Renoir and Matisse intermingled with contemporary masterpieces. Glancing into offices as he passed, he noted the flurry of activity in each one. He kept a small staff with an excellent work ethic who appreciated having offices that rivaled those of corporate CEOs.

When he turned right at the end of the hall, the entire wall on his left was a floor-to-ceiling glass view of an endless ocean. He'd found this location six years ago, and Josie had immediately suggested the perfect place for his office was facing the ocean rather than Brickell's business corridor. She'd been right.

Her blood was as blue as it got. The Silversteen banking dynasty stretched across the country with fingers in many financial pies. As a chosen daughter, she'd been groomed from birth to serve the Fratelli de il Sovrano and sent to the Fras at sixteen, but Vestavia had seen her potential. He'd convinced Fra Diablo she'd be perfect for fieldwork.

And she had been.

She was one of the few who knew Vestavia's true identity and his mission. That he was in fact an Angeli, an order older than the Fratelli.

He and six other Angeli would accomplish in one decade what their ancestors had failed to do in the past two millennia. And the Fratelli would do all the preparatory work without knowing they were being danced as puppets. The Fratelli really thought twelve Fras could rule each continent.

Had decision by committee or democracy ever worked? No.

As one of seven Angeli secretly infiltrating the Fratelli de il Sovrano on each continent, Vestavia had reached his position quickly. For the past year, he'd been pulling strings on the Fratelli, manipulating their extensive resources to begin laying the groundwork for the Renaissance. When Vestavia and his six Angeli counterparts were ready, they would step from the shadows and return this world to one of peace.

To do that, they had to first purge the planet of 80 percent of the population while not losing the core group who would rebuild after the devastation.

Starting over was the only way. His ancestors had tried with plagues and other devices that destroyed the beneficial with the slovenly.

His generation of Angeli would not make the same mistakes.

They would systematically bring each continent into line, create parity to ready the world for the Renaissance.

When Vestavia reached his office, the motion detector read his thermal image and unlocked the door, which disappeared into the wall.

He entered, his eyes going to the woman sitting on his low-profile white sofa with black embroidered stripes. "What happened?"

"Baby Face lost Mirage and got killed in the process." Josie stood, showcasing those amazing legs with a trim navy-and-gold skirt suit. Thick lashes and skin so smooth it didn't look real. Rich brunette hair tumbled lazily past her shoulders with each move of her head to brush against the crest of full breasts exposed by her scooped-neck jacket.

Every inch a creation of perfection.

Special Agent Josie Silversteen, his brilliant protégé at the DEA, now held a warrant for the arrest of fugitive Special Agent Robert Brady. Such irony.

"That's not a full report," he admonished.

"Of course." She rushed ahead. "Forgive me, Your Excellency. Baby Face was given access to our megacomputers he believed were part of an international tracking program within the DEA. He had no idea they belonged to the Trojan Prodigy, and greed led him to shop the Mirage once he located something. But we haven't been able to duplicate his electronic trail. Baby Face went to a house in Peachtree City, Georgia, owned by an elderly man for over twenty years who doesn't appear to have any computer skill. The woman who rented the house has disappeared. She's listed as Gabrielle Parker and appears— on paper—to be a widow living off a moderate trust fund. I have to believe she must know something about the informant for Baby Face to have gone there." Josie paused, then added, "I *will* find out."

Her husky voice combined with that fuck-me-where- I-stand look in her eyes reminded him how long they'd been apart.

Six days. An eternity.

His cock could tell him right down to the minute.

Vestavia pulled off his jacket and laid it over the arm of the sofa, then stepped past her. When he reached his desk, he turned around and sat back against the front edge, placing his hands casually on each side. If he got too close to her, he'd break his first rule between them—business before pleasure.

"Durand told me about Turga. What about his helicopter pilot?"

"I have a team tracking the pilot. I'll know more . . . tonight." She dropped that last word in her sex-against- the-wall voice and he got hard. She walked over, bold, gorgeous, raw confidence flowing through the three steps that brought her to stand between his outstretched legs.

His cock twitched toward her as if she were magnetized and he was pure steel.

"Do you have time to go ... deeper into this?" she asked, then ran her tongue around her lips.

Vestavia gripped the desk with taut fingers. "Not now. You know my rule."

She exhaled an exaggerated sigh. "Business comes first. . . . I just thought for once"—she smiled like the vixen she was—"you might like to come first."

He lifted his hand and ran a finger along her face, then down, following the edge of her jacket until his finger slid inside, the tip brushing across her nipple. She shivered. Her breathing hitched. A slender jaw muscle flexed with the effort of holding her control.

Vestavia smiled. No point in him being the only one uncomfortable until they got back together. "Hold that thought."

Her eyes were on fire when she backed away and lifted her laptop bag. Insatiable and demanding in bed. Another of her finer qualities. "I'll be back tonight."

"Don't disappoint me."

"Never," she promised softly with wicked heat that assured the hours of sex would be as satisfying as the late-night report.

She'd never let him down, in the bed or out of it, but if the Mirage slipped through her fingers, Josie knew the penalty. All Fratelli women had to pass through an indoctrination that guaranteed they understood the consequences of failing a Fra *and* understood there was no escaping the organization.

A program that assured compliance.

Nine years ago, Josie had passed without a whimper, convincing the Fras she was unbreakable, not showing a hint of weakness until she arrived at Vestavia's home hours later. The only time he'd ever seen Josie break down into tears had been afterward when she'd walked into his waiting arms.

She was strong, brilliant, and dedicated.

She would not fail him or she'd find out what the Fras had put her through would feel like a day at the spa compared to his sanction.

———

Gabrielle made the last step down into the basement meeting room and hesitated to go farther until Carlos stepped down right behind her. He barely touched her back with his fingers to prod her into movement. She took a breath and walked forward.

Centering the roughly twenty-foot-wide-by-thirty-foot-long room was a rectangle-shaped, black-lacquer conference table polished to a high gloss that seated ten. The two men and the woman who had arrived just minutes ago sat in plush almond-colored leather chairs. Both men were on the left side, peering at a laptop monitor.

In any other setting, the mahogany panels on the walls would give the room a warm and inviting feel.

The only female had positioned herself on the right, across from the men. At five feet eight flat-footed, she wore a pair of jeans like a runway model, her honey-brown hair cropped short and curt, much like her attitude had been upstairs.

"Have a seat there." Carlos pointed at the closest chair for Gabrielle, which was next to the female.

If he thought placing her beside this Amazon would raise her anxiety level . . . he was right, but not enough to force her into capitulating easily. Not yet.

She sat down and folded her hands in her lap.

Carlos introduced the other three, first names only, then sank into a chair at the head of the table on her left. "First, what's your real name, Gabrielle?"

"I told you I'm Gabrielle Parker."

"Cut the lies."

The steel edge of Carlos's words sliced her to the bone. She clutched her hands so tightly her nails were biting her soft palms. Guess the nice-guy routine was over and gone.

Gabrielle had moved to the States to insulate her family and wouldn't expose them now. And she had to protect her contacts in South America from being discovered, especially after the mistake she'd made that had exposed her identity.

"I want a lawyer." Gabrielle wished she'd said that with more force.

"We don't bother with lawyers." Rae gave that bit of scary news in a British accent and added an evil chuckle.

No lawyers. Next idea. Gabrielle did have contacts at the British embassy who could help her and might vouch for her, since she was technically a citizen of the United Kingdom—another layer placed between her and her family in France. But that would create as many problems as pointing out that she was the daughter of a government official in

France. Any try for diplomatic immunity would jeopardize her father's position and place his new family at risk.

She'd have to find her own way out of this mess.

And if the media were tipped off about what she'd been doing for the past ten years, ruining her father's reputation would be the least of her problems. Durand Anguis would find her immediately and retaliate in a heinous way, maybe harm her family.

But she hadn't been raised by a woman with a steel will just to fold over at the first sign of a crisis.

"Okay, if I'm not Gabrielle Parker, then who am I?" She'd built a solid background for Gabrielle Parker. That alone should take them a while to disentangle from all the layers she'd created to protect her identity.

"Gotthard, you get everything from headquarters, including my report?" Carlos said to the wide-body chap working at the laptop.

"Yes. Downloading the preliminary documents now."

"What documents?" Gabrielle asked, her hands clammy all of a sudden.

Carlos met her gaze with an unreadable one. "From running your fingerprints for starters."

Her fingerprints? Could this bunch have a resource at Interpol? Maybe. Probably. How fast could they confirm her true identity? Gabrielle frantically tried to figure out how much she should tell them. If she didn't tell them the truth and they found out first on their own, they'd never believe anything else she said.

Gotthard shook his head. "Nothing yet from our files. Still waiting on international replies."

Did they really have access to international records or were they bluffing?

Gabrielle clenched her hands together, fearful and furious. Carlos had taken her fingerprints while she slept. What else had he done? *Besides humiliating me when he ordered me to get out of his sight in the bedroom?* She was no beauty queen, but no man had ever ordered her to cover her body.

She studied him with new eyes, those of a woman who had trusted too quickly again.

"Who are your contacts?" Carlos asked with chilling quiet.

"If I am who you accuse me of being, do you really think I would put a resource in danger when you have yet to tell me who *you* work for?" she answered with a frigid reserve her mother would have been proud of.

Carlos crossed his arms. "Not like you have a lot of choices right now, is it?"

Her stomach churned. Acting compliant hadn't worked, so what could she lose by going on the offensive?

This was the United States after all. Individual rights had to be respected. Everyone answered to someone. She just had to figure out who that someone was for this bunch of operatives.

"You think not?" Her choices were admittedly dwindling, but agreeing out loud would only feed the arrogance permeating the room. "I can assure you my *resources* will bring the hammer down on any division of U.S. intelligence when they find out you've kidnapped me," Gabrielle charged, hoping she sounded as threatening as the Amazon next to her.

Carlos didn't so much as blink. "Go ahead. I don't care if you get the CIA in hot water. We're not the CIA, FBI, or any other acronym you might know."

Her indignant glower faltered, but she held on to enough anger to counter his attitude. "If you *are* an intelligence agency, I'll tell you whatever I can, but I'm in no mood to play semantics after last night. *Whoever* you are, I'll have your head on a pike for kidnapping me."

Carlos gave her a wry smile. "No, you won't. You may not even leave here a free person, and you sure as hell aren't getting near a phone you can operate anytime soon."

Okay, that severely limited her options. They acted like some form of intelligence or security operation, but they didn't use legal tactics. Of course, she doubted the CIA or MI6 would either. She hadn't been shoved into a chair and had a spotlight shone in her eyes, but that was so over-the-top American Hollywood she wouldn't have expected it either.

But neither had anyone pulled out a badge to prove they had the right to hold her. She'd point out that lack of protocol if she didn't believe they would laugh her out of the room.

"Then who are you people? Who do you work for?" she asked.

"I told you, we protect national security, but this organization doesn't exist as far as the United States government or any other government is concerned." Rich black lashes brushed Carlos's cheek with each slow, patient blink. "And, if that isn't enough to convince you that cooperating is in your best interest, no one knows we have you and we have the power to hand you over to any country that produces documents proving they have reason to prosecute you. Plus, we have the ability to provide any documentation to assist them."

Uh-oh. She'd run across some bizarre groups while entering different agency mainframes, but hadn't planned on a rogue bunch. Whom were they aligned with . . . or against?

Were they truly part of the American defense mechanism?

Dreadful as this was, it could be worse. She *could* be facing Durand Anguis, who wouldn't ask questions in so civilized a manner. Continuing to deny her identity for much longer was too risky since the fingerprints would turn up her last name as Saxe if they did indeed have access to international databases. Admitting that much might stop them from searching further and drawing her father into this.

"I'm Gabrielle Saxe," she finally admitted.

Silence invaded the room.

She waited for some acknowledgment. None.

An interrogation tactic? Most likely. Her skin chilled at facing an uncertain future.

She glanced at Carlos, and for a brief moment she could swear worry slipped into his gaze. Was it a sincere emotion or just part of his professional routine?

Whom was she kidding? He didn't care. This was his job.

"That's correct," Gotthard finally confirmed. "Just got the results of the search."

She let out a breath, glad she'd jumped ahead of the report coming back. That was too close.

"What exactly do you do all day?" Rae interjected.

"I use my computer skills to keep an eye on groups that threaten world peace," Gabrielle said. That had a positive spin, not too much and nothing they could call a lie.

"Who do you work for?" Rae asked.

"No one. I'm financially secure."

"Wait a minute." Korbin tapped a finger on the shiny obsidian surface of the table, then stared at her, eyes squinted. "Gabrielle Saxe, as in the Gabrielle Saxe that married Roberto Delacourte years back? The actor who knocks down about twenty-five million a movie?"

"Yes. We were married . . . for six months."

"That explains the financially secure part," Rae quipped.

"I have my *own* money." Gabrielle rarely discussed her finances, never in fact, but Rae had made it sound as though she'd been a gold-digging groupie. She'd been taken by Roberto's sexy smile and charm, but she'd never wanted anything but to be loved by him. In the end, she'd realized she'd rushed into marriage out of loneliness. He'd lied to her from day one, playing her like the naive fool she'd been back then.

She'd been faithful every miserable day of those six months, too. Every painful day.

Murmuring erupted in the room.

Carlos raised his hand. The room quieted immediately. "We're not interested in your tabloid love life, Gabrielle. You've established that you can afford to sit around all day playing on the computer."

Tabloid love life? Playing on the computer? She clamped her teeth so hard they clicked.

"But you have yet to explain how you know about the Anguis," Carlos continued. "Your blanket 'I want to help world peace' statement isn't going to fly. You've broken enough laws in enough places to end up in prison somewhere. If you don't have anything significant to share at this point, we *might* let you choose which country you'd prefer to be prosecuted in."

Could he really do that? Gabrielle knew a great deal about international law, having studied that on her own, and had felt relatively certain she'd covered her tracks well enough to never get caught. But this group had found her and possessed electronic evidence to prove what she'd done.

She had no training to deal with situations like this. Or yesterday. Understatement.

"Fine, I admit I'm Mirage." She leaned around, speaking to all of them. "Since I'm the one who shared information to begin with, I think it only fair you tell me what happened to Mandy." All of this had happened because she'd tried to help a young woman in trouble. "If you found me, then you have to know what happened to her. Was she rescued?"

Carlos wanted to shake some sense into Gabrielle. Hadn't she figured out her game was up and she had no more moves left? "We ask questions and you answer them. Understand?"

Gabrielle had been taking deep breaths and speaking calmly as if buying time to gather her thoughts and guarding her tone. But she answered through clenched teeth this time.

"I'm trying to cooperate, but if you want *any* answers from me, you'll at least tell me if Mandy is safe. She's the reason I took a risk that landed me here." Gabrielle held her posture as rigid as a school principal in a room filled with faces lacking compassion, but Carlos could see her hands clasped in her lap. White-knuckled.

She maintained that same regal calm in the face of the threat he'd lobbed at her about handing her over to a country that would prosecute her.

Damn if he didn't admire her spirit and backbone.

Her intense violet-blue eyes searched his for something. A degree of help or support?

Not now.

That silent reply must have come across loud and clear when disappointment dulled her bright gaze. She changed body language faster than most women switched shoes. Rattled earlier, then hurt, she now seemed determined to shield her emotions from everyone, or specifically him. To hide that she was terrified of her precarious future. She was wasting her time. She couldn't cloak the vulnerability he'd already witnessed that was eating at his insides.

He didn't want to feel anything for her, but those gorgeous eyes meeting his televised both compassion and fear for Mandy. The mistake would be allowing himself to see Gabrielle as anything other than what she was—a player in a deadly game.

One who should be answering questions to save her own butt.

Instead, she was worried about Mandy. So was he.

"Gotthard," Carlos said. "Got an update on Mandy?"

The air sobered with apprehension for the young girl.

"Mandy went into a coma from blood loss—" Gotthard read further, then finished with "Bottom line, she's still alive."

A collective release of sighs filled the room.

"A coma?" Gabrielle gasped. "What went wrong? Who screwed up the rescue?" She'd winged that at the whole room.

Anger visibly bristled in response to the criticism.

She blew all her sympathy points with that outburst.

"Look, Gabrielle." Carlos was not reining in his temper one inch. She'd leaped over a line into the proverbial fire. "We went wheels up twenty minutes after receiving your last message and made a HAHO jump into the French Alps at night during a damn blizzard to save Mandy." He'd leaned forward, stabbing his index finger against the desk on each point. "If we'd gotten the information sooner, we might have reached her before she broke a glass to cut her wrists. You're in *no* position to question anything my team did and had better start giving answers if you hope to ever see daylight again."

Carlos straightened away from her and crossed his arms to wrestle his calm back in place. He'd wonder for the rest of his life where he could have shaved minutes that might have put the team on-site faster. He would *not*, however, allow another person, particularly a civilian—a suspected felon—to criticize his team.

Gabrielle opened her mouth to speak, but he didn't give her a chance.

"Back to our questions," he snapped. "How did you know Mandy was being kidnapped or who the kidnappers were?"

Her rosy cheeks lost color, but he would not be swayed this time. Carlos questioned if Gabrielle was as vulnerable as he'd first thought or just a damn impressive actress.

"Guest arriving," announced from a hidden speaker in the room.

Who the hell was coming now? Had Joe traveled that fast?

Carlos turned to Gabrielle, whose face had washed out to the color of sand on a beach. If she didn't give them something soon, she'd be facing Joe. Or worse. Tee.

Carlos nodded at Korbin, who reached over to lift a remote sitting on a low, black-lacquer cabinet along the wall. He punched keys to activate the flat screen, generating an image from the camera covering the driveway.

A silver Lamborghini slashed through the gate.

"Why is *he* here?" Carlos asked the room in general.

"Don't know." Korbin clicked off the screen image and dropped the remote on the cabinet. "Joe said we had one more coming, so Hunter must be it."

The door upstairs opened and closed with quiet civility that fit one particular agent. Bootheels thumped down the steps.

Carlos turned to Hunter Wesley Thornton-Payne III, who always managed to piss Carlos off without even opening his aristocratic mouth. He detested aristocrats, anyone who believed bloodline granted you unearned respect.

Hunter angled his chin in that I'm-so-much-better-than-you-miscreants way that made Carlos want to test the arrogant agent in the barrio after midnight where attitude wouldn't save his ass. They'd use Hunter's blond hair to scrub the brick walls.

Ex-CIA or not.

"Morning, Rae, Korbin, Gotthard." Hunter lifted his chin to each, who nodded in return. Then he took in Gabrielle and shifted his gaze to Carlos. "I take it this is Mirage."

Carlos nodded.

"What have I missed?" Hunter eyed Gabrielle once more before he stepped past her to sit on the other side of Rae.

Carlos nodded at Gotthard, giving him the floor.

Gotthard leaned back from hunching over the laptop and faced Hunter. "Mandy is alive, but in a coma, and fingerprints confirm this is Gabrielle Saxe of Versailles, France."

"What have *you* got, Hunter?" Carlos crossed his arms, sending his best silent message of "Just give me the facts without the attitude."

"If she is our informant, she's no amateur," Hunter began. "She bounced that post through at least two different compromised servers. She might have hacked them herself or just bought them from one of the big hacker groups on an IRC network like Freenode or EFnet. *I* almost didn't find the address." A hint of respect and irritation entered his arrogance. "We had a forty-eight-hour window of authorization to monitor network traffic going to or from the compromised computer at a waste-disposal plant in Russia. The minute she replied to my post about the babe being in danger, we had her."

"I should have known that was a trap," she muttered.

Gotthard raised his wide head to face Hunter, deep furrows of concentration carving the bridge of his nose. "Was there any evidence on that Russian server, maybe something that might indicate who she's working with?"

Not much for the techno side of this business, Carlos enjoyed anytime someone who *was* an electronic wizard tweaking Hunter. And he doubted that had even been Gotthard's intention.

"I'm not working with anyone," Gabrielle interjected.

No one so much as blinked her way in acknowledgment.

Carlos might have suffered a weak moment for her last night, but he knew better than to believe anything she offered now. She could have told him her real name was Saxe last night.

"Let's just say I was thorough." Hunter angled his head slowly at Gotthard and pursed his lips with just enough vigor to let everyone present know he felt imposed upon to answer. "The origination point was a private IP that belonged to I. M. Agoste." He pronounced the last name with a heavy accent on the hard *e*. A smile of triumph glimmered on his too perfect lips.

"What?" Rae squinted in thought, tapping her pen against a notebook she'd been writing in. "I'm A. Ghost?" She paused, thinking, then nodded. "Bloody well is since you know she wouldn't use a real name."

"The puzzle queen's got you there, Hunter." Humor lifted one eyebrow and the corner of Gotthard's stern mouth.

Carlos smothered a chuckle. That son of a gun Gotthard *had* been poking at Hunter after all. The pompous agent's smile dissolved into a flat line. Getting one up on the never-wrong Hunter was a favorite pastime among the team.

"Gabrielle will now tell us how she knows Mandy and how she found out so much about the kidnapping." Not ready to play hardball just yet, Carlos coaxed, "This will go much easier if you cooperate."

The spark of anger she'd fired up earlier had dissipated, leaving a graceful statue, breathing so softly the material clinging to her breasts hardly moved.

He knew without a doubt she wore no bra. Don't look there.

His sigh came out tired. Anyone capable of hacking past firewalls should be bright enough to realize when she was getting a break. He hadn't threatened her . . . yet. "Gabrielle—"

"From a postale card."

Carlos gave her a dubious look. "I sent a scan of that postcard to headquarters this morning." He cut his eyes at Gotthard, then Hunter. "Anything back from decoding?"

The look of surprise that rolled into disappointment Gabrielle gave him shouldn't have cut, but he felt it just the same. Had she thought just because of what happened yesterday and last night he wouldn't search every possession she had?

"I got a text the postcard is indecipherable," Hunter interjected. "If that's all she has to offer, I say we call security and be done with her."

That got Gabrielle's attention. "I can explain the message on the card."

"Then explain," Carlos ordered.

"It's in code," Gabrielle said, glancing at everyone. Not a face around the table registered belief.

Gotthard rubbed a finger across one eye and read further. "I'm online with the decoding department right now. Nothing from the Monster." He looked at Gabrielle and simply said, "Our supercomputer."

Carlos stepped around Korbin and opened the low cabinet. He withdrew the postcard and a stack of copies he'd made of it for the meeting, then passed the copies to the BAD agents.

Gabrielle cringed when she realized one major downside she hadn't considered. The postage stamp indicated the card had been mailed a couple weeks ago.

Carlos raised a gaze flooded with suspicion. "Who sent this?"

Stalling wasn't helping her. Gabrielle accepted that she had to give him something for any hope of getting a break with this group. "A girl I knew in school a long time ago. She disappeared before I graduated. That card was the first time I've heard from her in eleven years."

Carlos tapped a finger on the table in a silent rhythm.

Sound bizarre? Welcome to her world for the past forty-eight hours.

"I'm in no mood to ask twenty questions to get one

answer," Carlos warned quietly. Distant and foreboding. Nothing like the seductive vibration she'd experienced from his sleep-roughened voice this morning.

He sat forward, close enough for her to smell his fresh shower and resent him for shoving her thoughts off track. "If you continue to lie, you won't like how this ends."

The whispered threat should have sent a shock of fear scurrying along her spine, and on some level it did, but she'd survived the unimaginable yesterday. That she sat here alive gave her strength and resolve to fight her way out of this, too.

Besides, showing emotions would be perceived as a weakness these operatives would exploit any way they could.

"I am not lying," she told Carlos in a tone intended to allow no room for dispute.

"Really? So you what?" Carlos sighed. He lifted his hand, palm up, as he turned to her. "Got a postcard from a long-lost girlfriend who figured you were the *one and only* person who could help an American diplomat's daughter being kidnapped?"

Sure, that sounded ridiculous, but he wanted the truth. "You ask me questions, then refuse to believe what I tell you. If you don't like my answers, don't ask questions."

Smooth eyebrows lowered over the two narrowed black slits with thick lashes. Carlos stood and paced away, fingers absently massaging his neck. He dropped his hand. Anger rippled off him so thick the air should have clogged the vent system.

Her heartbeat jumped in the silence.

"Why didn't you just contact the FBI or CIA?" Hunter asked.

She swiveled, pushing her gaze past Rae to take in the cocky new arrival. His burgundy turtleneck sweater created a beautiful base for a living bust of perfection she had no doubt women adored. He sat in profile, elbow on the table, head propped on his palm. Elegant golden hair styled just the right length to be daring, yet civilized.

She knew his kind all too well and was not impressed.

"That would have put Mandy at greater risk," Gabrielle answered, shifting back to address the whole room. "The FBI and CIA would have thought it was a hoax or just locked me up until they figured out if I was mentally imbalanced, which might have cost Mandy her life. Those agencies tend to act quicker if they believe they gained the information from a credible source. I think it's fair to say Mirage is known as a credible resource." Sure that had been snippy, but she'd earned that right.

"Who sent the card?" Korbin asked.

A fair question, but one Gabrielle really did not want to answer. "I told you, a girl at my school."

"What did you say yesterday?" Carlos asked her. "Don't be obtuse. We want the girl's full name."

Eleven

Gabrielle stood at the crossroads to her future and a chance of saving Linette. Tell Carlos Linette's name or not?

Would she put her friend in greater jeopardy by sharing her identity? Could these people possibly find Linette? Her friend was already in danger or at the very least being held against her will. Maybe this was a chance to save her.

If these operatives, and that had to be what they were, rescued Mandy, they had to be what they contended. Right? The anger behind Carlos's words when he'd said they'd made a jump in a blizzard had felt genuine.

"Gabrielle?" Carlos said pointedly.

"I'm not ignoring you." She addressed all of them with that before returning to Carlos. "I'm trying to answer your questions without compromising my friend's safety." She nibbled on her lower lip then had a thought. "Can you tell me what happened to the kidnappers after you rescued Mandy?"

"No!" echoed around the room.

Her shoulders drooped. "I see."

"What would be the threat to your friend?" Rae asked.

Gabrielle weighed her selection of replies and finally realized they would remain at an impasse forever if she didn't offer more. "A *fratelli*."

Tension snapped through the room at that admission.

"What do you mean by 'a *fratelli*'?" Carlos asked in a voice that doubled-stacked the chill bumps on her arm. If he sounded threatening yesterday, today he was downright lethal.

"I don't know," Gabrielle admitted. "It was referenced on the card."

"The card again," Hunter scoffed, then everyone jumped in.

"How was it referenced?" Rae wanted to know.

"Oh, please. The card is bullshit," Hunter countered before Gabrielle could speak.

"What if it's not?" Rae argued right back with plenty of heat. "Mandy *was* kidnapped. We *did* find her in a château in St. Gervais. The Anguis *were* the kidnappers."

Gabrielle noted everything Rae said, deciding this group couldn't know all of those details if they had not indeed saved the young girl.

Korbin jumped in with "Rae's got a point."

"Our people said the best they got out of the card text was gibberish," Hunter tossed right back. "The Monster didn't break it."

"I can—" Gabrielle started to say she could prove the text was not gibberish, but got cut off.

"What if . . . our people are wrong?" Carlos asked Hunter. "What if the card *is* in code? We can't pass up a chance for any lead on the fratelli."

Gabrielle tried to ignore how her heart jumped at the possibility that Carlos was finally supporting her position. That he might actually believe her. While the debate raged, she began to realize she had something to trade—decoding the card.

If she convinced them the card was in code, they had to believe she was not a criminal. That was logical.

Additionally, she now had a measure of belief—or call it an internal feeling she relied upon—that these people were not part of that *fratelli*. Logic implored that they would have feigned knowledge of the *fratelli* or any group they shielded, not argue over the credibility of her card that might be a lead.

The significance of how important it was that they locate this *fratelli* was not lost on her either. Finding the group could mean finding, and saving, Linette.

Gabrielle's instincts had kept her alive so far. She had to rely on them now more than ever.

"If you're not afraid of the truth, then let me prove it's in code," Gabrielle challenged Hunter, ready to take on all of them.

The arguing stopped as though someone had hit the pause button. When Hunter's gaze leveled with hers, he made no effort to hide the disparaging assessment in his eyes. Weapons and blood shook her to her toes, but she'd been raised around his kind—the arrogant and the affluent—and neither fazed her.

"Go ahead, decode it," Hunter said without a bit of concern in his voice. "And if you can't, you're of no value to us."

She didn't deserve his attitude or being held this way. Not after all she'd done to help Mandy and what she'd faced yesterday after they'd tricked her into exposing herself. "I helped you and you're all treating me like I'm the enemy."

Gotthard paused from typing on his laptop. "Until you give us a reason to think differently, you are."

She needed one ally in this room and Carlos was her best hope. "I can show you how the code works."

His gaze trapped hers and shifted from tense with impatience to an openness that surprised her. Carlos leaned against the wall. "Okay, start with explaining the address the card was sent to."

Licking her dry lips, Gabrielle dove in. "It was sent to my father, Louis Saxe IV, who lives in Versailles and is president of the National Assembly in France."

Gotthard interjected, "Correct. A powerful position in their government and he is well respected."

Gabrielle hoped that would be enough to stop them from searching further into her background.

"How much does he know about all of this?" Rae asked.

"Nothing." Gabrielle needed them to believe her on this point. "No one in the Saxe family knows about the Mirage or anything I've done."

"Miss Sex, huh? Fits you." The darkly handsome Korbin grinned at his play on her French pronunciation of *Saxe*. Like Carlos, he was of Latin descent and similar in size, but Korbin's facial structure made her think he was a mix of Mexican and Anglo, whereas Carlos had sharper angles . . . more South American.

Korbin gave her such a smoldering look she stiffened.

"Cut it out," Carlos snapped.

When Korbin smiled at him with a bit of taunt in his expression, Carlos sent back a warning glare that was deadly.

What was that all about?

"Besides, you haven't reached the *R*'s yet," Rae said to Korbin with a tongue so sharp she could draw blood.

Gabrielle tried to keep up with all the pointed comments and narrowed glances flying.

"I'll let *you* know as soon as I do," Korbin said, the full power of his charm directed at Rae now. He broke out a rascal's smile that had to stop women in their tracks.

"What are the *R*'s?" Gabrielle asked.

"Back to the postcard." Carlos ignored her question and pinned Gabrielle with a no-nonsense stare. "Why did it take you so long to send the first message?"

What had made her think his eyes had ever been a warm brown earlier? Mr. Nice had evaporated. The black look Carlos gave her boiled with the fury of a midnight storm on the sea.

Things had been going good. What had riled him?

"I received the card two days ago, or maybe it's three by now . . . I have no idea what time it is." Gabrielle swiped loose hair off her face. "Anyhow, my friend had no way to find me other than sending the card to my father's home in Versailles. He has my mail forwarded to my address in London that then sends it to a mail center in Peachtree City. That's why it took so long to get to me. My friend was careful, addressing it only to Gabrielle with no last name. That way if the card was intercepted with the 'gibberish,' as you put it, most people would assume Gabrielle was someone on my father's staff. My friend did not include a return address so I have no idea where to find her."

Gotthard asked, "Why didn't you tell us about the Anguis trying to kidnap Mandy when you sent the first message? If we'd known sooner, we probably could have caught them before they reached France."

"I didn't know the Anguis were the kidnappers when I sent the first message," Gabrielle answered carefully. She couldn't share her South American contacts on the Anguis family with any of these people, no matter what they threatened. Innocent Venezuelans only trying to help her rid the world of the Anguis murderers would be in jeopardy.

"You didn't answer his question," Carlos pressed.

"Because all I knew from the card was that Mandy would be kidnapped in South America." Gabrielle chose her words carefully. "I didn't find out that Anguis was behind the kidnapping until I did some research with resources in South America. And please don't ask who because I don't have their names, we contact each other electronically through an elaborate system." Fairly close to the truth.

Carlos tapped fingers against his upper arm. No expression as if he contemplated how to squeeze more out of her.

Gabrielle ran her fingers into her hair, knocking her twisted bob loose. The plastic clamp bounced on the floor. Long strands tumbled across her shoulders when she squatted down to pick up the clasp and shove it into her pants pocket.

"I'm not some kind of trained personnel like the rest of you," Gabrielle muttered, trying to figure out what would get through to this stubborn lot. "If you want me to admit I'm intimidated by all of you, fine, I admit it. I don't know who you are or what you want, but you're obviously the ones who helped Mandy, so I'm going to go out on a limb and say I believe you're working with the right side of the law. In exchange, I wish you'd show me the same courtesy. If I prove to you the text on the card is in code, will you believe I'm trying to be honest with you and I'm not a threat to the United States?"

She kept her gaze on the table, refusing to meet eyes watching her like silent predators ready for the kill.

The postcard from Linette slid onto the table surface into her view guided by Carlos's fingers.

A tiny victory. Gabrielle was not ready to sing hallelujah, but this was a start. Her chest muscles relaxed with the quick shot of relief.

Gabrielle explained, "My friend and I wrote the code first in ancient Latin. We then reversed the sequential alignment, deleting the first letter of the first word, the second letter of the second word, and so on through five words when there were an appropriate number of letters. We changed the code halfway through to Italian. Numbers corresponded to days of the week and colors—"

"Are you serious?" Gotthard stared at her in either disbelief or amazement.

Gabrielle prayed it wasn't lack of belief or she'd never get out of this place. "Yes, I am serious. I'll read off the code and interpret each word so you can follow the translation."

A noise came out of Hunter that was a cross between a snort of derision and a chuckle that said *This should be good.*

Gabrielle's burst of confidence pushed her to lean forward so she could look around Rae and speak to Hunter. She smiled first. "If you can't keep up, take notes."

Hunter mirrored her smile with a confident one of his own and said in a gentleman's voice, "If you fail to prove it's a bona fide code, you'll be headed for a cell buried so deep in our containment facility you'll never see daylight again."

Gabrielle swallowed her cockiness at that.

She hadn't used the complicated code in a long time. Carlos and his team—had to be a team—clearly had access to extensive equipment. Anyone capable of deciphering a code would not accept her version if she made one mistake in the convoluted steps she and Linette had created just for the purpose of making it impossible to break.

She leaned back in her seat, studied the words, then went for it, reading slowly, stopping to answer questions from Gotthard, Rae, and Korbin, then moving along. She hit a rhythm on the second line, feeling comfortable.

At least she was fine until she caught Carlos staring at her with a warm appraising gaze. Gabrielle lost her place.

Everyone glanced up at her verbal stumble.

"Pardon me," she said. "I'll start the last sentence over."

She gritted her teeth over the flush of heat that rushed through her, then didn't pause until she'd finished.

"Assessment?" Carlos issued that order to the room.

"It's a code," Rae answered.

"I'm sold." Korbin winked at Gabrielle, the scoundrel.

"One hell of a code," Gotthard muttered, admiration flooding his words.

Everyone turned to Hunter, who arched a beautiful male eyebrow and said, "I stand corrected. Impressive."

Gabrielle released a pent-up breath, ready to relax until Carlos asked her, "What did your friend mean by 'I am bound by the fratelli'?"

"I don't know," she replied quickly.

Gotthard stopped typing and became stone still, along with the rest of the room.

"*Fratelli* is Italian for 'brotherhood,' but that's not a code, for heaven's sake," Gabrielle added.

"You're sure you don't know anything more?" A lock of black hair fingered Carlos's smooth brow now drawn tight with lines of question.

He still didn't believe she was telling the truth.

"Really, that's *it*." Gabrielle wondered at the grim faces. What exactly was this *fratelli*?

"How are the Anguis tied to all of this?" Korbin asked.

"What do you mean?" Gabrielle wanted a more specific question before she said much about them. She glanced at Carlos, who seemed to have pulled back inside himself.

He was a study of ruthless control.

She sensed more than saw the entire room focus

expectant gazes on Carlos, who leaned the palms of his hands on the table inches away from her.

Those perfectly formed lips parted when he said, "Don't. Be. Coy. You have no allies in this room at the moment. Our team just risked their lives on a tip from you without even knowing who you were or if they were walking into a trap. If you hope to leave here, then you need to be more forthcoming."

She jerked back as if slapped by the deadly tone.

No one had talked to her in that way, threatening her outright, since her miserable excuse for an ex-husband had played her like a fool. She'd spent too many nights alone, frustrated over having no life and no family because of the ax both her ex and Durand Anguis dangled over her head. All that frustration rolled into one large knot of anger.

She slapped a hand on the table, then fisted her fingers. "I've been very damned forthcoming. I've risked my life to help put away criminals. What do *I* know about the Anguis? They're a bunch of murdering bastards driven by money and power. Why hasn't *your* organization done anything about them?"

Carlos stood away from the table. A muscle in his neck pulsed. He stared at her for a long moment, then his chest expanded with a slow breath. That tight control hid whatever he was thinking.

When he spoke, his voice was quiet, but demanding. "Give me the name of the person who sent you the card."

She'd put this off as long as she could. "My friend is Linette Tassone, and we attended the École d'Ascension in Carcassonne, France, at the same time. We shared a dorm room and common study interests. Like me, she had a knack for computers." Gabrielle noticed Gotthard typing. Taking her statement? "When I graduated, I went on to receive a degree in computer science in the UK, then I decided to search for Linette. That's when I found out about her . . . death, but I always questioned the story of her disappearance and now I feel justified."

"What story?" Carlos asked.

"Linette's father said she'd run away and had taken up with a bunch of degenerates. He said her stupid actions got her killed, but he didn't tell me more. I was shocked and eighteen when I made the trip to see her family, too young to press her father for details."

"Why don't you believe him?" Rae asked.

Gabrielle waved her hands in exasperation. "First of all, Linette would never have defied her father because she was terrified of him and an obedient child. Second, she was so shy it took us three months of seeing each other every day to finally speak, and I spoke first. Third, Linette was far from stupid. She was brilliant. And, fourth, she would never have just disappeared without saying a word to me."

"So what do you think happened?" Carlos watched her as though he judged every word, trying to come up with a verdict.

"I don't know," Gabrielle admitted quietly. "I didn't so much accept what her father had said as I finally accepted that Linette was gone forever after years of searching for her. But now I believe something happened to her she couldn't avoid, like she was kidnapped or coerced to go somewhere.

I just can't figure out the grave in the family plot with her headstone or her father's story. If Linette isn't dead, then who did he bury?" She sent that last question to Carlos, who didn't show any reaction, so Gabrielle went on.

"Anyhow, I had planned to work somewhere until—" She took a deep breath. The strain of the last few days and now having people pry into her private life weighed her down emotionally. "Until I married Roberto. After our divorce, I was attacked and decided to work from my home." Hiding like a criminal after he'd first terrified her with his fists. She'd been ready to divorce and then imprison him until he explained how he'd publicly smear her and her family's name, which would have destroyed her father, who was at the time in a tight campaign for his new position. Roberto had secretly filmed her the few times she'd shared his bed and manipulated the video to something so degrading she got nauseous just thinking about the copy he'd given her.

Her father's career would be destroyed and her stepsisters would live under a cloud of shame by association to her. So she'd agreed to Roberto's terms, which painted him as the victim of a loveless marriage who divorced her.

If only conceding her pride had ended it all. She suspected the enormous insurance policy Roberto carried on her listing him as the beneficiary was the motivation for the attacks, but if she went after him, he'd turn on her family.

As it was, he was content to either wait on her to die or only make attempts that appeared as accidents and could not be traced to him.

"I picked up on an odd posting on a Web site message board and realized it had to be some sort of code," she continued, explaining why she was in hiding beyond fear of Roberto. "I was shocked at what I learned when I broke the code. I watched the posts for a couple weeks, trying to decide if it was someone *playing* or seriously planning an attack on a flight from Heathrow to Wales—"

"The prime minister's flight that was diverted in '99?" Gotthard had stopped typing.

She slowly nodded her head.

"MI5 picked up posts from the terrorists that tipped them off—" Gotthard's words died when she shook her head.

"I figured no one would believe me if I just called up to tell them, and I didn't want to become the target of terrorists. So I set up a network to send e-mails with enough markers to alert MI5. If I have to, I can quote the text in each e-mail. I began using an alias to protect myself after that."

She paused, hoping for some words of understanding. None. "I started looking for information then since the Internet was such an easy place for criminals to maintain contact and pass plans. When I found things that might affect a country's security, I then had to find a way to get this information to *worthy* intelligence groups." She gave Carlos a peeved glance. "Someone who would have shown more respect to an informant."

Carlos lifted an eyebrow in a don't-get-snippy look.

She shrugged. "I didn't want the information to land in the wrong hands. If you believe I'm Mirage, then you should know how much I've helped in the Middle East."

Guarded looks passed around the room.

"Why do you think Linette didn't include her return address?" Gotthard asked Gabrielle.

"She's probably worried that I might try to find her and land in the same place she's in or get into some kind of trouble hunting her down." Which was exactly what Gabrielle had been contemplating, but these people didn't need that information. "I think she's a prisoner somewhere and it has something to do with that *fratelli* reference." She didn't want these people thinking Linette was a criminal.

Carlos paused his tapping fingers. "What about your resources in South America. How did you find them?"

"In a chat room for an underground operation in South America that is part of an organized watchdog group, for lack of a better description. They want to rid their country of the drug lords, which may not be a realistic goal, but at least they are doing something. I created a communication path with someone there in a way that would not lead anyone to me in case it was a trap."

Gabrielle would share all she could, but not a word about how the Anguis were responsible for her mother's death. She'd kept the secret safe for the first few years in deference to her father's demand. But now she had to keep it secret to protect her own life.

Who knew where the information from this room would go after this meeting? If Durand Anguis learned the whole story and couldn't find her, he'd go after her family.

She rubbed her tired eyes, thinking. "I don't know what to say that will convince you, but I've risked my neck to help intelligence agencies and now you, even though I don't know who or what you are. I'd never heard of Mandy before getting the postcard."

"Guest arriving," the mechanical voice announced again.

All eyes turned to the flat screen where a red Ducati Monster S4R motorcycle entered the gate.

"Who's that?" Gabrielle asked, nibbling on her fingernail.

"The boss." Rae tapped her pen on the table. "You said Linette disappeared while you were at school. What did everyone say about her missing?"

"Nothing really. It wasn't that unusual." Gabrielle stopped fidgeting with her fingernail, swiped a hand over her hair, and explained, "Linette wasn't in class one day. When I went to our room to check on her, all her possessions were gone. I asked questions, but no one would tell me anything, not even her family's address so I could write her. The school is very strict. They don't tolerate being questioned."

"Wait," Carlos said, staring over her head in concentration. "You said nothing really happened when Linette went missing and that it wasn't that unusual? Did you mean it wasn't unusual for Linette or for others to go missing?"

Footsteps approached from the top of the stairs.

"Others," Gabrielle answered, keeping her eyes on the stairwell. "Students dropped out all the time without notice."

When another towering hunk in a leather motorcycle jacket entered, the room came to attention. He was maybe late thirties and wore jeans in a way any woman would appreciate. Just as imposing as the rest of this bunch with his dark brown hair pulled back in a ponytail and blue eyes so intense she felt as though he expected her to give up her secrets with a look.

Carlos took a seat beside Gotthard.

"Gabrielle, I'm Joe," the new man said politely, before he addressed the others in the room. "Hell of a jump you made. Good job. Gotthard has kept me posted on this morning's conversation and running a deep profile on Gabrielle, cross-checking her story."

She glanced at Gotthard, who had leaned an elbow on the table and propped his head with a meaty hand. He nodded at Joe. "Everything she said checks out."

Gabrielle frowned. "Given my situation, did you really think I'd try to lie my way out of this?"

Joe's narrowed gaze tightened. His voice was whisper soft. "I expect anything at any time, just as everyone else in this room. Underestimating an adversary would be a stupid mistake for those in our line of work, and I assure you I don't hire stupid people."

"*Excusez-moi,*" she murmured in apology.

Joe nodded and continued, "Gotthard turned up some interesting cross-references. Unlike most of the other elite schools in France, the one Gabrielle went to was a private operation, funded by private investors and donations. Many graduates from there went on to have distinguished careers. The school is in a castle that has belonged to a local family for umpteen generations. But there seems to be a high percentage of dropouts. I'll let him explain further."

Gotthard thumped his thumb against the laptop. "I wouldn't have thought much about the dropout rate since these are privileged and spoiled kids who probably don't finish anything."

Gabrielle stiffened at the insult. She'd worked her bum off her whole life to prove she was not some indulged child.

"I expected to see them popping up anywhere from news articles to job status to marriage announcements," Gotthard went on. "Out of the six that disappeared the year Gabrielle was in school, only two have turned up. Both male. The four females are all listed as deceased."

Gabrielle's heart pounded. More confirmation that something had happened to Linette. "Why would her father say she was dead if she wasn't?"

Carlos answered, "He either believes she is buried in that grave or can't risk telling the truth. Was there anything special or different about Linette—or you—we should know?"

Yes, but the less everyone knew about her the better Gabrielle felt her chances were of getting out of this. "No."

"So what do you think happened to Linette?" Rae asked.

"I imagined everything over the years, even that her father might have sent her to a convent where she wouldn't have been able to contact me." Gabrielle took a breath. Her gaze sought out and didn't waver from Carlos's. "But I can't conceive that he might be a party to something that would have hurt her physically, so he must believe she is dead."

"Or she did something he considered the same as being dead to him," Rae suggested.

"Not Linette." Gabrielle didn't even try to hide her exasperation. "This *fratelli* must know something."

Silence fell over the room suddenly, no exhale of breath, no tapping keys, no rustle of paper.

Carlos could feel the panic seizing Gabrielle in spite of the strong front she was putting up, but could do little about it since he wouldn't see her again after this meeting.

Once Joe had a plan, they would all head out. Carlos would normally walk away without looking back, no sleep lost over a prisoner. But he'd heard enough to convince him Gabrielle had landed here out of honorable reasons and had no idea just how bad a spot she was in and that her freedom might be nothing more than a memory after today.

He'd argue in Gabrielle's favor for Joe to keep her in protective custody at a BAD safe house until all of this was over, but she'd have to show Joe she had a value for that concession.

And he doubted she had anything left to barter with.

"Gabrielle?" Carlos waited until her gaze met his and hoped like hell she got his drift. He warned her, "If there's anything you haven't shared yet, don't hold it back from Joe."

Her eyes widened for a flash before a resigned mask settled across her face. He had no idea if she understood or not, but he'd do his best to help her.

"What is this *fratelli*?" Gabrielle asked carefully.

"In for a penny, in for a pound," Rae said softly, but her words were clear in the total quiet.

Carlos faced Joe. "Might as well tell her since she isn't

going anywhere until we get to the bottom of all this, and the more she understands, the more she can share."

Joe appeared to think for a minute, then gave a short nod. "The Fratelli is a ghost group behind the viral deaths last year in India and the U.S., plus a couple other earlier attacks."

Gabrielle frowned. "I thought the media said India was an anomaly and a pharmaceutical company was behind the U.S. attack?"

"You haven't hacked quite as deep into intelligence mainframes as you thought," Hunter pointed out. "The public thinks the same thing you do, which is what they need to think while we search for this group, or paranoia will create chaos and likely play into whatever the Fratelli is planning."

"What *do* they want?" Gabrielle asked.

"That's the million-dollar question," Joe said. "The only reason I'm willing to discuss any of this with you is because that postcard is the first significant lead we've gotten on this group. So the more important question is what are they going to do next, and how did Mandy play into those plans?"

"Mandy was enrolled in the École d'Ascension, too," Gotthard interjected.

"Really?" Gabrielle whispered with a tremor of unease.

"That's not all," Joe added. "Another girl left with Mandy, signed out for a week."

Gotthard lifted his gaze to Gabrielle along with everyone else.

"I don't know about another girl," Gabrielle answered before someone asked her.

"Give us a rundown on the second girl," Carlos told Gotthard.

"Amelia Fuentes. Family is the third-largest coffee-bean producer in Columbia. The school records show she was heading home and taking Mandy with her, but no one has reported her missing. She's due back in three days."

Joe interjected, "I had operations place a call the phone ID service would show as the school calling the Fuentes home and asked if Amelia was available to come to the phone. The housekeeper said Amelia had a change of plans and decided to vacation in Germany for a few days."

"We need to find out what she knows about Mandy," Rae pointed out. "In fact, that school seems to be a common denominator."

"Exactly." Joe checked his watch, then told Carlos, "That's why I need your team rolling by tonight."

"What are you going to do with her?" Carlos said, indicating Gabrielle, who watched in silence.

"Security is on the way to pick her up and take her to holding," Joe said.

"No." Gabrielle stood.

Joe faced her, legs apart and arms crossed.

Carlos pressed, "Got something else to tell us?"

"Yes." Gabrielle's effort to scramble for a plan showed so clearly it was pitiful, but her eyes brightened all of a sudden. "You'll need help getting inside the school campus."

"Not really," Gotthard answered. "I can access the plans."

"But, uh—" She lifted a hand to her head, fingers clenching her hair. "You can't just walk onto the property."

"I thought you'd figured out that we're covert operatives," Rae told her drily.

Gabrielle swung an irritated glare at Rae. "I do understand that much, but I doubt you can recon that property by the time Amelia is due to return. The institution's security is superior to that of a UN meeting."

"Guest arriving," the speaker announced again.

Gabrielle turned wild eyes to the monitor, where a black panel van pulled into the drive. Then she faced Joe with determination in her voice. "Breaking the school's security systems will take more expertise than deciphering the code on Linette's card."

"How would you know?" Hunter asked.

"Because I created software for their security division," Gabrielle fired right back.

"So you'll just give the administrative control to us." Gotthard hefted one shoulder in a negligent shrug.

"You'll need more than that, like a good reason to be on the property." She met Carlos's gaze, the hope for support so strong in her eyes it was all he could do to stand in place.

The door upstairs opened and heavy footsteps entered.

"You can't just walk on the property," Gabrielle said in a flurry of panicked words. "The students are chosen to go there. Nothing, not even more money, can change the rule that every student has to wait at least six months to be allowed admittance once they are accepted. Instructors go through a twelve-month evaluation phase. Most of the staff has been there for over twenty years, and new staff must go through the same twelve-month vetting period.

They have their own maintenance people. Visitors must be invited, and no one comes to visit, not even family, with less than a two-week notice."

Boots pounded down the stairs, each thump sounding as menacing as a death knell.

"So there's no way to get inside unnoticed?" Carlos asked.

Two men dressed in black gear similar to that of SWAT teams trudged into the room. The only identifying mark on their clothing was a bold SECURITY written across the front of their jackets.

Gabrielle took a step back.

Carlos hated to watch her in terror, backing away like an animal expecting attack. She knew they were going to lock her up somewhere with no contact to the outside world. But it sounded as if even with the information she could supply, they had only a slim chance of gaining access to the school.

She planted her feet. "There is *one* way."

He wanted to hug her for coming up with a bargaining chip, until she added, "I have to go with you."

TWELVE

Carlos uncrossed his arms. "No."

He couldn't help this crazy woman if she was determined to keep digging herself deeper into this mess. Joe would use any resource, even Gabrielle, to get closer to the Fratelli.

And Tee would . . . better not to consider the limitless ways she'd use a resource who landed in their camp. The whole team was committed to taking down the Fratelli, and Carlos would gladly lead the charge, but putting this woman in the middle of a mission was not going to happen.

"Then as they say here in the States," Gabrielle said with assured finality, "you're screwed."

"You would let another young girl be hurt?" Carlos pressed.

"No, but undoubtedly you would by not at least entertaining my plan." Gabrielle wiped her eyes with graceful hands, the action feminine and gentle, which translated as vulnerable in Carlos's book. "You should at least consider—"

"Why?" Hunter asked.

Gabrielle set her jaw in a way that said she was tired of Hunter cutting her off.

"Let's hear your plan," Joe told her, ending all debate.

"*Merci.*" Gabrielle looked at Carlos with unsure eyes. She licked her lips in a dainty way as if she'd been taught how to do so properly in a Miss Manners class. Waves of brunette hair fell in tousled strands, tumbling with no real direction other than down to brush her shoulder.

Too soft-looking to be dangerous.

Too tired to be a threat.

The urge to bundle her off to a room where she could lie down and rest swamped him. He'd watched her go from fear to outrage to fear again. She definitely wasn't trained for this.

What was he going to do with her?

A confidence he hadn't seen before blossomed in her face.

"In addition to the school's accounting systems being in severe need of upgrading," Gabrielle started. "The books are opened to outside auditing firms during a break in mid-November each year for the fiscal report to all the investors."

"Hold it," Hunter interrupted. "I thought you said no one from the outside could get in. But they let auditors in?"

Gabrielle sighed and narrowed weary eyes at him.

Carlos couldn't wait to see how this one played out.

He'd noticed the more tired and hungry Gabrielle became, the testier she got.

"How very observant of you to recall my precise words," Gabrielle told Hunter in a cultured voice that could snap the royal guard into line. "If, however, you'll allow me to actually *finish* a thought, I'll explain why even if you could gain entry as an auditor, it would be a useless endeavor."

"All-righty then." Rae twisted her mouth in a half attempt to hide a laugh.

Gabrielle picked up where she'd left off. "An outside accounting firm has to go through the same vetting gauntlet, a more difficult one in fact, for no less than six months prior to being chosen. If your phony auditing firm was chosen, which would be a miracle, you wouldn't have access for another month at the soonest. And *if* you passed that test, your team would be under constant scrutiny, confined to the accounting department. This would undoubtedly handcuff anyone hoping to covertly investigate other areas, thereby making the entire mission a waste of time. I hope I've satisfied your fruitless inquisition."

Hunter answered her with a mild roll of his eyes and waved his hands dismissively. "Continue."

"The audit occurs between November twelfth and fifteenth, but the Board of Regents requires a pre-audit the last weekend before the outside auditors are given access."

"This weekend?" Gotthard asked.

Gabrielle nodded.

"So what's your idea?" Joe showed no sign of leaning one way or another, so far.

She folded her hands neatly at her waist as though she

were speaking to the principal. "Their computer systems are in dire need of upgrading that they've been fighting. They are loath to deal with the problem since it would mean allowing someone access to their records."

"How does this help us?" Korbin sounded unconvinced.

Gabrielle explained, "I've been discussing a software program with the school for the past year that allows one person to sync all electronic files within a day or two. If a virus was introduced to the system in a careful way, their computers would shut down and react as though the entire system had been crashed, when in truth it would be a managed crash."

Korbin drummed his fingers on the table surface, dark eyes fixed in concentration. "If they run as tight a ship as you say, there's no telling how many weeks it would take to find a way into that system without detection to set up this crash."

"Actually, I know *exactly* how long it will take," Gabrielle answered without hesitation.

Carlos noted the confidence in her voice. This was her territory, but she'd still have to convince Gotthard and Hunter that the school systems could be breached. Even he knew the complexity of what she was suggesting.

"They want the program I wrote specifically for them," she added. "The only possible way to gain quick entrance to the school would be to throw a kink into their accounting program since everything in an audit revolves around money. Once that happens, I believe they'll contact me since I have history with the school and prior clearance."

"We *can* throw a kink into their systems," Gotthard confirmed. "*If* we can get into their systems."

"That's a big if," Hunter muttered.

Carlos didn't see this as a viable option if Hunter and Gotthard doubted they could gain entry into the school's computers. And there was no way they could insert someone who hadn't been cleared if what she described about the school's vetting of outsiders was true.

"There is no if. This can be done." Gabrielle nodded, then turned to Joe. "But only if you make me a deal."

"What deal?" Joe asked.

"I'll help you access the school's records if you assure me you won't turn me over to Interpol or any other country and you try to find Linette."

Carlos ground his back teeth. She had no idea what she was doing. He'd gag her if he could do it right now to prevent Gabrielle from getting herself in any deeper. Did she really think Joe would let her walk out of here with an agreement that she'd gain access to the school's computers for them?

Joe asked, "How do we know you really can do any of this?"

"Think I have that for you," Gotthard chipped in. "You were in classes with Linette, right, Gabrielle?"

"Yes." She sounded tired and out of patience.

Gotthard looked up at Joe. "Linette was brilliant. Her profile indicates she was in the top ten percent of Mensa. Genius." Gotthard cut his eyes at Gabrielle. "Your IQ?"

"Two points higher."

When she raised those beautiful eyes in challenge to Carlos, he saw only a woman.

Not an informant. Not a threat to the world.

Just a woman who could bleed and die.

He would not put her in danger.

Joe spoke up. "I'm convinced and your plan has merit, but only if my people can go in."

That was more like it, but Carlos doubted Gabrielle would give in so easily and she didn't.

"Won't happen with as little time as you have," Gabrielle countered. "I can get you inside the campus because I'm an alumnus they know, but more importantly, the reason I can help you get inside their computers is because when I wrote the current programs, I incorporated a back door into the system. Without me, you don't have a chance."

That did it. How would Carlos talk Joe out of using her now? "And you think we'll just let you go do this alone?"

"No," she admitted.

"So we're back to this plan not working." Carlos expected her to admit defeat, not lift her chin a notch in defiance.

"I can get someone inside with me as a bodyguard," Gabrielle suggested, confidence in her voice picking up speed.

"Has to be someone with electronic capability," Hunter pointed out.

"No, it doesn't," she replied quickly.

Hunter opened his mouth to protest, but Carlos cut him off. "Let her explain."

The look of thanks Gabrielle sent him curled soft fingers around his heart.

"I need someone who looks like a bodyguard and

isn't well-known in aristocracy, such as yourself, I would assume," she told Hunter.

Carlos smiled. She had him there. Part of Hunter's use to BAD as an agent was his social contacts and ability to gain access to the criminally rich.

Hunter growled, then inclined his head, conceding the point.

"If no one knows about your secret life as Mirage, why would the school believe you need protection?" Korbin asked.

"I can answer that, too," Gotthard said without looking up from his laptop as he typed. "Because . . . she's not just Gabrielle Saxe. Just got a full report on her prints."

She covered her face with her hands and groaned.

Gotthard read from his monitor, "She's Gabrielle Tynte Saxe, heir to the Tynte dynasty, and she's had two attacks on her life before she disappeared following her divorce."

Carlos blinked. He'd known something was not just average about her, but her entire family was imperial lineage?

She was way up the freakin' royal food chain.

"You told me there was nothing different or special about you." Carlos waited until she uncovered her face to add, "When you tell a lie, it's a whopper. Now we have even more reason to keep you here in protective custody."

"No!" Her eyes rounded in panic. She jerked toward Joe. "I can get inside with one of your people . . . by tomorrow."

"We'd be sending a civilian into danger and risking our

people while doing it," Carlos argued, not liking the way Joe was considering her offer.

"You'll waste the best chance you have to get answers on Mandy and the other teens . . . and finding out who the Fratelli are," she threw right back.

"Hard to argue with that," Joe finally said.

"But I won't help unless you make me a deal." Gabrielle's sable eyebrows lowered over a stubborn gaze. She rushed ahead before Carlos could shut her down. "I'll do whatever is necessary to help you if you promise to look for Linette and free me once I'm through and you see that I'm not a criminal."

Joe didn't hesitate. "Deal."

THIRTEEN

Carlos stood in the kitchen with his back to the rolling mountains beyond the cabin and leaned against the sink counter. He'd run out of arguments to prevent Gabrielle from going. The mission should be his only concern, but she had no one else to watch out for her.

"She walked into this." Joe paced along the opposite side of the island as he justified the decision. "We're just doing what BAD does best—capitalizing on resources and assets wherever we can find them."

"Baby Face considered himself a white-collar criminal who didn't dirty his hands and had never worked with Durand before. Makes me wonder why he was picking up Gabrielle on his own, and how did he find her?"

"All good questions, but Baby Face is dead so he can't help us, and we can't pass up this opportunity." Joe paused and rocked back on his heels, arms crossed, thinking.

Carlos finished his coffee and placed the cup in the

sink. He'd issued orders to the team, dispersing Rae and Korbin in one direction to get ready to leave and Hunter back to the IT to start processing information on the school.

Joe glanced over his shoulder at the sound of footsteps and voices coming up the stairs from the basement.

Gotthard appeared with Gabrielle right behind him, saying something about a secondary retrieval something or other. When they both entered the room, she fell silent.

"We've breeched the school programs." The smile Gotthard rarely sported underlined the significance of their success.

"I need my laptop to check for messages from the school." Gabrielle's excitement flashed in her eyes, not as tired now that she'd eaten a sandwich.

"Why can't you use ours?" Joe had put her with Gotthard to monitor her moves.

"My e-mail system is complicated and all my passwords are loaded into my laptop." Embarrassment flushed her cheeks with rosy color before her lips curved. That's when she glanced at Carlos and dimples showed up with the fairy smile.

Her eyes reflected a deep loneliness when her guard was down. Unremarkable in so many ways, but the dimples and smile rearranged her nondescript features into adorable.

Carlos breathed out a long, miserable sigh.

She was *not* adorable, dammit. When was he going to get it straight in his mind that she was a potential threat to American security? And people he cared about?

This woman had a connection to the Anguis she'd yet to explain to his satisfaction. Just as she'd been told earlier, Gabrielle was the enemy until proven otherwise. One who could be a danger to others.

Right. And he was the Easter Bunny.

Joe nodded at Gotthard. "Let her boot up."

When she turned to follow Gotthard downstairs, Carlos said, "Gabrielle?"

She swung back wide-eyed with a look of fear as if she thought something had changed. "What?"

"We're leaving as soon as you get an invitation from the school."

Her relief reached out and touched Carlos. She moved as if to take a step toward him and caught herself, making him wonder what had been on her mind. She grinned. "Gotthard came up with a particularly nasty way to fubar the computers, so they should be looking for me now."

She hurried from the room before Carlos raised his eyebrows at her last comment. Did Miss Priss even know what the acronym *fubar* stood for?

Joe lifted his phone, which must have buzzed, and answered it, paused, then muttered something low that sounded like a curse and hung up. "Based on all the information you sent yesterday, we managed to track down the helicopter."

"You found Turga's pilot?"

"We caught up with him in South America. He made a fuel stop near Caracas and disappeared while the chopper was being serviced. The station belongs to one of Durand's legitimate companies, and the pilot's flight plan indicated Durand's compound as his last stop. He may be lost to us."

Carlos drummed his fingers on the counter, thinking. "That doesn't fit Durand's MO."

"Why not?"

"At least it wouldn't have fit at one time." Carlos scratched his jaw. Joe and Retter, BAD's top agent, knew he was Anguis, but not that he was related by blood. Sad to remember more about the ways his family killed people than anything else. "Durand wouldn't kill or kidnap someone with a trail like that to his compound. He liked everything kept low profile, unless he really wanted to make a statement." Like bombing the vehicle of a competitor trying to move into his territory. The explosion sixteen years ago took out a van full of female teachers just trying to help South America's underprivileged.

Durand tried to explain the deaths on the bus as an unintentional accident.

Carlos disagreed, but in the end the teachers were just four more deaths he felt to his soul.

"So you think . . . ?" Joe prompted.

"Whoever took the pilot might have been snatching him away from Durand." Carlos scratched his chin, thinking.

"Another player in the mix." The grim set of Joe's jaw crept into his words.

"I'm betting the Fratelli are involved, maybe payback for losing Mandy, but that almost doesn't fit either. Why the pilot? Why not have someone shadow Baby Face and grab Gabrielle if they knew about Durand's plans? I wonder if whoever grabbed the pilot knows that Gabrielle is the informant?"

"Don't know, but that pilot *can* finger you and Gabrielle."

Carlos chewed on that, considering the implications and risks. "Maybe Gabrielle would be safer with someone else." He'd tried to sound all business, to hide his lack of conviction. The idea of sending her out with anyone else dug under his skin and irritated him more than it should have.

"*She* won't be any safer with someone else, but *you're* going to be exposed with no immediate backup on-site, but I'd rather have you on this just because of your knowledge of the Anguis."

"I realize that." Carlos met Joe's gaze that shared nothing. Guilt almost pushed him to tell Joe just how well he knew the Anguis, but Joe and Retter knew as much as BAD needed to know. He'd told them years ago about how the Anguis soldiers were tattooed like him.

He just hadn't explained the significance of the scar.

"The closest we can get anyone to that school is going to be half a kilometer away, which might as well be a continent away if things go to shit." Joe drummed his fingers on the counter. "I *could* send Retter, but I had other plans for him."

Carlos shook his head. "She'd never listen to Retter." And the idea of Retter alone with her didn't sit well at all.

"Not listen to *him*?" Joe smiled in disbelief. He clearly couldn't imagine anyone denying his top gun and one of the most intimidating agents to come out of BAD. "Retter's pretty intimidating."

"That's why she'd never listen to him," Carlos explained. "Gabrielle runs hot and cold. One minute she'll bite your head off and the next she's terrified. If you snap at her at the wrong time, she'll just freeze up." It surprised Carlos that he was beginning to understand her fluctuating personality so well, but he did. She developed more backbone and attitude when she was exhausted, but catch her rested or just after eating and she was gentle as a kitten.

"I've got orders to cover a media event in a congressional hearing room that's been on the books for the past five months. Basically, it's a media blitz for the two presidential parties." Joe's long sigh telegraphed how much he hated expending trained agents he desperately needed in less threatened places right now. "We're going to be stretched thin on manpower. Retter's pulling together a team to take into Venezuela. I need him to find out who's attacking their oil minister and fingering the U.S. as the money behind the hits before this oil crisis turns into an international conflict."

Carlos held up his hand. "I'm on board. We'll leave as soon as I can get Gabrielle packed and out of here."

What had Turga's pilot told Durand about him and Gabrielle? Carlos had to keep her safe, which was going to be a trick if Durand sent his guns after them. One more thing came to mind.

"So you're going to let her go when we get back from the school?" Carlos was surprised, but glad she'd cut that deal.

Joe started toward the steps, then stopped and lifted his eyebrows in surprise. "I agreed to search for Linette and let her go once we were convinced she wasn't a criminal. We'll search for Linette because we would anyhow. But the minute you're done in France, Gabrielle comes back here. I can't just wave my hand and declare she's innocent. We're not the only ones looking for her. I had to cut a deal with Interpol to get her prints processed. They want her next."

———

"What do you mean Turga's pilot is gone?" Durand dropped the file he was reviewing and stared in disbelief. "What happened?"

Julio's wiry body tensed. He gripped the large envelope in his hands tighter. "His flight plans to Venezuela indicated he would arrive in Caracas today. I had men in place to intercept him, but at his last fuel stop the pilot leaves his helicopter and no returns. Authorities are all over the airport right now. I think he ran from something."

"Why?" Durand stood behind his desk, scratching the side of his chin.

Julio waved the envelope in exasperation and shook his head. "Have no answer, yet. Maybe he did no go willingly. Maybe we learn more when we find the leader of the black-ops team from France."

"Sí." Durand studied that a moment, then asked, "What have you got?"

"More photos, better angles on the face of the man who led them, though the lighting was no so good in these."

Durand took the photos Julio handed him and laid the shots across his desk. The last photo showed a four-person team of three men and a woman. The leader appeared to be Hispanic, raising the hairs along Durand's arms, but the shot had not been full face.

He fingered the glossy photos, separating them four across. Vague images with the low lighting, but that one in particular made him look twice.

"Do you recognize him?" Julio pointed at one picture.

"Maybe, maybe no. From this angle, his eyes look familiar," Durand muttered more to himself. Did he know this man? "Show these pictures around. See if someone recognizes him." The man was definitely familiar, but Durand could not place the face right now. Soon he would have answers.

"*Sí.*"

"In the meantime, I want the person who dared to betray me and cost my men their lives." Durand seethed every time he thought of his brother's death. "We will set a trap and see what we catch."

———

Carlos shifted in his seat, caught between sleep and consciousness. First class offered more room for his legs and arm space, but nothing for stiff muscles and memories too dark and twisted to be mere nightmares.

He breathed deeply, trying to use this time to rest.

The subtle scent of a female swirled near his nose. He might have gone back to sleep at that point if not for noticing the arm draped across his middle.

He opened his eyes to find Gabrielle beneath his left arm, hugging him as she slept. Her chest expanded and contracted softly against him with each steady breath.

When had she lifted the center console and scooted under his arm?

From his vantage point it was hard not to glance straight down where a gold, oval-shaped locket had slid into the valley between the gentle swell of her breasts. Sure, an antique locket had drawn his attention. He lifted his right hand to cover his eyes, then propped his elbow against the aisle armrest. Everything about this mission was wrong or off-key.

Starting with Gabrielle's being practically royalty. An aristocrat with a bloodline that could be traced all the way back to the thirteenth century.

Men had fought wars over women like her.

She might not be a runway beauty, but Carlos now understood why he'd sensed an inherent grace about Gabrielle.

And she *was* attractive, in an understated, natural way without all the fuss. He rarely met women who would go out in public without makeup or clothes in perfect order, but Gabrielle had changed from her wrinkled warm-ups to a pair of jeans and pink knit top without a peep of protest. She accepted the plain clothes as standard fare, then braided her hair and twisted the single length up on her head with a clamp.

No muss or fuss.

A simple yet elegant look on her.

She *could* dress and live like a queen with round-the-clock protection. Why didn't she?

His mother—and that was stretching the definition—would never have forsaken a life of luxury to live in anonymity or moderation. Alena Anguis had considered herself royalty and expected everyone to treat her as such. For a while, Carlos and his brother had been the favored princes in the household, until Carlos realized how much blood the Anguis dynasty floated upon.

He uncovered his eyes. He stared at the sun rising beyond the window, trying to bury the painful memories back where they belonged. Forever forgotten. He hadn't thought about his biological mother in many years, intentionally. The woman had cared more about the latest fashions and keeping her body perfect than children whose births cluttered her life. She refused to be soiled by a messy kid or to consider having another baby after Carlos's brother. Pregnancy was an imposition she bore like a martyr.

Her obsession turned into bulimia, killing her by the time Carlos was ten.

His father, Durand, had sold his soul to the Salvatore family when he married Alena, only daughter of the powerful Salvatore cartel. Durand owed all he had gained to them.

When Salvatore withdrew his support of the Anguis upon Alena's death, claiming she'd died from mistreatment, Durand declared war between the families. From that point on, Durand was determined to prove the Salvatore don had made a mistake in snubbing him.

For the bloodline of a spoiled princess, Durand turned every male in his family into soldiers for his personal war.

The only real mother Carlos ever had was his aunt Maria, Durand's sister.

For her, Carlos would carry a secret to the grave that would likely send him to an early one. But that's what a man did for the ones he truly loved.

His gaze settled on the woman clinging to him.

Mirage—Gabrielle—had passed on more information on the Anguis than any intelligence agency for over eight years. Carlos had to know what she knew. Had to know if there was any way she might expose his secret.

He'd treat her as a temporary ally, for now.

Gabrielle gripped his chest and started breathing in gasps.

A nightmare had her. Odd, but he was as sure about that as he was about what it would take to calm her before she began screaming.

He unclipped her seat belt and turned her until he could hold her face against his chest. Her rapid breathing indicated she was closing in on full panic. He whispered into her ear, "Wake up. Come on, baby, wake up. Just a dream."

She trembled against him, her fear so real he could see it on her skin. God, he hated that.

He rubbed her back slowly and whispered again, giving her a little shake to break her away from whatever grisly images played through her captured mind.

Her arms had locked around him when he'd turned her to face him. Fingers clutched at his side. He hissed at the recent wound she'd grabbed and reached down to move her hand.

Slowly, her breathing evened out again. Before thinking better of it, he kissed the top of her head and continued moving his hand along her back and arms.

The flight attendant stopped next to him with a silent

offer for the blanket in her hand. He nodded and smiled his thanks when she draped it over Gabrielle then moved away, checking other passengers.

Gabrielle peeked out between her lashes, not ready to admit she was awake. This was not where she'd been when she went to sleep. She remembered lifting the console so she could get comfortable, but not how she ended up in Carlos's arms. Again.

His hand moved slowly up and down her spine. Her body preened under the comfort, refusing to break contact and turn away from what he freely offered. If she closed her eyes, she could pretend she was in the arms of a man who cared for her.

But she wasn't fooling herself about why he was here or her value to him. She had some freedom of movement for as along as he perceived a value, but what about once she had nothing more to offer?

Would Joe really set her free?

She shivered at the possibility of remaining a prisoner of this black-ops group who didn't exist in the known world of espionage.

"Are you okay?"

Gabrielle stilled at his deep voice so close to her ear, then pushed herself away from his chest. His gaze was both sharp and tired. She wondered if he ever rested.

He was here with her in spite of not agreeing with this mission. He'd told her he wouldn't let anyone hurt her. She believed him.

"I'm fine. How did I end up *this* way?" She glanced between them.

"You were having a nightmare. I didn't think you'd want to scream and put the entire airplane into a panic."

She flushed with embarrassment at the definite possibility since she'd been deep into a blood-drenched nightmare when she'd heard him trying to wake her. He'd saved her that humiliation.

"No, of course not. *Merci.*" Gabrielle shifted away until she sat properly in her own seat and brushed loose hairs off her face. Her stomach rumbled softly. She must have slept through breakfast. "How close are we to landing?"

"About twenty minutes." Carlos dropped his chin down as though he wanted only her to hear him, so she leaned close again. "When we arrive, follow the instructions I gave you."

She nodded, paying more attention to the perfect shape of his mouth at eye level. So firm and male, and kissable. She wished he'd never kissed her and shouldn't be thinking about that right now.

Had to be hormones waking from too long in hibernation that kept her wondering if he'd kiss her again.

"Need me to go over it once more?" he asked.

"What?" She raised her eyes to meet his curious ones. He sighed. "When we exit the plane—"

Gabrielle's mind whipped back into gear. "I got it the first time we went through this," she said, cutting him off, but keeping her voice low. "Stay next to you. Don't talk to anyone. Tell you if I see anyone I recognize. Don't use your name or give mine unless it is absolutely necessary. Tell customs we're here on vacation, et cetera and so on." She frowned at him. "I got the other fifty dos and don'ts, too. I'm not a moron."

His eyes twinkled in spite of her harpy tone. "Are you hungry?"

"Yes, but I probably slept past breakfast."

Carlos waved at the flight attendant. She came right over, brilliant smile on her pretty face when she leaned down to hear him. She nodded and returned to the galley.

"What was that all about?" Gabrielle cringed at her crabby attitude, but the woman had been ogling Carlos.

And he seemed fine with it. Men.

"I asked her to bring you some food." His mouth twitched, fighting a smile.

How could she fault any woman for ogling a man who looked that good in a black, button-down shirt and black jeans after flying all night?

She wanted to shrink and hide in the blanket. Mornings weren't her best time of day. She rarely spoke to anyone before having a shower, tea, and breakfast.

She felt the need to apologize, but not to the person who had taken her prisoner. In a compromise with her conscience, she said, "That might improve my mood."

"I've noticed." The smile that broke free reached his eyes this time. Gorgeous deep brown eyes fringed with black lashes.

She couldn't hold on to her anger in the face of his good nature and smiled back. "I'm sorry to be so grumpy. But I'm used to being alone in the morning. I normally have time to acquire a personality before I leave the house."

Something she said drew an odd look through his eyes, but the fleeting expression vanished just as quickly.

The flight attendant brought her breakfast and nicely reminded Gabrielle she only had about ten minutes to eat.

"*Merci.*" Gabrielle finished quickly, handing her tray to the flight attendant on the last pass through before landing.

Other than popping a couple mints in his mouth from the tin he shared with her, Carlos remained quiet throughout the landing and changing airplanes to the one for Carcassonne. He kept her close to him, his eyes constantly scanning.

But his eyes showed the lack of rest. Based on what she'd heard during the meeting, he hadn't slept much in several days.

Gabrielle feigned sleep until Carlos dropped his head back and let his eyes close. She doubted he was ever in a deep sleep, but sensed he wouldn't even try to rest when she was alert. She could tell he watched her constantly, even when he didn't seem to be noticing her.

How would she slip away with him so vigilant?

Why did she feel so guilty about planning her escape? She'd do her part of this mission first to assure they were able to protect the young girls being targeted.

But she had to find a way to leave because she doubted Joe would let her walk around with knowledge of his group even if she didn't have a name for them.

When she escaped, Gabrielle had to disappear permanently.

—⚬—

"You're never home when I am so why does it matter how much I'm gone?" Gotthard asked, regretting the call he'd made home. He should have realized his wife, Martina, wouldn't see it as an effort on his part to stay in touch, but rather an opening to rag on him.

"I might not mind if I could find you once in a while."

"You have my cell phone and I return calls when I can." Gotthard used his Bluetooth so he could type hands-free, but this call would be short. No one at the BAD operations center made a call to anyone on a cell phone long enough to be traced, no matter if they were talking to their ninety-year-old grandmother.

"Why can't I at least know where you are? What can be so top secret about working on the interior design of an airplane?"

"For one thing, the design is for another country, and number two, I signed a security agreement. I'd breach the contract by telling anyone, including you."

"At least—"

"I'm sorry, Martina, but I have someone buzzing me. I've got to go. I . . ." *Just say it. I love you.* He wanted to, really, but . . . "Miss you. Talk to you later."

Gotthard hung up, waded through a few moments of guilt, then returned to toying with the code from Linette's postcard. He'd been sending messages out through a system he'd created that sent postings in several mixed forms to different blogs and electronic-board sites. He signed each message with *Bee Happee* at the bottom and included a code word in the text.

"What you got, big guy?" Hunter sauntered into the IT center at BAD, located beneath the city of Nashville and connected by underground tunnels to the high-rise

AT&T building, which housed the business front for BAD.

"Not much new, except for this." Gotthard turned and lifted several documents he'd printed out. "I've been cross-referencing names and found a common link between the three teens, Linette, and Gabrielle."

Hunter took the papers and started reading. "What is it?"

"Look at the ancestry. There's a *D-ange-ruese* notation showing up in each direct lineage of a firstborn or an only child. What I've found online indicates it's a bloodline that might go back two thousand years."

"Sounds like one of the zillion myths being peddled on the Net." Hunter leaned down, studying the notations, then shook his head. "Damn Internet is the best and worst thing that ever happened to this world."

"Myth or not, Amelia, Gabrielle, Linette, and the two other teens we can't locate all have that designation in common plus they're all either an only child or a firstborn. Mandy is the only exception, but it's something."

Hunter squinted his eyes in thought. "Huh. I've got friends in Europe who specialize in really obscure ancestry. Let me put some professionals on this."

--- ⚍ ---

Once she deplaned in Carcassonne, Gabrielle breathed easier again, aware of Carlos only by the occasional touch of his hand to guide her back to him if she strayed.

Was it her imagination or had he withdrawn from her?

He hadn't joked or touched her unnecessarily since leaving the Charles de Gaulle Airport.

Now she was thinking like a high school teenager, worried the hot guy in school didn't notice her. Her cheeks heated at the memory of this hot guy running her into a bathroom to put clothes on at the cabin.

He'd noticed her, but not in a flattering way.

She pulled a carry-on bag Joe's people had packed for her after she'd listed all the things she needed. How had anyone shopped that fast? Every item she'd requested had been included, no questions asked.

At the first ladies' room they reached, Gabrielle moved out of the flow, but stopped short of the entrance when Carlos caught her arm.

Swinging a glare first at his hand, then at his face, she kept her voice low and didn't soften the bite of annoyance sparking intentionally. "Do you really expect me to endure this trip without using the loo?"

The crowd noise swallowed a sound that accompanied the scowling curl of his lips. He took a breath, seeming to draw patience from that simple act, and leaned close when he spoke.

"I hadn't planned to give you this until later."

He drew her into his arms intimately, as if . . . to kiss her?

Gabrielle held her breath, all thoughts of the ladies' room vanishing at the prospect of another kiss. She had no idea what had prompted this and would normally be worried over acting inappropriately in public, but they were anonymous to this crowd.

One thought ventured to the surface. *I might not get this chance again.* She'd denied herself the simplest of joys over the past ten years. What was the harm in a kiss?

When he slid a hand around her back, she turned her face up to his, staring into eyes dark as charred whiskey. He paused and his gaze burned with something she was afraid to give a name. She swallowed, her breathing shallow and expectant.

Her skin rippled with anticipation. Want.

His jaw tensed. He glanced over her head and slipped a hand under the back of her sweater, raising a gasp from her when his warm fingers touched her skin.

A quick kiss was okay, but nothing overly demonstrative. "What are you doing?" she whispered.

"Just be still and put your head against my shoulder."

She frowned, then complied. He hugged her closer with one arm while his fingers on the other hand moved around and clipped something on her waistband at her right hip.

She ground her teeth. He was putting a tracking device on her. "Do you really think I'll just leave it stuck there if I want to run?"

Another deep sigh fluttered her hair, sending a brush of mint breath past her nose. "It's not . . . that type of unit. I have no way to check a public bathroom to make sure it's safe for you so I put a panic button on your jeans. Don't put your hand on your hip unless you need help. It only takes a touch to send an alert to my receiver."

Now she really felt like a witch for sniping at him.

He added, "If you ran, I'd find you and return you to Joe, who would lock you up for a very long time. Your chances of getting out of all this are better if you stay with me."

Any warm feeling she'd tendered for him disappeared under a blow of irritation. She stepped out of his arms, feeling justified in her foul mood.

"I need some time so don't come rushing in to check on me," she warned.

"How long?"

"I have to freshen up and change clothes if we're going straight to the school. I'm not in proper attire."

Carlos eyed her suspiciously.

She'd shared all she considered necessary.

He checked his watch. "You have ten minutes. Tops."

She couldn't possibly do everything she had in mind in ten minutes. Maybe with a little practice, but she hadn't tried this execution in the past two years. The last thing she wanted was for Carlos to come charging into the ladies' room at the wrong moment. He'd intimidated her into going along with him when they'd first met and he wanted the key to her Jeep. Maybe she could use the same strategy on him.

Gabrielle gripped the handle of her luggage tightly and stepped up to push her face close to his, hoping she sounded as threatening as her frame of mind.

"I have been knocked overboard, shot at, kidnapped, handcuffed, terrified, and held prisoner. I will *not* be told how long to take in the loo."

His eyebrows lifted in surprise. "Sure you got enough to eat on the plane?"

She growled and stomped away toward the bathroom entrance.

"Ten minutes, Gabrielle, or I *will* come get you."

FOURTEEN

Vestavia stood near the door to the conference room at Trojan Prodigy. He shook the hands of the four Fras arriving for a meeting he'd requested. He took his time with each wrinkled, but firm, hand he gripped.

The wall of glass on this side of the thirty-second floor overlooked the Brickell business district. Bulletproof glass had been installed inside the tinted windows, assuring safety. In addition, a fine mesh was interwoven into the extra glass that prevented any viewing from outside during daylight or such as now, when darkness wrapped the bustling city.

Coming from D.C., Chicago, New York, and Seattle, these four Fras were the backbone of the North American Fratelli, the ones who swayed the others.

This was the perfect example of why a group of twelve Fras could never rule one continent successfully. Too easy for one man to manipulate the power.

"You each have a copy of the file on our current project." Vestavia waved his hand at the five place settings with folders. Once the men were seated around one end of the fourteen-foot-long walnut conference table and reviewing the files, Vestavia served them each their preferred beverage, which meant Scotch, whiskey, or gin.

At thirty-eight, he was the youngest of all twelve Fras, the present group ranging from fifty-two to seventy years of age. Another reminder that he was the most recent follower elevated to this level, which had come on the heels of the unexpected death of Fra Bacchus last year.

This North American contingent believed poor Bacchus had succumbed to a heart attack in his sleep.

That was *a* version of the truth.

Had they suspected foul play in any way, an autopsy would have been scheduled at a private clinic. That would have revealed a synthetic chemical in a blood sample from Bacchus, the catalyst for the heart failure.

But Vestavia had been careful when he eliminated the only Fra who had suspected his every move from the outset and constantly questioned his allegiance to the Fratelli.

Now, *he* was the celebrated brother and Bacchus was off meeting his maker.

Some of the most powerful men in North America sat at the table, none of whom had any idea an Angeli sat among them.

They believed the Angeli had been a myth, but Vestavia was very real. The Fras would know his power when he and six more Angeli emerged to guide a new world once the groundwork had been completed. For now, he would pretend deference to men unworthy to sit in the same room with him.

He had been the first Angeli to infiltrate the Fratelli, the most powerful organization in the world—at the moment. A collection of brilliant men flush with geniuses, but the Fras were not capable of a true Renaissance. They understood the mechanics of collapsing major industrial nations, but not the art of overtaking each nation methodically.

"Everything will be in place for Friday." Vestavia took the open seat at the head of the table. "To assure success, we must not allow the United States to lose focus on the oil issues."

Fra Diablo, the senior of the group, who could influence the votes, had supported Vestavia's promotion to Fra. Drooping jowls moved when he lifted his head and shoved a bushy white eyebrow up. Skin sagged under his eyes, and his nose turned down, stopping short of being a hook. He drew deep breaths, his exhales wheezing slightly.

"With fuel prices climbing higher than any country anticipated, particularly the United States, that shouldn't be a problem," Diablo noted. "What about the teenagers?"

"The last one will be picked up this week," Vestavia assured him.

"Isn't that cutting it a little close with the presidential election next week?" Fra Benedict, the Banker as Vestavia thought of him, was always first to criticize. More round than tall, Benedict could always be counted on for a frown and a negative attitude. He pointed out every potential fault, no matter how minuscule, so he could be the one to claim to have foreseen a failure when it occurred.

Temper, temper. Vestavia had climbed quickly by presenting a sincere mix of humility and confidence to the Fras, but to hold a meek front in the face of inferior beings was a test of his discipline.

"Everything will be in place in time," Vestavia said with a finality he hoped would end that discussion. "Timing is the key to success, just as timing was crucial five months ago in orchestrating the meeting that takes place this week in the Capitol Building." He let that sink in, reminding them none of this would have happened without his ability to plan. "To rush any part of this schedule is as dangerous as running behind. We are currently *on time*."

None of this bunch would insult another Fra or behave improperly. They believed in order and respect. As contradictory as it sounded, they would kill for the order but allowed "no unnecessary deaths." No unnecessary actions that would draw attention to the order.

To commit such an act would show a lack of respect for the Fratelli.

At least Vestavia had the sense to see the absurdity in that thinking since deaths were unavoidable when conquering.

Fra Morton had the habit of lifting his hand a couple inches off the table, index finger extended, every time he spoke, as if to mark his place. "No one suspects the teens disappearing?"

Vestavia shook his head. "No. We've been very careful in our selection and solicitations. They each appear to leave the school willingly."

Morton nodded his balding head, lips pinched in

thought, and placed his hand flat on the table. He wore the understated brown suit of a nobody on his gangly body, which matched his nondescript face. A casual observance would dismiss his simple question and quiet acceptance as a pushover, but Vestavia never took anything casually. He'd investigated every one of them thoroughly.

Morton sat on the boards of six international firms, three of which held major defense contracts.

He was no pushover.

Fra Dempsey made notes during every meeting. He paused in writing. "What about the Venezuelan? Is he suspicious about what the teens will be used for?"

"No." Vestavia rested his arms on each side of his file, making a show of being relaxed. "I've assured that Durand Anguis has more to worry about than the fate of the teens and ensured he will perform his tasks on time."

"Impressive . . . if all goes as expected." At fifty-two, Dempsey was one of the most accomplished Fra whose holdings included high-rise buildings all over the world and a luxury yacht manufacturer that custom-built vessels for world leaders as well as ships for international trade . . . and private submarines. Trim body, thick gray hair, and deep tan, he reminded Vestavia of a movie star known for that look whose name he couldn't bring to mind.

"All will go as I explained in the original presentation for this project." Vestavia would have preferred Mandy had been delivered to him, but she knew nothing significant and had been a sacrificial lamb. He'd only ordered the kidnapping to draw the attention of the Mirage, who took the bait the minute Durand's involvement was leaked.

The only mistake in that plan had been in not capturing Mirage, but Vestavia would find this freelance informant soon and silence the rat.

"I sense a concern, my brothers." Stilted quiet fingered across the table and got under Vestavia's skin. Were they questioning him? *Him*. Fighting the urge to snap at them, Vestavia turned to the strength his ancestors had passed down through genetics rich with strategic ability and showed a tranquil countenance.

Benedict never wrote a thing in the meetings, but lifted a gold pen in his pudgy hand, fingering it like worry beads. "What if the Venezuelan fails or if one of the teens doesn't come through or—"

What if you got laid by a woman who looked like Josie? Vestavia wanted to counter. The percentage of possibility had to be the same. Hard to imagine Benedict the Banker controlled 20 percent of all the money transfers between the United States and overseas.

Vestavia lifted a hand to stop Benedict the Banker before he bit his lip trying to get another worry on the table. "As I explained last time, we have three teens and only need one. The other two are insurance. This is a simple plan, but a well-constructed one that will have far-reaching results."

Diablo had supported Vestavia's rise to this level and proved to be the strongest voice in the group. He cleared his throat, effectively taking the floor.

"I hope I speak for all present to say I think you've done an outstanding job of planning this next step." Diablo paused as if waiting to see if anyone would contra-

dict him before continuing. "Of all the places we tested
the biological agents in the last three years, the United
States bounced back the quickest. We'll see faster results
of future testing once we have this country in a more ten-
able position. After Friday, the world will get a firsthand
look at how the greatest industrial nation handles a crisis
with longer impact than airplanes ripping through high-
rise towers. And we shall see which of the predators on
other continents make the first move."

"Good." Vestavia held a calm face though he wanted to
smile, to enjoy the moment, but he'd celebrate for a week
with Josie at his private island. Soon. "I'm ready for the
second half of the funds." But it took a majority to move
the funds, and the four Fras in the room besides him held
proxies from the other seven not present.

"If we are all in agreement, the eleven million will be
moved in twenty-four hours." Fra Diablo passed a pointed
gaze around the table, waiting for a response from each.

Morton lifted the one finger again and nodded.
Dempsey tapped his pen against the leather cover to his
writing pad, but gave a dip of his head in acknowledgment.

All eyes turned to Benedict, who sighed heavily, making a production of any decision, then finally said, "I'm
agreed."

When they stood to leave, Vestavia caught the severe
glance Diablo sent him that was just as pointed and full
of warning, his message clear. *Don't make me regret supporting you.*

The men rose and filed out. All except Diablo, who
extended his hand.

When they shook, Vestavia leaned close. "There's no reason to worry, but I needed to see you today for another issue as well. I need your support for one more thing."

"What's that?" Diablo's eyes relayed his hesitance.

"A necessary death."

"Beyond what is already proposed?"

"Yes. One that is not entirely related to the event Friday, but is important to the security of our organization."

"Who? Why didn't you bring this up in the meeting so all the Fras would be included in the decision?"

Vestavia took care with his words so as not to insult a Fra directly, but they were all suspect in his book. "Because there's been an operation breach on the teens and Mirage. We have a mole working for one of our Fras who is leaking information and must be dealt with . . . *if* it isn't a Fra."

— ⁓ —

A steady flow of passengers moved past Carlos in both directions through the airport in Carcassonne. Conversation was a blurred mix of languages, but most sounded French.

He gave the second hand on his watch one extra round past ten minutes, then shook his head. Gabrielle had taken less time to shower and change before they left the cabin, so freshening up shouldn't take this long.

He'd started toward the ladies' room, one spot no man wanted to enter uninvited. With any luck, using the excuse he was checking on his traveling companion, who had been ill, would save him some grief.

As he reached the entrance, two young ladies strolled out, wheeling their suitcases behind them and chatting.

They glanced up annoyed, then their eyes widened. They ran slow gazes over him, smiled and murmured something in French with a seductive tone.

Carlos winked. They blushed and scurried off.

Right behind them, a shapely woman in a deep-cinnamon-colored skirt suit with gorgeous legs and matching short pumps exited the room. She was looking down, grumbling about something while she fiddled with a button on her coat.

A coat like Gabrielle's and pulling an identical suitcase.

Carlos hesitated in step at the same moment she stopped abruptly in front of him and looked up. He worked to find his voice. "Gabrielle?"

"Take this." She shoved the luggage handle at him, muttering, "You can pull that while I finish dressing. C'est des conneries! You should try doing all this in ten minutes."

She stalked off, then glanced to each side of her and swung around to face him. Her hair was swept up into a chic twist that showed off her high cheekbones. The angry gaze she shot him narrowed the longer she stood there waiting.

"Now what?" Her accent deepened.

Carlos caught himself and stepped forward next to her, surprised by the change that flowed over her like a thundering rain. She'd gone into the bathroom a cute, frumpy mess and emerged a polished butterfly with sharp teeth.

"You look . . . nice," he finally managed to say. Not really. She looked stunning in that getup and sexy as hell.

He bet she'd look even better out of it.

"That compliment does not negate rushing me," she snapped. "And *don't* ask me if I'm hungry."

"Are you?" He grinned. She was a bossy little thing at the oddest times.

Her answer was an indignant huff. She straightened her back and held her hand out for the handle of her luggage, pursed lips now the ripe color of a split watermelon.

All at once, he was hungry. Another look at those legs and he was starving in a way that wouldn't be sated by food.

She moved her hands toward her hips.

Carlos tensed. "Don't."

"It's okay." She stuck her hands on each hip and nothing happened, no alarm buzzed on his phone. "I moved the little bugger to a more suitable spot."

Carlos tapped a thumb against the handle of her suitcase, seeing this next couple days as a battle of wills. An annoying prospect, but with an upside. Pretentious women with snobby attitudes generally turned him off.

The more she took on the air of nobility, the less he'd have to worry about this wild attraction to her.

He passed her the handle of her suitcase. "We'll discuss that later, but don't change anything I do ever again."

That should get her back up a bit, bring out the truly obnoxious arrogance he expected from the highly born.

Instead, the air went out of Gabrielle with that one reprimand. "I'm sorry, I was just, you know, worried I would bump the thing and cause a commotion." Her eyes were skittering around anywhere but his face.

He'd embarrassed her, again. Seemed to be his specialty with her. Carlos took her chin to make her look at him. "No harm done, really."

Doubt stared back at him so he added, "I had no idea you were doing all that, but you look very pretty." Compliments fed a woman's confidence, but in this case he meant every word.

Her gaze softened. Those melon-colored lips puckered, then rounded.

Stupid comment, because now he was thinking about how attractive she really was and how much he'd like to kiss her again. She looked more kissable than she had when she woke in his arms on the first flight. Hard to imagine, but true. When she'd come out of the nightmare, he'd stared into eyes puffy from heavy sleep, hair mussed, and a face so innocent he had to remind himself why she was with him and fought with every muscle to keep from crushing his mouth to hers.

Gabrielle's lips parted. Her tongue slipped out and brushed her bottom lip, leaving a slick path.

Carlos's body clenched. This was going to be a problem.

A man wearing an overcoat made an abrupt turn next to her.

Carlos snatched Gabrielle to his side.

"You're going to wrinkle my clothes worse than the luggage has," she groused, and smoothed her jacket.

He couldn't believe how fast her mood switched from angry to hurt to irritated. "Wrinkling your clothes is the least of my concerns when someone makes a quick move near you."

She twisted, eyes searching the crowd. "Who?"

"Nobody, this time," he whispered. "But you have to be on guard from here on and do what I tell you." He gave her that last order in a nicer tone.

For all his effort, he got a droll look in return that said she was getting tired of being told what to do. This was exactly why Carlos had to escort her. Retter would have lost patience by now and intimidated her into submission, which could have turned her catatonic or screaming.

Or Retter would have seduced her to get his way.

That would have worked, but just the idea of Retter getting his hands on her in any way unleashed a black mood Carlos didn't want to identify the source of.

Korbin and Rae passed by, but Korbin slowed and ran an appraising gaze up and down Gabrielle.

That just pissed Carlos off, which didn't improve his tone when he told Gabrielle, "Let's go."

She made another huffy noise that he translated as she'd go but that he hadn't heard the end of her complaints. He nudged her toward baggage claim again.

Carlos kept stealing glances, trying to decide what was different about Gabrielle beyond her clothes, hair pinned up in a sexy twist, and the light makeup that brought out her crystal eyes.

Male heads turned, but she didn't appear to notice.

Carlos put on his aviator sunshades and scanned constantly, not really expecting a threat here, but always prepared. When she shifted toward the corral of limo drivers, he stepped ahead of her, blocking Gabrielle from a short man dressed in a tailored black suit that reeked of money.

The little man held a white card with ASCENSION below a gold crest with a flying falcon.

Gabrielle stepped up next to Carlos.

The driver said, "Mademoiselle S?"

"*Oui*, but I prefer English since my companion does not speak French fluently." Her terse tone indicated any other action would be unacceptable.

Carlos considered giving this guy a shorter nose when the driver sniffed in disdain at his not speaking the local language.

"As you wish, Mademoiselle S, and I will call ahead to inform the office of your request." The driver took over the luggage except for Gabrielle's computer bag, which Carlos kept.

He leaned close to her so the driver wouldn't hear. "You just keep impressing me."

The smile she tried to smother spread her full lips wide. The dimples winked again. She was the vision of a young, carefree, sophisticated woman in that moment, taking his breath.

A woman who might have more secrets than him.

Dangerous combination.

Carlos and Gabrielle loaded into a black stretch limo and rode silently as the car left the airport. He rarely saw cities from this vantage point. Normally he came in under the cover of darkness and left just as silently.

He had expected his cell phone to ding with incoming text messages, but when he checked, he had no signal. "Is there no cellular service here?"

"Yes, but the service has been affected this week by major repairs being made to aging towers. It will normally return quickly . . . within an hour."

When the driver headed due east instead of turning north, Gabrielle questioned his route.

"There is a detour for a repair being done on the direct route that would detain us longer than taking the road through *la cité*," the driver explained, using a local term for "the city."

A tiny gasp escaped Gabrielle and Carlos smiled at her excitement.

"The castle was built in the 1100s," she told him, quietly explaining how there had been a bloody crusade here at one time. The driver kept to the paved highway to Carcassonne and turned north, driving them past one side of the castle. Visitors walked dusty roads up to the walled fortress and towers that seemed to float above the ground in the hazy morning.

"Sixty towers and barbicans," she continued, playing his personal tour guide.

Carlos had to admit the sight of such a well-preserved medieval city with miles of walls was an incredible vision, and he'd have asked what a barbican was if not for enjoying her voice too much to interrupt. The castle took on a magical quality when she described it.

"When the apples fall and rot on the ground, it can smell like cider," she went on.

"Mmm." But Carlos was inhaling the delicate perfume she must have put on in the airport. And his sightseeing had narrowed to observing the graceful shape of her slender neck. So inviting and so damn kissable. He should have been looking at the cobbled streets and landscape, but nothing beyond the window held his attention like the woman next to him.

"This castle was supposedly the inspiration for the movie *Sleeping Beauty* and I think they used it in *Robin Hood*," she finished breathlessly as they exited Carcassonne and drove along roads snaking through an expanse of flatlands and vineyards. She sat back against the seat and added, "As grand as that is, the École d'Ascension castle is magnificent."

"Looking forward to seeing it again?" He wanted to run his finger along her neck, to feel the smooth skin.

To touch so much more.

"*Oui*," she whispered, then met his gaze. Her eyes flared for an instant. Just enough to let him know she'd picked up on his thoughts.

He silently cursed himself for letting her see that when he had more to think about than how much he wanted her. He let a blank mask drop over his face. She blinked as if she'd been confused, then shrugged.

The driver cruised northeast for the next forty minutes. Gabrielle returned to pointing out everything from flowering hedge roses to two-hundred-year-old plane trees along the narrow highway they traveled that had no shoulders. Poplar trees cut across rolling hills carpeted with vineyards before they turned down a dusty road that could use some of the rain threatening.

Even the gloomy weather couldn't dampen her spirits. When the castle housing the school came into view,

Gabrielle sat up. "It rises from the mist like something in a storybook."

"Yep, just like a fairy tale," Carlos muttered, seeing it differently. More like a logistic nightmare for Korbin and Rae, who wouldn't be able to get close. Formidable stone walls wrapped a fortress that probably covered twenty-five acres. Low-hanging clouds hovered above the castle. Not a tree grew on the land immediately surrounding the compound. Great defense strategy from back when they cleared the surrounding area so guards could see an enemy approaching.

The École d'Ascension had the distinct privilege of being one of the only private grand schools of France where heads of state and royalty had studied. The other schools were government-owned and just as exclusive.

"I used to have picnics over there when the school allowed us outside the walls with security." She pointed at where a string of trees ran alongside a stream half a kilometer away. The closest cover. "The gardens inside are wonderful, but I always wanted a fountain. I wanted a place inside with running water where I could just walk out to the courtyard anytime without security hovering."

Carlos ignored the scenery when he noticed the tremble in her fingers.

The driver was speaking into his cell phone so Carlos leaned over and whispered close to her cheek. "What are you worried about?"

She nibbled on her bottom lip, then turned her face to him and said, "I know it's silly, but I spent most of the years here terrified of being sent to LaCrosse's office, and now I'm going to face the man I worked so hard to avoid as a student." She smiled sheepishly. "He's brilliant and dedicated to the school. I make him sound like an ogre, but it was probably more his size and position that had scared us as children."

Carlos moved his hand to cover hers.

She glanced at her hand, then at him.

"It'll be okay," he whispered. "I won't leave your side."

She smiled and nodded. "I can do this."

There was the strength he'd glimpsed in her. He hoped it would be enough to keep them from being caught.

Inside the castle walls Carlos saw what Gabrielle had been trying to tell him. The gardens within view were so perfectly sculpted he wondered if the gardeners were engineers as well as artists. When the limo driver parked, Carlos stepped out and circled the car on cobblestones to open Gabrielle's door before the driver could. He got another miffed sound for that.

Carlos offered a sinister smile at the little bastard, who shrank back with a frown.

At the top of stone steps was a pair of arched oak doors with heavy black hinges and a family crest with birds scrolled on the weathered surface. When the left door swung open, a fiftyish man with a dour face and thick lips too rosy for a guy appeared. His charcoal-gray suit was no more inviting than the stern set of his graying caterpillar eyebrows. He waited patiently while Gabrielle and Carlos climbed the steps.

"Welcome, Mademoiselle Saxe," he said to her, then

turned to Carlos. "You must be her security." The slur came through in his words.

Carlos said nothing since he was the only person accompanying Gabrielle and the statement was meant to lower him to the level of hired help. Did this bunch really think their snubbing would cut him? He wanted to laugh.

"Please follow me." Their guide inclined his head and walked away with them right behind.

The hall they entered had arched ceilings over twenty feet high that were painted in trompe l'oeil, basically a bunch of butt-naked baby angels pointing at each other. Their guide wound his way through more arched walkways with elaborately carved borders gold-leafed in what was likely real gold. The place could be a museum for all the intricate craftsmanship that had gone into every piece of structure and painted surface. Chandeliers so delicately designed they reminded him of lace glass hung in every open space.

They followed the guide up blue-gray marble steps of a sweeping staircase with gold-and-black rails of vines twisted around spear-shaped vertical braces. At the upper landing, which sprawled in a semicircle with halls off each side, plush handwoven rugs with scenes of ancient France covered the floors.

More impressive was the narrow cut Carlos had detected within the arched entrance to each area they had passed through. Had to be where this school hid their security-screening device since no one had asked him to empty his pockets or her purse.

He had no gun, but living on the streets alone as a teen

had taught him how to find a weapon anywhere in any place.

A man in his late twenties with well-behaved short brown hair sat at a mahogany desk in the center of the area they'd reached. Priceless tapestries covered the walls on each side of him. He was facing a computer monitor until they neared, then he looked up and rose to his feet. He fixed a practiced smile on his clean-shaven face and dismissed their guide with a nod before he spoke.

"Mademoiselle Saxe. How nice to meet you. I'm Pierre Prudhomme." He smiled at her.

Gabrielle angled her head in polite acknowledgment. "Monsieur."

"One moment." Pierre lifted a phone receiver, spoke too softly to be heard, then hung up and ushered Gabrielle toward a door several steps away. After two taps, he opened the door and stepped back and faced her.

"Monsieur LaCrosse is expecting you and has been informed of your preference for English."

Gabrielle's posture stiffened, to the point Carlos began to wonder if she could handle the pressure sitting on her shoulders. When she entered, he stepped inside, then stood out of the way, playing the role of bodyguard with his feet apart and hands behind his back. He left the dark shades in place.

No point in spoiling their image of hired security.

LaCrosse stood behind a dark-mahogany desk with intricate inlaid designs and birds carved into the corners. The piece had to be over two hundred years old and would dwarf a smaller man. But LaCrosse was close to six feet six and wore a tree-bark-brown suit that evened out the angles on his bony frame. Thinning hair cut in short layers matched his suit color. For all the blandness of his scholarly image, green eyes sharp as a cat's took in everything with precision.

Carlos could see how this man's size alone would terrify a young girl, but Gabrielle was now an adult.

Still, he regretted putting her in this spot.

"Mademoiselle Saxe, how nice to see you again." LaCrosse stepped forward, took her hand, and pecked a polite kiss on the back of her fingers before releasing her. "I trust you traveled well?"

"Yes, *merci.*"

The hesitance in her submissive tone worried Carlos. If she failed this first test, they were screwed.

"Please, have a seat," LaCrosse said to her. "I appreciate your coming to help us with this problem. I understand you've lived somewhat reclusively for a long time."

"I'm happy to help my school," she said with plenty of sincerity. "That's why I continue the IT chat boards for your students." She shrugged out of her coat, draping it over her lap when she sat.

"Yes, yes. We're quite grateful for your assistance." LaCrosse leaned back in a high-back leather chair. "Our IT department is eager to observe as you institute the new system."

Gabrielle sat silently for a moment, then said, "I'll instruct them *after* I've completed my work."

Carlos was glad for the dark shades or LaCrosse might have caught *his* surprise, too, at her curt tone.

"You only have four days," LaCrosse pointed out.

"I see no problem," Gabrielle answered with less edge.

"Surely, you'll need assistance while making the repairs and changes," LaCrosse countered congenially, but his annoyance at being rebuffed showed.

Having others nosing around would complicate things, but Carlos would figure out how to cover for her.

"If I do, I'll inform you of such." Another sharp reply from her that wiped the smile from LaCrosse's eyes.

Carlos cut his gaze at Gabrielle. If she rebuffed this guy a little too hard, they might get tossed out on their ears. What had happened to her fear of this man?

LaCrosse leaned forward, hands clasped together in front of him. "We *prefer* that everyone be escorted while visiting here."

In other words, he would not allow Gabrielle free run of the estate.

Silence piled into the space between them while LaCrosse waited on her to acknowledge his decree, clearly not pleased with her countermanding his rules.

Gabrielle lifted her head, eyes calm and unwavering. "I came in good faith, as an alumni who walked these halls for many years unescorted. I still remember how to traverse the compound without getting lost, so I appreciate the offer of a guide, but respectfully decline."

Carlos was torn between wanting to tell her "Atta girl" and wishing he was close enough to give her a warning nudge. Didn't she realize he could keep any escort distracted while she worked? She was obviously making a valiant effort to maneuver an optimum situation, but getting tossed off the property wouldn't aid their cause.

That's when the difference in her dawned on Carlos. It was as if the clothes she'd donned beneath her coat were her armor and gave her confidence that came with her position in life.

LaCrosse studied her a moment, deliberating on something, then offered her a smile that looked as though he had a mouthful of tacks. "As you wish." He stood. "Would you like to get settled in your quarters then take a look at the system?"

"Yes, that sounds fine." Her voice had returned to that of the demure woman who had entered. She stood as LaCrosse stepped around his desk.

When he reached her, she said, "I'd like to introduce my security companion—"

"That won't be necessary," LaCrosse cut her off. "We have exceptional security and you know our six-month review protocol for allowing anyone on this property. I'll have the driver drop your man in Carcassonne and pick him up in four days when he takes you to the airport."

FIFTEEN

Gabrielle was not staying here alone.

Carlos had agreed to let her handle LaCrosse when she assured him she understood the man's personality, but it was time for him to step in. He opened his mouth to tell LaCrosse they would both stay in Carcassonne when Gabrielle pinned LaCrosse with a deadly glare.

"*What?*" She served that cutting reply with a dose of outrage. "I *thought* you were in a dire situation. That's why I dropped everything and came immediately. I do this for you and you *insult* me?"

LaCrosse's hard gaze didn't budge. "Mademoiselle Saxe—," he started in a clenched-jaw, you-must-understand tone.

"It's Mademoiselle *Tynte* Saxe." The razor edge she delivered that on was meant to cut a man off at the knees. "*The* Tynte family who have donated to this institution for almost two decades, building an entire wing for the IT department, re-creating the historic design of this structure right down to hand-cut stones. I've had two attempts on my life in the past ten years. I do not travel without personal security and took a risk just to make this trip. I assure you *your* background checks are nothing compared to my family's vetting process for my protection. Your security is much appreciated, but nothing will give me the comfort of being away from the safety of my home except my bodyguard, Mr. Delgado, to whom I expect to have the same welcome extended if you want my help. If not, I can arrange for accommodations in Carcassonne for both of us and catch a flight home tomorrow."

Sweat beaded along the smooth skin on LaCrosse's forehead.

Damn. Carlos stared at Gabrielle through new eyes. She was terrified and he knew it, but she'd given that speech with all the passion of a queen tossing a gauntlet at the feet of her worst enemy.

"Mademoiselle Sax—Tynte Saxe, I beg your pardon. I meant no insult." LaCrosse swallowed hard, his Adam's apple convulsing. His pale skin turned a greenish cast.

A verbal kick in the nuts did that to a man.

"Oh, well." Gabrielle turned to Carlos, her voice firm. "To use your favorite line, let's go." She stepped toward the door and Carlos moved ahead of her to reach for the knob.

"Wait, please." LaCrosse cleared his throat. "Allow me to make a phone call." He reached over and dialed the phone with decisive punches to each key, but his hand trembled. When someone on the other end answered, he covered his mouth and whispered tersely, shaking his head as if the other person could see him, then sighing right before he hung up.

"We can accommodate Mr. Delgado as well." He'd agreed with polite grace, but he wasn't particularly happy. Someone had him by the short hairs and was braiding them.

Carlos waited for Gabrielle to make the next move. This was her show and she'd been running it like a pro. He couldn't find the words to describe the respect he had for her at the moment.

That was one gutsy female.

She sighed dramatically and turned to face LaCrosse. "If you're sure. I wouldn't want to insult you either."

"You're positive you can get us back running in four days?"

"Perhaps sooner if things go well, but four days are the most I'll need," she assured him.

Carlos moved to the side again, guard position stance.

LaCrosse strode to the door and opened it to his assistant. "Pierre, please show Mademoiselle Saxe and her security companion to their accommodations."

A moment of surprise flickered on Pierre's face before he stood, a polite mask slapped over his pale features. "Of course. Please follow me."

Gabrielle forced her breathing not to escalate, but her blood pressure was another matter as she walked behind Pierre. Her rapidly thumping heartbeat should be loud enough to echo against the stone-and-mortar walls of the hallway and betray her false confidence. She clutched the coat in her arms to keep her hands from shaking. That whole threat to leave had been a bluff, but Carlos would not stay without her and she couldn't ruin this chance to win her freedom.

She had four days to complete her work on the computer system, then find a way to elude Carlos. The thought of leaving him knocked a massive hole in her confidence.

Could she survive without him right now?

What would he do if she did try and he caught her?

Pierre paused at a door, punching a code into a panel to unlock it, then turned to her. "This will be your quarters."

Gabrielle entered, her eyes trying to take it all in at once. This was the first time she'd ever set foot in the inner sanctum where senior staff and dignitaries stayed. The sort of suite her family would normally stay in when they traveled, but she hadn't in a long time. The ceiling soared to twelve feet. A gilt, eight-foot-wide wall-console table along the left end of the room had a Sarrancolin marble top and matching carved mirror that would overpower an average sitting room.

Gabrielle had crossed to the beveled-glass window and turned in time to see Pierre start to step forward, then pause.

Carlos lowered a dark-shade-covered gaze at Pierre.

Powerful in every respect and with a confidence Gabrielle found enviable, Carlos just stood there, pulsing with intimidation.

Pierre gulped and lifted his hand in a motion for Carlos to enter next, then followed. He cleared his throat, but his voice was a notch high. "We didn't know which bag was yours, Mademoiselle, so both were delivered here."

Gabrielle stepped back through the sitting area, decorated with seventeenth-century furnishings, ignoring for the moment the double doors that opened into what had to be the bedroom.

She hid her giddy feeling and turned a solemn demeanor to Pierre. "This will be acceptable. *Merci.*"

"Your room is across the hall," Pierre said to Carlos, and moved toward the suitcases. "Which one is yours?"

Carlos strode over as if to point it out for him, but didn't. "I stay where she stays. We'll make this work."

Pierre's appalled expression was nothing compared to what Gabrielle was feeling. Didn't Carlos realize how that would look or what the administration would think?

"But, monsieur, this is not, uh, this is not—" Pierre's worried gaze ran to her for help.

"Acceptable?" Carlos finished for him. "I'm not concerned with decorum, only her safety. Her reputation will remain intact . . . or I'll know who soiled it."

Clearly not used to dealing with an alpha male, Pierre backed up two steps.

Gabrielle had to help the poor guy or he'd have a seizure. "This is quite all right, Pierre." She walked over to Carlos and hooked her hand around his thick biceps and said, "I prefer that he stays," with just enough inflection for anyone to read between the lines that they were intimate.

Her body jumped at the mere idea of being intimate with a man like Carlos.

"If you say so," Pierre mumbled, confused. He finally regained his composure and gave them the four-digit code to open their door and dismissed himself, backing out.

Carlos chortled, then turned those dark glasses on her.

Gabrielle released his arm and let out the breath that had been strangled by the lump of fear in her throat. *"Mon Dieu . . ."*

Carlos covered her mouth and she panicked. What was wrong?

He leaned close to whisper. "Let me engage a bug jammer until I can sweep the room."

She nodded and waited while he pulled out something that looked like an iPod and pressed several buttons. Her gaze strayed to the double doors open to the bedroom where a poster bed stood with a black brocade headboard. Gold, burgundy, and black pillows embroidered with alternating colors were piled at the head of the bed covered in black silk. She might have to make a running start to reach that mattress covered in black satin. The only other thing she could see from here was a rosewood chest-on-chest.

Carlos stepped between her and the bedroom view, speaking quietly. "Okay, we can talk. What was that '*Mon Dieu*' about?"

"LaCrosse was close to a stroke when we left him." She kept her voice down just to be careful. "This might put him over the edge. I was afraid I said too much."

Carlos's smile softened. He removed his glasses and stuck them in his jacket pocket and cupped her face with his hands. "Stop fretting. You did great. Do you always wield your family name like a sledgehammer?"

His compliment stroked a balm across her fears, calming her. "No. I've never used my family's power before, but I remember how my mother would react when anyone tried to push her around. She was amazing so I just tried to act and speak the way I thought she would in my shoes. But I feel a little embarrassed at bullying a man I respect so much." Her voice trailed off with a fading memory of the woman she'd admired and lost at far too early an age.

Carlos took her hands, rubbing his thumb across the delicate skin. Her heart took off racing again for an entirely new reason.

She was alone with this gorgeous man whose touch was driving her crazy. Gabrielle leaned forward, her body taking the initiative she was terrified to consciously do.

He lowered his head slightly.

Her pulse pounded with anticipation. He was finally going to kiss her. She lifted up on her tiptoes. Her eyes fluttered closed.

Carlos froze when he realized he was an inch from kissing Gabrielle. He'd been so surprised to see her confidence fly out the door behind Pierre after that show of force in LaCrosse's office. He'd meant to comfort her by holding her cold hands until she relaxed.

She'd been pretending, and doing a damn good job of it.

Her lips were so close he could feel her fast breaths on his neck. She wanted him to kiss her. It was written all over her face, but kissing her was not part of the plan. Peeling her out of that sexy suit sure as hell wasn't part of the plan, even if she might share more about what she knew.

He'd never use a woman that way.

Welcome to four days of hell.

She moved until her hips met his.

Carlos gritted his teeth and eased back, whispering, "You ready to get to work?"

Gabrielle's eyes flew open, filled with disappointment. Then accusation. And finally, the worst blow, hurt.

Just kill me now. He wanted her, dammit, but letting her in on that would only complicate this further.

"The sooner you finish your work here, the sooner this is over with." Carlos maintained a façade of hard determination, feeling like a snake for giving her the false impression that she'd get her life back if they succeeded at finding a link between Mandy and Amelia.

He couldn't tell her Joe had lied to her.

BAD generally brought felons into custody for a short time, then they became someone else's problem.

He couldn't look at her and think felon.

Gabrielle swung away from him, grabbed the handle of her suitcase, and disappeared into the bedroom, slamming the door.

Yep, four days of hell.

Carlos sighed. He used the psuedo-iPod to search for bugs while he waited on Gabrielle to regroup and walk out of the bedroom. He found one bug, then returned it to the white marble base of a crystal sculpture centrally located on the low coffee table.

Phone had to be tapped as well.

When the door opened again, Gabrielle emerged dressed in navy slacks and a white, scooped-neck sweater. Her hair was falling loose around her shoulders in thick waves.

Everything had changed, except the hurt in her eyes.

He needed her to trust him without question while here or he couldn't protect her since neither of them knew what dangers lurked inside this ancient pile of stones.

Carlos walked over to her.

She crossed her arms and looked away.

"You forgot your earrings," he told her.

She frowned at him, lifting a hand to her ear. "What?"

He lifted his finger to his lips and pointed at the bedroom. She backed into the room and he closed the door, then ran a quick scan over the room for a bug. None.

Whoever set the bug hadn't figured on her having company.

He stepped close to her, but she backed away. He put his hands on her shoulders, holding her in place when he leaned down to whisper, "There's a listening device in the sitting area next to the phone."

She stiffened.

"Since we know where the bug is, we'll be careful. And, about earlier, I didn't mean to—"

"What? You didn't mean to what?" She turned her face to his, eyes first hopeful, then waiting to be hurt again.

Her lip trembled.

He couldn't build trust if he trounced on her feelings.

"You didn't mean to kiss me," she continued. "Why? Because I'm not good at it?"

Ah, hell.

Her forehead squeezed with a frown. "Or was there something else you had in mind to tell me? Like how you don't like having to be here with me or . . ." Her voice was turning more heartbroken by the minute. "Or how I'm not your type—"

The job had nothing to do with what he had in mind.

"I didn't mean to . . . do this." He drew her into his arms and kissed her.

Her hands slipped around his back, climbing up his spine, honing the edge of desire that charged through him.

The first time he'd kissed her had been an unexpected pleasure, but nothing like this one, that burned with a fever pitch. His mouth feasted on hers, taking all she gave to him willingly. If she'd held back or hesitated, he might have been able to pull out of the spinning nosedive, but she kept urging him for more.

He pulled her closer, loving the feel of her. A real woman with curves in all the right places and perfectly shaped. His fingers lifted the back of her cashmere sweater from the waistband of her pants, then he felt the smooth skin hidden beneath the gossamer fabric. Soft, like her. He inched his fingers up her back, nothing impeding his progress.

Nothing. As in, no bra.

Carlos groaned. She was practically naked in his hands.

She rubbed her hips against him, right where he was hard as the rock walls surrounding this compound.

The surge of heat that shot up through his groin shook him.

She wanted this as much as he did, so why not?

Clearly, the wrong brain had taken over doing the thinking.

Her hands moved between them, clutching at his

shirt, turning him on more even though her movements were awkward at times as if she had little experience. Definite turn-on.

He'd had women who knew every way to touch a man.

Gabrielle was fresh and eager in a way that felt innocent.

She lifted the bottom of his shirt. Her delicate hands sent shivers up his spine with the way she touched his abs, lightly, then more boldly. She shoved the material up farther and lowered her head to kiss his abdomen.

Her fingers moved ahead, playfully caressing his nipples then pausing at . . . the scar on his chest.

The Anguis tattoo.

If she found out . . . what little sanity he had left gnawed its way through the desire frying his brain. He still didn't know how much she knew about the Anguis. Carlos pulled his hands quickly to her shoulders before she lifted his shirt another inch. When he set her away as gently as he could, his shirttail dropped.

Hallelujah for gravity.

Confusion glazed her eyes.

A knock sounded at the front door.

Good thing, since he did not want to answer the questions percolating behind that gaze. He didn't want to lose the ground he'd gained either. Carlos dipped his head and gave her a quick kiss, then whispered, "I'll answer the door. You straighten your clothes."

She gasped, looking down at herself, where the worst part was her knit top pulled loose, but it bought him a quick out.

He shoved his shirttail into his pants and slipped on the shades as he strode to the door, then opened it. "Yes?"

Pierre was back. "Is Mademoiselle ready?" He tried to peer around Carlos.

"She'll be right out." Carlos closed the door without another word and turned as Gabrielle walked out of the bedroom, neat as a pin.

She had that look, as if she wanted to talk, but he put his finger to his lips to spare himself a conversation he really didn't want right now. He winked at her.

Gabrielle rolled her eyes. She was fully composed when he opened the door wide to reveal Pierre still standing in the same place.

"Hello, Pierre." Gabrielle stepped forward, forcing the little squirt to back up. "I'd like to see the IT center and get started."

The efficient Pierre nodded and turned to leave.

Carlos stepped out behind Gabrielle and closed the door, but when he turned around, she hadn't moved.

She covered her mouth with her palm and leaned toward Carlos, speaking for his ears only. "If you plan to stay in there with me, we're not finished with that conversation."

Sixteen

I'd like our meal sent up to the room at eight thirty," Gabrielle told Pierre, who'd written the order on a notepad as she'd dictated. She kept her step brisk, her heels snapping against the hard floors on her way back to her room.

"*Oui.* Will there be anything else for this evening?"

"No, thank you." She checked her watch. That would give her and Carlos a little over an hour when no one should bother them. She glanced back at her bodyguard, whose hard expression hadn't changed since walking out of the room seven hours ago.

What was going on behind those bloody sunshades?

At the last hallway leading to her room, Pierre peeled off in a different direction.

Carlos reached the door first, punching in the code, then let her step inside. "Stay here while I check everything."

Did he really think someone would be lurking inside?

She waited until he stepped out of the bedroom and crooked a finger for her to come to him.

She walked forward, but he stepped back into the bedroom before she reached him. When she got inside, he pulled her close to him. Gabrielle slapped both hands on his chest and shoved her face up into his.

"Not until we talk," she warned, disgusted that every nerve in her body had just jumped into high gear, ready to let him get away with kissing her again.

To get away with a lot more.

She had some pride left. No more hot kisses until he explained why he'd stopped the last time.

The only reason she could figure was that he got caught up in the moment, but wasn't interested in anything sexual with her. That possibility stung almost as bad as having him yell at her to put clothes on in the cabin.

He didn't find her physically attractive.

Carlos didn't say a word, but he didn't intimidate her either. He'd never harm her, physically. She knew that with a certainty she'd never felt about any other man, which weighed heavily in his favor when it came to kissing him.

They had been halfway to the part where they fell into bed together. She hadn't dated a man in forever, and sex had become a distant memory.

But she wanted him to feel the same heat for her.

Her moral compass spun out of control over the idea of sleeping with a man she didn't know anything about, whom he worked for, where he came from, or what would happen once this was over. But she'd married a man she knew all that about only to be treated like a bank account with legs. Roberto had used her in more ways than one, leaving her emotionally bankrupt.

Just once, she'd like to experience true passion.

But she and Carlos only had an hour, so she didn't have time for a discussion. She had to get down to business.

"We have to hurry," she started in a hushed voice.

"About that kiss—," he murmured. Was that guilt rippling through his voice?

"We don't have time for *that* right now." She almost smiled at his confusion. "First, I have to take this panic button off. When I stepped near a communication console, it buzzed and everyone looked up. I don't know why it happened. Next, I got into Amelia's records. She's expected back, at least on paper. I found the plans for this compound in the archives and the floor her room is on."

Understanding dawned in his eyes. "Stick the panic button in my bag. Put on soft-soled shoes. Tell me you're taking a nap and don't want to be bothered. Speak loud enough to be heard in the living room and use that snobby tone again."

Snobby? She curled her lip in what she hoped was a feral look.

His eyes crinkled, but he didn't laugh. "I'm not criticizing. I was impressed."

Her insides melted over the compliment. She backed out of his arms and quietly pulled her sneakers from the suitcase. Once she had those on, she took a fortifying breath before speaking loud enough for anyone listening to hear.

"Jet lag is catching up to me. I need a nap and I *don't* want to be disturbed."

Carlos walked out into the living room so she followed him. He closed the bedroom door with a solid thump, then pulled her over to the powder room and closed that door softly once they were both inside.

"This room is safe. What about the plans?" he asked.

"When the IT center was built, the engineers needed the plans so they could run additional power and so forth. I recall a worker talking about how they couldn't set a beam in one spot because of the underground tunnels. So I dug around for the plans today and found how the wires had been run underground between this building and student housing for women. I think they took the easy way and ran the wiring through the tunnels."

"Okay, so what does that do for us?"

She cocked her head in a smug angle. "While you were looking all hot and dangerous outside the glass window to the IT center, I was locating Amelia's room and creating a loop for the security cameras we'd pass. She's in the high-priority residence area, same section where Linette and I stayed. If we're quick, we can check out the room to see if she's coming back, but they'll become suspicious if the camera loops run too long. We may see some students since this is mealtime, but once they shut the building for the night, security walks the halls."

"Will you be able to tell if anything looks wrong about the room?"

"Yes. When Linette left without notice, her half of our room was clean within a day. If Amelia is gone against her will, I'm thinking at least one-half of the room will be spotless."

"Good idea. Nice job."

"Thanks." She preened inside and started to reach for the handle when he said, "Hot and dangerous?"

Gabrielle cut her eyes up at him. "Like you weren't playing up the sexy bodyguard bit to the hilt for the females ogling you?"

"Just doing my job." His eyes crinkled with humor that downplayed the stern frown he gave her, then his face turned all serious. "Tell me how we get to the tunnel."

She explained the back way to the stairs and the room where the access point to the tunnel should be if it was still there.

"What about the code to our door?" he asked.

She smiled. "I've set it so we can bypass security by keying in a secondary code that will not show up on their panel. But the original code will still go through if someone tries to come in."

"I'll leave a set of eyes to catch anyone who might try, but I doubt they'll bother Mademoiselle Tynte Saxe." He winked and her blood pressure spiked. "The minute we step out of here, don't say a word and do everything I tell you to do."

"Like that ever changes?"

Carlos ignored Gabrielle's jab and took her hand, opening the door, then leading her into the living room, where he positioned her next to the exit door. He didn't like her ditching the panic button, but they didn't need to draw attention either. He was not letting her out of arm's reach from here on out, which would be an issue later tonight, but he'd face that then.

Opening the glass doors to the patio where the wind was blowing, he placed an open magazine next to the glass figurine where the bug was planted. The pages fluttered intermittently from the breeze.

He placed his psuedo-iPod on the top of a cabinet with a laser beam set to trigger the video recorder in the unit if the door opened.

At the door to the hallway, he entered the secondary code, then pulled her out behind him. Carlos kept a steady pace, moving them down the hall silent as a shadow. The door to the stairs creaked, but no one appeared in the thirty seconds he waited, so they descended three floors down to the basement. Carlos flipped on a small LED light and let Gabrielle lead him to a room that smelled as damp and musty as it looked.

"It should be on this wall." Her whisper echoed and she froze.

"No one should hear anything down here unless there's a bug, and they have no reason to put one in this spot. Stand still while I check." He shone the light across the wall, running his hands over the stones. No obvious breaks. Cobwebs reached across the walls with wispy fingers, tying several weathered trunks to a long cabinet that hit Carlos chest high. He carefully moved the trunks, checking behind them. Nothing. The cabinet weighed as much as a full refrigerator. He gripped the side at the back and put everything he had behind, pulling it away from the wall.

"There's a panel," Gabrielle whispered, softer this time.

He put a foot against the wall for leverage and strained every muscle to widen the gap to three feet. Enough for them to squeeze into the opening.

Four tarnished brass pins held the panel on the wall. He unscrewed the pins, then put the panel on the cabinet and forced his body through the angle into the dark hole. Reaching a hand behind him, he waved her forward.

She touched his fingers, letting him know she was there.

He pinched the LED light and stood up, banging his head on the hard ceiling. He held back the curse he wanted to yell and caught her by the shoulder before she made the same mistake. "Don't stand up too quick."

Wasted effort since she was able to stand without touching the ceiling.

"Must have been a damn small bunch of warriors living here back when," he muttered, drawing her along behind him.

Gabrielle whispered about the two turns they had to find to reach the student housing. Her slender hand was cold in his, gripping his fingers with all her strength.

He towed her along, wanting to chuckle at the fast flip in personality. She was a study in contradictions. One minute she was quiet and flush with embarrassment, then the next she was taking him to task over not finishing the kiss.

She had to think she'd done something wrong. He owed her an explanation or at least an apology for being a jerk.

Or a kiss. He wouldn't mind owing her a kiss if not for it sending the wrong message and crossing all over the lines of a mission. He'd never had this issue with a prisoner, and never with any one woman.

But all he had to do was hear her voice or get a whiff of her perfume or the smell of her shampoo and he wanted her.

"This is where it should be," she murmured when they reached the middle of a long passage with no doors.

At the next corner, Carlos saw a dust of light breaking through from above.

"There it is." He let go of her hand and shone his light up the opening that rose eight feet above them. Long fingers of light pierced through a grate at the top. Rows of spikes had been driven into the wall at one-foot intervals from the grate, forming a ladder that ran down to waist-high above the ground.

He pulled her close. "I can't put you up there first since I don't know what's on the other side."

"Go ahead. I can get up the ladder by myself."

"Okay, I'll wave you up as soon as it's clear. Keep this." He handed her the light and reached two rungs up so he could catch his foot on the last one, then started climbing. When he reached the grate, it appeared to open into a storage room with hot-water heaters and cleaning equipment.

He used one hand to push up on the grate, holding himself to the ladder with the other. He put his shoulder into inching the heavy metal to the side. It slid on a track.

That was the good news.

The bad news was a squeak caused by friction at one point.

He listened. No footsteps came running. Once the grate was open far enough he climbed through and turned to wave a hand at Gabrielle. All he could see was a black hole until his light flashed twice. Smart woman.

A scuffling noise was followed by a feminine grunt, then her face appeared. He took her arm and helped her onto the floor, then to her feet. She immediately started dusting off her pants. Every bit the lady until she realized he was waiting.

"Oh." She glanced around. "We go up the stairs."

"Tell me now what the upper-floor layout is before we get there so we won't have to talk."

She explained, using her hands. "Amelia's room is 210. If nothing has changed, everyone should be in their room or at the meal hall, because we were never allowed to linger in the hallways. But we might run into someone coming or going."

"We'll deal with that if it happens." Carlos took her hand and led the way. When he pulled open the wooden exit door to the second floor, the hinges whined.

She held her breath, then shoved up close to see past his shoulder. A metal door twenty feet away on his right closed off the hallway, with an alarm-code panel on the side. A sign above stated NO ACCESS.

Gabrielle whispered, "That's the staff quarters and security entrance for this building. Go left to the first turn, take a right, and 210 should be halfway down on your left."

He nodded and eased into the hallway, where hand-blown glass sconces lit the passageway, painted a dusty rose and white. Each door was still marked with metal numbers in gold. She stayed close behind Carlos, careful not to make a sound. When they turned the corner, a door shut with a click in the hallway.

Her whole body shook with the fear of getting caught. On some buried level, she was still the frightened teen who never broke a rule or took a risk while here. She'd never wanted to be taken to the "special building" at the back of the property. The place she'd once thought was for exceptional students until a rumor floated around of someone screaming out a window.

Could have been a fabricated rumor just to scare students, but she hadn't risked finding out.

Carlos reached back, taking her hand as if he'd sensed the terror she felt and knew the simple touch would ease her fears. He moved forward, forcing her from her spot. At the door to Amelia's room, he listened, then tapped his knuckles lightly. No answer. He slipped something from his pocket.

Feeling clingy all of a sudden, she released his hands so he was free to jimmy the lock while watching both ways. He opened the door and she followed him into the room.

The room hadn't changed much other than newer floral brocade linens, the priceless French Provençal antiques still elegant and feminine. Clothes were tossed across one bed just as she and Linette had done on weekends, though they'd kept the room neat all week. Nostalgia flowed over her in slow waves, reminding her of happy nights sharing dreams and sad times once Linette disappeared.

Carlos moved around the room silent as a ghost.

Both of these beds and dressers had photos, books, nail polish, hairbrushes, and other items scattered about. If one bed was Amelia's, the school still expected her to return.

A humming noise drew her attention to the loo. The fan was on, which meant . . .

Carlos stepped backward just as the commode flushed. She cringed at the noise.

He had her out in the hallway in half a second. The sound of the bathroom door opening and shutting came through the wood separating them. They barely got out fast enough.

Carlos took a step the way they had come when a door to another room between them and the turn for the stair-well opened.

A young woman with long, silky brown hair backed out of the room, closing the door behind her. She fiddled with the lock.

Something whispered from Carlos's lips that Gabrielle bet was a curse. If they went the other way, the student might report strangers in the hall and LaCrosse would immediately know who they were by the description.

If they walked forward, they'd have to interact, and any lie might hang Gabrielle if the student told someone.

She clenched Carlos's hand, fighting a panic attack. Didn't take a genius to figure the probability of escaping without notice was too small to calculate.

What would LaCrosse do if he heard about this?

Sweat trickled down her collar.

Carlos started forward, pulling her with him. Her heart bounced in her chest. What was he going to do?

When they were within ten feet of the girl, she must have heard them approaching. She swung around with a wide-eyed look that washed away when surprise burst across her face.

"Gabrielle, what are *you* doing here?"

SEVENTEEN

"Me? What are *you* doing here?" Gabrielle demanded.

Babette flung herself into Gabrielle's arms. "I sent you an e-mail that I was being exiled. Why didn't you call me?"

"Who is she?" Carlos asked at the same moment Babette said, "Who is he?"

Gabrielle took a breath, hugged her half sister to her, then looked around. "Oh, dear. Do you have a roommate?" she asked Babette quietly.

"Yes, but she's eating right now. I don't like the food in the meal hall so I keep snacks stashed here." Babette kept her voice down, picking up quickly on the conspiratorial atmosphere.

Gabrielle bet her sister's resistance to dining in the common area had more to do with being new than the food since the school had fabulous chefs.

"Let's talk in your room." Gabrielle glanced at Carlos. His lips were drawn in one unhappy line, but he nodded.

"Sure." Babette opened the door and closed it as soon as everyone was inside. "So what's going on? How did you get permission to visit? I was told that would take forever and an act of parliament to get approved."

"Babette is my sister," Gabrielle told Carlos, stalling while she came up with an answer for why she was in the dorm. She turned to Babette. "He is—"

"—her bodyguard," Carlos answered for Gabrielle, which reminded her to be careful about what she shared.

"Really?" Babette's animated face crumpled with worry. "Has that scumbag tried to hurt you?"

"No, I, uh . . ." Gabrielle looked to Carlos for help.

"Scumbag?" he asked, not helping one bloody bit.

"Roberto, her ex-husband, I told Gabby he had to be behind those attacks. Don't you know who you're protecting her from?" Babette glowered at Carlos, who cut his eyes at Gabrielle as if she should now help him.

She crossed her arms in silence.

"Yes, I do know about him," Carlos lied since Gabrielle hadn't shared that much about Roberto with him or his black-op friends. "I'm here to ensure he doesn't even try. Gabrielle's here to help the school with their computer system and wanted to see her old dorm room again, but there's a couple girls in it. This is a stuffed-up bunch so we don't want them to know we were over here. LaCrosse would probably get his panties in a wad."

What a brilliant story. Gabrielle's knees were weak with relief.

"You can trust me. I won't tell a soul, especially not the head troll." Babette delivered that with all the sincerity of an accomplice. Then her gaze softened when she took full measure of Carlos to the point of ogling.

"Don't speak disrespectfully of Monsieur LaCrosse." Annoyance heated Gabrielle's neck at yet another female drooling over Carlos, but she couldn't fault an impressionable teen.

It was *his* fault anyhow. A woman couldn't possibly take in all of him in just one glance. But her younger sister had been taught better manners. Gabrielle cleared her throat, pulling Babette's focus back to her.

"Why didn't LaCrosse mention your sister?" Carlos asked.

"He probably assumed I knew." Gabrielle shrugged.

"Do you know the girls in Gabrielle's old room?" he said in a voice as smooth as fine cognac and loaded with just as much intoxicating charm.

Gabrielle sent a sharp glance of warning at him for turning that power on her little sister.

He winked at her. The bugger.

"*I* wanted Gabrielle's room, but all Papa remembered was that she had been on this floor." Babette's attention never moved from Carlos as she pushed the long sleeves of her gray T-shirt back to her wrists and smoothed her hands over the jeans she wore. "Papa never said much about *her* time in this dungeon. Which room?"

"Two ten." Carlos smiled and Babette's cheeks flushed pink, then she looked away.

Gabrielle knew he was trying to get information while

they were here, but her maternal instincts surfaced when it came to her sisters. She kicked her foot against his ankle.

His jaw clenched, but his understanding expression never wavered except for the eyebrow he lifted.

Babette missed the silent exchange. She was staring off in thought, nibbling on the corner of a fingernail, then pulled her hand away and snapped her fingers. "Beatrice and Amelia. Beatrice and I have classes together. She'd probably let you take a look at your old room if she's there. I've only met Amelia at lunch a couple times. Talk about an extreme mouth. She's got an opinion on everything to do with civil rights."

Gabrielle smothered a chuckle. Babette had to be sorely put out to meet someone more opinionated than herself. Carlos was far better at this espionage part than her, but she picked up the thread he'd started and guided Babette back on topic.

"No, no, I don't want anyone to see me here," Gabrielle assured her sister. "So these girls are friends of yours?"

"Beatrice is okay." Always animated, Babette moved her hands up, shoving hair off her face, then she fiddled with the edge of her T-shirt and finally settled her hands at her hips, fingers hooking the top of her jeans. "Her mum is a duchess who just remarried, so she got dumped here while the *luuuv* birds have a first year alone. Bet she's here longer. Amelia's a dorfy one. Beatrice doesn't really know her since they just got moved in together. I'm betting Amelia probably got tossed by her last roomie. I don't want anything to do with her."

"Why?" Gabrielle asked.

"Because the one time I tried to have a conversation with her she said . . ." Babette paused then straightened her posture, lifted her chin, and pulled her hands together in front of herself emulating a formal stance that was in direct contrast with her usual slouch. She raised her voice and said in an overdone snippy accent, "Biting one's nails is a terrible habit and socially unacceptable."

Babette made a face. "I haven't missed Miss Prim and Proper Salsa one bit since she left last week. Beatrice says Amelia's okay, just programmed that way because her dad is some big-deal coffee guy in South America."

"Was there a school break last week?" Gabrielle asked conversationally.

"Not really. Beatrice and Amelia are ahead in credits for the quarter so they could take off, but Beatrice got the same answer I did when she called home to ask for a vacation—no way, no how." Babette's eyes shone with dampness, but she shook it off. "She's been stuck here with me, but Amelia got six school days off. She left with some girl who got hurt or sick while they were gone, so it sounds like her trip got screwed."

"Do you know if anyone else is gone right now?" Gabrielle asked.

"I don't know that many kids yet. Why do you want to know?"

Gabrielle cut her eyes to Carlos. Had she said too much?

He answered Babette, "Your sister is helping them cross-reference files. It seems a few high-profile students like Amelia have slipped out without permission, but that doesn't mean Amelia did. Anything you hear could help Gabrielle, make her look good to the management here so they might ask her to come back and work some more."

Gabrielle narrowed her gaze at him for raising Babette's hopes, but his trick worked to enlist her sister's help.

"I'll keep my ears open for anyone coming and going in this building."

Carlos checked his watch. "We have to get back."

Babette lost all interest in him and turned to Gabrielle with pleading eyes. "Are you coming back to see me?"

Gabrielle's heart broke at the realization she didn't have a clue if she'd be free to visit her sister again. But she wouldn't worry the child. "As soon as I can, but I've got to keep a low profile right now because of . . ." What could she say and not cause alarm?

"The scumbag," Babette finished for her, and turned to Carlos. "If he comes near her, I hope you plow his face down to his socks."

The smile of assurance Carlos gave her was outright evil. "If anyone tries to hurt her, I'll do worse than that."

Babette sighed with adoration for Carlos.

Gabrielle jerked his sleeve. "We going or not?"

"Getting testy?" he murmured.

Babette launched herself into Gabrielle's arms again. "Come back as soon as you can and call me."

"I don't have my cell phone with me," Gabrielle told her. *Because the guy you're mooning over destroyed it.*

"Why not?" Babette looked up at her worried. "What if I need to reach you?"

"We use mine when she travels," Carlos explained. "I'll give you the number."

"Good." Babette snatched up a pen and paper. "I'm ready." She jotted the numbers down, then stuck the paper in her pocket and smiled. "I won't tell a soul about this either."

"Call if you have any . . . problem." Gabrielle wanted to say *if someone tries to kidnap you*, but why should anyone want Babette?

Why should anyone want Mandy or Amelia for that matter?

Worry clawed a hole in her stomach.

"Nice to meet you," Carlos told Babette, and she almost swooned. Gabrielle wouldn't have thought the little hellion had it in her to behave so girly.

Carlos opened the dorm door and slipped out.

Gabrielle waved to Babette and rushed out behind him. They made it to the stairwell and the creaky door to the stairs was swinging closed behind them when the staff door at the end of the hall opened.

A woman shouted, "Where are you going?" Footsteps pounded in pursuit.

Carlos yanked Gabrielle's hand and flew down the stairs through pitch dark. She slipped twice but he kept her from falling. As they reached the second landing, the door above them squealed open. Carlos pressed her against the wall with his arm. She couldn't see her fingers in front of her face.

"Who's down there?" a matronly voice bellowed. A flashlight beam glowed down the center of the stairwell, but the black hole gobbled up the light. One heavy plod after another hit each step as the woman slowly descended. "Stay where you are."

That order wasn't necessary. Gabrielle was glued in place, fear paralyzing her.

Carlos opened and shut the access door to the first-floor rooms but didn't make a move to exit through them. He lifted Gabrielle and hoisted her onto his shoulder fireman-style, then tiptoed down the steps.

How did he move so easily and not make a sound?

He stopped at the basement landing when the footsteps above them reached the first floor. A radio crackled to life.

The woman above them said, "I'm in the first-floor stairwell. I heard this door open and close, but can't be sure anyone went through it. I'm going to do a room check on this floor. You search the stairwell all the way."

Gabrielle clutched at Carlos's waist to steady herself while he moved through the dark with careful but quick steps. He set her on her feet, then she heard a rustling noise as if he moved something.

"Give me back the light," he told her softly.

She dug out the small plastic case in trembling hands. "Here."

He caught her arm with one hand and took the light with the other.

A door at the top of the stairs squeaked again and slammed shut. Footsteps pounded downward much more quickly than those of the woman who had chased them.

Carlos flipped on the light, showing Gabrielle the opening to the grate. "Be careful. Don't rush."

Was he kidding? Don't rush. She swung around and he caught her under her arms as her feet floundered, trying to hit one of the spikes. Her toe caught.

The door on the landing one floor above opened and a man shouted, "Find anything?"

The answer he got was too muffled for Gabrielle to hear.

"Watch what you're doing," Carlos told her calmly as she pulled out of his grasp and moved to each lower step.

The door above slammed shut. Then the footsteps pounded downward again.

She dropped one foot at a time, clutching the spike above her as she made her way down what seemed like an endless ladder.

Carlos prayed for enough time to get them to safety and stuck the light in his pocket. He swung through the hole backward, catching the spikes with his foot. Holding the grate with one hand, he used all his strength again to lift it off the track while he slid the metal covering into place. The grate snagged on something and stopped an inch short, but he couldn't spend the time or risk the noise shoving it into place. He climbed down the last steps and dropped to the floor.

The grate screeched with the friction of metal against metal when their pursuer slid it aside.

Carlos grabbed Gabrielle and yanked her out from beneath the open shaft just before a beacon of light showered down the hole. He held her close to his chest, willing their pursuer not to climb down.

Radio noise crackled above, but he doubted the guy could transmit from this far belowground.

Carlos moved Gabrielle away and started walking slowly until he heard the guy growling and banging the grate aside.

He was following them into the tunnel.

"Stay close," Carlos whispered, then took her hand and ran. He made the first turn before a light beamed in the tunnel behind them.

The guy had to figure out which direction to go first.

Carlos hoped that would buy them enough of a head start to reach the administration building before security either caught them or called to alert the central office.

When he reached the cabinet in the basement of the administration building, he squeezed through the opening then pulled Gabrielle through.

Brisk steps heading toward them echoed through the tunnel.

Carlos gave the huge storage unit one adrenaline-powered shove and the piece flew back against the wall with a thud.

He snatched her hand and kept her moving before panic turned to shock and she stopped. If he could leave her alone, he'd have hidden her and gone on his own to draw their pursuer away. But she knew the territory and he couldn't risk letting her out of his sight.

When they reached the third floor, he towed her into the brightly lit hallway where he could pick up the pace.

And took a quick look at Gabrielle.

Her face was smudged with dirt and her hair was askew.

Eyes bright from excitement, she looked wild and free. When her gaze met his, she grinned.

Not the careful smile of earlier, but a full-fledged grin.

Carlos rushed up to the door of their room. The phone inside was ringing. He punched in the code to disengage the lock. Voices and footsteps approached from around the corner at the end of the hall, the sound bouncing against stone walls.

He whipped the door open, pulled her through, and closed it softly.

Gabrielle dove for the phone, but the ringer had silenced.

Carlos rubbed his head. Who had tried to reach them?

A knock sounded at the door.

He swung around and pointed at the bedroom, mouthing the word *shower* and rubbing himself to get the message across quickly.

A second knock sounded. She nodded and rushed out of the room as he jerked off his dusty jacket and tossed it on the floor.

Heartened to hear the shower running, Carlos slowed his breathing and opened the door with a hard-faced "What?"

"Security." A robust fellow in his midforties stood there. The school name was embroidered on the shirt half of his starched brown uniform. He had a radio hooked to his belt and a stun gun clipped in a holster. "Have you been in Student Building A tonight?"

"No."

"No one from this room was there?" the guard persisted.

The sound of a cart rolling up to the door was followed by Pierre's face next to the security personnel. "What's going on?"

Carlos caught a too casual note in Pierre's question. He was acting and not good at it. "Sounds like your security is doing a dorm check."

Pierre eyed Carlos curiously, then told the guard, "It's probably just new students testing limits. Please don't disturb Mademoiselle Saxe again."

The security guard didn't care for that suggestion, but nodded and left.

Pierre waved the older man pushing the food cart forward, then turned to Carlos. Once again, Pierre sported a superior look that Carlos would like to rearrange for him. "I called twice to say the food was ready early. Where was Mademoiselle?"

"Showering. She doesn't like to be rushed," Carlos answered as bored as he could sound considering his heartbeat was still clamoring from the run.

"Where were you?"

"Right here."

"Why didn't you answer?"

"First, it's not my job to take phone messages. Second, I don't answer her phone at home, so why should I here?" Carlos shoved his gaze over to the cart. "I'll take that."

Pierre frowned. "You don't want him to serve?"

"No." Carlos tugged the cart into the room while he blocked Pierre from moving in behind it. He swung around and stared at the pair. "Anything else?"

"I'd prefer to confirm that Mademoiselle Saxe finds everything acceptable before I leave."

"That's too bad. I prefer you not see Miss Saxe in a towel, which is her favorite way to eat a meal." Carlos did all he could to maintain a straight face at Pierre's shocked expression and the wide-eyed look of his food staff. "We'll call if we need anything." He closed the door and let out a sigh of relief as the footsteps receded.

Too close.

He retrieved his fake iPod and walked into the bedroom, scanning for bugs. Clean. And . . . the shower had ended.

"Gabrielle," he called out, then stepped toward the bathroom to let her know everything was okay. The door flew open and she rushed out wearing nothing but said towel.

"They're gone?" she asked on a hushed breath.

"Coast is clear."

He might have kept his hands off her if she hadn't burst out laughing and launched herself at him, whispering excitedly, "We did it!"

Carlos caught her as her arms went around his neck.

And the towel came loose, falling to a puddle at her feet.

Oh, man, he wanted to look, to feel, to kiss every spot. *She's off-limits.*

Gabrielle kissed him and he let her for about thirty seconds while what little control he had just sifted through his fingers faster than fine sand. Then he took over, kissing soft lips that tore apart every reason his mind dug up to stop.

A shaft of light from where she'd left the bathroom door ajar speared into the dark room.

Gabrielle tasted like toothpaste and happiness.

And every touch of her fingers said she wanted much more from him than a kiss to celebrate their daring race.

She cupped his face, kissing him back with sweetness that hit him low in the gut. He claimed her mouth over and over. He'd been in a semi-aroused state for so long her intentional rub against the front of his jeans stroked him past the point a cold shower would be of any benefit.

The growl that rumbled should have warned her.

His tongue joined hers in an erotic glide.

The need to have her floored him. She was unlike any other woman, passionate about everything. He wanted to feel that passion unleashed. He scooped her up and she curled toward him. Bashful? Two steps and he dropped her on the bed, ready to play.

She whipped the covers up and over her body, her face turned toward the mattress.

The abrupt change in her knocked his senses back into working order again. Why was she hiding herself?

The moment shifted so quickly from let's-get-naked to don't-look-at-me his brain had a chance to catch up with his body. He couldn't do this, and even if he did, not with the light on where she could see the Anguis tattoo on his chest. Carlos took a reflexive step back.

The movement drew her attention to him. "Please. Don't."

Anguish needled through her voice and tore at his heart. What was going on? He slowly moved back to the bed and knelt on the edge.

When she sat up, disillusionment filled her eyes.

Carlos didn't want to be the reason for the wounded look but knew he had to be, and that was killing him.

He pressed his palm along her cheek. "What's wrong?"

Gabrielle curled a hand around his wrist, but didn't say a thing at first, just nibbled on her lip, worried about something. She glanced away, then back at him. "I thought maybe, I mean I know I'm not . . . not like the women you probably have all the time, not a perfect shape, or sexy, but I just . . ."

She thought he wasn't interested. That he was rejecting her?

His heart ripped at the possibility he'd caused this remarkable woman to doubt herself or her attraction.

If she reached down to cup him, she'd know the truth, but if she touched him now, backing away from her would be a test he doubted he could pass.

She held his gaze silently, waiting to see what he'd do.

Watching the dejection in her face peeled his resolve one layer at a time. Most women played games, never willing to expose what they honestly thought.

Gabrielle had just laid her soul bare for him.

"I know you don't—," she mumbled, her gaze shifting away, embarrassed.

He turned her face to him with one finger. "I don't know where you got the idea you aren't exceptional, because you are."

"Sure." She dismissed his words with a dainty snort. "You don't have to lie to me."

"I'm not lying." He brushed the hair off her face.

"You don't think I'm exceptional. You made it clear

back at the cabin you weren't interested in doing . . . this . . . with me."

He shook his head. "I was trying to let you know I wouldn't take advantage of you."

"You yelled at me to go in the bathroom when I jumped off the bed that morning in the cabin." Hurt coursed through her voice and face.

Carlos played with her hair, then smoothed his hand over her cheek, hoping he was wrong but needing to know just how much damage he'd done. "And you thought I didn't like the way you looked half naked, didn't find you attractive?"

"Yes."

The tiny answer poured salt on the rip in his heart. He trailed a finger along her chin and down her neck then fanned his fingers over the delicate skin along her collarbone. He stopped just short of her breasts.

She shivered.

He met her gaze and couldn't deny her the truth. "I ran you into the bathroom so I could get my pants on without injuring myself. I was so turned on you were killing me."

She stared openmouthed at him. "Really?"

"How can you be so intelligent and dense at the same time?" he asked, smiling, then he lowered his mouth to her.

But she pulled away. "You don't have to—"

He stopped her with his hands on each side of her face. "You're right. I *don't* have to, but I want to kiss you." What would be the problem in telling her the real truth since no one knew what was going on in this room?

"In fact, I want you. Period." He covered her lips, kissing her tenderly, giving her his apology. Slipping a hand around her neck, he cradled her like the fragile treasure she was and slowly slid the silky covering away from her body.

She stared at him with a trust he didn't deserve, but intended to honor.

He eased her down onto her back, where he could savor each kiss he placed along her face, her soft throat . . . her shoulders.

If he took his time—and he planned to do just that— the room would be dark before he took off his shirt so he could avoid a discussion about the damn tattoo. He kissed her, slowly, gently, as he explored her skin. His fingers molded around her elegant shoulders, gliding along skin so smooth she could be a living crème puff.

Gabrielle gasped when he brushed lightly along her abdomen, then lower, where his fingers grazed the curls between her legs. She quivered and his body clenched at the passion simmering beneath him.

He knew without a doubt she would surprise him since nothing about this woman had been predictable from their first meeting.

And he wanted that passion, to feel this amazing woman in his arms, screaming her release.

She was half on and half off the bed. He inched his hands under her sexy bottom and scooped her into his arms, rolling over to the center of the bed.

When he stopped, she was on top of him.

Gabrielle lifted her head, staring at him with a question in her eyes.

Was she having second thoughts about this? About him?

She was from the bloodline of kings.

He was from the bloodline of killers.

"Are you sure you want to do this . . . with me?" he asked, hating the sick feeling that struck him at the thought *she* might now change her mind. But he wouldn't fault her if she backed away.

"I'm . . . not sure—," she mumbled.

"That you want to do this?" he finished.

"Oh, no." She shook her head once. "I know I want to make love with you . . . if *you're* sure?"

The tight band across his chest relaxed with that nervous admission.

She still didn't believe he wanted her?

Carlos grasped her hand and guided her fingers down to his arousal. He hissed at the contact. An ache surged in his heavy groin.

"Still wonder?" he teased, his voice husky with wanting her.

Her beautiful violet-blue eyes widened, then twinkled with happiness. How could something as simple as seeing her happy make his heart jump in joy?

She massaged her fingers along the front of his jeans, stroking his cock, experimenting with gentle pressure until he clenched his teeth against the sweet torment.

When he eased her hand away, she smiled shyly. She kissed him with tentative lips, testing, nipping, then moved to his neck. Her timid exploration drove him crazy with every second that passed waiting to feel her.

He didn't get involved with women, kept things light.

He'd probably be damned for all eternity, but he wasn't backing away.

Dainty fingers inched along his collarbone to his chest and carefully released one button from his shirt. His breath seized. He should stop her right there, but curiosity held him captive. She had an innocence he hadn't found in another adult female, an intoxicating freshness in her inexperienced moves.

But he sensed she wanted, or needed, the control, to feel the power over him. He moved his hands from her waist, letting his arms fall by his side.

Would he see the bold Gabrielle who had raced through tunnels tonight or the demure woman of sophistication who could be so reserved and proper?

Her butterfly-like touches moved down his shirt, leaving the other buttons, but pulling the shirt free before she smoothed her hands up his sides and across his chest.

He sucked in a breath and should have been ready, but when her fingers raced over his jeans to cup him again, a shock of electricity bolted through his core. He clasped her round bottom and rubbed his cock against her inquisitive fingers.

Hallelujah, the bold Gabrielle had shown up.

She unzipped his fly, delving her fingers inside, curving around him. Carlos clenched against her hungry hands and fought to remain still for as long as he could, then flipped her over.

He kissed her, his mouth urging her to not back down now.

She gripped his hair, drawing them close, her tongue meeting his, daring him to show her more.

Heat singed the air, stoking the scent of hot bodies in a primal dance. The smell of fresh bath and feminine musk clouded his senses until all he could hear, see, feel, was Gabrielle.

The room was dark as night now, except for a strip of light slicing past the almost closed bathroom door. He was past worrying about her seeing the Anguis tattoo. Doubted she even knew about it.

He could just focus on her pleasure.

His hands roamed over her, seeing every curve and soft shape as a blind sculptor. He eased his fingers between her thighs and gently played until she clenched and shuddered.

Oh, yes, she would be like no other.

He fingered the fragile folds, so sweet and delicate.

Her breathing hitched and she lifted up. Not yet.

Gabrielle tried to catch her breath. She wanted to pinch herself to be sure this was real. This gorgeous, sexy man wanted her. She held Carlos close, reveling in the feel of his embrace. He kissed her as if she were the only woman on Earth.

That he did so challenged her to take what he offered. She'd grown up believing she would marry her Prince Charming, but exchanged rings with a snake. Her dreams had been stolen along with her hope for a normal life.

She'd lived by everyone else's directives for as long as she could recall. Even her slimy ex-husband forced her to live in hiding. Didn't she deserve the chance to be intimate with a man who really wanted her? Maybe even cared about her?

Carlos had convinced her he burned for her.

He'd called her exceptional. Attractive.

Her. Naked.

Gabrielle pushed her hands down, shoving herself up to him. She unbuttoned his shirt and pushed the cloth off his arms.

He lifted up on his elbows, then shed the shirt before he circled his arms around her back and pulled her to him lovingly. She swallowed the lump that jumped into her throat. He framed her face with his hands, paused, then kissed her tenderly on her cheeks, her eyelids, barely touching her lips.

He was treating her as if he cherished her.

She'd melt all over him if he did that again.

Easing back up onto her knees, she reached down, working the jeans past his hips and freeing him. She tossed them aside.

A masculine sound raw with need escaped.

She'd never felt so wanted, so confident.

In one of his liquid moves, he was up on his knees, facing her. He pulled her forward, always keeping her close. She grasped him. The feel of velvet skin over his hard erection was pure sensual decadence. Gripping him lightly, she moved her fingers up until her thumb brushed over the damp tip.

The blitz of Spanish he muttered would have singed the ears of her language instructor. She blushed to her roots from the erotic meaning.

Gabrielle tried to smother her laugh of pleasure, but couldn't hide her joy at his earthy flattery.

"*Dios mío*, you are a she-devil come to kill me." Carlos drew a deep breath and lowered her across the bed, covering her with his wide body.

She ran her hands across the cut muscles and toned shapes.

Her fingertips brushed over a scar on his chest, just over his heart. She replaced her fingers with her lips.

He stilled.

Was the scar ugly? Why did her touching it make him uncomfortable? A scar didn't matter to her.

She moved her lips along his neck and cheek, finding his mouth and losing herself in the scorching kiss.

Black night surrounded them, heightening her senses and lowering the walls of her restraint with a man. But she'd had so little experience—if the unremarkable sex with Roberto even counted—she felt unsure of how to move forward.

So when Carlos asked her in a husky voice, "What do you want me to do?" she panicked for an answer and said, "Surprise me."

He chuckled. A low, riveting masculine sound that held a warning. "I'm not sure you want to give that suggestion to a man like me, princess."

EIGHTEEN

Princess?

Gabrielle had never cared for being treated like royalty growing up, but from Carlos's lips *princess* sounded so intimate.

An endearment.

She caught his warning about "a man like me." A man she couldn't get starry-eyed over, but she was beyond caring.

She wanted this man. Tonight was hers to take. "What's it going to take to get you deep inside me?"

He stilled, again, and tense silence swirled around them.

Had she said the wrong thing? She hated being so inexperienced, but then his fingers curved around her breast, lifting the nipple to his mouth. He suckled her and all thoughts ceased.

The burst of heat that streaked across her skin pooled between her legs.

She might die if he stopped. A low moan of yearning seeped from deep inside her chest. She clutched his shoulders, clinging to him and her sanity with the same fierce grip.

His fingers cupped her other breast, then his lips were there, his tongue torturing her nipple. She squirmed, needing more, so much more.

The nimble fingers left one breast and drew circles along her abdomen, lower, teasing the curls. She pushed up off her knees and he swiped a finger up her thigh, inside her, dipping in again and again.

Mon Dieu! She shuddered and cried out, spinning toward a flame that threatened to burn her to the core.

Then all at once he touched that point where everything in her body was now connected. He teased up and down with torturous control, so agonizingly slowly she was close to losing it. Then the movement changed to a swirling friction.

"Please, please . . ." She couldn't finish the thought. For the first time in her life, her mind was of no help.

He whispered sweet words in Spanish, assuring her she was beautiful and desired. The room filled with his ragged voice, which stirred something deep inside her. Something wholly feminine she'd never felt so completely before. His masculine smell, hot and damp from sweat glistening against his skin where her body met his.

His fingers crazed her wet heat.

She arched, strung tight with a need so demanding she expected to rip apart from head to toe.

He moved to her side, one leg hooked around hers,

spreading her legs apart. His mouth found hers, kissing hot and hard. When his tongue pushed between her lips and rushed to hers, he pressed his finger deep inside her, then pulled out, then repeated the motion, mimicking it with his tongue.

She gripped his shoulder, clinging for her life, so close to losing her mind she didn't realize he'd quit kissing her until his mouth replaced his fingers.

The tongue that had tangled with hers now brushed back and forth over her most sensitive spot. Her heart raced. A frenzy of nerves scrambled for release. She arched up.

Her body clenched tight, then shattered, free from the strain.

Stars blistered across her vision.

His tongue pressed her for more.

Unable to refuse him, she cried out again and again until her muscles quit contracting.

Spent beyond her wildest imagination, she could only lie there, her chest moving with each long, exhausted breath.

Then he was holding her, cuddling her to him the way she'd always dreamed the man she'd love would do. Carlos whispered in her ear how special she was, how hot she made him, how much he wanted her.

But he never pushed for more as he held her close while she found her way back into her body again. His big hands wrapped her against his warm chest. Gentle lips touched her forehead, her cheek, and brushed her lips.

She rubbed her hips against him like the wanton woman she was at the moment.

He answered by reaching a hand between her legs from behind to tease her, then plunged two fingers inside.

How could she want more after that?

She didn't know, but there it was.

He laid her down on the mattress. "Don't move."

"As if I could."

His deep chuckle rumbled all the way to the bathroom just before the light flashed when he opened and closed the door. Her mouth went bone-dry at the vision of his gorgeous backside in that moment.

He rummaged through something, then flipped off the light on his way back.

What had he been looking for . . .

Protection?

"Did you have a condom with you?" She was cheered and suspicious at the same time. Had he really planned on this?

"I always carry a few," he admitted, answering her unspoken question.

She heard the hesitation in his voice, as if he thought he'd insulted her. Not even.

"I would have been sorely disappointed if you hadn't." She reached blindly until her fingers encountered his sheathed erection.

The growl that followed had an edge, warning her he wouldn't hold back much longer.

She didn't want him to.

She was more than ready for him.

He kissed her, moving his lips to her ear and whispering, "*Exceptional* is too understated for you. I'll have to search for a better word."

She shut her eyes tightly, not wanting a tear to streak loose. This man could touch a place inside her she'd shielded from others for a long time. No man had ever gotten close to her, not even Roberto. She'd been too young to know the difference between love and lust the last time.

She knew the difference this time.

When Carlos moved between her legs and kissed the inside of her thighs, all sane thought fled.

She gasped, gripping fistfuls of the plush duvet. The muscles inside her legs were taut, ready to snap. His mouth moved away, kissing a path to her navel.

He leaned over her and kissed her sweetly at first, then with heat. The tip of his erection prodded her, pulsing against her slick opening. He waited, then thrust a little harder.

Warmth rushed her when he pressed deeper. She locked her legs around him. He plunged all the way inside, filling her, then pulled back.

With each stroke of him sliding deep within her, his fingers worked magic, driving her back to that edge where she wanted to leap off into oblivion again. She met him stroke for stroke, determined that he reach the same mindless plane where he was sending her.

He moved his arms to support his body above her. She clutched his biceps that flexed hard beneath her fingers, his breathing harsh.

"I need you so much," she rasped on a strained breath, then he moved one hand between them and fingered that one spot, taking her breath.

Her world broke into a thousand pieces. She cried out his name until she couldn't anymore.

With both arms supporting him, Carlos lifted away, then shoved deep, again and again, powerful strokes. He growled his release, pumping relentlessly as he climaxed. Nothing would ever be as incredible as making love to him.

Carlos shuddered, finally collapsing and rolling to the side, taking her with him so they stayed joined.

He kissed her tenderly, his lips barely touching hers.

"I need to tell you something." She ran her fingers across his face and damp forehead where she brushed a lock of hair back, wishing the lights were on so she could see his face.

"What?" he asked with a hint of concern.

"I don't just do this . . . I mean, I haven't done *this* since my divorce. Haven't really dated."

Carlos wasn't moving again, his breathing as quiet as his thoughts. "I know you aren't the kind of woman to play the field, but what stopped you from at least dating?"

"For one thing, I withdrew after divorcing Roberto and didn't want much to do with men for a while. Then I had a couple near-miss accidents that scared me so I couldn't risk meeting someone." And she sure as the devil wouldn't have met anyone who made her feel the way Carlos did, but she wasn't saying that.

"Attacks on your life by the scumbag?" Carlos interjected.

"Yes."

"Why do you think your ex is behind the accidents?"

"Because when we split up, he had an insurance policy

on me for twenty million dollars we took out right after getting married that stays in effect as long as the premiums are paid. He made it very clear what would happen if I tried to cancel it."

Carlos hugged her to him and muttered, "That bastard. But he has to know he'd be suspect even if you died in an accident."

"No, he blackmailed me into keeping a joint life-insurance policy so it looks like we have one on each other, like we had an amiable breakup and kept those policies. If I hadn't, he would have trashed me and my family in the tabloids, which would have had a devastating impact on my father."

His lips touched her forehead sweetly, then he pulled back. "You were loose as Jell-O a minute ago and now you're tense. What's wrong?"

"It's nothing."

"Tell me." He added a kiss to soften the gentle demand.

"I should have more experience by now. Roberto wasn't much of a lover and rarely came home at night. I feel like I'm stunted in this department and I hate not excelling at something."

"You've got it all wrong," he whispered in a voice so erotic goose bumps pebbled along her skin. His hands ran along her back, stroking her. "Making love with you felt like a gift being shared. As for being good at something, I'm afraid to think how much better you could be in bed."

Her glow of happiness returned.

Carlos embodied everything a woman could want in a man.

A man of honor.

A man capable of helping her take down Durand Anguis.

—⁓—

Carlos spun the shower faucets off and snagged the towel folded on a shelf above his head to dry off. The hot water had done nothing to help him regroup after the last few hours of making love to Gabrielle. He should sleep like the dead tonight, but damn his body, he wanted her again.

She wouldn't be able to walk if they went another round.

Humming on the other side of the curtain let him know Gabrielle was still in the room with him.

Guilt jumped him the minute his lust cooled. He shouldn't have stepped over that line and made love to her. Not just because of his position with BAD.

Because she was no onetime wham-bam-thank-you-ma'am kind of woman. He hadn't thought she was, but neither had he been prepared for just how much she'd come to mean to him. How much he didn't want her hurt by anyone.

Especially by him.

He'd guessed she hadn't been with many men before she told him. One other man, to be exact, and the scumbag might as well have been nonexistent if not for the emotional scars he'd left.

Carlos smiled. She'd told him to surprise her. He might have done something more provocative with an experienced woman, but his instincts had been right to warn him to take care how he made love to Gabrielle.

He never expected to care for another woman. Not after watching one die sixteen years ago.

Pain and pleasure rolled around in his heart, banging the organ with an ache for his lost love and desire for the woman who gave life to something dangerously close to joy.

He'd enjoyed plenty of women, sweet ladies he'd met who clearly wanted no more than he had—a few days of rousing sex.

But Gabrielle was not like any other woman he'd met. Tonight with her had been different in a way that was hard to ignore. She was spectacular and naïve at the same time.

He flinched over recalling how he'd thought the same thing after making love to sixteen-year-old Helena when he'd been seventeen.

Helena Suarez, Salvatore's goddaughter.

Her face had faded over the years, but not the painful memory from the last time Carlos looked into her eyes as the life seeped from her body.

And Helena had died because she'd been involved with him.

He wanted Gabrielle now with that same burning desire he'd had for Helena, but this time as a man who knew the risks they both faced.

Gabrielle would never be safe around him.

The best thing he could do to protect her would be to convince her to stop sending intel on people like Durand Anguis to security agencies and for Joe to put her into the WITSEC program if they could figure out how to do it without causing an international clash over hiding an heir to a dynasty.

That was *if* Carlos could prevent BAD from handing her over to Interpol.

"Are you going to come out?" she asked. The snicker of laughter that followed had him smiling.

"How about grabbing my phone for me?" He had to get her out of the room so he could put a shirt on. Getting into the shower without exposing the tattoo on his chest had been a chore in itself.

"Sure, sweetie."

He peeked past the curtain. The minute she cleared the door into the bedroom, he was out and pulling clothes on.

Sweetie. That was something his aunt would have said to her husband when Carlos's uncle had been alive. He'd been the only role model of a decent man in Carlos's life. His uncle had told him once that a woman was a gift from heaven to be cherished.

Gabrielle deserved so much more than he could offer, but that didn't change that she felt like his gift from heaven. He swallowed, hating the decisions racing toward him any day now. What was he going to do when it was time to take her back to Joe? He owed Joe and BAD for saving him from destroying any hope of living out his life a free man. He'd walked away from Durand when it became clear his father was grooming him to run the family business, built on murder and torture. He saw it all so clearly the day Helena died.

So how was he going to keep Gabrielle safe and fulfill his commitment to BAD? He'd face that decision when the time came, but he was not going to let anyone harm her.

But she was in danger the longer she stayed around

him because anywhere Carlos went was an unsafe zone as long as Durand lived.

"Where's your phone?" she called.

He stuck his head out the door and waited until she turned around to point at his duffel bag, then at his ear to remind her they might hear.

She mouthed *Oh* and went to the duffel. By the time she returned, he was dressed in jeans and a gray T-shirt. He combed his fingers through his hair, then closed the door and turned on the faucet for the sink before he punched Korbin's number.

Korbin answered. "Any news?"

"We confirmed that Amelia is expected back, so she hasn't disappeared yet. What have you got?"

"A stiff back from sleeping outside with an unaccommodating partner."

Carlos chuckled. "Couldn't convince her you were willing to skip ahead to the *R*'s?"

"No, I told her—"

The phone must have been snatched out of his hand because Rae was on the line. Gabrielle watched him with a curious lift of her eyebrow and arms crossed over the tank top she wore.

With no bra.

Carlos looked up at the ceiling to keep his mind off her and no bra.

Rae's tired and annoyed voice came through the line. "If I were disposed to do something so stupid as to have sex with Korbin, he'd be too bloody drained to do his job. I doubt he could handle what I have to offer."

Carlos caught something that was a cross between a comment and a growl. "What did Korbin say?"

"Some nonsense about being up for the challenge. He should keep his mind on the mission, which reminds me, Gotthard wants to talk to you and Gabrielle. How's she doing on the computers?"

"So far so good, but what she excelled at was getting us in here. She was right about the tight security clearance. They wanted to boot me, but she pulled the Tynte power card and stood her ground." He smiled at her round-eyed expression.

Gabrielle's cheeks pinked with embarrassment. Cute, definitely cute. She deserved the compliment, and he hoped her success here played in her favor when time came for Joe to make a decision on her future.

"No kidding?" Rae sounded just as impressed.

"I'll touch base as soon as we know when we're leaving."

After hanging up, Carlos told Gabrielle to wait in the bathroom. He went out to his duffel and dug out a headset rigged with a splitter so he and Gabrielle could both talk to Gotthard.

Once he had two earpieces wired into the phone, he got Gotthard on the line.

Before they started sharing data, Gabrielle asked, "How is Mandy?"

"She's still in a coma, but her vitals are better." Gotthard moved on to the job at hand. "The remote access Gabrielle set up for me while she was coding the programs is working perfectly."

Carlos looked at Gabrielle, surprised she hadn't mentioned how much she'd done for BAD while in the IT area, but they hadn't had the chance to discuss much since leaving there.

"Hunter and I have been chasing lineages," Gotthard continued. "From what we can tell, Linette, Gabrielle, Amelia, and two other students currently MIA have similar markers from their ancestry. Have you ever heard of a D-ange-ruese line in your family history, Gabrielle?"

"No, but I never searched either." She stared in thought for a moment, then snapped her fingers. "I meant to tell you two something. I don't know if this is significant or not, but Amelia, Joshua, and Evelyn have student identification numbers that identify them as being physically challenged."

"That was in their bios, but it isn't consistent with you, Mandy, and, I assume, Linette," Gotthard pointed out.

"True," Gabrielle muttered. "Was there any other connection, Gotthard?"

"Only that so far each of you with this D-ange-ruese notation is either firstborn or an only child."

"What else have you got on the teens?" Carlos asked.

"The other two not accounted for are Joshua Williams, the son of a Massachusetts congressman, and Evelyn Abrams, the daughter of an international financial broker in Israel. According to the online schedule, Amelia is due back tomorrow. Joshua was listed as visiting friends in Germany, and his passport went through the Frankfurt airport so that seems to check out. Evelyn is listed only as visiting family in Israel, and her passport was logged at the Tel Aviv airport. But Joshua and Evelyn should be checked in by tomorrow morning. All the teens, Linette, and Gabrielle have ancestries that can be traced back practically to Noah's ark, all five are exceptional students with high IQs, and all five come from families that are above reproach. All except Mandy, who was a hellion and adopted. She doesn't fit the MO."

"What do you think this means?" Gabrielle stared past Carlos's shoulder, focused, as that brain of hers processed information.

"I don't know." Gotthard sounded as though he hadn't rested in days, which was probably the case. "We can't come up with any scenario that makes sense, and that worries us the most since the Fratelli's attack last year on the U.S. never culminated in a threat or demand. Retter found leads on the attacks on the Venezuelan oil minister, but doesn't trust them."

"Why not?" Carlos put his arm around Gabrielle when she shivered.

"Retter said the leads were too easy to find and follow, like they might be planted, but the local sentiment is real, and most believe someone in the U.S. is financing the attacks. This could be all about some plan to cripple the U.S. by inflating the fuel problems in America to a crisis that rivals last fall when gas prices shot through the roof and the stock market was crazy, but no scenario makes sense so far. I'm sending photos and bios on Mandy, Amelia, Joshua, and Evelyn next, but nothing on Linette just in case Gabrielle's laptop is ever compromised. We'd have no way to warn Linette. You'll have everything in ten minutes."

Gabrielle thanked Gotthard before Carlos cut the connection. He wished the hope in her heart wasn't written so plainly across her face. Gotthard probably had as slim a possibility of finding Linette online as Gabrielle and hated the false hope his teammate's efforts spawned.

"Why don't you see what the chef whipped up for your highness?" Carlos got a wry look for that, but she headed for the living room wearing a gray tank top and black warm-up pants, damp hair hanging loose around her shoulders.

Her lack of vanity surprised him for someone with her background. The aristocrats he'd known were more like Hunter, who spent a fortune to have every hair planned out for the day.

She was so intent on snooping through the dishes he snuck up and dropped a kiss on her bare shoulder.

She jumped and almost head-butted him.

He caught her before she knocked the food off the table. "Hungry, Miss Saxe?" Then he glanced up at the shelf where the activation light glowed on his jammer, indicating they could talk freely.

When she turned around, a chocolate-covered strawberry hovered near her mouth. She held it between two fingers, and instead of biting down she ran her tongue over the tip and sucked the chocolate on the strawberry.

He went rock hard and whispered, "If you want to eat any of that food, you'd better stop teasing me."

A wicked gleam twinkled in her eyes.

Seeing her feminine confidence return warmed him. Her ex-husband had to be some kind of idiot to have gone looking for something more than this woman. He should have his head spun around to face backward just for undermining her femininity.

If the bastard ever got close to her again, he'd get more than his body rearranged.

"I am hungry," she finally admitted after eating the strawberry and licking her fingers.

If she didn't stop licking things with that tongue, he'd run out of condoms tonight. He'd only brought his standard four.

Wasn't as if he'd expected to use them on this trip.

She laughed and pulled out of his arms. "Let's eat or I *will* be . . . what do you say? Cranky?"

"That's for sure." He couldn't believe the change from timid to relaxed. Men just never realized how easily their words and actions could break a woman's spirit or power up her confidence. Gabrielle was brilliant, heir to a fortune, and had protected herself alone for the past decade.

But what had she been doing during that time to know so much about the Anguis? Where was she getting her information?

"Here's yours. I'll take a water if you don't mind." She handed him a plate loaded with carved beef that would probably melt in his mouth, a potato soufflé, green vegetables with almonds, bread, and a radish shaped into a flower.

He grabbed a cola and bottle of water from the minifridge, then sauntered over to the sofa. She bounced around the serving table, clearly delighted, as if she never dined so well. She pranced over to the sofa with a plate piled just as high as his and plopped down with the one-person buffet in her lap.

Then ate without hesitation.

When Gabrielle paused, she licked her fingers again. She lifted her head, eyes bright as those of an elf on a mischievous mission. Dimples winked when she smiled, and she covered her mouth shyly with one hand, hiding cheeks round with food.

But that she hadn't been the least bit concerned over devouring a full plate in front of him tugged on his heart.

What was he going to do about Gabrielle?

He couldn't keep her with him, but neither could he let Joe and Tee send her to Interpol. If he went against BAD, he would have no refuge left in this world because he would be hunted as a threat to the organization.

Hard decisions were as much a part of his life as breathing. He'd make this one when the time came.

———※———

An insistent buzz interrupted his sleep.

Vestavia came awake, instantly assessing his surroundings as he always did even in his Miami penthouse, as he was now. He read the caller ID, then lifted the phone receiver to stop the noise before it woke Josie.

"What's going on?" He cradled the phone against his ear with one hand and used the fingers on his other to toy with Josie's hair. She slept like an angel beside him. His contact at the École d'Ascension wouldn't have called unless he had an emergency.

"We've had a small glitch here, Fra Vestavia," his contact warned.

"As in?" Vestavia asked quietly. Josie snuggled close and burrowed into the pillow. His gaze strayed to the solid-gold pocket watch that rested on a rectangular onyx pedestal on the nightstand. A birthday gift from Josie. She'd found the antique treasure in Switzerland last year.

"Our computer systems have crashed," his contact at the school continued. "No one on our IT staff has been able to resolve the problem so we brought in outside help."

"Who?" Vestavia ignored Josie for a moment and stared out the window where stars winked in the black sky over the ocean.

"That's the good news. It's an alumni we've been in communication with for over a year about a custom program she's written that will upgrade all of our systems without needing so many fingers involved."

"So she's cleared to visit the school?"

"Absolutely. I've personally reviewed her records. She was a quiet little geek of a prominent family. Actually she was one of the D-ange-ruese line, but her mother's death was suspect so you struck her name from consideration. Her father is a respected member of the French government and rumored to be our next prime minister."

"I'm not crazy about it," Vestavia grumbled. His man inside the École d'Ascension was completely trustworthy, and the school had been a favorite Fratelli hunting ground for many generations due to its security and exclusivity, but this broke protocol. "Keep an eye on her and inform me immediately about anything unusual."

"Of course."

"What is the status of the three students?" Vestavia

asked, swinging the conversation back to his utmost concern.

"Everything is in order. They are all listed as off campus with permission, except for the last one."

"As soon as the last teenager is picked up, you'll receive word to adjust her records to reflect a voluntary leave."

"I had a call from one parent this week."

Josie stirred awake and moved over to stroke Vestavia's hard cock. He tensed, then managed to answer, "Which one?"

"Someone on staff at the Fuentes estate checked to see that Amelia's leave was approved by the school. I assured them it was, that she's an exceptional student, and that Amelia indicated when she left that she'd be visiting a friend in Germany. They accepted that without question."

"The next girl will be the last one, and everything must be in place by this Thursday," Vestavia emphasized. "The U.S. economy and infrastructure will be put to a real test by next Tuesday for the presidential elections. We'll see if this country is the superpower it contends." He hung up as Josie's skilled hands pushed any lingering stress from his body. With the success of this next test, he'd have the North American Fras agreeing to anything he suggested.

But he still had to find the mole and Mirage. An informant could be anyone close to a Fra, which included women.

Josie was the most capable woman he'd known in the order. He sucked in his breath when her lips closed around him and hoped like hell she wasn't the leak.

NINETEEN

Gabrielle sat cross-legged on the bed with her laptop propped on a pillow in her lap. "Do you want to see the files again before I delete them?" she called softly toward the half-open bathroom door between her and Carlos. The bedroom door to the living area was closed and music played in the other room, but they were both careful about saying anything loud enough for the listening device to intercept.

The door opened and he walked into the bedroom buttoning his cuffs.

Correction. He swaggered, dressed in a black cotton business shirt and black pants, looking sexy, deadly, and every bit the man who had used two more condoms last night.

The man she intended to escape.

She played a dangerous game with her sanity every time she touched him, knowing she'd have to walk away. But if that was the price to pay for this stolen time with

Carlos, so be it. Didn't she deserve a little happiness, no matter how temporary? She'd take what he'd give her now over nothing.

Gabrielle quaffed the longing she'd suffered all night, the burning desire to stay with him. Her verbal deal with Joe was as flimsy as the air it had been written on. Smart advice would be to prepare herself for the inevitable and start visualizing walking away from Carlos, disappearing without a word once she'd gained his trust.

"Why? You worried about leaving the files on your laptop?" He tucked his shirttail in his pants and finished buckling his belt. When he lifted his gaze to hers, he smiled.

How could she walk away from him? "Yes, Gotthard set up access for me at a data-vault facility where I can upload and download files from the school or my laptop. I want to send them there before I close this."

"Good idea. How much longer do you really need to get the school's computers up and running?"

Once the files were uploaded, she used a secure deletion program to overwrite the files on her local system multiple times, removing all traces of their existence from her hard drive. She'd have to be just as thorough covering her tracks when she vanished, but not until she knew Babette was safe.

Gabrielle closed the laptop. "I could be finished in two hours. I put all the necessary parts in the data vault before we left Georgia. All I have to do is launch the remaining parts of the program. And once I leave, if Gotthard needs anything more from here, he's set up to use a remote access without being detected by the IT staff." She stood and walked over to him. "What's that odd look all about?"

"You did all that yesterday?"

"Of course. I didn't know how soon we might have to leave, but I can make it still appear as though I need another two days if necessary."

"You are one hot techno babe."

The grin he gave her hugged her heart. Her stomach fluttered with a sudden happiness that left her weak in the knees. Forget about later or tomorrow for now. The only guarantee in her life was each minute she drew a breath.

"You better get dressed if you don't want the principal to call you into his office for being late," Carlos warned.

She rolled her eyes. "LaCrosse doesn't really worry me so much anymore, but there's no need to be late. So I'll get dressed." Untying the robe, she let it fall to her feet.

Leaving the only scrap of clothing she wore beneath the terry robe. Black lace panties.

"Holy mother of—" He covered his eyes with his hand. "We only have one condom left."

She sighed loud enough for him to hear. "Fine. I'm dressing." At the closet, she slowly flipped through the few choices she had. And wiggled her butt a couple times just to see if he was watching her.

Vain, yes, but she'd never had this kind of male attention.

She felt his body at her back as one hand came around to her breast and the other slid down her abdomen, weaving a finger beneath the lace of her panties and touching *the* spot as if he had it marked from last night.

Her knees did buckle this time.

He caught her and murmured, "I warned you to get dressed."

"I was ... trying ... to—," she gasped.

He lifted her back against his front and moved around until he sat down in the armed chair with her in his lap.

"Grab the chair arms and don't let go," he whispered.

She did, shivering at the promise in his voice. One condom left or not, he wanted her.

He hooked her legs with one arm, lifting them toward her chest, and slid her panties off. Tossing those aside, he lowered her legs and pushed them apart with his knees. His lips grazed her neck. The hand he held her with now toyed with her breasts. Her nipples became taut, aching buds.

When his fingers between her legs started moving, she arched at the shock that ran through her. Her knuckles tightened. She gripped the chair, every muscle in her body clenched. Her nails dug into the plush upholstery.

He whispered something erotic in Spanish, but she was lost to anything except the sensations that washed over her and vibrated between her legs. All her focus was on his fingers. He'd take her so close to the edge then pull her back, then dip one finger inside her and start it all over again.

His fingers abandoned her breast. She wanted to cry out, but his next move banished any complaint when both hands glided over her naked skin to part her legs gently. He used fingers of both hands, caressing the sensitive area he'd exposed. He teased her folds, but this time without any hint of stopping.

She started climbing higher, reaching for that pinnacle, her body bowed up for release.

He plunged another finger inside and massaged a spot deep within her.

This time she exploded with a force like she'd never felt before. She called his name, begged him not to stop. The power of her release shook her to the core. When the tremors subsided, she lay gasping and limp in his arms.

He held her wrapped within his protective embrace.

"What ..." *Take a breath.* She took two. "Did ... you ... do to me?"

He snuggled his face into her hair. "You smell like something I want for breakfast. I'd say we located your G-spot." The laughter in his voice was pure male arrogance, but she had to give the devil his due.

She hadn't even known she had a G-spot, so he'd earned the right to sound cocky.

"I'm really late now." Late and not interested in computers. She wanted to climb back into bed with him wrapped around her. Worse, she wanted to stay with him.

If only there was a way, she would.

"Good thing or we'd use that last condom. If we don't finish up here soon, I'll have to get even more creative."

That sounded like a great idea once the feeling returned to her lower half.

He stood her up, setting her on her feet, and walked her to the bathroom or she'd have fallen flat on her face. While she stood there dazed, he stepped away and returned with her underwear and some clothes on hangers.

When she took them, he caught her chin and said, "So

don't get in a huff this time when I tell you not to come out until you're dressed." He kissed her quickly and closed the door.

She stood there, her heart breaking. How could she leave this man? He embodied everything she'd wanted in a man she could care about.

Hooking the hanger on the towel rack, she chuckled sadly. In what alternative universe would she be able to be with someone like Carlos? His first responsibility was to his duty, which meant handing her back to Joe as soon as this was done.

If that was to happen, better to keep her feelings private and not let Carlos know how much he was coming to mean to her. He was only doing his duty, protecting the world. He wouldn't have met her if she hadn't put herself at risk.

Gabrielle managed to put on clothes and straighten her hair, but she was nothing more than a dressed linguine noodle that had been overcooked by the time she emerged from the bedroom to find Carlos in the living area.

"Your sister called," Carlos told her. "She's fine, just wants to talk to you." Carlos pressed a button and handed her the phone. "It's dialing her and I've got the bug jammer working right now so no one can hear what you say."

Gabrielle lifted the phone to her ear.

"Fauteur de Trouble," her sister sang out upon answering.

"I hope you are not being a troublemaker."

"Who, me?" Her sister laughed, then turned serious. "Amelia's back."

"When?"

"Late last night. I saw her at breakfast. She said she'd left with Mandy Massey on a trip, but Mandy pretended to be friends so she could use Amelia to get out of school because Mandy said her dad wouldn't have let her go to South America alone. After Mandy and Amelia hit the airport, Mandy said she had tickets to meet some guy in South America so she bugged out on Amelia. Amelia says she heard Mandy got sick and her parents pulled her out of school. Is that any help on your student list?"

"Yes, that's a great help," Gabrielle said, cursing herself for having to lie to her sister and involve her in this. "Was Amelia upset?"

"Not really. She was more interested in showing off her new haircut and clothes. I admit she looks different, maybe even a little more with it, but nothing I'd call a press conference for."

Gabrielle smiled at her sister. Babette was such a spotlight queen and considered few bright enough to shine in her presence.

"She's leaving again in two days," Babette added.

"Why?"

"I'm not sure. Amelia is prattling on worse than ever from her latest soapbox on the fuel crisis and being physically challenged. I get that and know having a prosthetic leg is not easy to deal with, but she can be so obnoxious. And the only other thing she talks about is how important her father is and how only important people come to Columbia to see him and important meetings happen there. Come on. The girl needs to expand her vocabulary. How *important* can a man be who grows coffee beans?"

"I don't know, but I'm glad you called. Thanks for helping me. I'm running late. We'll talk later, okay?" Gabrielle hung up the phone and handed it back to Carlos, then told him everything Babette had shared.

"Your sister's got a point," he admitted. "How big a deal can be going on at a coffee plantation? But we'll pass that along for Retter and his team, and that's probably more than you or I would have gotten from Amelia."

"Do you think Joshua and Evelyn would talk to us?" Gabrielle asked.

"If I spoke to a student and LaCrosse heard about it, he'd be suspicious. I'm wondering how physically challenged teens play into all this. Are they a threat or will they be a threat? That's hard to imagine. I'm not sure there's anything more to be gotten from trying to talk to the kids. The Fratelli operate too abstractly to guess at what they are doing. Maybe the teens are just a diversion."

If Carlos thought nothing else was to be gained by staying, then he would have to take her back to the States. Gabrielle wasn't ready to face whatever Joe had in mind. Her best chance at freedom lay in staying as far from the States as possible.

A knock at the door made her jump. She looked at Carlos for direction. He lifted his hand in a palm-out "be calm" signal, then strode to the door and opened it.

"What?" Carlos snapped at someone.

Gabrielle stepped closer and heard Pierre say, "Monsieur LaCrosse assumes Mademoiselle Saxe is waiting for breakfast, but we've had no order placed for her meal."

"That's because—," Carlos started.

"—I wish to eat in the main dining room," Gabrielle answered, stepping into view.

Carlos moved aside when she did, which allowed her to see yet another appalled expression on Pierre's face.

"Got a problem with that?" Carlos asked in a tone that warned Pierre there was only one correct answer.

"Of course not." Pierre's scolding gaze contradicted his words. He addressed Gabrielle. "I assume you know the route."

"*Oui, merci.*" When Pierre backed up, spun, and walked away, she turned to Carlos and laughed. "I'm afraid Pierre finds me lacking."

"If he's stupid enough to let me know, he'll find his face lacking a nose. Why do you want to eat down there?"

Her eyes twinkled. "You have to see. It's like a fine restaurant and a training ground for chefs. And the students congregate there so we might get a look at Evelyn or Joshua."

"We can do that, then go ahead and finish the programming."

She smiled so he'd assume she was ready to do just that.

Carlos secured the room to his satisfaction, then she guided them down two long hallways to a split stairwell that converged in the central dining area.

"Looks like a place you'd need reservations six months in advance for," he murmured.

She smiled, recalling when she and Linette always sat

at one of the white-linen-covered, round tables that seated four, leaving the rectangular ones for eight to the cliques of popular students. Roses in narrow glass vases and silver condiment servers still centered each table. Hand-cut glass sparkled around six massive chandeliers hung from the soaring ceiling.

"My family donated those three framed pieces by fifteenth-century artists." She pointed at each one hung on the stone walls.

"From the smell of bacon, eggs, and breads baking, I'm thinking this was a great idea." Carlos took the last couple steps until he reached the floor. "How is it everyone here isn't overweight?"

"Exercise classes are required." She stopped next to him, scanning the room. She inhaled the aroma of rich sauces billowing in the air, waking her salivary glands. Tonight she would have cassoulet, practically the national meal in France.

"What's protocol here?" he asked.

"We choose a table and they bring us food."

She led the way with Carlos at her side and had almost given up finding one of the teens when she saw a red-headed boy sitting alone at a round table.

"There's Joshua," she said under her breath. "I'll ask if we can share his table." She waited while Carlos considered her suggestion. Would he trust her to make contact with the teen?

"Okay."

She enjoyed a surge from the confidence he was placing in her and moved toward Joshua.

"May we share your table?" she asked the boy.

He lifted his head. Freckles marched across his blunt nose. Eyes too sad to be a child's stared out from under a shock of golden red hair. He ate with perfect manners, only his right hand in sight.

"Sure." Joshua stared fleetingly at her and Carlos. "Are you new teachers?"

"No, we're guests." Gabrielle smiled, hoping he'd warm up to her. "I'm installing a new computer program." She searched for a common interest. "I was a student here once."

Joshua said nothing while they settled and a waiter took their orders, then brought them coffee and tea. Joshua glanced around as though looking for someone or to see if someone was watching him.

"Have you been here long?" Gabrielle added honey to her tea, keeping her tone casual.

"Not long."

"Where does your family live?"

"America. My dad is a congressman in the United States."

Gabrielle caught herself listening to the inflection in his words. He sounded as though he was reciting information, his answers so quick and automatic.

"Is this your first time in France?" Gabrielle smiled, trying to think of more mundane questions that would not frighten him off. This had seemed simpler when she came up with the idea of trying to find the teens.

"Yes, my first time. I love the country. The school is excellent." He stopped abruptly as though that was the end of the answer. He was clearly nervous.

"I know some people in Congress," Carlos said while buttering a croissant. "Who's your dad?"

Joshua was stark white. He glanced at Gabrielle, who couldn't figure out why he was so nervous.

"I'm going to be late," Joshua muttered. "Please excuse me." He stood up, lifting the still half-full plate, and turned to leave. That's when she saw his left arm. A prosthetic forearm and hand he used awkwardly, favoring his right side.

"Thank you for allowing us to sit with you," she told him, and he said something she couldn't hear, then hurried away.

She turned to Carlos. "I feel bad asking him questions. I think we terrified him. He didn't even eat his meal."

"Something was off with him and I don't think it was just us." Carlos leaned forward and spoke low. "Now I understand even less how the kids factor into all this."

"I don't either." She kept an eye on the half of the room she could see behind Carlos and finished her omelet.

She wasn't very good at this investigation thing and had to try harder if she was ever going to find a way to prevent going back to the States yet.

"There's Evelyn three tables away," Carlos said softly, his gaze caught on someone past Gabrielle's shoulder. "She's talking on her cell phone and stacking her food like she's ready to leave."

Swinging around slowly, Gabrielle took in the room from the corner of her eye. "Got her." Another chance to find out something, but she wasn't exactly sure what she needed to ask.

Carlos placed his napkin on the table. "Let's go."

She was up and moving with him. They were ten tables away from where Evelyn sat with two more female students. Evelyn wore narrow, rectangle glasses with tortoiseshell rims, so distinct against her pale skin and light brown hair bobbed short.

Gabrielle's attention was snagged by an attractive woman with short blond hair wearing an aqua-colored pants suit approaching from the other direction. She appeared to be in her midthirties and moved with an athletic grace.

As they neared Evelyn's table, the blonde slowed and stepped behind Evelyn, who swung around and smiled.

But Gabrielle recognized the smile on Evelyn's face as a practiced one they all seemed to have as teens in a school full of strangers. A polite smile taught from the moment she could understand the word *protocol* and what family duty meant.

Gabrielle slowed her pace so they wouldn't pass the table before Evelyn was ready to leave.

"That confirms her," Carlos murmured when the blonde lifted a sweater draped over the back of Evelyn's chair and helped her put it on.

Evelyn was in a wheelchair. The blonde maneuvered Evelyn's wheelchair between tables, but something on the metal chair caught on a tablecloth and yanked the linen. Glasses tumbled.

Carlos stepped forward and broke out a smile packed full of charm. "Let me give you a hand." He squatted down and unhooked the cloth.

The blond assistant's eyes narrowed in concern then impatient acceptance.

Not the usual female response to Carlos.

When he finished disengaging the chair, the blonde lifted a perfunctory smile and thanked him before Carlos backed out of her way.

Gabrielle looked at Carlos, who moved away as though pulling back. In fact, he turned to walk away from the woman and Evelyn, tilting his head to tell Gabrielle to go, too.

"Hi, I'm Gabrielle Saxe." She ignored Carlos's frown and stepped toward the blonde. "I'm working in the IT department."

A twinge of annoyance creased the woman's forehead before she broke out a practiced smile of her own. "I'm Kathryn Collupy and this is Evelyn. Nice to meet you."

She'd given that with the clipped precision of rank and serial number in a British accent that didn't sound natural.

Mon Dieu, Gabrielle wished she were better at this. She took a wide step and angled her head to speak to Evelyn. "I went to school here a long time ago so I'm enjoying meeting students. Is this your first year?"

"I've been here three months." Evelyn's hands were folded together in her lap, posture perfect. She had a blanket over her legs down to where the toes of brown leather shoes peeked out.

"Where are you from?" Gabrielle asked the teenager.

"Israel," Evelyn answered. No enthusiasm for the conversation whatsoever.

Kathryn pushed her chair in the direction of the elevators.

Now what? Gabrielle mentally raced for something to keep the conversation going as she fell into step with Kathryn.

"Have you chosen an elective to study, something special you enjoy?" Gabrielle angled her head toward the student.

Evelyn didn't answer, studying her hands in her lap.

Kathryn cleared her throat. "She plays the violin." Then added, "Beautifully."

Gabrielle smiled at Kathryn, who ignored it. "Really? I love the violin. When do you have music class, Evelyn? I'd love to come by and hear you play." She was reaching for straws, but didn't know what else to do since Kathryn never slowed her hurried pace.

"Evelyn can't play this week," Kathryn said. "Her violin is being restrung and having a minor repair. She plays *only* her instrument. Check the school bulletin for her next recital date."

Gabrielle knew when she was being dismissed, but Mirage would never have become so well-known if she hadn't been tenacious about gaining information.

"Where are *you* from, Kathryn?"

Evelyn's assistant stopped in front of the elevator bank and pressed the button quickly. "I've lived all over Europe. My father's job required we move often."

"Really? What does he do?" Gabrielle smiled brightly in spite of the tension building from Kathryn.

The elevator doors swooshed open and Gabrielle

could swear Kathryn released a breath she'd been holding. "Please excuse us. I don't want Evelyn to be late."

Carlos walked up as the doors hushed shut. "What do you think?"

"I need to get to the IT center." Gabrielle couldn't tell him more right now, but both teens had acted withdrawn and nervous. What was Kathryn Collupy's story? Gabrielle wanted to dig into Collupy's file while she still had access with no one bothering her.

Eyes taking in everything around them first, Carlos tilted his head to the left, instructing her silently to go. He didn't say a word while she led the way to the IT center.

Where LaCrosse was waiting for her in the hallway next to the glass observation windows.

TWENTY

"Bonjour, Gabrielle."

"And good morning to you, Monsieur LaCrosse." She hoped her smile didn't appear as stiff and plastic as it felt. The IT staff moved with purpose, intent on their individual jobs on the other side of the glass window next to where she stood in the hallway.

Aviator sunshades in place and arms crossed, Carlos was doing his tough-guy bodyguard routine.

She wanted to smile when LaCrosse cast a wary gaze at Carlos and murmured, "Monsieur."

Carlos gave him a half nod of acknowledgment. No smile.

She did love how Carlos intimidated this group that had made her quake in her sneakers as a teenager, but LaCrosse was only a threat when it came to falling grades. He expected excellence and cared only about the future of his students.

"I understand you are making good progress."

LaCrosse's shoulders were tense, much like the muscles in his drawn face. More worry creased his forehead than yesterday. Was the chancellor pressing him to get her out of there quicker?

"Yes, I'm pleasantly surprised by how well this is going." She infused that with a casualness she sure as the devil didn't feel. "I think it's a testament to the exceptional job your IT team has been doing. I see many of the suggestions I've made in past resource articles instituted here."

His squared shoulders lifted with pride. The lines in his face relaxed. "That is excellent news. I'll leave you to your work." He dropped a curt nod and backed around, walking away.

As she started to move past Carlos to enter the IT center, he said, "Wait a minute." Several of the staff working on the other side of the glass window behind him had paused a moment ago to watch the exchange between her and LaCrosse.

The students were just as interested in her and Carlos.

He spoke softly, barely moving his lips. "Smile like you're happy to hear what I'm telling you."

She did, keeping her eyes on his face.

"Be very careful today," Carlos warned. "Don't take any chances. LaCrosse is clearly catching heat from someone." Carlos's shaded gaze dropped to her face.

"I will, but something was odd about the teens and that Kathryn Collupy. Evelyn seemed to wait for her assistant to speak for her. I want to see Kathryn's file."

Carlos's mouth tightened. "Like I said, just be careful. I don't trust LaCrosse one bit."

—⁓—

Carlos held the door for Gabrielle to enter their suite ahead of him. She looked over her shoulder, waiting as he'd instructed. Once he had his psuedo-iPod in place to interfere with the bug, he gave her the nod to start talking.

"I can't find anything new on the teens. But Kathryn Collupy is interesting. I found a memo on her. She was just recently approved as a replacement assistant for Evelyn only because Kathryn was already on the approved list to start here as a physical-therapy instructor later this year. When Evelyn's last assistant quit without notice, the school asked Kathryn to fill in for sixty days."

Carlos scratched his jaw. "Based on what you've said about this group's security clearance, that doesn't seem too odd."

"No, but what does is that Evelyn's last assistant quit so abruptly after four years together. I sent a message to Gotthard so he could research her. He'd left me a message in the data vault to go ahead and finish the installation, which I did. He said Joe sent instructions to you. What do we do next?"

Carlos hadn't been looking forward to this at all. "Joe wants us back in the U.S." He'd been dreading this moment when he had to really decide if he was going to hand her over to Joe and Interpol.

"What?" Her excitement deflated like an abandoned party balloon. "You're kidding. We don't have anything firm yet.

"Don't do this, Carlos." She backed up a step. "Do you really believe he's going to let me go free?"

No, worse. Unless Carlos came up with something to negotiate with—and right now they had squat—Joe was going to hand her over to Interpol, the International Criminal Police Organization supported by over 180 countries and located in France. Only the United Nations was more powerful.

"I'll take your silence to mean you either don't believe him or can't tell me." She walked away, then turned around, disappointment pouring off her. "Just tell me what you want me to do and I'll do it."

She was killing him. "You've done a great job, but—" He had a duty. That had never sounded so cold in his head.

"Then don't take me out of the picture to sit somewhere waiting for God knows how long until someone decides my fate. I don't believe Joe is going to release me." Her voice went up a notch with her fear.

"Interpol does want to meet with you." Carlos painted that less threatening than the truth—Interpol had no tolerance for electronic criminals and could turn a simple interrogation into a five-year investigation with all their bureaucratic red tape.

"You're going to give me over to *them?*" The disbelief in Gabrielle's voice slashed through him right behind the look of betrayal in her eyes. "If they find any proof of what I've done and consider it criminal, I'll go to prison and my father will be destroyed. They would never allow him to remain in his position."

Carlos wanted to lock her away somewhere safe, but not in someone else's custody.

"I—" His cell phone dinged with an incoming text

message. Carlos unclipped it, read the message, then closed the phone and looked at Gabrielle. "Gotthard wants us to pull up a message from the data vault marked URGENT."

She didn't ask why, just rushed into the bedroom to where her laptop sat on the lace doily covering the top of the dresser. Carlos followed, waiting until she booted up and accessed the storage site to read behind her.

Gotthard's message read:

> *Another assassination attempt was made on the oil minister in Venezuela. Everything points to the Salvatore family, but Retter found the shooter, who had been killed execution-style.*

Carlos frowned. "If anything, Dominic Salvatore prefers to be Switzerland when it comes to political battles or conflict with the government. He has people inside the government to do his bidding. Why would he attack the ministry?"

"I don't know." Gabrielle scrolled the message.

> *Rumors continue to surface that the US and Venezuela are trying to form a partnership for oil production. Retter says the word behind closed doors in South America is that Venezuela is going to pull out of the deal, because they think the US is behind the attacks on the oil minister and a possible coup attempt to overthrow the government. The oil minister believes his country is being used*

in a political war with our presidential elections
coming in another week. OPEC isn't any happier
and has walked away from discussions with US
representatives. If Venezuela can prove the US is
behind the attacks, OPEC will be forced to make a
show of support to appease their members.

Carlos drew a deep breath and let it out. "The Fratelli *has* to be behind this."

"What do they hope to gain?" Gabrielle asked.

"I don't know. The concern is if OPEC gets pushed in a corner, they might do something that would have a catastrophic effect on the U.S. economy. Analysts speculate something like the crash last year to the power of ten, especially if this turns into an international conflict. The viral attacks orchestrated by the Fratelli last year affected other countries, just like this fuel situation does. My guess would be whatever they're up to is much larger than just sending the U.S. into chaos, bad as that would be."

Gabrielle rubbed her arms and glanced over her shoulder at Carlos. "Do you realize how large an operation they have to be if they are behind all this?"

"Yes, and the scary part is I'm betting our estimate is not even close."

She scrolled the next part into view.

Retter thinks there's a meeting of some sort being
organized in either Columbia or Venezuela to cool
tempers, but Joe can't find out who from Washington
would go as the liaison from the US.

Carlos searched mentally for possible choices. "The obvious liaison would be someone in good standing with all parties who has a stake in the partnership succeeding. Petroleum refinery and distribution groups come to mind first. Could be someone from the State Department or the president's cabinet."

Evelyn's last personal assistant disappeared two days after she quit—looks suspicious. Joe sent a local person to canvas Linette's family home, but they couldn't get past the housekeeper. He wants any information Gabrielle has on Linette's family that will help. He'll discuss Gabrielle's status when she returns.

Gabrielle scrolled down, but that was the end. When she turned to look at Carlos, her bright blue eyes teemed with a thought. "If Joe wants information on Linette's family, take me to Bergamo."

"That's probably not what he had in mind," Carlos started.

"The minute I return, I lose any chance of proving my innocence in all this. I didn't do anything wrong, Carlos, and Joe knows it, but he doesn't want me to be his problem."

It just never got any easier. Carlos was torn between doing the job he'd sworn to do and keeping her safe from everyone. Was there any value in going to see Linette's parents? He doubted it, but he didn't want to take her back yet either.

"Post a message for Gotthard to tell Joe you've convinced me we might find out something by going to see Linette's parents in Bergamo, and if Joe agrees, I'll be in touch after we land in Milano."

She leaped into his arms, kissing his cheek. "*Merci!*"

"Don't thank me until we hear from Joe." Carlos hugged her close, hoping this wasn't a mistake he'd regret. Joe would probably agree. Durand still had a bounty on her head, and no one had found the pilot that could identify them.

She pulled out of his arms and swung around, typing with lightning keystrokes. He packed his bag while she stared at the laptop for several minutes, then hit a couple keys quickly and closed it down.

When she finished and turned to him, trust was written so clearly in her eyes, his first, last, and only thought was to protect her. "Gotthard said Joe approved the trip."

I Ie'd get a text from Joe soon, confirming that.

Carlos lifted his hand to brush his fingers across her cheek. "You call LaCrosse and tell him you're done. Get him to send a car. We'll deal with tickets at the airport."

"Okay." She rushed out to the living room where he heard her dialing and her soft voice giving LaCrosse the good news.

He hated exposing her further, but a group with an agenda that would rival that of the worst terrorist was threatening everyone's safety. BAD and America needed Gabrielle for any hope of uncovering the Fratelli's plan.

Once that was done, he'd find a way to free her even if it meant never seeing her again.

She entered the bedroom and headed for the closet as

he passed her on his way to retrieve his observation camera. When he had everything back to the original condition, Carlos walked into the bedroom.

The bed was made. Her packed suitcase sat next to his duffel bag, the open closet empty and the bathroom neat as a pin. He should have been surprised by how quickly she'd packed, but he wasn't.

Gabrielle stood in front of the window, staring out, her quiet profile sad and distant.

She'd lived in hiding for the last ten years. Not the pampered life of most women with her position and money. She had a strong core he'd only found in the agents he'd worked with at BAD. Gabrielle hadn't been trained to do this type of work, but she was gutsy and determined to do her part.

He clicked on the CD player to cover any low conversation and walked to her. She didn't turn around. He put his hands on her shoulders and kissed the back of her neck, which was tight with tension. If she weren't dressed so perfectly, he could have her relaxed in ten minutes. Probably just as well. If he was going to burn that last condom, he didn't want to rush.

In fact, the next time he peeled her down to bare skin he planned to have a case of condoms on hand.

"I also gave Gotthard a couple new things I found before finishing the installation," Gabrielle murmured.

Carlos kissed her neck and she shivered. "What else?"

"I"—Gabrielle paused for a sigh—"can't find Amelia's itinerary for when she leaves again, so I'm wondering if she's staying here after all. But I did find where Evelyn and

Joshua are scheduled to travel to the U.S. later today with a group of students. Both of their parents are in the U.S. right now, too. Amelia may be going as well, but her schedule hasn't been listed. Babette said the group of students leaving this afternoon is on a ten-country tour where they will speak to political leaders regarding the fuel crisis's impact on the physically challenged. The first stop is the U.S., then Brazil. Maybe there's a tie between the teens going to Brazil and the meeting your people think is happening in South America with the oil minister."

"We'd have a thread to follow if Amelia's father was involved in oil drilling or fuel distribution, but he's in coffee bean production."

Gabrielle shrugged. "It's all so bizarre, but I believe in Linette. I have a sick feeling these kids are targeted for something dangerous. Maybe after all these years Linette's father will have mellowed some and let her mother talk to me."

"What do you think you'll find out?" Carlos stared over her shoulder at the quiet hills and trees, wishing he could stop time long enough to enjoy a stroll with her.

Another gentle shrug. "I don't know, but maybe something that would shed light on what really happened to Linette. She's involved on some level with the people behind this, and I believe it's involuntarily."

Carlos reserved judgment since he couldn't place unquestioned faith in someone he'd never met, but Gabrielle's trust weighed heavily toward convincing him she was right.

He wrapped his arms around her, pulling this incredible woman against his chest. Holding her felt so right, so natural, as if they had always been together.

She sighed heavily.

"What?" he asked.

"Italy is just a speed bump, right? Joe will still hand me over to Interpol."

He closed his eyes, wishing for an answer that would ease her worry, but he wouldn't lie to her. That would be cruel.

"Maybe not." That was the best he could offer, for now.

Gabrielle was silent for a long time.

He turned her to face him. "What are you thinking about?"

Worried eyes met his. "It's silly, but we have to fly to Milano. Roberto lives there. I met him the first time while searching for Linette. He spends the bulk of his time there."

"Milano is a huge city and we'll be leaving the airport immediately to go north to Bergamo, but you don't have to go."

She hesitated before admitting, "You're right. He can't know that I'm there. I doubt any paparazzi even remember what I look like since I've been in hiding so many years."

She answered too quickly to suit Carlos. The idea of being that close to Roberto clearly scared Gabrielle. He closed his eyes for a second, cursing the dog for the fear he'd instilled in her. "I won't let him near you."

"Oh, *he* isn't the problem," she scoffed. "Roberto would never risk getting injured, not so much as a scratch that might lower his screen-star value. He would, however, send someone else to do his dirty work."

"Then you aren't going."

She pulled back. "Yes, I am. I'm not worried about me. I don't want to put you at risk. You won't know what to watch out for. You don't even have a gun with you."

"If that's all you're worried about, then don't." He trailed a finger along her face. "I've faced worse than anyone he could send, and I'm just as dangerous without a gun as with one. He's an amateur, and besides, he'd have to know you were here or that we're going to Milano."

"Good point." She gave Carlos a wan smile.

His insides were telling him not to take Gabrielle to Bergamo, but he had to find out what the Fratelli were planning.

Last year's viral attack appeared to have been some sort of test.

What was happening now could be the real thing. But what?

A knock at the door ended the debate. They had to go. Carlos and Gabrielle followed a rigid Pierre and a porter who carried their luggage to the waiting limousine.

LaCrosse stood near the open door to the car. "Please accept our deep appreciation for your expertise and coming to help us, Mademoiselle Tynte Saxe." He extended an envelope to her.

Gabrielle started to accept the funds, then paused, seeing LaCrosse through adult eyes. She admired him for his dedication to the school and students. She believed he would spend the money as a treat for the students if she requested it.

"I have an idea for how to use this payment," she said,

pulling her hand back. "Keep the money and build a fountain with a sitting area where the students may study outside."

"That's very generous of you," LaCrosse said with warm eyes that had Carlos wondering if this guy was as genuine as Gabrielle believed him to be. "I'll pass your request along to the Board of Regents."

"Wouldn't you rather see that money go to the endowment fund than something so frivolous?" Pierre interjected. His question was purely criticism of her idea, not a suggestion for a better donation vehicle.

LaCrosse slid a controlled glare at Pierre.

Carlos tightened his grip on her computer bag, considering how best to put the sniveling little bastard in his place for insulting her generous idea.

But Gabrielle handled it when she swung a formidable gaze at Pierre. "No, I *don't* think the endowment fund needs to be fattened. Those coffers are filled annually by alumni and their families. I think this fabulous school deserves a spectacular fountain and sitting area." She turned a softer look at LaCrosse. "Please understand that it isn't a request. I'm entrusting those funds to be spent according to my wish. There is more than enough to complete the project. I'll expect to see the fountain upon my return."

Carlos grinned, not giving a damn what any of them thought. He loved watching her in action.

LaCrosse nodded and seemed pleased with her offer. "Of course. When do you plan to return?"

Carlos told LaCrosse and Pierre, "Sharing that information would interfere with keeping her safe. Best thing you can do is get busy building that fountain." He curled one side of his mouth just to let Pierre know he enjoyed watching the scrawny pip-squeak be denied.

"We need to go," Carlos told Gabrielle, who climbed into the backseat with him.

LaCrosse shut the door without another word and the car moved forward. Once they were on the open road, the driver received a call, spoke softly, then hung up. His eyes filled the rearview mirror.

"Mademoiselle, I have a message about your flight."

Carlos hadn't made flight reservations yet. He didn't want anyone to have advance knowledge of Gabrielle's schedule. What the hell was that all about?

"Yes?" Gabrielle asked with polite interest as she lifted a notepad and pen from her purse.

"Your private jet has arrived. The pilot wanted you to know the repairs were completed sooner than he'd expected so you will not have to travel on a commercial airline."

"Excellent news. *Merci.*" She smiled until the driver's eyes disappeared from the mirror, then tapped the pad with her pen to draw Carlos's gaze down to what she'd written.

I don't have a pilot or a private jet.

TWENTY-ONE

"Park here," Carlos told the limousine driver when they reached the airport in Carcassonne. He'd tried texting Korbin and Rae for backup, but had kept getting a busy signal. Were the damn towers down being repaired again?

When the car stopped moving, Carlos added, "Keep the doors locked and stay with Miss Saxe while I do a security check."

"You think the airplane is a danger?" the driver asked.

"Not necessarily. This is just standard operating procedure." Carlos reached over and squeezed Gabrielle's hand to let her know to sit tight. He didn't like that her skin felt like ice.

"I'll be fine," she said in a voice so small he really hated to leave her.

But he'd written instructions on the pad for her to order the driver to leave immediately if anything happened or if he didn't come all the way back to the car to get her.

If he waved her to the plane, that was a sign to leave.

Carlos got out and strolled over to the lowered steps, waiting for passengers. The engines hummed and the white fuselage of the Learjet gleamed like a polished pearl.

He climbed the steps slowly, wishing he'd had a chance to alert Korbin and Rae or had a weapon in his hand, but anything other than riding to the airport as planned would have caused suspicion he didn't want to create with the school.

At the door, he stuck his head inside.

Plush and sleek. A corporate fly toy.

He'd just stepped all the way inside to inspect the cabin further when the cockpit door opened. Carlos swung around, prepared to fight.

Jake Malone, one of BAD's more versatile agents, stood with hands on hips and a grin that split his face from ear to ear. His buzz cut was hidden by a captain's hat cocked a little to the side. He'd stuffed that wide body into an airline pilot's dark-coat-and-pants uniform, perfectly outfitted right down to the white shirt and tie.

"Slick ride, huh?" Jake grinned, just as comfortable wearing official-looking gold bars on the shoulders of his jacket as jeans and sandals.

"What are you doing here?" Carlos was relieved, but annoyed.

"Joe bought some time by letting Interpol think the CIA is investigating Gabrielle, not that he had her in custody. But Interpol issued a warrant early this morning to bring Gabrielle in for questioning. Joe didn't want to risk her passport photo being recognized, especially with the false name. He figured no one at the school would question Gabrielle having a private jet."

"Good thinking. She just finished the computer work this morning. Are Korbin and Rae up to speed?"

"Gotthard sent them the message you two were going to Milano next. Korbin had problems with his cell today so he called me via sat-phone to let me know they saw you two leave a half hour ago. He and Rae should just be arriving at the commercial terminal about now."

"Would have been nice to know this wasn't someone *else* waiting for us," Carlos said, scowling.

"Hey, I got one of Joe's usual orders a couple hours ago—find a plush private jet, get here before you arrived, and get in touch with you as soon as I had everything lined up. I sent a text. Two out of three isn't bad. That's batting over .600."

"I'll remember that next time I have to cover your ass in a firefight."

"When I didn't get a confirmation back from you, I sent a message through the school. You must have gotten that or you wouldn't be here. I knew you'd at least come to see who had delivered a jet to you."

"That's some screwed-up logic, but it fits, considering the source." Carlos paused, squinting in thought. "You said *us*. Who's your copilot?"

Jake shook his head. "You don't want to know."

The door at the back of the cabin opened, revealing a bed. Jeremy Sunn strolled out, looking like a surfer parading as a pilot in his jazzed-up outfit.

He stretched, yawning. Sun-bleached hair curled along

the collar of his starched white shirt that glowed against the bronze tan. Carlos had never seen the jean-clad Jeremy in navy slacks or a pressed long-sleeved dress shirt.

"When'd *you* get a pilot's license?" Carlos asked.

Jeremy lifted his diver wristwatch into view and shrugged. "Don't know. Maybe an hour ago, depending on which time zone we're in right now." He flashed a bright grin.

Oh, hell, no. Carlos rubbed his forehead where a throb had started, then glared at Jake.

"I *said* you didn't want to know," Jake reminded him.

"I'll get Gabrielle and you get ready to fly us out of here as fast as you can," Carlos told Jake, then turned to Jeremy. "And you, don't push a button or touch a knob, not even in the bathroom."

Jeremy raised his hands in surrender. "I'm just here for decoration." He turned around and headed for the sofa facing two cushy-looking side chairs.

Carlos stopped him with, "I don't think so. We need someone to carry bags for Miss Saxe."

"Your arm broke?" Jeremy spouted off.

"No, mine's just fine. Yours may end up snapped if you don't get over here and act like someone employed by a woman who is heir to a fortune."

Jeremy scowled, but got to his feet and stormed past Carlos, who started to jerk him back inside to clarify his role.

But the minute Jeremy's feet hit the steps going down, the guy turned like a chameleon, marching ahead of Carlos with military-straight posture. That was saying something since Carlos knew Jeremy had never been near the military and they wouldn't have taken the surf hound with Jeremy's prison record.

At the car, Carlos tapped for the driver to open the locks, then he helped Gabrielle to her feet. She took in everything going on in silence.

Jeremy removed the bags from the car and stepped around to face Gabrielle. "Nice to have you back on board, Miss Saxe."

"*Merci*. Nice to meet you, too." She glanced at Carlos, but kept up the charade while he closed the trunk.

When Carlos stepped back around the limousine, Jeremy was saying, "I'm at your service, day . . . or night."

The minute the limo pulled away, Carlos leaned close and said, "Don't even think about acting on what I see in your eyes if you want to return home with all your parts in working order." Then Carlos told Gabrielle, "This is Jeremy, one of our people who you will not see again after we land."

"Nice to meet you, Gabrielle." Jeremy smirked and carried the bags to the airplane.

Gabrielle laughed. "He's sweet."

"No, he's not *sweet*." Carlos wanted to wring his neck. "Jeremy is just as dangerous as every other operative in this group, maybe more so since we never know what he's going to do. Joe must have been desperate for a copilot to send him."

"So he's a pilot, too?"

The admiration in her voice hiked Carlos's irritation another notch. "No, he's *not* a pilot. Jeremy is as much use in that cockpit as a blow-up doll. Actually, that's not fair since the blow-up doll could be used as an air bag."

At the top of the steps, Jake had the door to the cockpit open. Carlos introduced Gabrielle to Jake, saying, "He's the only real pilot on board."

"So you don't need a copilot?" Gabrielle sounded worried.

"No way."

Her shoulders relaxed.

"I've got autopilot for when I need to grab some shut-eye."

"What?" She stabbed that question at Carlos.

"Much as I hate to admit it in front of him since we barely have room for his ego in the cockpit as it is, he's the one pilot you want flying in any situation."

Jake gave her a Southern-fried grin. "Yes, ma'am. Don't worry about a thing. We'll be landing in Milano in time for lunch."

Carlos led her into the cabin, considering how Interpol's international APB had thrown a new kink into the plans. BAD played by their own rules, and Interpol had no idea whom they were dealing with.

He sent a silent thanks to Joe for the quick plan he'd created to shield Gabrielle's identity for now, but that wouldn't last.

— ∞ —

Vestavia paced the marble floor of the hallway between the kitchen and living room of his Miami penthouse. At four in the morning this was a damn lonely place without Josie.

His cell phone rang. Vestavia glared at the sound, anticipating a call from that arrogant prick in South America. He had to find Mirage before Durand did. But when he checked the caller ID, it was his contact at the École d'Ascension, telling him that Saxe woman had finished converting their computer programs to the new system.

"She finished the software conversion this quickly?" Vestavia was both glad and suspicious.

"*Oui*. She and her bodyguard just left."

"Where are they headed?"

"To Carcassonne airport, but they aren't taking a commercial flight as we'd assumed since she arrived that way. We received a call that her private jet had just been released from repairs and was waiting on them at the airport."

"I want their destination," Vestavia demanded.

"Not a problem. I have a cousin who is an air traffic controller. They are going to Milano, but I have no idea what their final destination will be."

"That's good enough," Vestavia assured him, then considered the next move. "Your IT team is satisfied they understand the program and don't need her again?"

"Absolutely. She left them an online instructional guide to troubleshoot anything that came up and default plans for if they had to reinstall any part."

"Okay, I can live with that."

A sound of relief hushed through the lines. "I'm so glad. I was worried her access to the computers presented a problem."

"No. Carry on and keep me informed, Pierre."

"Of course, Fra."

Vestavia closed his cell phone on the way to the silver leather sofa in his living room. He sat down heavily and flipped open the file on his glass coffee table. Everything on Gabrielle Saxe anyone wanted to know was in there, including the one person who could tidy up for him.

He hadn't survived this long by being careless. Allowing someone with her level of computer expertise access to the school records could be harmless, or not. He had too much depending on the successful movement of those teens to risk allowing one computer geek to walk around free who might have access to those files.

The school was only one ripe hunting ground in hundreds they'd found for D-ange-ruese connections, but Vestavia hated to lose a valuable resource.

If the Saxe woman could program all that, she could infiltrate the program for someone else, voluntarily or involuntarily. He couldn't risk that.

Sifting through the file on the Saxe woman, he stopped at the page with a list of every significant person she'd associated with since entering and leaving the school. Saxe had become a recluse after she'd almost died from two suspicious accidents. The authorities would have figured out who was behind the accidents if she'd reported them, but she'd never said a word in complaint or about the life insurance policies.

Given a chance, her ex-husband would finish the job.

Vestavia smiled. He was all about giving a person a chance.

"So does Linette's family own much property?" Carlos split his attention between Gabrielle's nervousness and guiding their rental car along the winding roads that had started to climb once they left Bergamo. She'd been so silent, speaking only to give directions.

"They have a hilltop home and land that covers probably a thousand acres." Gabrielle stared out the window where the scenery had changed over the past couple miles from a lush valley to rocky outcroppings. "Most people do not own so much land, but this estate has been in her father's family since the sixteenth century."

Gabrielle fiddled with the small gold locket that appeared as old as her friend's family home. She had laughed off her worry about being recognized by anyone as some misplaced vanity.

He thought she'd brought up a valid concern, one he'd passed on to Rae by cell phone while Gabrielle had freshened up in a restaurant ladies' room after landing. Now he had more to worry about than Gabrielle trying to take flight.

Carlos had kept a close eye on her the whole trip, but he felt pretty certain she wouldn't stray far from him now that he knew her sister Babette was at the school. Otherwise, Gabrielle would try to escape the first chance she had. He'd do the same in her shoes, but she wouldn't risk BAD using her sister as leverage.

What Gabrielle didn't know was that Carlos hadn't said a word about Babette to anyone at BAD.

"Sure you remember how to get there?" he joked. "We haven't seen another car since that last turn twenty minutes ago."

"That's because we've been on Tassone property most of that time." Gabrielle studied the landscape for a moment, then said, "Linette used to tell me how isolated she felt up there. She was fairly athletic, good at running and climbing since that was the only way she could meet other children to play games with."

"She must have been lonely to make the trek up and down these hills," Carlos muttered. "What about the Tynte home? Has it been owned by one family just as long?"

The smile left Gabrielle's eyes first. "Yes, my mother was the last Tynte heir before me."

Was. He let her ride quietly for a few minutes, then asked, "What happened to your mother?"

"She was killed . . . in an accident. I was eleven."

"Sorry, I didn't mean to open a wound." He'd lost his biological mother the day he was born even though she really didn't die for another ten years, so Carlos couldn't relate to Gabrielle's loss of a mother.

If anything happened to his aunt Maria, yes.

"No, it's fine," Gabrielle said. "I just don't think on it often."

When she didn't say more, he went for a change in subject to something he felt she could expound on. "You seem to have solid resources in South America." He glanced over when her fingers curled tight. "I'm not asking for your contacts, Gabrielle. I'd just like to hear what else you know about the Anguis. Anything you could tell me about Durand and his men could be helpful on this mission."

Her hand relaxed and she chewed on one corner of

her lip. "I hate to say this in a way that sounds flattering, but Durand's really good at what he does. He expects one hundred percent loyalty from his people."

"You know what any of his men look like?" The road he followed climbed through stunning vistas. Wide blue sky backdropped each outer curve of switchbacks up the mountain.

"Durand marks his men."

"How?" Carlos gripped the steering wheel tightly.

"With a tattoo . . . on their chest."

His heartbeat thumped faster. "What kind of tattoo?"

"I don't know, just that it's on their chest. My contacts either don't know or are afraid to tell me that much."

He exhaled slowly, relieved to finally have that answer. "Lots of men have tattoos on their chest . . . even me."

"Really? What does yours look like?"

"Snake and dagger. Had it done when I was really young," he said dismissively. "What made you research the Anguis the first time?"

"Nothing in particular."

She'd answered too quickly. Gabrielle was hiding something, but pushing her more right now would be a bad tactical move that might make her cautious about discussing more with him.

He slowed as they approached two short walls on each side of a drive made of yellow and white rocks. Naked vines spiderwebbed across the barriers. Weeds grew thick in front of the walls and sprouted between the stones of the drive.

"That's the formal entrance to the property." Her eyes lit with anticipation, then dimmed. "Linette said her father was anal about keeping the landscape perfect to the point she had to spend her Saturdays doing gardening."

Carlos drove through the entrance, proceeding slowly as Gabrielle pointed out the trees lining the drive as umbrella pines. The impressive three-story structure with pale gray stone walls and a terra-cotta roof had been tucked into the hillside for so many years the house appeared to be part of the terrain. The afternoon sun cast deep shadows beneath an arched walkway hugging one side of the house.

But again, the lack of maintenance in weathered shutters and rusting wrought iron along the gabled windows and the balconies didn't fit with Gabrielle's recollection of Linette's anal father.

Gabrielle had fallen silent again.

Carlos parked next to a tiered fountain of cherubs pouring water from one vase to another, but no water flowed through this fountain. Invasive vines crept along the statue. He circled the car and helped Gabrielle out.

When they reached the top of the decaying stone steps, he lifted the heavy, unpolished doorknocker shaped as a lion's head and banged three times.

Gabrielle told herself to focus on the mission and not the disturbing condition of the property. But worry over Linette's father kept cramping her thoughts.

The door opened to a short dumpling of a woman with more gray than black hair and a plump face that had aged well for being around sixty. *"Bon giorno. Come stai?"*

"Parla inglese?" Gabrielle asked, requesting English to be spoken.

"*Sí.* I know pretty good English."

"You are?" Gabrielle prompted.

"Housekeeper."

That couldn't be right, but Gabrielle moved ahead. "I'm looking for the Tassone family."

"Signore Tassone and his wife traveling."

"Really? Where did they go? I'd like to contact them." Gabrielle tried to imagine Linette's parents spending a nickel to travel far since her friend had often bemoaned her father's overly frugal attitude.

"They cruise Mediterranean. Signore Tassone gave strict orders. No bother him."

"Do you know when they'll return?" Gabrielle glanced past the woman, but saw little in the dark room behind the half-open door.

"Who know?" The housekeeper kept her gaze averted and shrugged. "Sometimes few weeks, sometimes few months. Just left this week."

Carlos took Gabrielle's arm. "Okay, we better hit the road if we want to get back to the airport in time for that flight."

"Yes, let's go. *Grazie,*" Gabrielle told the woman, then turned to leave.

"Signora? What your name?"

Gabrielle stopped, and as she turned to answer the woman, Carlos grabbed her hand and squeezed. She understood his message not to share her name.

"My mama was Madame Gervais. She met Signora Tassone on a cruise and asked me to stop by when I came to Milano, but Mama died six months ago. I just wanted to tell the signora hello and that Mama enjoyed their conversations. *Grazie. Bon giorno.*"

Carlos had the car in gear and was driving away from the house when he said, "So what's going on?"

"Linette's father was very tight with the family purse. Her mother rarely came to visit Linette because she got motion sick when she rode in cars for a long time, airsick on airplanes, and was too afraid of the water to cruise. I don't know who that woman was at the house, but she does not know the Tassone family."

Carlos slowed as they passed through the entrance and started back down the drive that would take over a half hour to get off the mountain. He didn't like this one way up and one way down, but that might just be a case of paranoia over having Gabrielle with him and no backup nearby.

"Linette's father would never have given up that home," Gabrielle added, wringing her hands together, then stopped and looked up at Carlos. "Linette said once when she asked her father if they could move to a new house, he told her the only way he was leaving his home was in a wooden box. Do you think they are dead?" she whispered.

"I don't know." He drove on, creeping slowly around a tight turn that leveled out for a kilometer.

She took in the tense muscles in his face. "What's wrong?"

"Nothing, but I'll feel better once we reach the main roads. Rae and Korbin should have a place scouted out for us to stay tonight in Milano. We'll give Gotthard this information and see what he can track down."

Gabrielle sat back and thought about Linette's parents, searching for a logical reason they would have changed so much.

Carlos maneuvered the car through a tight right-hand turn around a wall of rock and bushes hanging close to the road that blocked any view through the curve. On the other side was another long stretch of road with dips in the hills bordering the right side and a sheer drop-off for several hundred feet down the left.

A compact, red Italian sports car had spun out, blocking the road farther down. The driver's door was wide-open and a man slumped over the wheel.

Slowing down, Carlos parked four car lengths away.

"It looks like the driver is hurt." Gabrielle started to reach for the door handle.

"Don't get out of the car." Carlos opened his door and stepped out.

"Give me your cell phone. We need an ambulance." Gabrielle extended an open palm to him for the phone.

She realized why he hesitated. If he left her the phone and walked away, she could call someone to help her escape. To hand over his phone would show a trust in her she doubted this man allowed any person.

He didn't move to lift the phone from the clip on his belt.

Gabrielle lowered her hand, hurt more than she wanted to admit by his lack of faith.

"Here." Carlos snatched up the phone and keyed a button, then flipped it to her. She caught the phone in midair, shocked and heartened by the trust he'd shown her.

"It's ready to dial," he said, and walked away.

She pressed the emergency number that went through, but the minute the operator answered she lost the call. Gabrielle checked the connection. No cell tower.

How could she lose a tower without moving?

One of the great mysteries of cell phones.

She grumbled and reached around for her laptop out of habit before she got out of the car. She could use her blouse to make a bandage since it was warm enough to just wear the silk top she had on with her linen pants.

When she glanced ahead again, Carlos was almost to the car.

The driver sat up and jumped from the car, running for a valley in the hills lining the road.

Carlos spun and took off at a full run. His face went from furious to frightened when he saw her. "Run!"

She did, just as fast as she could. He caught up to her and grabbed her by the waist, yanking her off the ground, charging toward a dip in the hills on their side.

The explosion knocked him into the air.

She hit the ground sideways wrapped in his arms. Compression from the blast rushed across the open space like an invisible tidal wave of pressure to slam their bodies again. A second explosion shook the ground beneath her. Crashing banged and banged again right behind the explosion's initial impact.

She couldn't breathe. Gabrielle wheezed, fighting for air.

"It's okay, try to calm down." Carlos's voice sounded so far away. Her chest and lungs hurt like the devil. "You've had the wind knocked out of you," he told her.

He sat up, holding her in his arms. His face had scrapes and cuts, but he was alive. Oh, dear God, he could have died.

She tried to talk. Nothing came out.

"Shhh. Just work on breathing."

When she could finally fill her lungs, she drew a shaky breath, then nodded to let him know she was okay for the moment. He helped her stand. They turned around.

Their rental car was gone.

Vanished. Poof. No car.

"Where is it?" she croaked.

Carlos led her to the side of the road where their lovely Mercedes had rolled all the way down the ravine. The explosion must have blown it off the road.

"If I'd have stayed in the car, I'd be dead now," she whispered. Gabrielle's knees folded.

"Whoa. Don't pass out on me." Carlos lifted her into his arms and walked to the cut in the hills where he found a shady spot and sat down. "I have to assume they aren't going to shoot us or they wouldn't have gone through that much trouble to make it look like an accident. The other car had to be full of aircraft fuel for that kind of explosion."

Helicopter blades whomped overhead.

"Oh, God. Are they coming back?" Gabrielle cringed.

"No, that should be my people."

"How would they know?"

"I keyed an emergency call to Jake before I gave you the phone. Jeremy had a tracking device on this car for insurance to find us if anything happened."

"And the helicopter?"

"I told you Jake is the man to have when it comes to flying anything. He's also the one person who can confiscate something that flies at any time. Before we left, he located a small airport close to here and said he'd be prepared."

By the time they reached the airport in Milano and climbed out of the helicopter, Gabrielle was sorely missing her rental house on the lake back in Georgia.

"Want to fly somewhere else tonight?" Jake asked Carlos, then handed Jeremy their suitcases he'd kept stowed until now.

"No. Rae and Korbin have already reconned the city. I'd rather stay here where I have four of you close to help protect Gabrielle while we update the office and figure out where we're going from here."

"Okay, I volunteer for the first shift of protecting Gabrielle tonight." Jeremy walked back up giving that offer in his Boy Scout voice, but Gabrielle doubted he'd been one.

Carlos stepped close and said something to Jeremy too low for her to hear, but she'd seen his fury once already today when he'd turned around and yelled at her to run.

And he'd only played at intimidating Pierre and the others at the school.

This was not the playful side of Carlos. Veins stuck out the side of his neck. His hands were clenched into fists.

Jeremy took a step back. Probably a healthy decision.

Carlos finished whatever he was saying and just stood there, glaring at Jeremy, who lifted his hands in a confused motion. "You don't want a volunteer, fine. I'll sleep in." He backed up another couple steps.

Jake took in everything between Carlos and Jeremy without a word, but his eyebrows were staked high with interest.

Carlos drew in a breath and scratched his chin, then told Jeremy in a calmer voice, "Thanks for the offer just the same."

Jake chuckled.

Carlos cut a look at him that could maim, then turned a warm gaze to Gabrielle. "Ready to get cleaned up?"

"*Oui.*" She walked with him to another car, this one an identical copy of the silver sedan they'd lost. When they got inside, she asked, "What was that all about?"

"Just clarifying Jeremy's role in this mission." Carlos lifted his hand to her forehead, his fingers gently brushing a tender spot. "How are you doing?"

"Ouch. Fine, until you showed me I'd hit my head." She felt the lump with her fingers. Must have been adrenaline keeping the ache at bay. Now her head throbbed all at once.

"Korbin and Rae have us already checked into the hotel and they'll be in a room close by."

"I'm okay, really. I don't break easily." Not physically, but she made no guarantee about her heart.

Once she was in the car, he leaned over and clipped her seat belt, then kissed her on the cheek and straightened. "Fifteen minutes and we'll be there."

"Do you think it was Durand?" she asked, voicing the worry that had nagged her.

"Not his style."

She thought on that for a moment until it hit her whom

the person behind the attack had to be. Roberto. But how did he know she was here? And . . . would he try again?

When they reached the hotel, Carlos had her upstairs and in the bathroom showering before she could count to ten. Her relief at being here with him was short-lived when he refused to shower with her.

What had changed since this morning?

———

Carlos closed the door to the bathroom, which was modest compared to what they'd left in France, and walked into the contemporarily furnished living room with a cream-colored, overstuffed, six-foot sofa and matching chair. He flipped the wall switch, turning on a pair of circular lamps hung from the ten-foot ceiling on chains above glass and metal end tables.

A double tap sounded at the door to the suite. He opened it to Rae and Korbin, both in jeans and looking a little worn down. Camping out hadn't been a treat for either of them.

"Where's Gabrielle?" Rae walked in, looking around. Her hair was still damp from a shower. She carried a lap-top case.

"In the shower. I'll be back in a couple hours." Carlos accepted the 9 mm Korbin handed him on his way into the suite and shoved the weapon between the small of his back and his jeans, covered by a long-sleeved denim shirt he'd left untucked.

"So where are you going?" Rae asked Carlos, but the sinister glare brooding on her face shifted to Korbin. "What have you two discussed?"

Carlos didn't answer her right away. He looked at Korbin, who just shrugged and told Carlos, "You've got until daylight before I have to check in with Joe."

"Thanks. I owe you." Carlos would pay that marker in the future to Korbin without question for giving him a window of time to go off the grid tonight. And for keeping Gabrielle safe while he was gone. He turned to Rae. "I'm preventing any future accidents from happening and eliminating one person from trying to kill Gabrielle."

"It's like that, huh?" Rae's eyes lit with understanding and a gleam of warmth he wouldn't have expected from the hard-nosed operative.

Carlos could deny what she insinuated—that this was now personal for him—but he'd be wasting his breath since Rae had already put together the puzzle pieces. That was her specialty. She would have scanned Gotthard's report, which likely included Roberto's history and residences since he'd been married to Gabrielle. Rae would then have added that information to Gabrielle's barely escaping two previous mysterious accidents that had sent her into hiding, then Rae would have tied it all together with the insurance policies Gotthard had no doubt located.

Yes, Rae knew where Carlos was headed, but oddly she wasn't in his face about how dealing with Roberto had nothing to do with the BAD mission.

"Just tell Gabrielle I'll be back tonight." Carlos wished he could do this without involving others, but BAD agents backed each other in any situation. Another reason they were like no other teams on the globe. "I know it's not fair to ask this, but I'd appreciate it if we kept this between the three of us."

Rae smiled. "You got it, luv. I admire a man who fights for what is his." She sent a pointed look at Korbin.

Korbin's face was a mix of humor and confusion. Carlos did a double take at her since he'd never heard Rae make an overtly feminine comment to a male agent, and on a job to boot.

"Thanks, but she isn't mine." Carlos turned to leave.

"And here I'd given you credit for not trying to wonk me with a line of bullshit," Rae added. "Be safe. We'll take care of your woman."

Carlos sighed and left.

Gabrielle wasn't his to keep, but he intended to ensure Roberto never bothered her again.

———❧———

Gabrielle walked out of the bathroom in a terry robe provided by the hotel. She was drying her hair with a towel when she stopped in the middle of the living area.

"And where is Carlos?" she asked Rae and Korbin.

"He's busy, luv." Rae flipped through the magazine in her lap. Korbin didn't move from his reclined position. Head back, eyes shut, and breathing almost undetectable. Was he asleep?

So Carlos refused to shower with her, then just left without a word? What was going on with him? Gabrielle strangled the towel in her tight grip, sick of sly and evasive answers.

"That's not enough of an answer, *luv*," Gabrielle snapped back.

Rae paused in scanning the magazine, lifted a curious gaze, sighed, then continued flipping through the bloody magazine.

"Where. Is. He?" Gabrielle demanded.

"Busy," Korbin said without opening his eyes. "That's all we can tell you right now, but he should be back by daylight."

Cracking a bank safe would be easier than pulling anything out of those two.

"Fine." Gabrielle hated the disappointment so thick in her throat it crowded that one word. She turned back to the bedroom and closed the door.

By the time she'd finished dressing in jeans and a white sweater, Gabrielle heard what sounded like food being served. Stay in the room and pout over being blown off by Carlos or go out and see what she could squeeze out of those two in the other room while she ate?

She thought clearer on a full stomach anyhow.

Gabrielle opened the door to the succulent aroma of dishes being uncovered and placed around a table with four chairs. Rae and Korbin were already digging in.

Gabrielle sat in front of the only unclaimed meal on the table. "So you don't expect Carlos back in time to eat?"

Korbin shoved a piece of steak into his mouth, conveniently sidestepping the conversation.

"Not sure." Rae pushed each food on her plate apart so that nothing touched. "We'd like to discuss some things while he's gone."

That played into what Gabrielle had in mind. "Sure. I've got a few questions of my own."

Rae finished sorting her food and raised her vivid gaze to Gabrielle's. "I give you points for persistence, but you lose a few for being slow on the uptake. We don't answer questions. We ask them. To begin with, tell me about Babette Saxe."

Gabrielle's mouth gaped open. She might have earned Carlos's trust, but he'd lost hers by exposing Babette to this group.

—⁂—

Carlos walked softly through the ostentatious bedroom cast in twilight from the lights of Milano outside a wall of glass overlooking the city. Roberto's security was all show and little substance.

What idiot stayed in a place this vulnerable?

An arrogant one.

If Carlos had faced dealing with more than one bodyguard to gain access to the penthouse, he could just as easily have rappelled one floor to the balcony beyond the glass doors.

Hell, he could probably have jumped from the roof.

When he reached the bed, it was all he could do not to break out laughing. Roberto's dark brown hair was thick, just below his ears, styled and sprayed into the perfect shape. The guy lay spread eagle on top of red silk sheets. He wore skimpy black underwear.

Was that a thong for men? Ugh.

That *would* make what Carlos had in mind even easier to execute.

Roberto's toned form was too lightweight to have been the ripped body in that billboard ad Carlos had seen on the way here. Guess that was why they employ stuntmen and body doubles.

No stuntman to take the fall for Roberto tonight.

Carlos stepped close and flicked on the lamp next to the bed. The light glowed red. He rolled his eyes, imagining the lamp being used for mood lighting for the women this fool brought here.

"Wake up, Roberto," Carlos ordered in a normal voice.

Roberto muttered something like "Go away."

Carlos retrieved his switchblade and hit the release. He used the razor-sharp blade to flip a lock of hair onto the actor's forehead. Roberto swatted, hitting himself in the face and coming awake growling.

He glanced at Carlos, then his eyes widened. "Bruno!"

"Your bodyguard is sound asleep."

"Who are you? What do you want?" Roberto made those demands while scooting backward a few inches.

Carlos pointed the knife tip at Roberto's face, freezing the weasel in place. "Be very still or I'll be forced to contain you. Understand?"

Roberto nodded like a bobblehead doll on speed.

"Good. I'm here for one reason and don't have a lot of time to waste on this. I know about all three attacks on Gabrielle and that you're behind them. That ends now."

"I don't know what you're—"

Carlos touched the knife tip to Roberto's lips, stalling the denial.

"Remember the part about me being in a hurry?" Carlos lifted the knife from Roberto's face and waited on the fast nod again before going on. He moved the blade down until he slipped it under one strap of Roberto's thong.

"Oh, no . . . please, don't." Roberto sucked a sharp breath, trembling. His eyes stared at where the knife was a sneeze away from cutting Big Jim.

Or in this guy's case, nipping Junior.

"I had no idea they could make a male thong that small," Carlos taunted.

"Who are you?"

"Gabrielle's new bodyguard, and I take my job seriously."

"What the hell do you want?" Roberto yelled, the power in his voice fueled by a healthy load of fear.

That was more like it. This bastard had to pay for what he'd put Gabrielle through for the past ten years . . . and almost killing her today.

"What do I want?" Carlos echoed. "Very simple. Don't ever bother Gabrielle again. Don't even think about her in the future. Don't go near her and don't send any of your idiots to try to harm her again."

"Okay, okay. I'm not admitting to anything," Roberto added quickly. "But I swear not to have anything to do with Gabrielle in any way again." The color started coming back into his face too fast to suit Carlos.

"You don't really think I'd just take your word for this, do you?"

"Come on. I don't even know what you're talking about."

Carlos slid the knife closer, nicking the skin.

Roberto wailed as if his leg had been cut off. Big mistake to let an enemy know how easily you bleed.

"Shut up or I *will* cut something off."

Silence. Well, whimpering was quieter than Roberto screaming like a toddler who wanted a bottle.

"I'm going to give you a choice." Carlos waited until he had Roberto's full attention. "I can either carve a scar from your forehead, across your nose and down around your cheek to your ear or take your left nut."

"Are you crazy?" Roberto ruined his insult by crying. "I'll give you money, anything. Tell her I'm sorry. I'll give her money. I never wanted to hurt her. . . ."

Carlos rolled his eyes, waiting on the hysteria to subside.

Roberto sniffled, swollen eyes streaked with tears, body shaking uncontrollably, and if this went much longer, he'd probably need a clean thong.

When he quieted again, Carlos told him, "It's an easy choice, really. Lose your nut, you'll bleed a little, but you can still do the big-screen movies. However, it's probably going to cut into your love life, but from what I can see—" He glanced at the shriveling pouch on Roberto's thong. "Based on that dinky sac, you really ought to keep your face in prime shape."

Roberto started swearing all over again how he wouldn't touch Gabrielle.

Carlos flipped the knife quickly to Roberto's cheek. That shut him up. "I'm not leaving here until I'm convinced you really believe me when I say I will come back and there will be no choices the next time."

TWENTY-TWO

When Carlos opened the door to the hotel room, he expected Gabrielle to be in the bedroom asleep, Korbin catnapping in a chair, and Rae most likely online communicating with Gotthard.

He was really banking on Gabrielle to be asleep so that once he got rid of Rae and Korbin, he'd have a chance to wash off the residual scum he felt from tonight in a scalding shower. Then slide into bed and make love to Gabrielle.

Instead she stood in the middle of the living room with her arms crossed.

"Did you kill Roberto?" Gabrielle asked point-blank.

There went that fantasy.

Carlos glared at Rae. He pitched the paper sack in his hand to the corner near the door and crossed his arms.

"Before you go wonker, not my fault." Rae stood and looked at Korbin, who got up from where he'd been sitting in a side chair.

Korbin sauntered toward the door with one of those can't-help-you-with-this-one looks. He slowed long enough next to Carlos to say, "Gabrielle figured that out for herself, but that's not the only reason she's pissed. She knows that we know about Babette."

"How?" Carlos snapped, but kept his voice low so only Korbin and Rae could hear.

Rae had followed close behind. She stepped up as Korbin opened the door and told Carlos, "That *would* be my fault. Gotthard sent me a rundown on a list of students and figured out there was a connection between Gabrielle and Babette even though your girl buried Babette's records."

Ah, hell. Carlos saw a long night ahead of him. "She thinks I told you, right?"

"I tried to convince her otherwise, but you *should* have told us." Rae's pissy, narrowed look was nothing compared to the heat coming off Gabrielle's glare.

"I intended to as soon as I had a chance." Like once Carlos finished this mission and Gabrielle was somewhere safe.

Rae scoffed. "This one's going to be a problem for you."

"Too late to do anything about that."

"How'd you come out tonight?" Korbin asked. "Do we need to cover that front any longer?"

"No." Carlos shook his head. "Everything is handled. He won't bother us again."

Korbin nodded and moved through the doorway, turning to wait on Rae. She paused in front of Carlos and glanced over her shoulder at Gabrielle, who now stood tapping her foot. "Looks like a long night on the floor for you, but I did spare you one headache right now."

Carlos almost hated to ask. "What?"

"I didn't tell Gabrielle why Babette's name hit our radar. She's on a list of teens listed as not checked in as of tonight's meal."

His stomach sank. Not Babette. Carlos took in Gabrielle's angry gaze, wondering how much to tell her. He whispered to Rae, "Maybe Babette is off the reservation playing. If we don't find her by morning, I'll have Gabrielle try to reach her."

"Call us," Korbin said, then ushered Rae on out the door.

When the door shut, the silence was like a vacuum sucking the walls in close.

"You think I'm a cold-blooded killer that took out Roberto while he slept?" Carlos would deal with one problem at a time.

Gabrielle flinched, but the frown lines didn't leave her forehead. "No . . . but what did you do?"

"I convinced Roberto it would be a bad idea to ever bother you again."

He could feel each second tick slowly as she passed judgment, trying to decide if he was lying. Carlos took one careful step at a time forward, needing to hold her. He *had* wanted to kill that bastard for almost killing Gabrielle.

But Roberto still breathed, for now.

"Stop." She held up a hand, palm out when he was six feet away. "Why should I believe you after exposing Babette to all this."

"I *didn't* tell them about your sister."

The fight to choose between believing him or not deepened the lines of anxiety across her worried face.

Carlos took another step. "I can't prove it until tomorrow, but I didn't tell them. The last thing I want is for anyone to involve her or use her against you."

Gabrielle's lip trembled. "Are you telling me the truth?"

"Yes. I'm not using you." There. He laid the real issue out on the table. She wanted to know he wasn't sleeping with her to manipulate her.

Another reason he shouldn't have broken that rule, but now was a little late to be concerned about that.

"Do you know how worried I've been?" she asked in complete conflict with everything else she'd said.

But that was enough to tell him he hadn't destroyed the fragile trust between them.

"I'm sorry I didn't tell you I was leaving. I didn't want you to worry." Carlos opened his arms, and that's all it took for her to rush into them.

His heart started pumping again at the feel of her against his chest. He cupped her head and rubbed his cheek along her hair.

A minute ago, he'd been ready to convince himself keeping away from her was the best thing he could do.

Not now. He couldn't let go of Gabrielle even if doing so would save his life.

She hugged him hard, her hands gripping his back.

Nothing in his world had felt so right in so long. Somewhere his feeling for Gabrielle had crossed from one of protection to one of possession he shouldn't be feeling.

But he was just realizing how much he could care for a woman. For this woman.

And that freaked him out at the same time since this could lead nowhere but to disaster.

She lifted her head and held his gaze for a long moment. "I believe you and I trust you. Don't make me regret that."

Not much to ask of a man with a normal life, but he lived miles outside the realm of normal. Still, he meant it with all his heart and soul when he said, "I don't want to hurt you, and I don't want you to ever think I made love to you for any reason other than the simple fact that I wanted you."

She lifted up, touching her lips to his. He kissed her back with care, then pulled away.

"I don't regret what we've done," he said. "But I'll understand if you don't want to sleep together . . . anymore."

"Really?" She lifted a hand to his cheek, but he couldn't read what churned behind that intense gaze.

He had to give her space to figure out what she wanted to do. Right now wasn't the best time to touch her anyhow since he still had to shake off his fury from dealing with Roberto. He'd take her like a wild man if he didn't move back.

"I need a shower." Carlos disengaged from her arms and she let him. When he stepped away, she crossed her arms and looked down.

He'd survived almost getting blown to pieces earlier, the gut-wrenching fear he might not have gotten Gabrielle away in time, and fighting a goon half again his size tonight with little thought.

But the picture of Gabrielle's dejected face pummeled

him with steel fists. He'd had no idea until now how much it was going to hurt to lose her.

Carlos crossed the room to pick up the paper bag with a box of condoms that had been a waste of money and tossed the bag next to his duffel on the way to the bathroom. He stripped out of his clothes and climbed into the shower, cranking the water temperature up so high he couldn't see through the steam.

The scalding water badgered his muscles, but images of Gabrielle's terror-filled face after the explosion kept breathing life into his dark thoughts. He didn't realize he was squeezing the bar of soap until it snapped in half.

If anyone else harmed Gabrielle, he'd . . .

Carlos took a breath and rolled his shoulders, trying to not think about what he'd do.

He already missed her desperately. How was he going to let her go when all this was over? Music filtered into the bathroom from the bedroom. The shower curtain had a clear strip across the top where he saw the door open all the way just before the lights clicked off.

A puff of candlelight glowed on the other side of the shower around the sink. His vision adjusted just as he guessed what might be happening. What he hoped like hell was happening.

The shower curtain slid open a foot and Gabrielle stepped in. Gloriously naked.

His heart pumped hard with hope.

"I got a little candle off the food cart that probably won't last long," she said just loud enough for him to hear over the water battering his back. "Is this okay?"

Carlos studied her, wished he could see her eyes that televised her emotions. "Does this mean you made a decision?"

She chuckled. "No, I took my clothes off and came in here to tell you I wasn't going to make love with you. To use your words, 'for someone so intelligent, you can be pretty dense.' I'm angry, not stupid."

"What do you mean?"

"We both know my future is up in the air. I'm not giving up a minute with you."

The smile warming his chest reached up to touch his lips. "What do you plan to do with your minutes?"

She moved forward until he could see the glow of white around her irises through the steam.

Her fingers closed around his erection.

Carlos drew in a breath. "Careful, woman, or we won't need those condoms I picked up while I was out."

"Really?"

The enthusiasm in that one word pinged a tender spot inside him.

"And here I thought"—she paused and sheathed him—"I had the only one left."

He sucked in sharply at the jolt of pleasure from her touch. Water poured across his shoulders and sluiced between their bodies. He wrapped her in his arms. "You're incredible."

"The funny thing is, I feel like I am when I'm with you," she whispered.

"Never doubt it." He wanted to be careful with her tonight, not let the beast still roaming inside him loose.

He dipped his mouth down to kiss her, and she wrapped her arms around his neck, loving him with each nip of her sweet lips.

She tasted like wicked honey. When he teased his fingers over her slick body and slowed to toy with her breasts, she moaned her appreciation.

He reached down and scooped her up. Her legs went around his waist.

His heavy groin ached from the strain of waiting, holding back from driving into her until all he could feel was Gabrielle. No rage at the hand he'd been dealt, no fury over how close she'd come to dying today.

He wanted to feel just her.

With his hands underneath her, he pressed a finger inside. She clenched against him.

"Carlos?"

"What, sweetheart?"

She rubbed against him. "I am so ready. Now."

He lifted her, gently positioning the tip of his erection to ease inside, slowly, carefully. The need to drive into her clawed at him.

She wiggled her bottom, forcing him close to the frayed edge of his control.

"Carlos, stop being so careful. I'm not crystal. I don't want slow and easy. Don't hold back on me tonight."

Merde. The buried fury roared to life.

———

Durand opened the solid-metal door and entered the outbuilding on his property within sight of his home. He called it a *granero*, the shed, back when he brought his sons here to discipline them. When he'd had sons to be proud of. But this was not like most sheds. Constructed to match the house right down to the stucco finish, this building was eighty feet long and fifty feet wide, with rooms for extracting the truth.

No one was allowed inside without him or Julio. Durand's right-hand man stood next to a bloated body dangling from chains hooked to the ceiling.

Julio had gotten a man unknown in the region inside a group of local antidrug zealots over the past year. On Durand's behalf, Julio offered the man a great deal of money to convince the secret group to create a special team that would bear arms against the Anguis. He gave the man a bag full of money to prove to his followers he had financial support.

Men showed up slowly until an Anguis soldier appeared the night the leader called for a show of arms from everyone.

Durand walked over to take a look at what his trap had caught. "*Dios*, Julio. He smells dead. Is he?"

"No." Julio prodded the body with a sharp stick.

"*Por favor.*" The plea floated from the body as if spoken by a ghost. For a man closing in on fifty-eight, Ferdinand was a strapping guy, still fit and strong. Or he had been until spending the last twenty hours with Julio.

Now his eyelids were shut and puffy red lumps. His swollen and yellow skin looked like that of an obese alien.

Durand breathed through his mouth and stepped up to the body. "Ferdinand, spare your son this. Tell me all you know of Mirage."

"I . . . told . . . him." Ferdinand's words fluttered.

Julio shook his head. "He gave us *nada*."

Why were some men fools? Durand shrugged. "Bring his son."

"Nooo," the old guy cried.

Julio reached for a chain running to a hoist mounted to the ceiling and pulled the hook on the end over to a metal box eight feet square and four feet tall. When he opened the box, Julio pushed the hook inside, fitting it into a metal loop, then walked over to the wall and pressed a button.

A wail spewed from the box harboring Ferdinand's twenty-nine-year-old son.

"What a waste," Durand told Ferdinand. "I could have used a boy like yours with my men. You work for me, what, fifteen years? Why would you betray me like this?"

Durand shook his head, disgusted.

Raised from the box, Ferdinand's son howled in pain from the moment the chain tightened until Julio dropped him just close enough to let the pads of his bare feet touch the concrete floor. The son was turned away from his father. He wore only a pair of filthy shorts now soiled from his having been in the box over twenty hours. Dried streaks of sweat and grime fingered across his dirty body, but he no longer had enough water in his system to perspire.

Durand stepped in front of the young man and wrinkled his nose at the acrid smell. He made a mental note to give Julio a raise.

"*Agua*," the young man pleaded in a hoarse voice.

"Julio controls your water," Durand explained. "First,

tell me what you and your father have told Mirage about me."

"I no know . . . what you mean." The voice was rough as nails scraped over rusted metal.

"Julio, turn him around so he will see we are busy men and have no time to play games."

Julio spun Ferdinand's son, who squinted at his father. His eyes bulged. "Papa, Papa. Wh-what you do to him?"

"Your father's eyelids and every orifice are glued shut. Except the mouth, which he has failed to make good use of," Durand patiently answered. "Maybe we glue your eyelids open so you can watch yourself change if you no tell us the truth."

Ferdinand hung like a silent slab.

His son screamed and jerked against his bindings.

Julio walked over to the table and brought back a syringe he jabbed into the boy's hip. When he withdrew it, he turned to Durand. "This will last about a half hour. Long enough to prepare his body for interrogation."

"Take photos. I want my men to know what it means to betray me."

"Sí."

Durand walked out of the building, where dark clouds swarmed from the north. Wind stirred leaves on the trees lining the walkway to the hacienda.

Maria headed toward him pushing her useless son through the gardens. She stopped when they met.

"How is my favorite nephew today?" Durand asked, hiding his revulsion. His sister should have let the boy go when he was in the hospital after being injured years ago.

No man wants to live his life as a cripple.

Unfortunate collateral damage from the bombing attempt on Salavatore's life. Another debt owed by Alejandro when Durand found him.

"*Bien,* Uncle." Eduardo kept his eyes on the book in his lap. Always reading. Always the same answer.

The boy never looked him in the eye. Probably too hard to look up at men all the time.

"All is ready for tomorrow?" Durand asked Maria.

"*Sí.* Thank you for use of your jet." His sister's eyes didn't meet Durand's either.

She made him feel guilty for her son's problems. This was no *his* fault. The fault lay at Alejandro's feet.

She knew that.

"You don't have to thank me for everything, Sister. Blood always takes care of blood." Durand sighed. She asked for so little and only for Eduardo. Just one of many reasons he could deny her no request.

She nodded. "We still thank you for the roof over our heads and the medical treatments."

"*Sí, gracias,* Uncle," Eduardo mumbled on cue as he always did right after his mother.

Durand clamped down on the guilt creeping up his spine. He had provided well for them, been a loving brother to her and loving uncle to his broken nephew.

He had no reason to feel shame.

"I pray this surgery will be the last one for you, Eduardo," Durand said, changing the subject.

"*Gracias.*" Her son's gaze remained on the book in his lap. What could be that interesting?

"Thank you for finding a new doctor," Maria added.

Dios. Durand wanted to yell at her to stop thanking him. But he reached over and hugged her instead.

"I will see you tonight." Durand walked off, deciding it was time for Julio to find a place to care for Eduardo around the clock. Maybe leave him in the States, then his sister would have to get on with her life. Maria might fight him on it, but in the end he controlled the checkbook for Eduardo's care, and this *was* the last surgery.

Just as soon as he found and dealt with Mirage.

That would happen as soon as Julio broke Ferdinand's son.

———

His arms were a safe zone where nothing could touch her.

Gabrielle sighed, happy even if she was living a fool's dream. She snuggled her back closer against Carlos's warm chest. After all the years alone and unloved, she refused to face the possibility that she and Carlos might not be able to stay together. What would Joe do after this was all over?

What would he do if he knew that she and Carlos had been intimate? Would Rae or Korbin say anything? She didn't think so after seeing this team work together.

There were so many more things she didn't know.

Such as whom Carlos, Joe, and all these people worked for. Who was this Fratelli group they were trying to stop, and what exactly were they trying to stop? Where was Linette and how did her friend fit into all of this? And one big question.

Had Durand learned the true identity of Mirage?

She didn't know a lot of things, but deep in her heart she believed one thing. Carlos might not be the kind of man who would get seriously involved with a woman, but she believed he cared for her. That didn't change that he had orders to bring her back.

Carlos kissed the top of her head. A hand brushed over her hair, stroke after stroke.

She smiled. He was so affectionate she could fall hard for a man like him. As if she hadn't already?

Mon Dieu. Her mind could deny it, but her heart wouldn't.

"Why aren't you asleep?" he asked in a voice thick with exhaustion.

"I don't know. Just thinking."

"How can you have any energy after the last three hours?"

"The Tynte women are made of stronger stuff than other women," she teased.

"Yes, they are, and if you're the signature design, they're all beautiful, sweet, and intelligent."

Her whole body sighed with pleasure.

"What's bothering you?" he asked.

"Nothing really. I haven't even worried about Durand Anguis catching me for a while."

His breathing slowed, then his chest moved with one deep breath. "Why are you so focused on the Anguis?"

She'd sidestepped some of his questions earlier.

That was before he'd saved her life yet again. Carlos and his people fought dangerous groups such as the Anguis, so they'd have no reason to share her story or expose her. She'd wanted to tell someone for the longest time, but couldn't. Carlos knew exactly who she was, so where would be the harm in telling him?

"I've targeted the Anguis for a long time," she started. "My mother believed in being more than a figurehead for a dynasty. She was a bit of a rebel for her era. Her parents didn't understand the depth of Mama's humanitarian commitment. Neither did Papa. Against his orders, she slipped away and traveled to South America incognito with a group of teachers who were going to open a new school in Venezuela, but her real plan was to help a very dear friend escape a dangerous man her friend unknowingly married."

Carlos stopped brushing his hand over her hair and seemed intensely focused on her story. She appreciated his interest and that he didn't give her a standard "Just leave this to the authorities," as so many others had said years ago.

"Mama's friend lived in the Venezuelan town where the teachers were going to set up a school," Gabrielle continued. "On the way there, the bus passed through a small town near Caracas. Reports said a big black sedan ahead of them was stopped by goats in the road. Just as the bus caught up to the car, bystanders said grenades were launched at the vehicle from a rooftop. The explosion lifted the car into the air and ripped the bus apart." She'd kept this inside for so long she could hardly share it now without strangling on the pain.

"All the teachers were killed," she continued, reciting the events she'd played over and over in her mind from memory. "Mama had left a letter for the maid to give Papa two days after she left so he wouldn't panic when he returned home from a trip and found her missing. Papa sent a highly skilled tracker immediately to find Mama and bring her home. This man did catch up to her, but not until just after the bombing. Papa was devastated when he got the news." Gabrielle hesitated. "We all were. The man Papa sent to Venezuela was much like your people, with many resources. He arranged for documents that proved the body was his wife, which wasn't hard to do since Mama was . . . unrecognizable."

Carlos rubbed her arm, but remained silent.

Now that she'd started she wanted to get it all out.

"Papa wouldn't let me tell anyone what really happened since Mama had entered the country illegally. He said the media would focus on that and not the fact that Durand had killed innocent women when he attacked a competitor trying to move into his territory. Papa said Durand would be punished for killing Mama and the teachers. We told everyone Mama had been in a bad car crash while traveling and buried her along with the secret."

That had been a lifetime ago. Gabrielle still remembered standing in the rain at the cemetery, soaked to the bone, while she waited for everything to go back to normal.

As if it had all just been a bad dream.

"So you went after the Anguis?" Carlos said softly.

"Not exactly. I just got frustrated when as years passed it became clear Durand was not going to be held accountable. No one could prove he'd been behind the bombing even though eyewitnesses swore his men were on-site. The world forgot a month after the bombings, but I didn't. I didn't get serious about trying to do something until after I'd graduated, married Roberto, then divorced him and went into hiding, where I spent so much time on the computer."

"Because of being afraid of Roberto," Carlos muttered.

"*Oui*. So I turned to what gave me comfort, researching things. I used my skills to find out everything I could on Durand and the bombings."

"What exactly did you find?"

"That Durand Anguis was definitely behind the bombing. He'd wanted to make a statement so others wouldn't try to enter his area. He's killed many innocents, not just my mother."

Carlos turned rigid as a statue at that, which she understood because of his protective nature around a woman. Considering his line of work, Carlos was probably more aware of Durand's atrocities than her.

"Over time, I established a reliable contact," Gabrielle continued. "Thanks to this person, I have the name of the son who Durand credits with many of the murders."

The room was so quiet for a moment, Gabrielle could hear the air circulating.

"Who?" Carlos asked so softly it raised the fine hairs along her neck. When she shivered, he lifted the sheet up to cover her and drew her back closer against his chest.

She could feel Carlos's heart beating powerfully. The heart of a warrior who fought to protect the world.

"Alejandro Anguis, the man I hope to see one day die for his crimes."

TWENTY-THREE

"Why don't you give Babette a call?" Carlos tossed his cell phone on the bed for Gabrielle, who stood on the other side buttoning her blouse. In hindsight, he should have had her try to reach her sister last night, but hoped he'd have received word on Babette by now.

Gabrielle looked up, eyes wary. "Why? It's not even five in the morning yet. Did she text you?"

"No. Just give her a call and see if she's okay." He wasn't ready to tell Gabrielle her sister was missing. After last night, anything he said or did was a land mine waiting to be tripped.

She knew the name Alejandro, but didn't know that the Anguis tattoo was a snake and dagger. If BAD or Interpol freed her, she'd eventually find out about the tattoo and . . .

What had he thought? That the day would come where he'd really be free of his past? That there was a chance of ever having more of a life than a box of memories tucked away in a safe house?

Face it, hombre. The only hope you have to stay alive is to remain unencumbered to run and hide . . . and kill when necessary.

His best-case outcome scenario was to secure her freedom, then to disappear himself into the bottomless recess of BAD's network, become a deep-undercover operative only.

Family was everything and he had to stay alive to assure his was safe, so that one day he could free Maria and Eduardo.

Gabrielle gave him a curious glance, then finally lifted the phone and keyed in a number. She held the phone to her ear, amused by something she listened to before she spoke.

"Cute recording, Babette. This is Gabrielle. Just wanted to say hello. Call me." She hung up and tossed the phone back.

"Why don't you text her, too?" Carlos suggested.

The humor drained from Gabrielle's eyes. "What's this all about?"

Well, hell, subtle wasn't working. "Don't get upset until Gotthard gets us an update, but Babette's security card was not scanned through the school system last night."

"Oh, *mon Dieu!*" Gabrielle grabbed the phone, frantically texting, then looked at him. "I said it was an emergency. To call immediately. What are we going to do?"

The panic growing in her eyes was the reason he'd waited as long as possible to tell her about her sister. He walked over and put his hands on her shoulders. "We don't know that anything has happened. She might have lost her card."

Gabrielle studied his face, then narrowed her eyes. "Rae knew this last night. Didn't she?"

This was where things would go from bad to shit bad. "Yes, but she's probably been up half the night working on this."

"Which means *you* knew, too," Gabrielle accused, ignoring the rest of what he'd told her.

"Yes, but—"

"But you didn't think I needed to know last night?"

"No. There was nothing any of us could do until we determined Babette was definitely missing."

Fury burned away the panic. "News flash. She's missing! So what are you going to do?"

He wanted to snap right back at her over his frustration at another teenage girl being in danger, but couldn't when worry for her sister was behind Gabrielle's acidic tone.

Someone knocked at the door. Carlos walked away, glad for the short reprieve from how her shoulders sagged next. He could handle anger, but his insides clenched at the disappointment in her voice. That he'd let her down.

When he opened the door, Rae stalked into the room with a weary-looking Korbin right behind.

"Long night?" Carlos asked him.

Korbin shoved a droll look his way. "Yes, and not due to anything physically draining. Rae is a maniac when it comes to something she can't solve."

"Why didn't you tell me about Babette?" Gabrielle yelled at Rae.

Rae gave Carlos a pointed look. "Leash her until I have coffee or I may have to kill her."

Gabrielle launched at Rae, but Carlos caught her around the waist before she committed suicide.

Rae didn't move a muscle as Gabrielle flailed her arms and kicked, yelling, "Let me go. I'm flying back to the school."

"Calm down and I'll take you." Carlos struggled to hold her without causing a bruise.

When she settled down at that offer, he set her on her feet. "Get packed and we'll go."

"Bad idea." Korbin scratched the beard shadow on his face.

"Why?" Gabrielle demanded.

"Could be a trap. Someone could have figured out what Gabrielle did in the computers and be waiting for both of you."

"No one could have followed what I did in the IT center," Gabrielle argued.

"Someone tracked you to Peachtree City and let your ex know you were going to be in Milano," Rae reminded her.

"I don't care. I'm going to get my sister."

Carlos's phone dinged with a new text message. Gabrielle rushed into the bedroom and dove for the phone, punching the keys and reading. When Carlos caught up to her, relief burst with her next exhale.

"Babette sent me a text message."

"Call her." Carlos wasn't so quick to accept a text message as being from her sister.

Worry swept across Gabrielle's gaze when she caught his insinuation the text could be from anyone. She punched the keys and waited, then her eyes lit with happiness.

"Babette, are you okay?" Gabrielle's face ran the gamut from relief to concerned to annoyed. "You cut class? No! Do *not* cut class or leave without permission again." Pause. "Well, you deserve the penalty. You scared me. I didn't know where you were." Pause. "I was cross-checking something in the computer for their security and saw you listed as missing."

Gabrielle glanced at Carlos during that lie.

He wanted to say, *See, sometimes a small lie is better than a complicated truth*. Instead, he walked out to the living room while she finished talking to her sister.

"Now that the drama is over, let's get back to the mission." Rae poured a mug of coffee from the carafe that had been delivered earlier. She must be pretty spent. Drinking anything other than her standard tea was a sign of the strain she was functioning under.

"Gabrielle's just worried about her sister and she's not trained to do this," Carlos defended.

"She's a risk to you and this mission." Laptop open and typing, Rae sipped on the coffee, twisting her mouth at the taste.

"I'll worry about both of those." Carlos added that to the list of everything else, including not putting his team at risk.

When Gabrielle walked into the room, Carlos gave Rae a let's-drop-it look the female operative considered briefly, then shrugged.

"Babette's fine and I made sure she would not break any rules or disappear for the next month."

From where he stood at the window, gazing down, Korbin asked, "What did you have to promise to get that?"

"I said I'd visit soon," Gabrielle murmured, then glanced at Carlos, who couldn't give her the assurance she wanted.

"Okay, I've got Gotthard on-screen," Rae muttered, then told everyone in a clear voice, "Line up behind me if you want to talk to Gotthard."

Korbin stayed at the window. Carlos and Gabrielle stepped behind Rae within the range of the mounted video cam. Gotthard's face appeared on the monitor.

"Retter says security has been filing into Columbia since late last night. Someone from the U.S. is definitely meeting with the oil minister on neutral grounds to assure him our government is not behind the attacks on his life and possibly offer assistance in hunting down the assassins. We may at least have a date, if not a time frame for whatever is going down."

"How?" Rae and Carlos asked together.

Gotthard said, "We picked up Gabrielle's mail from the satellite box she used in Peachtree City."

"What?" Gabrielle shot eye-daggers at Carlos.

"I didn't do it," Carlos said out of reflex, though he wasn't the least surprised. BAD would miss nothing.

"*Your* people did," she countered.

"Gabrielle," Gotthard interrupted.

"What?" She glared at the monitor now.

"It's protocol, and you of all people should understand," Gotthard went on, not the least apologetic.

"Why?" She had her arms crossed.

"If we hadn't picked up your mail, we wouldn't have known that you got another card from Linette."

Her face lost color. "Another one? What did it say?"

Carlos lifted an arm to put around Gabrielle, then dropped it back to his side. Not knowing her friend's situation was killing her, but comforting her in front of team members would not help him when it came time to plead her case to Joe.

"Linette indicated that at least one of the teens is key to something that will happen by the end of this week, and the only place she's heard mentioned in separate conversations is Venezuela, but she's not sure that's related. She's worried about the teens. She doesn't know what will happen or how this fits into the plan, but a clinic in Zurich is involved. She apologized for not having more information but hoped you would pass it along to someone who could help since she believes the Fratelli are focused on the United States."

"Did she say anything else?" Gabrielle asked.

Carlos cringed at the hope in her voice.

Gotthard looked down, then back up. "Only that . . . well, at the end she said not to look for another card from her. It was too dangerous. She wouldn't put you at risk of the Fratelli finding out she'd contacted you."

"No more cards?" Gabrielle's voice broke.

Screw it. Carlos slipped an arm around her waist and hugged her. He figured Gabrielle had put some stock into this ending up with her locating Linette.

No more postcards shot that possibility to pieces.

"I'm working on finding Linette," Gotthard consoled.

"How?" Gabrielle asked, hope rising again in her voice.

"I've been sending out posts to community boards with a few key words thrown into my signature from your code."

"Oh." Gabrielle slumped. "I've tried for ten years, thinking she'd be online somewhere, and never got a hit."

"Did you try Web sites you thought would interest her?" Gotthard spoke to Gabrielle with a calm understanding Carlos rarely saw. The big guy was usually more abrupt.

"*Oui,*" Gabrielle answered.

Gotthard's eyes twinkled. "I'm not. And I have access to computers that can do fifty times the load your system could do. I have over three hundred signatures being sent to a wide cross section of community boards and blogs every six hours. My chances of getting a hit are much better, and I have programs that will catch it if she responds in code."

Gabrielle didn't appear sold on his plan. "But even in this era that is like finding one fish in the sea."

"True, but it's more than we had to start with." Gotthard's face returned to its usual gruff expression when he said, "The school has three different groups leaving today on trips, over sixty kids."

"That's what Babette was complaining about when she

called," Gabrielle interjected. "She said Amelia and some others were part of a peaceful international rally, so Amelia must be traveling with Joshua and Evelyn."

Gotthard's eyes flicked in Rae's direction. "Joe wants Rae and Korbin to go to Zurich and see what they can find out once I give you the name of the clinic."

"Got it." Rae scratched notes on a piece of paper she'd produced. "If Friday is still our target date, what do we think is going on tomorrow?"

Gotthard answered, "Retter's contacts have learned that the Fuentes compound just doubled its security. The staff is being prepared for a very important visitor, but they haven't been told who yet. Joe and Retter think that must be where the meeting will be in Columbia, and probably this Friday."

"Who do they think the U.S. is sending?" Rae tapped a finger against the desk, but Carlos could almost hear the gears in her mind turning with the puzzle.

"We're, uh, working on that." Not a muscle in Gotthard's face revealed his thoughts.

Carlos caught his hesitation to share something and figured his reticence had to do with a non-BAD agent being present. "Would you go get my phone," Carlos asked Gabrielle.

"Sure." She gave him an odd glance, then backed away. The minute she walked into the bedroom, Carlos turned back to the computer screen. "Who do we think is going to South America?"

"Maybe someone in the president's cabinet."

Gabrielle hurried back to stand behind Rae and

handed Carlos his phone. He took it, punched a couple numbers, then stuck it in his pocket as if he'd found what he was looking for and hadn't been pretending.

"Rae filled me in on the busted trip to Bergamo yesterday," Gotthard continued. "I'm searching for Linette's parents, but based on what Gabrielle shared, I wouldn't bet on finding them. There's a woman listed as having the power of attorney to manage the household expenses from a local account that is funded from an untraceable Swiss account."

"How long has that been going on?" Gabrielle asked.

Gotthard gave her a date from ten years ago.

"That was a week after I stopped by to ask them about Linette and they told me she was dead," Gabrielle whispered with the shock of that news.

"I'm still working on it," Gotthard said, reading something in front of him. "Joe wants to know if"—he glanced up—"Gabrielle still has electronic contact with her people in South America. Retter could use more local intel."

Gabrielle stood upright, then turned to Carlos. "Reaching them by Internet is a problem, because I included a poison pill in the last post I made about needing information on Mandy. I told them to close the IP server as soon as they posted and lie low since we were taking a big risk to communicate."

"How were you going to hook up again?" Carlos asked.

"They would watch for me to post an IT article under a specific pseudonym on a board, and the first letter of each sentence would spell the new site for them to post on again in code. It takes a week normally to set that up."

"Bloody hell," Rae muttered. "So that's a dead end."

"Not necessarily," Gabrielle corrected, frowning at the top of Rae's head.

Carlos touched Gabrielle's chin, drawing her gaze. "What are you saying?"

Gabrielle hesitated. "I know the identities and addresses of my contacts, but I'm not telling Retter."

TWENTY-FOUR

Vestavia lifted a file from his desk for the first phase of the Renaissance.

No one country could be a superpower. Not forever.

The only way the United States would ever become manageable was by cracking the infrastructure first to determine the strongest areas within the country, then undermining each of those.

What better way to bait a trap than their insatiable thirst for crude oil?

"You're sure all four of them are prepared?" he asked Josie, who was lounging on the oversize sofa he'd had the decorator put in his Miami office for late nights.

She stopped thumbing the touch-tone screen on her iPhone and brushed a length of deep-chestnut brown hair behind her shoulder when she lifted her head. Of all the exquisite international art in his south-Florida office, she was by far his finest acquisition.

"The teenagers are a little shaky, but we only need one for sure," she answered him, tapping her index finger against the iPhone case. "Since the other two are just backup and won't have to actually do anything, I think we're fine. And Kathryn still thinks she's working undercover to protect Evelyn, so she isn't going to give us any problem."

"Go on." Vestavia came around the desk and leaned against the front edge with his arms crossed. He drank in every inch of Josie in her red skirt suit and white, low-cut silk blouse.

"All the teens believe the story we've given them. And this"—she lifted a cell phone into view that matched her personal iPhone—"is programmed to send out three different transmissions at the same time."

Well aware of what made this electronic gadget special, Vestavia smiled. "You've done an excellent job, Josephine."

She preened under his compliment. This woman kicked in doors with a weapon drawn, but she was liquid sugar in his hand.

"This will solidify my position as the one to listen to within the North American Fratelli," he said. "No one should vote against the next plan I propose after this. It's annoying to be handcuffed by this ridiculous decision-by-committee the Fratelli use, but we can maneuver around them."

"We are all so fortunate to have you," she said in a voice bursting with admiration.

"What did you get out of Turga's pilot?"

A frown disturbed the smooth lines of her classic

beauty. "Everything possible before his heart gave out. The pilot was midtwenties and looked very fit. The medic's examination prior to interrogation did not pick up a heart murmur. As a side note, the medic has been relieved of duty." Her gaze hardened. "Permanently. But the pilot did give us the name of the man Turga had captured once he stopped blubbering about his wife and new baby needing him and the baby was sick and on and on. I reminded him that if his wife and baby ended up living under an overpass, they would still be better off than him . . . unless I ran out of patience and brought them in. That loosened him up. That and a method of skin removal I find very persuasive." Josie beamed a proud smile. "He said the man Turga captured was Carlos, but never heard a last name or a name for the woman that was Carlos's girlfriend."

"That's it?"

"Yes. That and some very good sketches of Carlos and the woman I've inputted into our imaging program. The woman's sketch is unremarkable, but we'll know soon if there is a hit on their faces." She tapped a scarlet fingernail on her lip. "I interrogated him myself."

No question Turga's pilot gave up everything.

"I'll be watching the national news tomorrow morning." Vestavia opened his arms to her when Josie stood. She glowed, flush with excitement, when she stepped into his embrace. He kissed her deeply. "Too bad you have to catch a plane or I'd lock the office door for a couple hours."

Her lips curled with a wicked thought. She stretched around him to hit the remote on his desk that locked the door to his office, then reached down to unzip him. "I'll use the helicopter instead of a cab . . . if you approve?" The whispered words followed her as she dropped down on her knees.

"Granted."

This was a woman worthy of an Angeli.

If she wasn't so competent in the field, he'd bring her inside permanently. Maybe in a couple years. The only time she allowed her feelings to show was around him, such as now, when she raised love-filled eyes to his.

He brushed his hand over her soft hair.

She lowered her head, putting that amazing mouth to immediate use. He gripped the desk behind him.

Truly an angel of mercy.

—⁂—

Carlos ended the call with Joe and closed his phone. He wiped hair damp from humidity off his forehead and guided Gabrielle along the tree-lined street in Caracas. Wearing dark sunshades in the bright sunlight of mid-morning allowed them some anonymity. They'd both opted for short-sleeved T-shirts and jeans to blend in, but he'd rather not have her in Venezuela at all.

She refused to tell anyone else how to locate the informants, which he understood. Joe hadn't fooled her with his easy agreement. Gabrielle was using every stall tactic she could find to avoid Joe and Interpol, plus she'd made a valid point about her being the only one capable of convincing Ferdinand to talk once they found him. The time line from Linette's last missive was the "end of this week," which Joe was taking as Friday, tomorrow—the reason he agreed to let Gabrielle go to Venezuela.

Time was the one nonnegotiable part of this mission.

And this trip was turning into another dead end, which might be literal if they were recognized.

"What did Joe say?" Gabrielle asked in a low voice, eyes moving back and forth nervously.

People were too close to her for Carlos's comfort, and dark was creeping over the end of another business day here.

"I'll tell you in a minute." He led her to a fountain near Plaza Bolivar, where the water would allow them to talk and misting cool air offered a reprieve from the heat.

"Sounds like he guessed right," Carlos answered once they stood with their back to the fountain so he could watch the streets crowded with bustling traffic. "Retter's last message confirmed the secret meeting in Columbia Friday afternoon will be at the Fuentes estate. Joe is starting to think this meeting might have been orchestrated by a third, unknown party who has plans to do something, like launch an attack on the meeting. If so, that would mean someone is trying to pull the U.S. and South America into a conflict."

"Who is representing the U.S. at the meeting?"

Carlos kept his eyes peeled for any threat and answered, "Joe was able to confirm both the president and vice president would remain in the U.S. The cabinet is still deciding who to send, but once they do, Joe will know. Retter has a dossier on Amelia so he's on the lookout for her in case she doesn't go to the U.S., plus in addition to the heavy security his team will cover the Fuentes home during the meeting to watch for anything unusual."

"This whole thing is too bizarre," Gabrielle marveled. "What could be happening with the teenagers? Brainwashing to commit some kind of crime?"

"I don't know, but experience has taught me to be prepared for the unexpected."

She released a deep breath and rubbed her forehead. "I'm worried about not finding Ferdinand and his son."

They should have found the men by now. The ever-resourceful Jake had confiscated an even better jet while he was grounded in Milano. This was a hybrid Lear that flew Mach speeds, getting them to Venezuela in record time, but three hours of searching for her contacts this morning had been fruitless.

She shook her head at some silent thought. "I spent a year tracking them and setting traps to prove to myself that they were trustworthy and to be able to locate them if necessary. I hate to think what may have happened to them. I can't find Ferdinand, Linette could be anywhere in the world if she's with this Fratelli group . . . I'm so tired of losing people."

Carlos reached out and lifted her chin with his fingers. "I won't tell you we can definitely find Linette, but our people are the best. As for your contacts, maybe there's a good reason they're missing." Man, what a liar. Ferdinand and his son were likely dead, but Carlos wanted to erase the misery eating at her for a while until they knew for sure.

"Someone should know where they are," she muttered, thinking out loud. "Why would Ferdinand's son close his pawnshop for several days during the week?" She shook her head. "This is a small community. People working in the neighboring stores were surprised he wasn't there. I don't like this."

Carlos didn't either, especially since they were only an hour's ride from Durand's compound. Something felt wrong.

But he wanted Gabrielle out of this country. Now.

"I agree." Carlos shifted to a more productive topic. "Joe said Korbin and Rae found the clinic in Zurich, but the entire place is full of teenagers."

"Wonder why?"

"Physical therapy. All the teens are physically challenged. Rae thinks she recognized one from her file photos that favors Evelyn. She and Korbin are searching for a way to get inside for a closer look."

"So what are we going to do?" Gabrielle asked that with all the enthusiasm of someone on death row. She'd run out of options and knew it.

"I told Joe we'd wrap up here and head to Zurich to help them identify the teens." That had caused a heated discussion, but Joe had finally agreed, reminding Carlos that Gabrielle had to come back to the States at some point.

Her quick intake of breath confirmed she hadn't expected a chance to dodge Joe again. "Good idea." Gabrielle frowned next. "But I don't want to leave without finding Ferdinand, to make sure he's safe."

"The longer we spend here asking about him, the more suspicion we'll arouse. Retter and his team will search for them without drawing attention. Ferdinand might have heard about you asking for him and is hiding."

"I hadn't considered that." When she didn't continue, he could see she was accepting the decision to leave.

Carlos took her hand and walked in the direction of where their car was parked two blocks away. They hadn't eaten since landing. He'd find a restaurant, then call Jake on the way to the car to give him a thirty-minute notice to prepare to leave.

"We're missing something significant and I feel like it's right under our noses," Gabrielle complained. "Why can't *your people* put this together faster?"

Carlos ignored her surly tone. He was just as frustrated as her. "My people are doing everything humanly possible right now. Let's grab something to eat before we get back."

She gave him a wry grin. "Trying to appease me? I can think of more interesting ways to put me in a better mood."

"Insatiable wench." Carlos smiled to hide the sick feeling in his gut over what she'd told him last night.

How could he possibly make love to her again with what he now knew? To do so without revealing his true identity *would* be using her. Never.

She laughed and gave him an exaggerated sigh, content to walk quietly alongside him.

He'd forgotten how intimate holding hands could feel. Such a simple gesture, but one he hadn't shared since losing Helena.

His and Gabrielle's destinies were never meant to cross. Now that his had intersected hers, they could not continue without causing harm to those he cared for.

Which included Gabrielle.

She'd shaken loose feelings he'd kept locked away for years out of survival instincts.

Gabrielle was sunshine warming his cold existence. He wanted to hold her in his arms for the rest of his life and wake up to her scent every morning.

But most important, she was the woman he had to find a way to shield forever from Durand and the Fratelli, then walk away from to protect. Hard to miss the irony in all this. Gabrielle had worked as hard to find Alejandro Anguis and bring him to justice as Carlos had worked to keep family secrets such as Alejandro's identity buried.

Losing Gabrielle would rip his soul into pieces and leave a heartless bastard not even Joe could save.

"How about this place?" Gabrielle stopped in front of a sports bar.

"Works for me." Carlos led her inside, where a short, black-haired girl in a rainbow-colored skirt and peasant top led them through a smoky room where several televisions dangled from the ceiling. He asked for a table in the corner so he could keep an eye on the entire room. A waiter brought two bottles of cola and took their order.

Gabrielle pretended everything was fine while she polished off her quesadilla before Carlos finished his last bite. She kept stealing glimpses of him. He was as solicitous as always, but she sensed a distance forming between them for some reason since they'd left Italy. What was he holding back from her? Something about the mission?

Carlos leaned back, eyes taking in everything.

But her.

Patrons spoke, ate their meals, and eyed the televisions

currently set on an American twenty-four-hour news station with a Spanish translation feed across the bottom.
Her Spanish was rough, but she could glean the general
information.

While Gabrielle had been racing across the world with
Carlos, little had changed back in the States. The fuel crisis
was churning political adversaries into a fever pitch. Candidates were battling fiercely for votes with the presidential
election coming up next week.

Fuel issues lay between the two political parties, an
intangible gauntlet with the power to drive even the most
apathetic U.S. citizen to cast a vote on Tuesday.

When the images on the television screen changed to
teenagers being interviewed, Gabrielle leaned close to Carlos and whispered, "Look."

He wiped his mouth with a napkin and raised his eyes
to the monitor. She read silently to herself.

The gist of the report was that teens of every income
level from all over the world were traveling to speak to
different countries as a unified group to ask nations to
provide relief for physically challenged individuals. Starting in America, they were addressing how the fuel crisis
impacted their lives.

The teens being interviewed said few people realized
the burden placed on those with physical impairments
who had a limited choice of vehicles, such as vans large
enough to carry wheelchairs. They were imploring all the
countries to offer aid in the form of gas credits and a list
of other suggestions.

"Oh, dear Lord." Gabrielle's eyes bulged when the

camera panned over three familiar teens and an adult—
Amelia with curly black hair, walking unevenly on her
prosthetic leg; the blond Kathryn Collupy, pushing Evelyn
in her wheelchair; and the redheaded Joshua, who shifted
his prosthetic arm as though to protect it . . . or to avoid
having to use it.

The dialogue scrolling below noted these were three
of ten students who would make a presentation this afternoon to members of Congress on how the fuel crisis is an
additional hardship on the physically challenged.

"Now I know what bothered me about Joshua," Gabrielle said under her breath.

"What?"

"The last report Gotthard sent included information on their injuries. Joshua lost his arm six years ago
in a car accident where his arm was crushed." Her heart
pounded as she realized what she was saying. "Children
adapt quickly. He should be proficient with the prosthetic
by now . . . or at least comfortable, but he acts awkward, as
though it's very new. Amelia lost her leg from cancer eight
years ago and walks as though she's just getting used to it."

Understanding dawned immediately in his face. Carlos
stood, threw way too much money on the table, and took
her arm. "Let's go."

"What do you think is going on?" she asked between
breaths.

"You saw what the rest of us missed. We've got it all
wrong." He gave that quiet answer as he walked them
calmly outside, then briskly toward the parking lot where
he'd left their rental car. "I'll call Joe in the car."

He barely slowed at the cross street, let several cars pass, then took off again. The gravel parking lot was crowded with vehicles and a few scooters. Their rental car was parked in a corner at the back of the lot, next to a building.

A van was parked on the driver's side and a sport utility with dark windows on the passenger side.

Carlos stopped and swung around, dragging her with him.

Three rugged-looking Hispanic men wearing jeans and boots strolled toward them. Carlos had more muscle and an inch on two of them, but the third was a brute. They all wore a mix of sleeveless shirts left unbuttoned with the tails hanging loose. They stepped from the shadow of the three-story building bordering one side of the lot. The wind whipped the left side of one unbuttoned shirt, exposing a weapon shoved between the man's barrel gut and the waist of his jeans.

Carlos might be able to take all three, but he had no defense she knew of against the gun.

She couldn't breathe past the fear gripping her throat.

Carlos looked over his shoulder and cursed. The swirling breeze fanned hair around her face when she turned to look as well. Two more men approached from behind, raising the ante on her panic.

When she looked forward again, the three men had stopped in front of her and Carlos. The brute with the gun said, "We are here to escort you to the Anguis estate."

—◆—

"We've lost contact with Carlos," Tee told Gotthard and Hunter over the videoconference line she'd set up in a hotel suite she and Joe were using as a mission headquarters in D.C. Gotthard and Hunter were in Joe's office that overlooked downtown Nashville from the AT&T building dubbed the Bat Tower by locals due to the two points sticking up at the top floor like the ears on Batman's mask.

"Retter, too." On one side of the monitor, Gotthard rubbed bloodshot eyes. He probably hadn't slept all night.

"Retter? His team is supposed to be staked around the Fuentes home." Tee tapped a long, dark purple fingernail against the innocuous brown hotel desk.

What the hell was going on in South America?

Hunter appeared next to Gotthard, leaning against a wall in his usual indifferent pose. "Retter got word of someone willing to sell intel on Salvatore's operation. He told his team to stick with the meeting at the Fuentes estate while he checked it out in person."

Tee flattened her hand, tapping each finger up and down in succession. Retter was their best gun, the one she and Joe sent into any situation without questioning the percentage of success. What had Retter gotten himself into? "What do we have on these teens?"

Hunter answered, "Mandy has come out of her coma and her prognosis is good, but has no idea why she was grabbed. The only interesting piece our people got from her was that she claims she did not abandon Amelia, but that Amelia abandoned her to meet someone in Germany, so they separated at the airport."

Tee interrupted, "Amelia is here in D.C. on the multi-national field trip with about sixty students, including Evelyn and Joshua, that were confirmed as being at school yesterday in France. All part of the media circus in a congressional hearing room today." In just a few hours.

"What kind of threat could the kids be?" Hunter asked.

"None of the teens are particularly athletic or have ever been difficult or dangerous." Tee shook her head and shoved her long hair past her shoulder. "Hell, they're model students."

"Hard to ignore a warning—," Gotthard pointed out, indicating the postcards from Linette.

"But," Hunter interrupted, "let's not forget we're working with information supplied by an unknown woman involved with the Fratelli who *no one* but Gabrielle has met."

"He's right," Tee agreed, though it didn't stop her from believing this Linette might be as real as Gabrielle claimed. "We've got a full contingent of BAD agents along with me and Joe attending the event to watch both political parties and the kids. Between us and the Secret Service everyone in that building is as safe as can be expected."

Tee didn't miss Gotthard's scowl at Hunter's attempt to discredit the information from Linette. Just as exceptional a computer terror as he was a dangerous operative, Gotthard hadn't backed off trying to find this mysterious woman online since Gabrielle had explained the code she and Linette used.

Linette was the only intel they'd had on the Fratelli so

far, but they had to proceed with caution when it came to this unconfirmed information.

Tee moved ahead. "I'm with Retter in thinking the teens are a diversion to draw attention away from the meeting at the Fuentes compound tomorrow, but we can't dismiss the threat to them. Once this dog and pony show is over, we'll send everyone we have tonight to find Carlos, Gabrielle, and Retter."

Gotthard was scratching his jaw, something Tee had figured out long ago meant their burly agent was mentally crunching on something. "What's up, Gotthard?"

"Just playing devil's advocate. What if Gabrielle was better than any of us realized and she's set up Carlos? Maybe even Retter?"

Tee didn't hesitate. "If any of my people are harmed because of her, I don't give a damn if she's a princess or a ditchdigger or what Interpol wants. She'll never see the light of day again."

—⁓—

Carlos stared through the open door to the desk in Durand's office. That room hadn't changed since Carlos had lived here. Same heavy, hand-carved desk shipped in from South Africa he'd helped three other boys carry inside when it arrived. The inside of the hacienda had changed some with new, more exotic decorations.

He had perfect recall of the layout and could find his way around the entire compound blindfolded.

The downside was that he wouldn't get the chance to put that knowledge to any use.

This was not going to be some happy family reunion. His father never forgave a slight, especially by blood.

Carlos tugged on the cable ties holding him to the chair, but Durand's men had put four of the thick black plastic straps on each arm, securing him to a chair bolted to the wall. This was a holding room for "interviews" with Durand. The soft leather seat and polished metal ladder-back chair didn't appear quite so daunting to get out of upon first glance.

He might have had a chance if his legs weren't just as well anchored.

Gabrielle sat in an identical chair to the side of him, trussed up equally secure. She kept turning her head to stare at him, as if she waited for him to save the day.

He'd promised to keep her safe.

She was now a prisoner of the one person she feared above all others.

The door leading from Durand's office to a hallway opened and closed with a snap.

"What is going on?" Durand's voice demanded from the next room. He walked past the gap where the door was partially open with a cell phone in hand, paying no attention to Carlos and Gabrielle, waiting in the dimly lit room.

No one had recognized Carlos, so far, and Durand didn't know—yet—he'd captured Mirage, but that would soon change.

From what Carlos had figured out on the ride here, his father must have grabbed Ferdinand and his son, then stationed an Anguis soldier to watch the pawnshop with orders to pick up anyone who seemed overly curious. No one would have anticipated the Mirage, an electronic informant, coming out in the open to make physical contact with a resource.

If not for BAD, she wouldn't have been here.

Carlos had given Gabrielle three hours, tops, to search for her contacts, thinking they'd get in and out without drawing attention.

But Durand had surprised even him.

"I lost men taking those kids for you," Durand said in a quiet voice, the one that was meant to raise the hairs on a man's arm. "It *is* my business when you put my family at risk. What are those kids doing in the United States? On television?"

Durand continued just as quietly, more so. "If you cannot answer that, then explain the meeting at Fuentes. I thought the point in the attacks was to keep these countries apart."

Silence filled the gap, then Durand replied in a low voice that belonged to the demon he was, "I know about the meeting with Fuentes because I make *everything* that happens down here my business." Pause. "Why can you no explain now? What happens tomorrow at noon?" A long pause followed. "I will give you until then, but you owe me, Vestavia. You have not handed over Mirage yet."

Vestavia? Could that be Durand's connection to the Fratelli?

Carlos could tell Durand had closed his phone. The click of a lighter sounded, then cigar smoke billowed past the opening. The pungent scent of high-grade tobacco rolled into the room, where Carlos finally put things together from Durand's conversation.

With so much negative press going on with the fuel crisis and presidential election only days away, everyone would show up for the dog and pony show at the Capitol this afternoon. A staggering list of political power would be present.

What better place to attack with so much of the world focused on South America right now?

The Fratelli could be planning two attacks.

Carlos hadn't worked out the whole plan, but Joe and Tee needed this information.

When Durand answered a call on his desk phone that sounded as if it was from one of his legitimate business accounts, Carlos whispered at Gabrielle, "Listen."

She zeroed in on him and waited.

"I think an attack is planned for D.C. today."

Gabrielle nodded. "Okay, but I still don't understand."

"I don't exactly either, but I think the meeting in Columbia is to draw the world's attention and national security focus away from a U.S. media show. Think about it. All the politicians will be on hand at the Capitol Building this afternoon, *both* presidential candidates, including the president and his cabinet. Plus children who belong to powerful people, allies to the U.S."

Her eyes widened with comprehension.

"I can get you out of here." He'd been scabbing together a plan since they were grabbed.

"No. I want to stay with you."

He knew she meant now, but the desperation in her words shoved past his stalwart defense, the barrier he'd constructed to keep him from wanting a life he could never have. He wanted to stay with her, too. To wake up every day and see this woman next to him, hear her laughter, and hold her close.

That would never happen. Not now, when he only had one hope of getting her out of here. The reality of losing her crashed in on him, clawed his insides with the savage pain of a wounded beast.

He'd spent a lifetime lying, but this one had to be exceptional to convince her to leave without him. "It will be easier for me to escape without you. I need you to get word to Joe and Retter that those kids and the president are in danger."

Her eyes glistened with worry. "What about you?"

"Retter will get inside here and help me escape." Not unless he brought an army with him, but let him enjoy the fantasy of Retter bringing in an army to stomp Durand.

"How are you going to get me out of here?"

"Durand's sister lives in the compound." Carlos prayed she would help him. "I can trust her to take you out."

If she's here.

"How do you know you can trust her?"

"I just can. She isn't anything like him."

Gabrielle opened her mouth to say something, then closed it and shook her head. She accepted his judgment of Durand's sister without question. He knew why. She trusted him and cared for him.

That wasn't going to last long.

Acid churned in his stomach over what he'd soon have to do.

"I don't know how much time we have before Durand comes to get us, so here's what I want you to do." Carlos gave her Joe's direct number that was answered 24-7. He told her exactly what to tell Joe to pass along to Retter, Korbin, and Rae for any hope of preventing an attack on the teens, the president, and members of Congress.

"What about you?" she asked. "You didn't tell me what to tell them for you."

"Tell Joe I'm at Durand's compound and it's a code black."

"Got it."

No, she didn't understand, but that was okay. He'd just told her to tell Joe he was dead to everyone since he would be by the time she was out of reach.

Durand ended his call, then clicked a button and said, "Julio, come here."

"One more thing," Carlos said to Gabrielle.

"What?" She focused on him, intent on whatever directions he gave her.

"No matter what happens . . . promise me you won't hate me."

Every line in her face softened. "I could never hate you. I love you." She stared at him with uncloaked love in her eyes.

Carlos couldn't believe he'd found a miracle like Gabrielle only to lose her. Hearing her declaration of love was almost too much to bear. He'd never intended to utter those words to another woman, but this would be his only chance.

"I love you, too, Gabrielle. You must believe that. Please, give me the promise I ask for." *So I can die in peace.*

"I'll do you one better. I promise to love you forever. I know there are things you haven't told me, but I trust you."

Hell. He'd be better off telling her now before she learned the truth in front of an audience. Carlos opened his mouth to speak, but heavy footsteps entering the dark room from Durand's office stopped him.

Julio walked in with four armed men. "We will untie you," he said to Carlos. "Make one wrong move and that one"—Julio pointed at a tall hombre with a severe mustache and attitude—"will blow her head off her shoulders. *Entienden?*"

"I understand." Carlos had one hand to play and it was winner take all. Once he was free from his bindings and standing, he reached over to help Gabrielle up.

Hammers on two weapons cocked loudly.

Carlos withdrew his hands, holding them up in the air. Gabrielle stood on her own, rubbing her arms, her fear palpable.

Julio led them into the office, then directed Carlos and Gabrielle to face Durand, who sat behind his desk.

"Who are you?" Durand asked Carlos.

"Tourists?"

Carlos got a gunstock in the back at his kidneys. He grunted and sucked down on the pain. He'd pee blood for a day or two, if he lived.

"It would be a shame for this young woman to pay for your back talk." Durand puffed on his cigar, staring intently at Carlos. "Julio says you were the black-ops leader who raided the château in St. Gervais. He was hidden belowground when you killed my men."

Just as Carlos had told Joe once years before, Durand Anguis operated like no other criminal. Carlos would bet Durand's men hadn't even known Julio was inside the château the whole time they were dying. He never lifted a finger to help his men.

Durand stepped around his desk, sucking on the cigar and studying Carlos. "I know you, *sí?*"

Rather than answer that, Carlos said, "I have a deal to offer you."

Durand smiled with deprecating humor. "Must I remind you that you are not in a position to negotiate?"

"You'll want to hear this offer."

"Really?" Durand laughed. He returned to his chair, where he leaned back and propped his feet on the desk. "I am intrigued. So tell me this offer."

"Not without your sister Maria present."

Durand's feet slammed the floor as he stood in a rare show of emotion. "What do you know of her?"

"That Maria is a good woman," Carlos said slowly. "She was kind to me once. I trust her and am willing to make a deal with you for something you want very badly."

Gabrielle gasped.

Carlos couldn't spare her a glance. He wasn't ready to see the hurt in her eyes at what she was assuming—that he was going to give her up as Mirage. He should be insulted, but by the time this was done, she'd look at him with much worse than hurt.

"I do *not* have to trade." Durand eyed Carlos like a snake deciding when to attack. "I can make you tell me all I want to know for free."

Julio and his men snickered.

Carlos shoved ahead. "You can try, but you'll be gambling that you can force someone with my training to talk, and there's always the small problem of believing me."

"You will talk if she is the one in pain."

Gabrielle stood so still Carlos thought she might break if he touched her.

"I thought Anguis did not harm innocent women." Carlos watched the eyes of Durand's men, who glanced at their leader for confirmation. When silence continued, Carlos tossed out bait he doubted Durand could pass up. "What does it cost you to hear my offer? I know about the teenagers kidnapped in addition to Mandy, and that you're being manipulated by a powerful group."

Durand's dark eyes blackened with annoyance. "What game are you playing? Tell me about this group."

"I'm just showing you that I'll cooperate if you agree to a simple deal and let your sister hear it so I know you'll keep your word."

"You *question* my word." Durand's low voice always warned of more danger than did another man's raging.

"No, but you respect blood above all else." Carlos drew on all he'd ever known about this man to get what he wanted.

Durand's eyes lit with interest. "You say my sister was kind to you once? Then she will know you." He turned to Julio. "Bring Maria."

While Julio was gone, Durand had his men move Carlos and Gabrielle to sit in the side chairs as if they were invited guests. Carlos maintained a blank face and kept his gaze away from Gabrielle. He had to believe she would keep her word to him and contact Joe, no matter what. He leaned forward with elbows on his knees and propped his chin on his cupped hands.

He knew Maria would not fail him. His aunt had been the only constant in his life, the one person who had ever cared that he existed.

But she hadn't seen him since he was a teenager . . . or since his facial surgery. What if she didn't recognize him?

Carlos had spent many nights at his aunt and uncle's house, where he'd had a male role model of a man with integrity who loved his family. But his uncle died too young. When Carlos met Helena, he envisioned a marriage like the one his aunt and uncle had shared. He would always consider his aunt his only mother. She'd bandaged his cuts, fed him as one of her own, and held him the only time he'd cried—over losing Helena. The same day Carlos had made a pact with Maria to hide the truth about the bombing, then walked away to keep his aunt and Eduardo safe.

When Maria walked into Durand's office, Carlos endured physical pain at not being able to hug her. The years had not changed her, but the warm brown gaze creased in confusion when she took in Carlos and Gabrielle.

"*Hola, querida Maria,*" Carlos said as he sat up, using his teenage greeting of "dear Maria" to give Carlos's aunt his identity immediately without Durand knowing.

Maria lifted trembling fingers to her forehead. She had to be trying to reconcile the voice and familiar greeting with the face.

Durand asked her, "You know this man?"

Before she could answer, Carlos took everyone back to the point of this meeting. "Now that your sister is here, let's discuss my offer."

Durand ignored him, waiting on his sister to answer.

The struggle to decide what to say warred in Maria's gaze. Carlos held his breath, praying she wouldn't say a word to undermine the deal he was cutting.

She nodded. "*Sí*. He is familiar, but I want to hear this offer he makes you."

Durand gave Maria a hard look. Carlos banked on the bond between these two to prevent Durand from forcing her to say more.

"Tell me!" Durand demanded.

"I'll give you Mirage—" Carlos flinched when Gabrielle sucked in a deep breath. But when he added, "And Alejandro Anguis," her muttered, "Bastard," cut deep.

Durand just stared at him mute.

Not a sound was made until Carlos heard sobbing and looked at Maria. She knew for sure now. Her watery gaze pleaded silently with Carlos to let her speak, but they'd made a deal and she had given her word.

"You can do this? Deliver both Alejandro and Mirage?" Durand demanded, amazement and excitement ripe in his question.

"Yes, but I want something in trade." Carlos hoped the next words would buy him some small redemption. "Let this woman"—he nodded at Gabrielle—"go free. Her only mistake was dating me. She knows nothing about any of this and will never risk saying a word once she leaves."

"Let her leave?" Durand stared in disbelief. "No."

"Durand," Maria said softly. "He has offered you what no one else has and asks far less than any other would in his place."

"You know this man, Maria?" Durand asked.

"I think so."

"Who is he?"

"I will no say unless you agree to his offer."

"*Dios!* You are family. How can you side with him?" Durand struggled to maintain his icy calm. He crushed his cigar in a glass tray.

"I will explain later, but first tell him you will make this deal. It is no so much to ask." His sister crossed her arms and jutted out that stubborn Anguis chin.

"His woman can cause me trouble," Durand pointed out.

Carlos chuckled sadly. "Take a look at her. Do you think she wants any part of this or that anyone will believe her? She has no proof of anything that has happened down here, and right about now she's ready to cut my throat for you."

Durand eyed Carlos curiously. "So why do you care about her safety and no yours?"

"Because I used her as cover to come search for an informant and owe her a safe return home."

No one spoke or moved for the next minute as Durand studied his dilemma.

"Who is your informant?" Durand crossed his arms, clearly not ready to make a deal.

"Like you haven't already gotten that information in

your *granero*?" Carlos didn't want to share Ferdinand's name, but he'd bet the father and son were somewhere in this compound. Most likely in the heavily guarded shed. Or already buried.

"How do you know so much about my operation?" Durand's gaze bounced to Julio, whose eyebrows lifted in curiosity, but he said nothing.

"Make the deal and I'll tell you." Carlos leaned back in the chair, arms crossed.

Durand finally pointed his cigar at Carlos. "I will agree to your deal, but if you no produce Alejandro and Mirage, I will find your woman and she will pay for your lies."

"I know that." Carlos turned to Gabrielle, whose horror was right up front for everyone to see. She knew, as everyone in this room knew, that Durand would hunt her down the minute Carlos was dead and his sister was home. Carlos prayed Joe and Tee would have Gabrielle safe by then. "Go stand with Maria."

When Gabrielle just sat there, Carlos added a firm "Now."

She stood and moved tentatively toward Maria, eyeing everyone in the room as she did.

Carlos said to his aunt, "Go with her to the airport and assure she is on a plane to the U.S. Once you call and tell me she is safe, I'll tell Durand everything."

"I will," his aunt assured him. "I am to leave very soon with Eduardo, who is seeing a doctor in the U.S."

Carlos smiled. "Damn. Rather be lucky than good any day."

"No one is going anywhere until you give me proof of at least *one* right now," Durand ordered.

Carlos sighed. "Can I lift my hands without getting shot?"

Durand nodded.

Carlos ripped his shirt open, exposing the Anguis tattoo with the scar. "I am Alejandro Anguis."

TWENTY-FIVE

Gabrielle stared at the inked design of a snake wrapped around a stiletto over Carlos's heart, with a scar.

"Alejandro?" Durand's shock stole his breath, then he wailed, *"Alejandro!"* His face contorted as he moved toward Carlos, his body shaking. He reached out with trembling hands, the muscles in his fingers tight as he cupped Carlos's face. Durand's head shook back and forth, disbelief in his harsh voice. "Why would you turn on family?"

Gabrielle's knees weakened. Carlos was Alejandro Anguis, the man who had killed her mother?

What happened to all the air in the room?

Maria covered her mouth, sobbing. Durand's men gripped their weapons, every visible muscle taut with anticipation.

Durand clutched Carlos's face, his fingers digging into the soft skin. His whole body shook with fury. His voice was raw. "You were blood. *My* blood."

Given any other situation, Gabrielle would have been moved by Durand's heart-wrenching keen at seeing his long-lost son.

But she couldn't find a smidgen of sympathy for this man.

Carlos said nothing, still as a statue. Durand let go of Carlos all at once as if touching him burned his hands and backed away. He'd left red welts where he'd gouged Carlos's cheeks.

The black eyes Durand turned on his son were crazy wild, and his raw voice was more threatening than anything he'd whispered before now. "You killed your own blood. My brother was in that château."

"Then *you* killed your blood, because I didn't send him into a death trap," Carlos replied in a voice as deadly soft as Durand's.

But then Durand and Carlos *were* father and son. Gabrielle felt sick.

Durand had been the monster in her nightmares for years. The blunt silence in the room felt as though the world had stopped spinning right here, this moment frozen.

After a long, tense stillness, Durand seemed to regain his composure and demanded, "Who is Mirage?"

"I'll tell you once Maria calls to say they have boarded the airplane," Carlos repeated without looking at anyone.

Gabrielle's chest hurt as though her heart had been ripped from her. How could Carlos be the man she loved? He had murdered innocent people in a bombing. Women. Her mother.

Her brain screamed with arguments in his favor. He couldn't possibly be that person. He would never harm a woman or kill without reason. But he'd just admitted as much. His aunt recognized him. Could he really trust his aunt?

Was Carlos now getting her to safety or just giving Gabrielle a head start before he told Durand she was Mirage?

Her head throbbed from trying to process the inconceivable, that she had been intimate with the man who had stolen her mother's life. That she'd fallen in love with a true mirage. Her heart bled from a thousand cuts. This was the man who had sworn he wouldn't let anyone hurt her.

Guess Carlos hadn't included himself in the list of possible threats.

"You are not in a position to negotiate, Alejandro," Durand warned in a deadly tone.

"That's why I asked for Maria." Carlos sat, stoic in the face of sure death. He wouldn't look at Gabrielle, his gaze landing on his father and staying there.

Durand wasn't happy about the position he was in, but couldn't back down now from his agreement. Gabrielle had learned from Ferdinand that Durand's power lay in the strength of his word.

"Maria, prepare your son for the trip," Durand ordered as calmly as sending her to make a glass of tea. His eyes reflected a disappointment in his sister Gabrielle didn't understand. "Julio, have the men take the woman with Maria and Eduardo to fly on my jet once my sister is ready."

"What will you do with him, Durand?" Maria asked, indicating Carlos.

"Do not interfere in business" was her brother's reply.

Gabrielle looked at Maria next to her. The woman turned imploring eyes to Carlos. What did his aunt want?

When Carlos averted his gaze, Maria sighed and walked out of the room. Durand ordered Julio to guard their prisoners, then he signaled his other men to follow him out the door.

Julio took a spot across the room, next to the desk. A strategic position so he could watch them both.

Gabrielle stood perfectly still, trying to breathe past the tightness in her chest. Carlos—or Alejandro—sat just as motionless across the room, avoiding eye contact with her.

Durand would kill him. She fought for a breath. An elephant was sitting on her chest. The thought of Carlos dying stripped her emotions raw. She should be glad to see Alejandro Anguis face his mortality, but her traitorous heart cried out to save Carlos.

At least until she could talk to him, find out why he'd lied to her. Then what? Turn him over to the authorities to be tried by a jury of his peers?

In his case, peers would be killers.

Carlos wanted her to get a message to Joe.

Now she had to question just whom Joe and his group of deadly operatives represented.

Carlos finally lifted his head to face her for the first time since entering Durand's office. The misery burrowed deep in his eyes twisted her heart in knots.

He'd made her promise not to hate him..

He was waiting for a sign of that promise.

She couldn't give it to a man who freely admitted being a murderer she'd spent a decade trying to bring to justice.

He looked away, but not before agony wrenched his grim face.

Gabrielle couldn't do it. She could not just leave him here to die. As if he'd heard her thoughts, his eyes cut back to hers. He gave a brief shake of his head she knew meant not to risk the deal he'd made. She checked Julio, who was staring at her. He hadn't noticed Carlos and couldn't see Carlos's face the way she could. When she looked back at Carlos, his lips moved as he mouthed the words *Please save them.*

He wanted to know she'd take the message to Joe that Carlos suspected something was going to happen while the teens were at Congress today . . . in a few hours.

No plea for himself, only for others.

Who was this man?

Durand strode back into the room. "Take her to the car, Julio."

"No, I—" Gabrielle stepped toward Carlos.

"Get out of here," Carlos snarled at Gabrielle. "I'm not apologizing for getting you into this because I needed you as a cover, but I'm also not going to put up with any more of your whining. Go home. Keep your mouth shut and he'll let you live. What part of that are you confused about?"

Gabrielle stood there, dazed by the angry outburst, until Julio crossed the room and touched her arm. She jumped. Her insides twisted in indecision. She couldn't accept any of this.

Carlos met her gaze, his dying request clear in his eyes. She fought back tears. It wasn't supposed to be like this. He waited for her acknowledgment.

She nodded, unable to deny him or speak.

The relief that spread across his face told her he was staking all on her not letting him down. That she'd get the message to Joe and save the teens.

But who would save Carlos? Oh, God, she couldn't do this.

Julio grasped her arm. Fury burst across Carlos's face. She couldn't let him put himself in more danger.

What exactly would be more danger?

"I'm going." Gabrielle swung around and walked from the room, fighting for control with each step. She tried to take a breath, told herself not to bolt back into that office and beg Durand to let Carlos go. Durand would use her against his son.

If she left, Carlos had no Mirage to give Durand unless he betrayed her. Would he?

He said Joe and Retter could get him out of there, but would his aunt allow her to contact anyone when they got to the jet? How long before she could try to reach Joe?

Outside, Gabrielle glanced around at the sprawling pale yellow house with a ten-foot-high stucco wall topped with spiked wrought iron surrounding the compound.

How could Retter get in here quickly enough to help Carlos?

When they reached a van outfitted with a hydraulic

lift at the rear doors, Julio swung his weapon from his shoulder and pointed it at her. She climbed inside, taking a seat that faced a wheelchair locked into place. A man with shoulder-length black hair close to Carlos's age sat silently staring at her.

Gabrielle turned to the driver, already behind the wheel. "Where is Maria?"

He ignored her.

So did the man in the wheelchair.

She lunged for the door, but the locks clicked shut.

※

Carlos couldn't move his eyes from the closed door of Durand's office. He'd never see Gabrielle again. Steel bands cinched around his chest with each second that passed.

Had he really thought Gabrielle wouldn't hate him?

No, he'd prayed she wouldn't.

But it was unfair to expect her to understand without telling her everything that had happened the day her mother died. That Gabrielle had hesitated to leave told him she still cared somewhere in her heart. Somewhere deep beneath all the hurt and disappointment she had to be going through, she did care.

He had to believe that so he could face what Durand would do to him once Maria called to say they were on the airplane.

Durand never just killed anyone. He believed examples should be made of any breach in loyalty. He'd do his best to bleed any information from Carlos first. Let them try.

Carlos scoped out the sole guard left, whose eyes were unfocused as a mannequin's, treating him as invisible as he'd been as a child in this household. But it only took one guard since the other one had secured Carlos to the heavy chair using cable ties again before leaving the room.

The door to Durand's office opened silently and closed. Carlos wasn't surprised to see Maria. He'd banked on it.

Maria told the guard, "Leave me with Alejandro."

When the guard hesitated, she added, "Durand sent orders. He's in the foyer should you wish to question him."

That ended any argument from the guard, who exited immediately.

Once the door closed, Maria crossed to Carlos and bent down to hug him. Her body shook with silent sobs.

She smelled of his past.

Tears stung his eyes. This was his true mother, the woman who had rocked him to sleep at night along with her own children and given him a safe haven from Durand's house. His aunt had loved him as one of her own when his birth mother couldn't tolerate being in the same room with him.

If only he could wrap his arms around his aunt one more time before he died.

"Alejandro, please let me tell Durand," she begged.

Carlos turned his face to her cheek and kissed the soft skin, then whispered, "No. This will be okay, just keep your word and don't tell Durand. Ever."

"He is not the boy I grew up with." Years of anguish and disappointment poured through her voice. She hugged Carlos once more, then sat down in the chair beside him, reaching over to entwine their fingers. "I can no longer look him in the eye or he will see my hatred."

His heart squeezed at the endearing touch of her fingers.

"My brother would not hurt Eduardo," she reasoned. She heaved a deep breath that held years of misery. "I can make Durand understand my son was a foolish boy who tried to kill Salvatore to impress him and you took the blame to protect us. He sees that Eduardo pays daily for his mistake with his broken spine. You have carried this burden alone for too long. Salvatore will no come for revenge. He would no harm a boy in a wheelchair and his mother. Eduardo begs you to know he is so sorry for what he did and wants to tell my brother the truth."

Carlos couldn't let her do it. Salvatore would pursue revenge for his goddaughter's death to the end of time. "You can't trust Durand or Salvatore not to retaliate in some way."

"What about you? Do you trust him to no kill you?"

Durand would do far worse to him. "I will be fine until you three are safe and my people show up," Carlos said quietly.

Her eyebrows lifted in surprise. "What do you mean?" She kept her voice just as soft.

"I would have gotten you out of here a long time ago if I could without Durand turning on you, but you have a chance to escape him now." Because Carlos trusted Joe and Tee to pull whatever strings it took to put Maria and Eduardo in the WITSEC program. BAD took care of its own, and they would do that if Gabrielle kept her word and warned them. Carlos expected Gabrielle to use the information she had to share about the teens to negotiate her own terms, but he didn't blame her.

"How can we escape and who is this woman?" Maria asked.

"Her name is Gabrielle. She's contacting powerful people who can protect you and Eduardo. An agency that took me in years ago and gave me a chance to do something good with my life." Carlos fought against fear that something would go wrong. He'd trusted BAD with his life hundreds of times. He had to trust them now.

He continued, "As soon as you get to the airport, Gabrielle has to make a call to the States. Children might be killed if she does not get a message to my boss in time. The minute you can talk to her with no one listening, tell Gabrielle I want Joe to bring you and Eduardo into protective custody. He'll make sure you're safe and that Eduardo has whatever he needs medically. Give Joe any information you can on Durand's operation. When you call Durand to say you're on the plane, make him let you talk to me and just say the words 'We're all set' to let me know Gabrielle got through to Joe."

Maria and Eduardo would finally be free of Durand. Carlos had set it up a long time ago for Joe to be the administrator of his will, which assigned his savings and the proceeds from a life insurance policy to Maria once Carlos died. Joe and Tee would hide Maria and Eduardo deep in the WITSEC program with enough funds to live comfortably forever.

Once Retter learned what happened to Carlos—

which he would because Durand would brag to ensure no one else crossed him—Joe could release Gabrielle, *if* he would. Carlos had left a note with Jake in case anything happened to him, asking Joe as a minimum to consider keeping Gabrielle in BAD since she'd be an amazing asset. Once Carlos buried Mirage forever, Gabrielle would be safe from anyone like Durand, and her ex-husband.

"And what about you?" Maria asked.

"The minute she reaches my friend Joe, he'll send a team in to get me." Carlos hoped Joe accepted his code black signal and did not risk sending in agents. He took a fortifying breath. Might as well put the finishing touch on his lies. "The sooner you leave here, the better it will be for me."

Maria made the sign of the cross. "Thank God you have someone who can help you. I am of no use." She squeezed his fingers.

"You're the best parts of me," he whispered, barely able to speak, then cleared his throat. "Please don't be angry with Gabrielle if she says she . . . hates me. I've hurt her even though I didn't mean to." He swallowed against the lump of emotion clogging his throat. "And tell Eduardo I forgave him a long time ago. We're blood. Family takes care of family. I love you. Now go before Durand gets any angrier with you."

"I love you as a son." She hugged him again, kissed his cheek, and left.

Julio stepped inside the room with three more men.

"I see you've elevated yourself in a pit of snakes," Carlos told Julio. "From a foot soldier to a mass murderer. Nice."

"I merely stepped in to help Durand when his own son turned his back on family."

"I can sleep at night. Can you?"

Julio ignored the question. "You have until they are on the airplane, Alejandro, then you will go with me to the *granero*. You remember the shed, no?"

—⁂—

At the Maiquetia International Airport in Caracas, Gabrielle climbed down from the sport utility parked next to a hangar with a private jet. Numb from everything that had happened, wind swept her unbound hair back and forth as she waited for instructions.

Black clouds joined forces and approached from the west, warning them to go airborne soon or be grounded.

The armed guard who had traveled in the rear of the van with Eduardo stepped out and swung the barrel of his automatic weapon to indicate a spot fifteen feet away. Gabrielle followed his silent directions and planted herself in the designated position. Satisfied with her acquiescence, the guard returned to the van and began unloading Maria's son.

Maria walked over to stand by Gabrielle. The woman hadn't even acknowledged her during the entire drive. Armed as heavily as the other guard, the driver strode across the tarmac to where they stood. He addressed Maria in Spanish, but Gabrielle caught enough to know he asked if she needed a weapon to prevent Gabrielle from running.

Carlos's aunt didn't answer right away, just stared in stony silence until the guard shuffled uneasily. Then she told him she was an Anguis and therefore capable of keeping one mousy female in place. When he bowed his head in deference, she then reminded him his immediate concern was to oversee the *safe* loading of Eduardo and his wheelchair. She arched an eyebrow and lifted her gaze past the driver to where the other guard struggled to wheel the chair and drag a bag to the plane.

The driver rushed away to assist.

Gabrielle was shocked when the older woman shoved a phone into her hand and whispered in clear English, "Make your call now before the guards come back."

"Do you know what—" Gabrielle started to ask what Durand would do to Carlos.

"Call *now* and follow his instructions," Maria insisted, her gaze going back to her son. Probably watching for any misstep in loading him onto the sleek, white private jet.

With her back to the plane as if she and Maria were in a conversation, Gabrielle punched the numbers and lifted the phone to her ear, which was hidden by her hair. "Thank you," she whispered to Maria while she waited on the call to go through.

"Do not think I am doing this to help you. If not for you, Alejandro would still be safe from Durand."

Gabrielle didn't know what was harder to handle—that Carlos's being in danger was her fault or realizing she had only a slim hope of helping him. She might be in no better position herself soon. Climbing on Durand's private airplane with his armed guards and his angry sister who clearly blamed her for Carlos's being captured didn't give her any sense of comfort.

Should she try to make a run for it the minute she finished the call? Would they gun her down at a public airport?

Maria leaned near. "The guards are coming back."

A series of clicks sounded in her ear, then the connection was made. "Hello?" she said quickly.

"Gabrielle? Where are you and Carlos?"

Somewhere between hell and damnation.

D urand entered his office. "Let us walk, Alejandro."

Julio issued orders. One soldier clipped the cable ties. The other guards stayed in place with weapons aimed at Carlos's head as the guard latched a pair of handcuffs on his wrists in front of him.

"Does Maria know why the *granero* is guarded?" Carlos asked, not at all surprised Durand wasn't waiting on the call.

The man who fathered him broke out a smug smile. "She believes the building hides drugs. She is so wrapped up in that boy she sees nothing."

Carlos stood, then followed him toward the door, but he paused in front of Durand. "At least Maria has a soul and cares about her family."

"You should talk." Durand's smile disappeared behind a mask of disgust. "Bad enough you fail against Salvatore, but you sneak off in the night and betray your family. I have protected this family alone since then." Durand nodded to the guard and they all filed out of the office, marching through the foyer and out the back door, where the gardens separated the house from the ominous outbuilding.

One thing Carlos noted—Durand was light on soldiers. Where were his men?

"We may share blood," Carlos said, shuffling along

behind Durand, "but you and I are *not* family. As for Salvatore, you sent a child to set a bomb. Eduardo didn't really know what he was doing. I stepped in to keep the blood off his hands." The lie had held up all these years and would now die with him, but at least Maria and Eduardo would be safe.

Durand stopped and turned to Carlos. "No. You left your cousin in pieces I have spent a fortune to put back together. And you allowed Salvatore to know I sent the bomb. If you had no failed, Salvatore would have blamed Valencia for the death of his goddaughter. Instead, those two mongrels united against me. I planned so well, knew that you would be in Cagua that day and would help Eduardo. I just did no plan on you failing me."

"How could you know I was going into Cagua that day?" Carlos's mind raced back through the years, trying to remember the details. "I told everyone I was going to Maracay."

"My men tracking Salvatore learned that Helena would accompany her godfather to pick up a package in Cagua." The blank stare on Durand's face was a study in patience.

Everything from the week Helena died came crashing in on Carlos. He looked away, staring into the distance as he pulled together the events of that day.

His father started nodding. "Yes, I knew you had been meeting Helena behind my back. She was a distraction for you and an enemy of this family. What were you thinking to get involved with Salvatore's goddaughter?" Durand shifted around and resumed walking to the barn.

A guard prodded Carlos, who fell into step, sorting through the new information on the bombing.

Carlos and Helena had believed they could find a way to mend the rift in the families that had been caused by his mother's death. An impossible dream, because Carlos had been too young to realize his father was insane.

Durand had intended to blame the death on the Valencia family so Salvatore would war with Valencia.

"You didn't . . . ," Carlos muttered in a deadly tone as it all came together. He snapped his gaze back to Durand, not wanting to believe what was gelling in his mind.

"What?" Durand glanced over his shoulder. "Kill Helena? *Sí.* Was necessary. Killing Salvatore's favorite goddaughter was key to gaining his support."

Carlos swallowed back the nausea that shot up his throat. All this time he'd believed if he'd arrived sooner he could have saved her. Even if she'd lived that day, Durand would have found another way to kill her and use her death to his benefit.

Because she'd been involved with Carlos.

"You are to blame for Helena's death and the trouble brought upon our family since then," Durand added. "I have built a strong army to protect our family, but we would have been even greater by now had you no failed us all."

Carlos accepted that his soul was damned beyond redemption when he started envisioning the painful ways he wanted to dismember and kill his own father.

A guard rushed ahead to open the double doors to the shed that hadn't changed much over the years. The innocent exterior of this two-story building hid soundproof walls and Durand's blackest secrets.

When Carlos stepped inside, he followed the wide-eyed

gazes of the silent guards. Two hideously bloated bodies hung inside a glassed-in box that had frost on the glass. Carlos had heard stories of how the infamous shed had been used after he left home. The hanging bodies accounted for the residual smell of death that no cleaning would remove.

The guards moved Carlos to where a thick metal hook dangled from a chain attached to the ceiling.

"Lift his hands," Julio ordered. When the guards complied, Julio caught the hook between the handcuffs and nodded at someone, who engaged a motor, lifting the chain until Carlos's feet barely touched the ground.

Durand's phone jingled. He answered, then said, "*Bien*." He pressed a button that put it on speaker. "Here is your call, Alejandro."

"We are on board and . . . all is set," Maria said, using the code to let him know Gabrielle made the call. "*Vaya con Dios*."

May God go with you.

Carlos doubted God would want to join him here. "And you."

"Touching," Durand said, closing the phone. "Now, who is Mirage?"

"Me." Carlos forced his mind past everything he'd just learned about the past and focused on saving Gabrielle. "Who else would have known as much about the Anguis?"

Durand asked Julio, "What you think?"

"Possible." Julio's eyes shifted toward the box with the two bodies. "He would have known how to contact Ferdinand."

Carlos pushed up on his toes to relieve the strain of his

body weight hanging and the handcuffs cutting into his wrists. That confirmed the two dead men were Ferdinand and his son, but they obviously hadn't given up Gabrielle.

"We'll know the truth soon enough." Durand walked across the room to a bowl-shaped fire pit like the one Carlos had seen on outdoor patios. Heat rose from this one, making him think it was full of hot embers.

Durand lifted a metal stick and walked back across the room. The end of the rod had a cutout design shaped as a circle with a line across the middle. A branding iron.

The emblem at the end glowed red.

"You don't need that," Carlos said. "I've agreed to tell you everything."

"This is no to make you talk, Alejandro. You can no longer wear the sign of an Anguis on your body. This will mark you as the traitor you are for all to see when I hang your carcass next to Ferdinand and his son."

Carlos clenched his teeth tight, preparing to have his skin burned to the bone.

Durand's radio hissed, then a voice said, "Don Anguis, there is an emergency call for you on the office line." He handed the branding iron to Julio and lifted the radio, depressing a button when he spoke. "Who is calling?"

"Vestavia. He says he needs to tell you who Mirage is."

"Forward his call to my cell phone." Durand handed Julio the iron, then turned to Carlos. "We'll both know soon if you tell the truth or if your girlfriend dies."

Had someone discovered Gabrielle was Mirage?

TWENTY-SIX

"Hello, Vestavia," Durand answered, then fingered the button on his phone to put it on speaker, placing them both on video feed. He preferred to see this man's face when they spoke.

"I have a lead on Mirage." Vestavia's face filled the screen.

"Really? What?"

"We think it's the man who killed your people in France. The photo Julio finally sent"—Vestavia paused, allowing his annoyance at Durand's delay to come through—"matches one we've confirmed that Baby Face and Turga were after for one thing."

"How are you sure?" Durand should thank Vestavia for corroborating Alejandro's claims, but this man was trustworthy as a rattlesnake.

"Took a while, but my people were able to cross-check every flight out of Europe each day after Mandy was taken. Our computers finally narrowed images from security cameras. We know who he is. Carlos Delgado."

Durand gave Vestavia credit for that, but he still had issues with the man. "That is good. Now, tell me the reason for these kidnappings."

"We agreed I'd explain tomorrow." Vestavia sounded testy, but he added, "Mandy served one purpose—to draw Mirage out, which worked. Mirage hasn't been online since then and he's clearly on the run. If Mandy could identify any of your men, the authorities would have visited you by now. Have you sent enough men to watch over the meeting in Columbia as we agreed?"

Durand mulled over Vestavia's evasive answer. The bastard's information was impressive. "I told you no question me. I agreed to send the men so they are in place."

"Don't get upset," Vestavia chided. "This will all pay off soon. We'll find Mirage any day now."

"Do no waste more time." Durand smiled at Vestavia's frown on the small monitor of his cell phone. "Mirage is hanging in front of me."

The silence stretched until Vestavia said, "Send me a picture of this man."

"I'll do one better." Durand turned the phone to face Carlos, whose eyes narrowed, then widened with recognition.

Dios, Carlos knew Vestavia.

Durand flipped the phone back around in time to see Vestavia's shock when he yelled, "What were you thinking to show him my face, you fool?"

"Take care with your words, Vestavia. *You* wanted to see Mirage," Durand warned quietly, danger percolating in his words. The video feed disappeared, leaving the usual "unknown caller" ID in its place, indicating the phone call was still active.

"I want my people to interrogate Mirage, so don't kill him," Vestavia ordered.

"Mirage belongs to me," Durand answered in a tight voice, and silently swore to kill Vestavia with his bare hands one day. "I will do as I please with him. As I told you before, you can have what is left when I am through, but I doubt a headless corpse can talk." Durand hung up, cursing Vestavia.

Carlos couldn't believe whose face he'd just seen on that phone display. Vestavia was former DEA agent Robert Brady, a fugitive BAD believed to have been connected to the viral attacks last year, and possibly the Fratelli. Carlos had just seen confirmation. He had to tell Joe, but doing so would be damned hard considering his predicament.

The single positive thing to come from that phone call was that Vestavia confirmed what Carlos had told Durand about Gabrielle. He had no reason to go after her.

"They've been setting you up," Carlos started, buying time in case he came up with a brilliant escape plan.

He could dream, right?

"What do you know of Vestavia?" Durand said, waving off Julio and the branding iron. "Put that back in the fire."

Carlos had at least piqued Durand's curiosity. "He's not someone you want to do business with. He uses people, then gets rid of them. Don't you wonder why he had you kidnap those teenagers who are now in D.C.?"

Durand fell silent for several moments, no doubt wondering how Carlos knew so much. "What do you know of that?"

"Mandy can't finger your men, so he's right about her not being a threat." Carlos didn't want Durand to have any reason to go after Mandy. She had enough nightmares to work through once she regained consciousness. "The other three are part of an attack he has planned for D.C."

"What kind of attack?"

Carlos could only feed him bits and pieces for so long before Durand figured out he was stalling for time. "I don't know exactly what he has in mind. I was only a conduit of information. I sent what I found out on him to people who are trying to protect the teens and the presidential cabinet."

Durand's eyebrows lifted. "Just who do you work with?"

"No one. I'm an independent contractor."

"So who pays you for this information?"

"Lots of people, but there was no way to trace the money back to them so I don't have any names for you."

"Why should I believe you?" Durand kept his anger controlled, but the rigid set of his jaw clearly showed that he believed Vestavia had played him.

"Why do you think Vestavia was upset when he saw me? He knows that I know he was behind the viral attack on the U.S. last year"—Carlos paused as that registered in the horrified frowns surrounding him—"and that he plans to make you the scapegoat for this attack. Don't believe any grand plan he told you would include the Anguis organization. This man is more mercenary than you ever hoped to be."

Something else came to Carlos while he was playing this hand. "And Salvatore is not going to be happy when he finds out who set him up to be blamed for the hits on your oil minister."

Durand's face flared with just enough surprise to confirm what Carlos had guessed. Vestavia probably paid Durand to make missed attempts on the oil minister in a way that placed the blame at Salvatore's feet. But why "missed" attempts?

"What do you know about Vestavia's organization?" Durand asked.

Carlos shook his head in disgust. Durand was so power hungry he'd let a dangerous man dupe him.

"I don't know for sure," Carlos hedged, unwilling to share anything unnecessary about the Fratelli. "But I believe he's part of a highly organized group who have the financial and political capability of wiping you off the face of the earth."

Durand's face changed colors from a sickly gray to mottled shades of red, but he still answered softly, "You lie."

"No, I don't. Check out my story." Fat chance of Durand's doing that. Carlos accepted that he'd reached the end of the time he could stall.

"Give me the damn iron," Durand ordered in a low voice without looking at Julio, who rushed over to the pit and retrieved the iron.

A siren blared through the building.

Radios crackled on the hips of Julio and his men: *"We are under attack!"* Weapons fired in the background.

Durand's face turned a deep purplish red. He crossed the room and took the branding iron from Julio's hand. "Go see what is happening and take the men. It could be someone trying to get Alejandro. Maybe that pig Vestavia."

Julio raced past Carlos to the door at his back, yelling orders at his men, who followed.

Carlos braced for the red-hot iron heading for his chest.

Durand stepped forward with the casual arrogance of a man who had always been in control.

When Durand got close, Carlos shoved up on the pads of his feet, grasping the chain in his sweaty hands. He kicked a boot up to knock the branding iron free. The end hit his thigh, frying a strip of skin before the rod hit the ground. He growled at the pain and swung his second boot right behind the first to connect with Durand's chin.

An explosion outside rocked the building. Carlos lost his grip and dropped hard to the floor, wrenching his wrists. He tried to twist around to see if anyone was coming, but couldn't.

If Vestavia had sent men for him, Carlos had a chance to fight another day.

Durand stumbled backward, caught his balance, then reached over to his left for the chain hoist control. He hit a button, yanking Carlos off the ground where he couldn't get traction to jump a second time. He lifted the branding iron off the floor and started walking.

"I was only going to mark you as a traitor, but now I'll let this burn all the way through to your black heart."

Durand moved forward, the branding iron chest high and coming at Carlos.

The door behind Carlos blasted open. Durand looked past him, eyes shocked. A gunshot boomed through the room.

The bullet struck Durand between the eyes, knocking him backward an inch before the iron reached Carlos.

Carlos sucked a couple fast breaths, then waited as heavy footsteps pounded up to him.

Dominic Salvatore held a .357 Magnum with the barrel pointed at Carlos's head. "Who are you?" Then his fierce gaze went to the tattoo and scar on Carlos's chest. He frowned, thinking. "Durand's brother died . . . there are no more family . . ." Recognition dawned.

"Alejandro?"

— ᴧᴧ —

A low buzz of conversation filled the hearing room that held an easy hundred people. Awed voices from teenagers on their first visit and adults shielding whispered words percolated the air.

Joe walked away from Dolinski, the Secret Service agent in charge of operations today, wishing he could tell the president's protective service the truth about his team. Since no one knew BAD existed, the president had personally cleared Joe's team as a private security group hired to watch for a kidnapping attempt on three physically challenged teenagers during their international travels. And Joe would have shared more if they had firm evidence of a threat, more than just a warning sent in a postcard from an unknown woman about teenagers with no history of violence.

The SS wouldn't believe him if he swore on Bibles.

The way Joe saw it, the children, the president's cabinet, and esteemed members of Congress were as safe as they could be with the SS and twelve BAD agents in the room including him and Tee. Speaking of his codirector, Tee finished texting a message on her cell phone as he walked up to her. The navy jacket and pants look they'd chosen for this mission had been custom-tailored for her petite size and fit her lethal business image. Straight hair fell to her shoulders in fine strands of sin black.

He envied how comfortable she looked in the strait-laced attire that matched his. Give him jeans and a T-shirt any day.

"I don't like this." Tee met his gaze with a severe one that missed little. "Feels too easy."

"What do you mean?" Joe surveyed the room, catching sight of his people as he took in each section. Two BAD agents stood within fifteen feet of the three teens. Joe had pointed out four of his people to the SS agent so if something happened and those two moved in to protect the teens, they wouldn't be shot by Dolinski's men.

"*Everyone* is here. What better way to lure so many powerful people into one spot than by using political hot buttons?" Tee grumbled, thinking out loud more than pointing out the obvious. "Just because the room is full of children doesn't mean it's safe enough to have the president, most of his cabinet, and an alarming number of congressional members present." Tee's cell phone buzzed. She thumbed a key and read a text message, then scowled. "Correction. Both presidential candidates and their running mates. This is a terrorist's wet dream."

Joe pointed out, "But nobody in an intelligence group has noticed any terrorist movement in the past two weeks, no one has entered the U.S., nothing has popped up on anyone's radar but what we've learned at BAD. And the SS swept for bombs." He frowned, thinking. Could they have missed something? "We can't put a hundred percent faith in a damn postcard from some woman no one can vouch for except Gabrielle."

"I know." Two small vertical lines broke the plane of Tee's exotic face, which was part Vietnamese, the tiny change a serious sign of her frustration. "Gotthard is running a breakdown between the list of everyone preregistered and anyone who came through security who was not on that list."

"Slipping in undetected would be hard to engineer."

"Not if that person was SS or another national security agency."

"What are you thinking?" Joe shoved his full attention to Tee now. She had the amazing ability to think not just outside the box, but to reach the outer limits of possibilities.

"We didn't find out until after the viral attacks last year that a DEA agent had been working as a mole."

"Brady. You think he's involved?" Joe asked, trying to follow Tee's thinking, which would be like keeping up with a beam of light at night.

"Not necessarily, but we are the only ones who know about the Fratelli and that he might be involved with them. We should consider everyone a suspect, even the Secret Service."

"Good point."

Hunter walked up to them, his eyes skimming the crowd, then settling on Joe and Tee. "Just got in. Gotthard is here, too. Korbin and Rae are inside the clinic in Switzerland, waiting for word to move. They've located three teens that match the ones we're watching."

Tee angled a perfectly shaped eyebrow the color of coal. "How could there be two sets of the same teens? We checked all the records. There isn't a possibility of a twin or even a sibling of the same sex."

"The tougher question is, which set of teens are the real ones and which set are fake?" Joe glanced at his watch. "We've only got thirty minutes before they address the energy committee. Who do Rae and Korbin have to back them up?" Joe had the best BAD agents available stateside covering this meeting inside and out.

"They have four contractors Retter set up before he disappeared." Hunter thumbed a message on his cell phone as he spoke. "They'll move to apprehend the teens in the clinic on your word." He looked at Joe.

"Not yet. Those teens are safe for the moment. We have to determine what's happening to this trio before we do anything there that might tip off whoever is behind this, whatever the hell *this* is." Joe would kill for a drop of solid intel right now. Carlos had sent word the teens were definitely in danger and that this meeting was the true target, not the one in South America. He just didn't know what the danger was, only that he believed the meeting in South America was a decoy.

And Carlos might be dead by now. Retter as well, so what the hell was going on in South America, too?

"We can't help Retter and Carlos yet," Tee said softly, reading Joe so easily it always surprised him. "As soon as this meeting is over or we've determined what is going on here, you and I will go after them. For now—" Her gaze shifted to the side, then she frowned. "What is *she* doing here?"

"Who?" Joe and Hunter asked together, turning their heads in the same direction.

"Silversteen, the DEA agent leading the search for Brady. Why would she be here or even in D.C. right now?"

"I don't know." Joe studied the sleek form of Josie Silversteen slipping through the crowd.

"Let's find out what official capacity she's here under." Tee lifted her cell phone, tiny fingers typing in a blur. Hands that knew how to kill a man in more ways than Joe wanted to count. She paused, typed again, paused, and raised a suspicious gaze to him. "Silversteen is supposed to be on leave today. Her office has her listed as being in Miami."

"Wonder if she knows something she isn't sharing with anyone else?" Joe said quietly. "She has a reputation of not playing well with others."

"Neither do I," Tee muttered, then flashed a wicked look at Joe. "I'm going to find out what she knows. Think you can handle this without me?"

Joe sighed. "I would say be careful, but I'd only mean for you to be careful not to kill her."

Tee patted his cheek. "Flattery will get you a night at the Ryman when we go home." She tugged on the bottom of her jacket as if straightening her armor for battle.

Joe ignored the tease about the building housing his favorite Grand Ole Opry entertainment in Nashville and snagged Tee by the arm. At the flash of anger in her eyes for being detained, he whispered, "Be careful. Really."

His codirector nodded, then moved away, her body moving with liquid grace.

Hunter said, "Everyone's in place. Twenty minutes to go."

"Let's hope this Linette hasn't steered us wrong." Joe scanned the room once more, his gaze settling on the three teens and the Collupy woman. "Are Jake and Jeremy back?"

"Yes, I told them to wait at Reagan Airport. Figured once this was over we were taking our best people to South America."

"That's the plan." Not much of one since Joe doubted they'd get to Carlos and Retter before the agents were killed.

———

Josie flashed her ID at one of the armed security guards overseeing the flood of people and teenagers being checked in and out of today's meeting in the hearing.

"I feel for you guys having to deal with so many physically challenged kids. Has to be a nightmare getting everyone scanned. You deserve bonus pay."

"Like that's going to happen." The closest security guard with a military buzz cut and buff physique to back up that dangerous look allowed a grin. He reviewed her ID and checked her off his list of approved law enforcement, noting the time she exited, then waved her on. "Have a good day."

She smiled, planning on an excellent day. Now that she'd confirmed the three teenagers and Kathryn Collupy were in place, Josie was on her way to a spot close enough to observe but not be affected by the blast. Keying in three phone numbers on her cell phone would trigger detonators for C-4 packed inside long, narrow tubes the teenagers had unknowingly passed through security.

Scientists in Fratelli labs had successfully tested the solid tubes of C-4 in security scanners identical to those here, then integrated the tubes into the prosthetic and wheelchair structures. The detonator had been camouflaged in the prosthetic mechanism and within the wheelchair design.

In less than an hour, the U.S. power structure would be crippled beyond belief. No one had ever considered the possibility of losing the sitting president, vice president, the next four directly in line to the presidency, and the other presidential candidate a week before Tuesday's polling.

This country would turn to number six in the government hierarchy, the secretary of the treasury, a Hispanic man with a spotless record who would be duly shocked by his new position. His opportune trip to Columbia would be called a miracle by some who would believe he was just one lucky bastard. From the ashes of a chaotic country desperate for a new president, he would show leadership in the interim that would prove him to be the best candidate once elections were resumed.

In spite of a twenty-two-year career in politics spent maneuvering himself into a position where he'd be appointed by the current administration, the man who would step into the president's shoes was truly neither left-wing nor right-wing.

Josie smiled over the brilliant plan for putting a Fratelli in the White House.

—⁂—

Tee shadowed Josie two blocks from the congressional meeting. Her target entered an office building and passed up the elevator for the stairwell.

At the third floor, Josie went through a doorway to a hall that was very empty for a D.C. office building. Tee made a mental note to have someone research the offices rented along the hallway, but she'd bet every agreement would lead back to the same renter, who would be non-existent by the time they located an address.

Tee mentally flipped through everything that could be going down. Kidnapping didn't seem likely with so much security onstage. And why would Josie leave the site if she was part of an operation? If Josie wasn't part of something going on here, then why would she lie to her office and show up at an event like this?

Trying to put herself in Josie's shoes, Tee realized the only reason she would be off-site in an operation was if . . . something was going to happen at the site. Like a bomb.

Tee started texting Joe frantically.

Up ahead, Josie opened a door and vanished inside an office.

—⁂—

Joe read the text message from Tee, then stepped back from where he observed the crowd to speak softly into his transmitter, which would reach his entire team. "Tell all three television stations to go to commercial break in five seconds. I don't care how you make it happen." He headed for Dolinski.

———

Not exactly the rescue Carlos had hoped for. Durand lay sprawled, a glassy-eyed stare fixed on his face. Carlos should feel something like remorse, but all he could muster was relief this monster would never harm Gabrielle, Maria, or Eduardo.

Salvatore hadn't moved since stopping in front of where Carlos hung.

"*Hola, Salvatore.*" Carlos didn't deny being Alejandro since lying in a situation like this wouldn't help him. At least Salvatore would probably kill him with another bullet between the eyes instead of torturing him.

"You are the one Helena went to meet the day of the bomb," Salvatore stated.

"Yes. I know you don't believe me, but I never wanted her harmed," Carlos told him, his voice thick.

The door slammed open again. Carlos kept his gaze on Salvatore since he couldn't imagine a bigger threat than the one he was facing.

Retter came into view . . . wearing more artillery than Rambo. Except Retter was so much taller than Stallone. He had black grease on his face. Arms bulging with roped muscle held a .50-caliber machine gun. Two belts of ammunition crisscrossed over the black tank shirt on his chest. Black cargo pants were ripped and dirty as though he'd crawled through mud. Blood was splattered over him.

He'd never looked better to Carlos.

Salvatore didn't blink an eye. In fact, he ignored Retter.

What the hell was going on? Carlos started to ask Retter when Salvatore spoke.

"I know you didn't kill Helena or try to kill me. Durand tried to convince me the Valencia family set the bomb and that his family suffered from the explosion. When that didn't work, he leaked that you had made the failed attempt on my life. He blamed his nephew's injury that made him a paraplegic on you. We searched Helena's diary for a clue on who had wanted her dead. I was not the only target, but I was warned not to go outside the store."

The pain from the handcuffs cutting into Carlos's wrists was nothing compared to the anguish shafting Salvatore's eyes.

Salvatore lowered his gun. "She wrote about how the two of you believed you could end the war between our families. That might not have convinced me if one of my security men hadn't told me what he heard on his radio. He scanned all channels that day and caught you yelling to your cousin, 'No, Eduardo, don't hurt Helena. Don't do this.' Then he heard your screams at Helena through the radio, telling her to turn and run."

Carlos wanted to say something, but all he could do was try to breathe through his constricted throat.

Retter was searching the room and found the control to the chain hoist, which he engaged to lower Carlos to the floor. He found a pair of bolt cutters and snapped the handcuff links.

"Thanks." Carlos stood, rubbing his wrists around the metal. "Want to tell me what the hell is going on?"

"Salvatore's man captured me," Retter stated as if that were an explanation.

Salvatore scoffed. "Because you let him."

"True." Retter's face split with a smile that turned the heads of women anywhere he went, regardless if he was decked out for a night on the town or wearing dirty fatigues as he was now. "I couldn't pass up a chance to meet with Salvatore. Once I did, I knew he wasn't behind the attacks on the oil minister. I had just explained that I thought someone else was trying to finger him for the attempts on the oil minister's life when he got a call from some guy named—"

"Vestavia," Carlos supplied.

"Yeah, you know him?" Retter asked.

"Sort of. Go on."

"He told Salvatore that Durand was behind the attempts, and if he didn't stop Durand now, Salvatore risked losing his political ties when he got fingered for the assassination. Vestavia also told Salvatore if he wanted to end the assaults on the oil minister, Durand was light on soldiers right now. But Salvatore knew that since he had men watching Anguis, it was no problem to mobilize quickly. So here we are."

So Vestavia sent Salvatore to take down Durand, but probably hadn't planned on Durand having Mirage.

Or the person Durand believed was Mirage.

"Where does that leave us, Salvatore?" Carlos had to know whether Salvatore would still chase revenge after today. "Does the fighting end here?"

"I want the man who killed my Helena."

Carlos shook his head. "I swear to you the one responsible forfeited his life that day as well."

Salvatore stared a moment, then nodded. "I have killed the head of the beast. His blood can no longer harm my family."

Carlos brushed both hands over his face and hair, then looked at Retter. "What about the teenagers?"

"What do you mean?" Retter asked. "I haven't talked to anyone. Salvatore said if I got his men inside here and he walked away alive, he'd let me go. You, too, if you lived."

Salvatore told them, "You're both free to go. I owe you for your help."

"You willing to repay that now?" Retter asked.

"How?"

"Cell phones, clothes, money . . . airplane?"

—⁓—

Tee turned the knob halfway, then shoved the door open, her weapon on Josie. The DEA agent was so focused trying to do something with her cell phone that her weapon was still holstered.

"What the hell are you doing here?"

"Drop the phone." Tee moved the laser beam on her weapon to the center of Josie's forehead.

Josie calmly lowered her hands and looked down her nose at Tee. "I'm a DEA agent, you fool." Her fingers still tried to press buttons on the phone.

Tee switched the beam to Josie's hand and blew off her thumb. Josie dropped the phone, screaming in pain.

Hunter and Gotthard rushed inside, weapons drawn.

"Cuff her and pat her down." Tee waited as Gotthard bound Josie's bloody hand and bound her wrists with flex cuffs. While he patted her down, Tee lifted Josie's phone, which showed the call would not connect.

That would be because Joe had Secret Service agent Dolinski jam all cellular service in a one-mile radius of the Capitol Building the minute he got Tee's text message. By now, the chambers would be almost cleared of occupants, the first shunted out being the president and his cabinet. Joe would have the three teens and the Collupy woman locked down in an underground holding facility as well.

Hunter contacted Rae and Korbin by sat-phone with authorization to take the other three teens into protective custody in Switzerland. Within the hour, they'd know who was real and who was not.

"You aren't cops or FBI. You haven't even read me my rights," Josie snarled.

Tee stepped close to Josie. "Here's your right. Open your mouth again and I'm going to pull your tongue over the back of your head." Tee motioned for her agents to move out. "Let's turn her over to the authorities she wants to see."

Outside, Gotthard and Hunter each had a hand wrapped around one of Josie's arms. The DEA agent glared in spite of the shock blanching her face, but never said another word.

Tee followed several steps behind, scanning for anyone who might try to help Josie.

"You have the target in sight?" Vestavia asked, staring out the tenth-floor window of a vacant D.C. office.

"Yes, sir. I'm ready," his sniper confirmed, waiting on the order to shoot. Another second passed. "Fra? Sir?"

Vestavia ventured one more look over the sniper's shoulder. "Take the shot."

The explosion might as well have ripped Vestavia in half. His whole body clinched as he watched Josie's beautiful head shatter like a ripe melon slammed with a sledgehammer.

He wanted to order the death of the Asian woman and the two men with her, but this shooter was a Fratelli sniper. Vestavia couldn't risk the Fras learning of an unnecessary death.

The reigning group of eleven North American Fras had ordered *this* sanction if Josie ever got caught.

And the removal of Pierre in France. Like his death mattered?

Vestavia had never thought anyone could trip up Josie.

He fought to maintain control, shield how difficult it was to get his breath. His Josie was dead. He would make everyone pay. His heart punched his chest with each painful beat.

Sweet Josie. Gone.

He had to face the Fras and explain what went wrong, but not tonight. Not now while he was so raw.

The sniper had broken down his weapon and stood. "Ready?"

Vestavia refused to betray any emotion. He choked

down the sick ball of agony in his gut and patted the shooter on his shoulder. "Nice job."

"Thank you, Fra."

Vestavia could find only one reason for failure today. There had to be a mole inside the Fratelli organization.

It clearly wasn't Josie, but he would find out who it was, and that person would pay dearly.

EPILOGUE

Carlos walked into Joe's office atop the Bat Tower in Nashville, ready to hurt people. "Where is she?"

"You mean Gabrielle?" Joe rose from behind his desk. He wore gray slacks and a sky-blue, button-down shirt.

Tee walked in from the door that connected their offices. She had her furry little Pomeranian, Petey, in her arms, snuggled against the cinnamon-red sweater she wore over a dash of black leather skirt. "She's gone, Carlos. She called when they landed to give us the airport where they arrived and was gone by the time we reached your aunt and cousin. We don't know where she is either."

He stared at both of them, wanting to call everyone liars who tried to tell him Gabrielle had vanished into thin air.

"You knew she could do it," Joe pointed out.

Carlos raked a hand over his head and clutched the back of his neck. "Maybe Gotthard can find her."

"I don't think so." Tee shook her head. "Not from what Gotthard said. He's impressed by her ability to manipulate anything electronic, and that's saying something."

This couldn't happen. Carlos just wanted a chance to explain to her, to tell her she was free forever from Durand, her ex, everyone. That he hadn't given her up and hadn't been using her.

What else could she think after finding out she'd been sleeping with the person she believed killed her mother?

"How's the burn on your leg?" Joe asked.

"Fine." Carlos waved it off, trying to figure out how to function now when the only thing that mattered in his world was gone forever.

"We just got in. What's the scoop?" Korbin asked, walking into the room with Rae on his heels.

Carlos backed out of the way and leaned against the wall so Korbin and Rae could take seats facing Joe's desk.

The idea of disappearing was starting to sound appealing.

"The teens you two rescued in Switzerland are the real McCoys," Joe started.

"The clinic had been told all three teens were severely depressed and delusional," Korbin added for everyone. "They had plenty of documentation that, of course, led nowhere."

Joe continued. "The teens in D.C. were copies who all thought they had been chosen to play decoys for the real teens, and Collupy believed she'd been employed by the CIA as an escort to watch over Evelyn. All three teens had been homeless or orphans who were involved in bad traffic wrecks in different countries in the last year. When they woke up in the hospital, each one had some physical damage that corresponded to the one on the real teen. They'd all had plastic surgery they were told was necessary as a result of their injuries, then speech and physical therapy."

Rae leaned forward, appalled. "You mean the Fratelli intentionally injured these kids, even put one in a wheelchair for life, and removed limbs on the others to make duplicates?"

"Yes, that's exactly what we've figured out has happened," Tee replied. "The teens all confirmed a photo of Josephine Silversteen as the contact person. She told each teen after the surgery that the organization she represented protected children and paid all their medical bills, but her people wanted them to help other children they resembled who were targeted for kidnapping by taking their place for a week. She assured them they'd be protected the entire way, and in return all their hospital and educational expenses would be paid."

Joe added, "The ability to find abandoned children that matched so close to the teens physically and in speech, and to infiltrate the DEA, proves the Fratelli are an even higher threat than we imagined. Kathryn Collupy was just as innocent. The planning on this was phenomenal since all of them went through surgery, rehab, and voice instruction during the last six months."

"What's going to happen to them now?" Rae asked.

"The teens have all been debriefed and are now in the WITSEC," Joe explained. "They've been placed with good families in the program and will receive what they were promised as a minimum. Now we know why Silversteen never caught Brady and why she was killed. They risk leaving no one who can talk."

"I just finished filling out a report. Brady is known as Vestavia, part of the Fratelli," Carlos interjected.

Everyone quieted and turned to him.

Carlos shared the phone call Durand received and how he saw Vestavia's face. He intended to add his connection to Durand in the report, but Retter had stopped him, saying he and Joe were the only two who needed to know that. Retter had refused Carlos's resignation this morning, telling him Joe wouldn't accept it until Carlos took some R and R.

They thought he'd stay. Would he? Carlos couldn't answer that right now.

"So Vestavia knows what I look like," Carlos finished.

"I don't think that's an issue if we don't put you out somewhere public or high profile," Tee interjected. "Salvatore burned the Anguis complex to the ground after you left and put out word he killed all the Anguis soldiers, including you." Tee gave Carlos an assessing look. "We'll build you a new profile."

"Right." Carlos had to get out of here. "Where are my aunt and cousin?"

"The Shepherd Spinal Center in Atlanta." Tee lifted a small box from Joe's desk and walked over to Carlos. "This is all the mail that came into Gabrielle's post office box in Peachtree City."

Carlos took it, thanked her, and headed for the door.

"Going to take some leave time?" Joe asked.

Carlos couldn't look him in the eye and lie so he just said, "Yes."

"When you coming back?" Rae tacked on to Joe's inquiry.

"Don't know." Carlos walked out.

―⁂―

Gotthard rubbed his tired eyes and glanced at the third missed call on his cell phone. All three from his wife, who only wanted to bitch him out for still being at work after midnight.

Like she was ever home when he went there? Shopping, girlfriends, and the spa came before a decent meal together.

The only light in this section of the IT offices at BAD came from the glow of multiple computer screens he'd watched for days.

Seven hits popped up next, replies to messages he'd sent out, searching for Linette. Multiple hits had come in constantly, but none with her signature. He clicked through the first five, then stopped on number six, shock paralyzing him.

He read the brief reply again, decoded the signature three more times until he slapped the desk. "Hot damn!"

The coded signature read "Jane of Art."

Linette had responded.

BAD now had contact with a mole inside the Fratelli.

―⁂―

Carlos drove his BMW down the driveway of the safe house in Hiawassee, Georgia. Fall had come and gone without him, speckling the mountains with dried orange, red, and brown. Wind swept discarded leaves in piles along the paved entrance.

All the security systems cleared without a warning light.

He grabbed the box with Gabrielle's mail he'd already gone through during the drive, hoping to find a clue to where she'd gone.

No chance. The only significant piece he did find was a manila envelope from the life insurance group that had carried the policy on her for the slimeball ex-husband. A document enclosed stated that the policy had been canceled and they had received a letter from Roberto claiming any future policy on her listing him as the beneficiary would be a false document he would willingly testify against.

That letter would be the fax Roberto had sent the night Carlos visited him. The guy lost his chance at a fortune, but he still had both nuts and his face.

And Carlos had a signed confession from Roberto.

Carlos climbed out of the car and went in search of his things.

One suitcase stored a week of clothes, and a two-foot-square cardboard box locked in the downstairs storage room held all the other possessions he owned.

He had enough money put away to find a place for his aunt and cousin once they finished with the treatments. With Durand dead and Salvatore appeased, no one should bother them.

What would he do then? Carlos didn't know, didn't care. What was life without Gabrielle?

He punched in the security code, then waited for a second beep before he punched in another set of numbers. Inside the house, he tossed his jacket aside and headed for the bedroom to retrieve the suitcase first.

When he stepped into the bedroom, he heard a movement in the bathroom and drew his weapon.

The door opened slowly and a body wrapped in a towel stepped out. Gabrielle.

Not possible.

"Don't shoot," she ordered. "I saw you coming up the drive on the monitor in the bathroom, but you got here before I could dress."

"What are you doing here?" He hadn't intended for that to sound so harsh, but pissed off had been his natural state for the last twenty-four hours.

"Obviously showering. Will you put that bloody gun down?" She wrenched the towel, covering half her body, tighter. The matching beige towel wrapped around her head flopped to one side when she angled her head.

He laid the gun on the nightstand. "How did you get in here?"

"Oh, that?" She shrugged and had to tuck the towel again. "I linked into the central house computer and ran the security codes when Gotthard let me check my e-mail on my computer. I fixed it so I could get in undetected, just like I did in our room at the school. I figured if your people brought me here again, I'd have a way to escape. When we left for the airport, I kept track of the route."

The little sneak. No one, not even Gotthard, had considered that she'd screw with BAD's security system in the house when she and Gotthard had been working to access the school computers from here.

"What are you doing here?" she asked.

"Getting my things." He was answering out of reflex, not really processing what was going on. Gabrielle was here. "I thought you'd disappeared."

"I did, but I needed somewhere to stay for a few days until I had clothes and a car again. I left South America with nothing—well, except for some money your aunt gave me I used to get here. It was the only place I felt for sure was safe."

It was now or never. He had one chance before he lost her again. "If you'll get dressed, I want to tell you something."

"Tell me now." She straightened her posture as if preparing to hear a lecture.

Carlos blew out a gush of air and jumped in with both feet. "I didn't tell anyone you were Mirage, and I didn't know about your mother when I made love to you. I wasn't using you."

Her face softened, giving him hope until she shook her head and said, "Now, tell me the rest of the truth."

Damn. She didn't believe him. "I just did."

"No, you didn't." Gabrielle took one step toward him, then another, slowly moving around the bed. "Tell me the truth about the day my mother died."

"I didn't mean to hurt anyone when I triggered the bomb," he said in a monotone, repeating the story he'd told a few times. "I didn't know the bomb would do so much damage."

Gabrielle kept coming closer. "That's not the truth either." She stopped a foot away from him, so close the next breath hurt when he smelled the familiar scent of her.

"That's the only one I know." He loved her beyond belief, but would not betray Eduardo so she'd have somewhere else to turn her wrath.

"Tell me how you pretended all these years that you were the one behind the bombing even though Eduardo was the one who really triggered the charge," she said gently. "Tell me how you carried the burden of those deaths and almost died yourself to keep the truth hidden. Tell me how you walked back into that snake pit to protect those you love . . . and lied to Durand to protect me."

His heart raced. "How could you—"

"Your aunt told me everything once we finally found common ground. I thought she was going to hand me over to Durand's men at the end of the flight, but she's like you. She'll fight to protect her own. She asked a lot of questions, then told me the tale of a young man she'd raised as her own son."

Gabrielle lifted a hand to his cheek. "Did you think I'd harm Eduardo in any way? She said she'd made an oath not to tell Durand the truth, but she figured I needed to know. Eduardo was with us when his mother shared the story. He cried and told me he was sorry about my mother. He's had to live with that and the guilt of knowing you shouldered his burden for the deaths all these years and how you've lived on the run to protect him and Maria. He lost his future that day, too. My mother would forgive him, so I can't do any less."

"I'm so sorry for your mother." Carlos couldn't believe the huge relief that washed over him now that Gabrielle knew.

"I'm sorry for Helena, too." Her eyes misted. "We all lost that day, including Maria. How about if we all build a new life together? Now, tell me you love me."

"I love you more than life," he whispered, pulling her into his arms and kissing her. In his next breath he sent thanks for this miracle.

Gabrielle hugged him to her. "I was so scared you wouldn't get away from Durand, but when I talked to Joe, he told me Retter had gone undercover to get inside and find you. Or I'd have gone back on the next flight."

Carlos owed Joe big-time for that lie or she'd have been killed if she'd returned to South America.

Her hands crawled along his back and up into his hair. He kissed her with all the love in his heart.

"You know what kind of blood I come from," he warned her.

"Yes, I do." She pulled away, her shimmering eyes filled with admiration he'd never have expected. "Not all the men in your family were like Durand. I know, because I traced the Anguis lineage at one time. You have the blood of warriors in your veins. The kind of men who protect what is theirs and love without restraint. I want that love and I want you."

"It's all yours." He kissed her, amazed to be holding her again. When he broke the kiss, he gave her one last warning. "You're not getting much out of this deal since all I own is what I can carry in two hands."

Her hands slid around front, between them. She moved her lips to his ear. "Great. That means I get to decorate the house the way I want." She giggled until her towel broke free and slid to the floor.

"Decorate away, princess, starting with the bedroom." Carlos lifted her in his arms, intending to show her just how much she meant to him. He draped her across the bed and stood up, slowly peeling out of his shirt.

He stared at his future, something he'd never expected to have.

Turn the page for a sneak peek of

SILENT TRUTH

By Sherrilyn Kenyon and Dianna Love

Coming soon from Pocket Books

CHAPTER ONE

Four years ago off the coast of Kauai, Hawaii

Hunter Wesley Thornton-Payne III didn't believe in premonitions of doom, but now might be an optimum time to reevaluate those beliefs. That last bone-jarring shudder of the thirty-year-old fishing trawler beneath him qualified as a preemptive warning.

Salt water sprayed across the deck from each side of the wheelhouse where he stood in a wetsuit. That didn't mean he wanted to be blasted with water every thirty seconds. For the past forty-five minutes this floating hazard had plowed south through the Pacific Ocean toward tonight's black-ops objective.

Failure would trigger hideous deaths for unsuspecting CIA agents over the next twenty-four hours.

A simple mission—on paper.

Scaling a sheer rock lava cliff rising two thousand feet out of windswept waves, and on a moonless night, might give him pause, if not for his partner, Eliot Sawyer. Having him on this mission should quiet any concerns.

But a dark shadow continued to hover over Hunter's psyche, a sixth sense he trusted almost as much as he trusted Eliot.

A ferocious wave broke across the starboard side, the tip of its watery tail lashing his face with cool spray. The faded teakwood deck quaked beneath his feet.

"This piece of shit better hold together long enough to get us into position." Hunter wiped water from his eyes again. "You can bet that sack-a-shit Retter is riding around out here in something that can do more than ten knots. I should be hauling *his* ass up that cliff since this was his idea."

Eliot laughed. The bastard laughed more than any other human Hunter had ever known. Even in college, humor had balanced out his mammoth size. "Thought you agreed this was the only way to slip inside Brugmann's compound."

Hunter hitched a shoulder in a don't-remind-me response. He'd come to the same conclusion as Retter—BAD's top gun and the lead on this operation—that approaching from the north under the guise of a decrepit fishing boat offered the optimum insertion point. Ehrlich Brugmann's private residence perched on a cliff above a vertical wall of volcanic rock overlooking the northern coast of Kauai. A home that had been in his wife's family for six generations.

Brugmann had traveled alone to Hawaii this trip. Had he thought the United States wouldn't notice him selling out the CIA and national security if he didn't do it in D.C. at his primary residence?

Hunter suffered another whiff of fishy stench permeating the wood, which a dousing in bleach wouldn't remove. He stared out over the starboard side at the last shred of light, as the sun sunk closer to the ocean. Twilight silhouetted a pair of fifty-footers bucking waves a mile off.

Two more boats held together with hope and slime.

Retter's doing as well.

Boats were okay in Hunter's book—the sleek half-million-dollar ocean racers he'd once piloted to trophy finishes.

But he hated the kind that tended to sink without notice.

Aging joints creaked in complaint when the deck pitched again. Hunter's grumble ended in a vicious curse.

"Good night for a swim, eh?" Even Eliot had to grab a handhold or bust his silly ass. Pale lights mounted to the wheelhouse cast a sallow glow over his wide body outfitted in a matching wetsuit and lit his crooked-tooth grin.

The same grin Hunter had run up against the night he bumped into Eliot while breaking into the dean's office at Harvard. Eliot had already disarmed the alarms when Hunter appeared beside him. Surprisingly, he and Eliot had broken in for the same reason—to correct the grades of a female student who had spurned the advances of a tenured professor and stood to lose her scholarship. Eliot had laughed in the dark and told Hunter to cover their butts, which he did. And was still doing.

Nothing bothered Eliot.

Not even the time the yacht they'd been on had stopped floating in the middle of the night. An explosion in the engine room had been at fault, but the reason really didn't matter when you had to tread water for the next nine hours.

"Not worried about tonight, are ya?" Eliot pushed and prodded until he got what he wanted, part of his personality that could be annoying as hell at times.

"Worried? Be serious." Hunter ran over the mission again in his mind. His brain assured him everything was a go. His gut argued, but failed to produce concrete evidence of a problem. Didn't matter either way. He and Eliot were going in. They thought as one brain and had faced missions more dangerous than this one. With an unmatched ability to breach any security and expert climbing skills, Eliot was the perfect partner.

But the deciding factor had come down to a matter of trust.

Hunter trusted no one, or at least he hadn't until Eliot took him rock climbing back in college. By the end of that first day, Hunter's life had been in Eliot's hands more times than he'd wanted to count. After that, he knew without question that Eliot had his back in any situation.

And he had Eliot's.

Of course, Eliot's heart was his greatest weakness.

"What about the CIA?" Eliot was back on track with the mission. "If they find out you've been here or seen their list of agents—"

"They won't. We're in. We're out. No one'll know. He's got two rent-a-guards. Stop worrying like an old woman. I got this," Hunter added, using their "end of discussion" phrase. With no choice but to insert, he wanted Eliot thinking only about breeching that security system. He gripped the vertical aluminum rail bolted to the wheelhouse and changed the subject. "Speaking of women, you still seeing that professor?"

"I am." Eliot's grin curved up, widened. Beamed.

Ah, hell. That silly look can't mean what I think.

"Was going to tell you this later, but—"

No, Eliot, we had a deal. What happened to the no-ties, no-commitments, no-baggage rule they'd shook hands on in college?

"I never could keep a secret from ya for long. Cynthia and I got married." Eliot shrugged. "I would have included ya in the wedding, but we did a quick trip to Vegas."

Married. Of all the stupid things to do. Hunter licked salt water from his dry lips. *Open mouth and say something, dammit. This is my best friend.*

Only friend.

"Congratulations. I guess?" Hunter scratched his chin. One thing for sure, he'd never complicate *his* life that way. Not for a woman. They all came with agendas. Like his mother, for one. "Wasn't a shotgun two-step to the altar, right?"

"No way. I'm crazy about Cynthia."

"What about what we do for BAD?" Hunter had joined the Bureau of American Defense after leaving the CIA. BAD operated as a covert agency that protected national security. They had no boundaries, no red tape, and no support if they got in trouble since their secret existence wouldn't be acknowledged. "Cynthia could be used against you if an enemy found out about her."

Eliot stopped smiling and swallowed so hard his Adam's apple pulsed. "My family's never met her, doesn't know she exists. You're the only one who knows about her and I trust you with my life, so she's safe."

What could he say to that? Hunter felt the weight of Eliot's confidence press down on his shoulders, but Eliot was right. Hunter would protect his friend—and any other BAD agent—with his life. "Have you told her what you do?"

"I told her I do investigative work for Interpol and that she can't say anything about my job without putting us both in danger. She's solid as a rock."

"And what about the risks we take?" With anyone else Hunter would let it go and wish the poor sucker good luck. But he'd been friends with Eliot too long to give him the patent superficial garbage Hunter's family considered the foundation of all relationships.

Eliot swayed with the rocking boat, moved his feet for balance, and wiped water off his face that dribbled from his buzz-cut head. "She thinks I'm teamed up with a guy named Leroy, which would be you. I told her you handle all the dangerous work. I'm just the on-site geek."

Like any good lie, that had a trace of truth. Eliot really had contracted from Interpol *after* a stint with the CIA, where he'd been trained along with Hunter. They were both proficient in electronic invasion, but in spite of looking like the bigger physical threat, Eliot's natural gift was cracking a safe or violating security systems, which left Hunter to neutralize opposition. Not a problem.

Hunter didn't mind getting his hands dirty on an op.

But he had no patience for bullshit, which had gotten him in deep trouble with the CIA on one particular job.

If the director of BAD hadn't intervened, Hunter would have disappeared like a puff of smoke in a strong wind.

The CIA allowed him to walk away—alive—as long as he stayed clear of any agency operation. They'd never know he was at the Brugmann compound tonight . . . unless something went wrong.

The FBI thought their people were coordinating with a covert CIA team. No one knew BAD existed, except the U.S. Executive Branch and no one there would admit such. Plus, the CIA wouldn't confess to having a team on U.S. soil, which made it easy to step in when an order came through secure channels.

He just had to insert, confirm the list of names, and exit.

"I didn't forget our deal in college." Eliot had spoken so softly Hunter almost didn't catch it over the rumble of diesel engines beneath his feet. "But I can't live my life without Cynthia and she deserves the respect of marriage."

The time to offer unwanted advice had passed, but Hunter believed his friend would regret the move down the line. This business punished anyone foolish enough to let emotions play into decision-making. He'd just have to do what he'd always done and cover Eliot's back by researching deeper on Cynthia than Hunter's initial scan to assure she wasn't a threat.

But he couldn't prevent her from breaking the fool's heart.

"Say what's on your mind," Eliot said. "Go ahead. Get it off your chest so we can celebrate later and get drunk."

Hunter wanted to be pissed off at Eliot, an easy feat with anyone else but this clown. "Just think it's an unnecessary risk. I mean, what're you going to do if she gets pregnant?"

The trawler engine sound changed abruptly, going from loud rumbling to silent when the captain cut back on power.

That was the sign for Hunter and Eliot to get humping.

They had two minutes before the props rotated again.

Hunter pulled his diving hood into place, checked his gear, then sat on the rail next to Eliot and rolled backward into cool water. He popped up in the inky liquid and paddled to the stern, where BAD's latest propulsion water sled floated.

Everything they needed was strapped in a watertight bag between two control arms. Hunter grabbed one arm and Eliot grabbed the other, both paddling away from the trawler while Eliot flipped on the power switch.

A tiny vibration in the handles indicated the electric turbo spun quietly within a cage.

The trawler engines rumbled to life and the boat moved off.

Unable to see Eliot's face, Hunter called, "Ready."

Eliot took a second to answer. "Cynthia *is* pregnant. I want you to be the godfather." He rolled on the accelerator before another word could be spoken.

Shit. Just like Hunter had suspected.

Another woman with an agenda.

He'd deal with this over beers later.

After thirty-eight minutes that passed with the speed of a stiletto slicing butter, Eliot anchored the water sled close to the access spot. Currents surged, yanking Hunter back and forth, trying to draw him down into the undertow first then bash him against jagged outcroppings of rock carved from weather and sea. He'd reconned the face of the cliff yesterday with a high-powered scope during a whale-watching cruise chartered for him and six agents.

The only dicey part would come when the wall angled out at a forty-five-degree slant two-thirds of the way up.

Once they cleared that area, the rest of the climb

would come down to memory of the mapped-out route, skill, and patience.

They'd executed these maneuvers many times in low-light conditions, and night-vision monoculars with the infrared illuminators would pick up every detail.

He climbed at a steady pace to reach the access point in the allotted time, but slow enough to avoid mistakes.

At the top of the cliff, Hunter reached up until he found a handhold on the steel structure supporting the massive teak observation deck that shot out four feet over the cliff's edge. He silently thanked the architect for Brugmann's home who included a deck and pool in the design. Climbing up into the framework, he unclipped from the rope connecting him to Eliot.

Spider-climbing sideways, Hunter reached the corner of the deck and huddled in a pocket of space to scan for threats while Eliot tied off the rope. He slipped on gloves that were like a second skin, then pressed a button to illuminate his watch face for a brief glance. Six minutes to eight. Better time than he'd thought. Enough to reach the house before one of the two guards on duty made his hourly perimeter walk.

But when he pushed away from the deck to recon the open ground they'd have to cover, something was not right.

A heavily armed guard in black fatigues stood between the rear wall of glass defining the two-story Mediterranean-style house and patio. He paced back and forth.

Something had changed since last night's intel.

A permanent guard on this side meant additional—unanticipated—security. Why so heavily armed?

Hunter turned back to Eliot and used hand signals to tell him the security had increased. Eliot would normally signal "what the hell?" right back, then grin.

This time he hesitated, no doubt thinking of his new family.

No room for baggage in this business.

As if catching the direction of Hunter's thoughts, Eliot gave the "let's go" signal.

Hunter moved out. They had four minutes to make it to the door on the pool cabana attached to the main structure before encountering the guard that *should* be circling the compound.

Plans always played out better on paper.

Hunter had just reached the corner of the cabana with Eliot tucked in close when heavy footsteps coming from the front of the house thudded toward them.

Damn guard was early.

The guy covering the rear of the house had reached the end of his pacing route at the opposite side and turned back in the direction of the cabana.

Either way Hunter went meant exposure to a threat.

He was supposed to insert and exit without alerting any security, a stealth op just to confirm documents were in the safe so the FBI could bust Brugmann, a CIA field coordinator, before he sold agency assets.

No noise, no sign of presence, and no blood.

Two out of three was better than dying.